CHIWAUKEE NIGHTS

Tower of Somnus Book Two

CALE PLAMANN

MOUNTAINDALE
PRESS

ACKNOWLEDGMENTS

For Marlo, Gage, Lola and Charlotte.

Also a big thank you to my wife for putting up with my antics during the writing and editing process. Also a big thank you to my patrons but especially Ari, James, and Sesharan.

Finally, but certainly not least, I want to thank the wonderful team at Mountaindale Press. Without their hard work over the course of months and months, none of this book would have been possible.

PREVIOUSLY ON TOWER OF SOMNUS

Katherine Debs is a young woman with a foot in three different worlds. Born as a hereditary employee and shackled to a life-time of debt to Ike Holdings, a subsidiary of one of the mega-corporations that took over the world after traditional countries collapsed. Her life should have been one of drudgery, working her hardest to maybe one day raise her station.

But she wasn't satisfied with that life. Sinking into an under-world of crime and smuggling, she joined one of the crews of mercenary 'independent contractors' that ran the poverty-stricken slums of the Shell that surrounded the Schaumburg Arcology where she was born and raised.

Then, Kat got her big break. A childhood friend gave her a subscription to *The Tower of Somnus*, a massively multiplayer role playing game that people could play in their sleep with living beings across the galaxy. More importantly, the abilities earned from completing dungeons and leveling up in the Tower carried over into the waking world, making subscriptions expensive status symbols as well as a path to power.

After gaining the subscription and making friends amongst the aliens, Dorrik, a four-armed lizard person of the lokkel race, and Kaleek, a giant otter warrior, Kat began to run into real world troubles. Apparently, a data trove she'd smuggled into her mercenary crew's base had vital information about the assassination of a corporate executive, Christopher Haupt.

The Tower provided Kat with a place where she could escape her oppressive day to day life, with beings she considered friends. While she bonded with them, Kat honed her fighting skills and earned paranormal powers, gradually becoming a force to be reckoned with.

Meanwhile, things became more serious in Kat's waking life with hired, cybernetically enhanced samurai interfering with her mercenary jobs, all the while a mysterious force seemed to maneuver against her.

Unfortunately, everything in the Tower wasn't as simple as it appeared. Before too long, Kat learned that an alien faction was looking to exploit humans and that they were willing to make deals to empower people in exchange for them cooperating with some sort of unknown plot against humanity as a whole.

Matters came to a head with Kat, her hacking support, Whippoorwill, and her boss, Xander, raiding the headquarters of Steel and Blood, a rival gang that the corporate interests were arming to eliminate them. In a pitched battle, they defeated Steel and Blood and obtained the evidence they needed to eliminate the executives that were seeking to destroy them.

Despite this, the likely mastermind behind the entire debacle, Belle Donnst, escaped. Rather than being punished for her misdeeds, she was promoted, in part for turning over 'evidence' implicating her own daughter in Christopher Haupt's killing.

The good news is that Belle doesn't hold a grudge against Kat. Her major promotion went a long way toward smoothing those ruffled feathers. The bad news is that Belle has a hold over Kat, sending her away to the megalopolis of Chiwaulkee for college, all the while explicitly hinting that she will have jobs for someone with Kat's particular skillset...

CHAPTER ONE

"Let's go over the plan one more time." Dorrik stood next to Kat on the rock face overlooking the beach, the wind rustling the giant lizard's crest.

She glanced at her companion. Her head only came up to the dusky scales of their upper shoulder, but the giant four-armed, muscle-bound lizard was more scholar than warrior. That didn't mean that Dorrik couldn't hold their own in a fight. Far from it. They were one of the most adept swords-beings that Kat had ever seen.

It was just that Kat suspected her companion thought their combat prowess secondary. At their heart, Dorrik was a scholar. History, anthropology, physics, the lizard devoured everything they could related to learning.

Dorrik was a skilled combatant almost without trying. Like her, they blended a casting class with combat prowess, but Kat wasn't sure she'd ever seen the lokkel practice with their swords. Like many of Dorrik's skills, swordplay was another thing that came to them with infuriating ease.

"We wade in and kill as many of the float fish as possible," Kaleek responded, his whiskers twitching. "Once enough of them are down, the Deep Terror will come partially to shore. At that point, I head into the water to attack it directly while Kat and you do your best to deal with its tentacles and deflate it."

Kaleek had been chosen for the direct attack for two reasons. First, he was a desoph, a semi-aquatic quasi-mammal that closely resembled a giant terrestrial otter. The three of them suspected that his experience swimming and fighting in the water would be useful in the coming battle.

Perhaps more importantly, Kaleek was the team's frontline fighter. The huge two-handed sword on his back was only a little smaller than Kat herself, but Kaleek could use it with deceptive speed and dexterity. Of course, it didn't hurt that he had stamina-based skills specifically to help him offset its weight and momentum.

"Just be careful," Kat replied, frowning. "I might be able to heal you if you get hurt, but Dorrik said that the tentacles carry a paralytic agent too. If you're waist deep in water and paralyzed, that sounds like a good way to drown."

"Desoph don't drown." Kaleek snorted. "Even our cubs spend more time in water than they do on land. It's unthinkable."

"Unthinkable or not," Kat crossed her arms as she stared him down sternly, "that's the sort of attitude that will end with you paralyzed and dead face down in a puddle."

"She is right, Kaleek," Dorrik said over the desoph's snort. "You won't be wearing your heavy armor so that you can fight in the water. If the Deep Terror even brushes you with a tentacle, that should be enough to paralyze you unless your fortitude attribute can overcome the poison."

"Come on." Kaleek wrinkled his whiskers at them. "In the past two months, we've blazed through four dungeons here on the second floor. I've been careful that entire time. Nothing is going to change just because we're challenging the floor guardian. Don't worry about it, I'm not going to let this thing tag me."

Kat just rolled her eyes. Kaleek could back his bold words up. Probably.

She called up her status.

Name: Katherine Debs
Class: Elementalist Initiate
Max Level: 2
425 Marks

HP: 22
MP: 29
STA: 24

Dodge: Insignificant
Damage Mitigation: Insignificant

Strength: 3
Agility: 4
Fortitude: 3
Endurance: 4
Mind: 3
Reaction: 5
Charisma: 4
Spirit: 3

Spells Known:
Gravity's Grasp
Levitation
Pseudopod
Dehydrate
Dazzle
Shadow
Water Jet
Gravity Spike

Skills Known:

Knife I - 8, 79%
Gravity I - 7, 42%
Water I - 8, 14%
Cat Step - 5, 61%
Light I - 5, 16%
Cure Wounds I - 2, 21%
Penetrate

Perks:
Nightvision
Leaping

Four dungeons worth of delving, and the awards had been a mixed bag. She'd only earned two attribute points, one in endurance and one in reaction. As for the other two dungeons? The three points in hit points and stamina she'd been awarded from their most recent adventure would be useful, but she was struggling to find a consistent use for the Leaping perk.

In theory, the perk was nice. It let her burn stamina to triple the force she put into a jump. Combined with Levitation, Leaping let her jump almost twenty feet into the air. A useful skill for climbing cliffs or buildings, but far too flashy for Kat.

"Are we ready?" Dorrik asked, pulling both of their swords free. Each blade was held casually in a two-handed grip consisting of each of the lizard-man's vertical hand pairs. "I believe that everyone is as prepared as we can be."

"Ready," Kat nodded, drawing her knife.

"Ready for this." Kaleek wrinkled his nose. "Not entirely ready for the third floor. The environment is a bit arid for me."

"Your preferences have been noted," Dorrik replied dryly as they began hopping from rock to rock to descend the ridge in front of them.

Kaleek and Kat joined them, scrambling down the boulders. Seconds later, the three of them were standing on the white sand of the beach. For a moment, the fake sun of *The*

Tower of Somnus beat down on them as the water lapped gently at the shore.

Then they spread out and began walking toward the float fish. Kat wasn't entirely sure about the translation software used by the Tower, because whatever float fish were, they didn't look like any fish she'd ever seen.

Each of the creatures was about the size of a beach ball, their mottled and slimy skin stretched tight over an air bladder filled with buoyant gas. A quartet of fins around their circumference let them steer themselves through the air, while a pair of tentacles ending in venomous barbs allowed them to collect and eat prey.

One of the five throwing knives Kat kept in a bandoleer across her chest whirred through the air, slashing deep into the side of a float fish. It popped like a balloon, deflating and sinking to the white sand.

With a follow up throwing knife held in the palm of her left hand, Kat approached her immobile foe. One of its tentacles rose from the sand, coiling and lunging toward her.

Kat half turned, her enhanced reflexes throwing her into motion almost the split second the dark green tentacle moved from the sand. She spun, using the momentum of her rotation to help drive her combat knife through the rubbery appendage.

Whether it was her form or her eight ranks in Knife I enhancing the effectiveness of the strike, the blade cut cleanly through the float fish's tentacle. A second later, her spare throwing knife was dropping to the sand as Kat grabbed the second tendril out of the air.

It struggled, slimy and writhing in her hand. Kat tried not to think about it as her knife flashed down, cutting off the venomous spike at its end.

After that, it was only a matter of stabbing the half-deflated orb of the float fish's main body a couple of times and retrieving her throwing knives. Leaving behind the dead float fish, Kat glanced at her companions.

Dorrik had already defeated their first opponent, severing

both tentacles before drawing an "X" with their swords through its body. Kaleek, on the other hand, was struggling. Each time he brought his sword up to handle one of the tentacles, the other would threaten him and force him back.

She shrugged, throwing her knife and popping another float fish. This time she didn't even bother walking toward it, instead standing out of its tentacles' range and throwing one knife after another into it.

Around four knives later, it stopped moving and she cautiously moved closer to retrieve her weapons. Neither of its tentacles stirred to stop her as she collected the daggers, and before long she found herself repeating the process.

A part of her felt bad for the floating blobs. She didn't know whether they were constructs of *The Tower of Somnus* or actual animals somewhere, but they clearly didn't know how to deal with a ranged opponent.

Her knife thwacked into yet another float fish, sending it sputtering to the sand. Really, they weren't even as smart as most animals on Earth. Even wild dogs would have run away by now, and as far as Kat could tell, there wasn't anything stopping the creatures from simply floating up into the sky and out of her reach.

Dagger after dagger followed it while the creature's tentacles twitched and searched fruitlessly for their assailant. Once the fourth hit, the tentacles dropped to the sand. Kat jogged over to collect them, but before she could reach the dead float fish, the ocean began to churn.

"This is it!" Dorrik yelled, squaring their stance and facing the water even as the waves began to wash much further up on the shore. "The float fish should begin fleeing as the Deep Terror pulls itself up onto the shore. Get ready!"

Kaleek stabbed his sword into a float fish that he'd trapped against the sand with his foot, twisting the blade slightly before he withdrew it. He cracked his neck and turned to the ocean. The beginnings of a semi-transparent sphere began to push itself out of the water some twenty paces from the shore.

Kat quickly stowed her throwing knives in their bandoleer, locking her eyes on the water. More of the Deep Terror splashed into view as it moved toward the shore, pulling itself from the water with six white tentacles, each as big around as her waist, grasping the shore and dragging its bulk.

It was a translucent hemisphere, as big as a small building and filled with vaguely defined organs and structures that Kat couldn't quite make sense of. The monster rippled slightly, its formless and pulpy flesh undulating rhythmically.

The second Kaleek touched the water, it seemed to sense him, the off-white tentacles pulling themselves off of the beach and curling backward toward the intrepid desoph as Kaleek splashed his way toward the creature's main body.

"Hit it now, Dorrik!" Kat shouted, whipping a throwing knife into the side of one of the giant tentacles even as she concentrated on another. Her mana stirred as it began flowing out of her. "We need to keep the tentacles off of Kaleek long enough for him to do some damage."

"Trying, Miss Kat," Dorrik grunted in response as they sprinted toward one of the tentacles that they had been sneaking up on. "*Nerve Lash.*"

Dorrik's eyes flashed purple a moment before the same glow appeared around a tentacle. The entire thing spasmed as Dorrik's psi energy ran down its length, activating whatever passed for a pain reflex in the Deep Terror.

Kat didn't envy the creature. After a fair amount of drunken coaxing and assurances that it wouldn't deal permanent damage, Kat convinced Dorrik to use the ability on her. For an agonizing second, it filled her lower body with white-hot pain so strong that Kat almost blacked out.

Her spell activated just as Kat was reaching for a second knife, and Gravity Spike sent two conflicting pulses of energy into the tentacle she was attacking. For a second, Kat could feel her magic simultaneously pulling on the rubbery length even as a handspan away it pushed.

With the sound of wet paper tearing, cyan blood erupted

from the tentacle as its surface rippled and crumpled. A second throwing knife dug deep into the tentacle's soft surface.

An angry, low crooning sound shook the beach. Kat stumbled slightly, dizzy as the deep sound made her teeth ache as they resonated. In the corner of her vision, a red indicator flashed into existence, a sure sign that she'd taken damage or received a status affliction.

A second later, she was spending stamina to use Leaping in order to clear a second tentacle whipping toward her at chest level while the one she'd injured curled its way gingerly toward the Deep Terror.

It passed under her, the wind ruffling Kat's clothing as she concentrated on firing another Gravity Spike into the retreating tentacle. The spell was slow to target and cast, but over the last couple of weeks since she'd learned it, Kat had come to accept that it was her most powerful magical ability.

Really, her only other direct attack was Dehydrate, a much quicker and more mana-efficient spell, but ultimately weaker spell. Of course, that wasn't against an ordinary opponent. It would likely be ineffective against a creature that appeared to be entirely made of water. Even if it could dry out the Deep Terror slightly, Kat suspected that the creature would be able to circulate more liquid into the afflicted area, negating any damage she could do.

Gravity Spike fired again just as she landed on the beach, once again ripping at the injured tentacle. This time, it went limp entirely as the invisible tempest of mana tore something important deep inside the muscular appendage.

Nearby, Dorrik hacked down with both of their swords, cutting a neat "V" halfway into the tentacle in front of them. Blue blood geysered from the gaping wound, but Dorrik's body glowed briefly purple as they boosted their physical attributes just enough to escape the torrent of ichor.

The remaining four tentacles writhed toward them, two circling to either side in order to hem Dorrik and Kat in. The other two crept toward them, tensed and ready to lash out at a moment's notice.

Without speaking, she found her back brushing up against Dorrik's rough scales. Out of the corner of her eye, they nodded at her, and Kat nodded back.

Then, Kaleek cut deep into the side of the monster, his sword passing easily through its mostly permeable skin. Clear, viscous goop began pouring out of its side even as Kaleek splashed deeper into the water. A second later, he stabbed it once again, shoving his blade so deep that the hilt slammed into the creature's pulpy flesh.

The tentacles around them twitched, and the mournful bass note from earlier began to swell once again. Kat could feel her concentration faltering slightly as the beach spun around her even as she tried to gather the mana for another spell.

"*Nerve Lash*," Dorrik's voice rang out, somehow clear and perfectly audible above the rumbling sound assaulting Kat's balance.

She clung onto the words, using them as an anchor to drag herself back to the real world and harness the mana she'd been gathering, pouring it into another Gravity Spike.

Dorrik and her abilities hit almost simultaneously. The left tentacle twitched and spasmed, unable to move as pain wracked it while the right had a basketball-sized area of its flesh crumple and begin leaking bright blue blood.

The mournful, pained sound cutoff abruptly. Kat spared the creature's main body a glance. Even as Kaleek was slashing it a third time, it began lifting its bulk from the ocean.

Kat frowned as she finally got a good look at the entirety of the creature. It truly was a half sphere, the bottom of its body edged with thousands of small white tendrils, almost like over-sized cilia. The strings of white monster flesh studded the perimeter of the monster, surrounding the much larger tentacles attacking the two of them.

The creature dripped water as it pulled itself up into the air, towering above Kaleek on a pair of newly revealed tentacles that were coiled together under it, rooting the Deep Terror to the ocean floor.

"Bring it down, Miss Kat!" Dorrik stepped in front of her. "I can hold the rest of the tentacles off for a couple of seconds. Kaleek needs it back on his level so he can finish it off."

Without responding, she changed her focus. A moment later, Gravity's Grasp pulled at the Deep Terror, causing its body to bow around the tentacles holding it up.

Its pseudo-leg began working against it. The Deep Terror's body was weak, usually supported by water as its tentacles did the dirty work of gathering prey. It could support itself out of the ocean, barely, its body forcefully sagging around the two tentacles that held it up.

Under the force of her spell, the 'leg' held up, but the rest of the Terror's body pulled toward the ocean, straining at its thin, translucent skin. Even at a distance, Kat could almost hear it creaking as the extra gravity began to tear at its borderline liquid flesh.

Cracks ripped in its body, leaking the Deep Terror's clear innards with distressing plops into the water below. Kat did her best to ignore Dorrik's whirling form as the giant lizard swung around her, glowing purple and hacking into the white tentacles that frantically quested toward her in an attempt to put an end to the magic.

Cyan blood spattered all around her as Dorrik danced back and forth. Their blades flashed in the light as they opened up great cuts in the tentacles, forcing them back one by one. Just as Kat was almost finished gathering her mana, one of Dorrik's weapons caught a tentacle too close to Kat, spraying her right side with its blue blood.

Almost immediately, a tingling chill seeped into her body, attacking Kat's concentration as she tried to finish the spell. She bit her lip hard enough that the iron taste of blood hit her tongue, focusing on the pain just long enough to finish another casting of Gravity's Grasp.

Her mana dropped into the single digits as the gravity magic rippled in a sphere over the monster's 'leg.' One of the two tentacles the Terror was standing on crumpled as the spell tore at it.

It toppled sideways into the water, only for Kaleek to leap at it, hacking into its dome with his sword and spilling even more of the translucent gunk that made up its blood into the ocean.

Kat shook her head, trying to fight the fuzziness creeping into her thoughts. Her right arm was completely numb, hanging limply from her side. Near her, Dorrik dragged a deadened leg, one of their swords in a single-handed grip as the lower arm flopped bonelessly.

They had done their damage though. Of the six tentacles that had originally attacked the two of them, only three were in any condition to continue fighting, and even those appendages were covered in deep gashes from the lokkel's swords.

Luckily, the tentacles were pulling back to fight Kaleek. Kat sighed, her vision fuzzing slightly as a vague sense of euphoria washed over her.

In the distance, Kaleek cackled maniacally, waist-deep inside the Deep Terror's deflating form, his sword hacking rhythmically as he worked his way through its inert goopy flesh and into the blurry organs deep inside its body.

"Should we be helping?" Kat asked, her tongue feeling like cotton in her mouth.

Dorrik blinked at her slowly, reaching down with their upper right arm to poke their lifeless lower left limb. It began swinging back and forth, clearly outside of the big lizard's control.

"Let him have his fun," Dorrik shrugged. Distantly, Kat noticed that their eyes were vaguely fogged as well. "There is no way that the creature will be able to stop him in time, and the third floor is one of his least favorite. Hopefully he'll complain less if we let him get it out of his system here."

"Why?" Kat asked hazily, blinking as she tried to fight the prickling chill invading her mind. "What's so bad about the third floor?"

"Nothing." Dorrik chuckled, watching as Kaleek ripped a handful of wriggling tubes out of the Terror with his bare hands and threw them into the ocean. At some point, the tentacles had stopped moving entirely. "It's just a gigantic desert. Wonderfully warm, dry, and sandy, with oasis cities made for players around the infrequent patches of water. My people love the place."

"No resting." Kat shook her head, grabbing one of Dorrik's hands as the big lizard prepared to sit down.

"If either of us rest right now, that venom is going to take over and we'll be out like a light." She heaved them back to their feet. "God, now that I think about it, that battle was closer than I'd like."

"That is the way of the dreamscape, Miss Kat." Dorrik's head lolled slightly to the side, their lids laying heavy on their eyes. "The Deep Terror is a foe designed by the Gardeners for six players. One to eliminate each leg. The paralytic agents in its tentacles are quite powerful, and the only way to fight it properly is to avoid getting hit. Average players struggle to avoid one tentacle at a time, especially when the blood spray carries similar properties."

"Defeating a floor guardian with a team of three grants an extra point because it is difficult." Dorrik smiled, a display of their massive needle teeth. "The Gardeners would not simply give us power for free. We just approached the monster with a good plan and a well-trained team."

"What are the Gardeners anyway?" Kat asked, frowning slightly. "I saw some sort of mention of them when we ascended our last level."

"An enigma." Dorrik shrugged, their eyes barely open. "Their existence is shrouded in myths and rumors. In fact, some of the more heretical groups such as the stallesp deny that they even exist. Still, many races have found murals of them in ancient ruins that predate spaceflight."

"Some even say—" Dorrik's voice cut out, replaced by an unintelligible string of snarls, hisses, and whistles.

Warning! As a probationary race on level 2, this information is prohibited. Your translation software has temporarily been disabled. Please contact an administrator if you wish to appeal this decision or if you believe it has been made in error.

Before Kat could respond, the first window disappeared, replaced by a much more welcome alert.

Congratulations, Adventurer!
You have defeated the Deep Terror and ascended past the second floor!
For achieving this feat with three or fewer players, a bonus attribute point has been awarded. Assign it wisely!
For ascending a level as an Elementalist Initiate, you gain the following benefits:

+2 Mana
+1 Stamina
+1 Mind

Keep climbing! Your answers and the Gardeners await you at the top!

Quietly, she assigned the extra point to Mind, immediately feeling some of the wooziness fade. In the distance, Kaleek whooped in pleasure, diving out of the caved-in monster and into the water of the ocean to clean its slime from his fur.

She'd address the translation issue later, but even with the cold numbness from the paralytic agent coursing through her veins, Kat couldn't help but feel a twinge of curiosity.

CHAPTER TWO

"Are you sure about this, Kat?" her mother, Penelope Debs, asked as she fidgeted. "I don't want to ask where you got it, but this is a lot of money we're talking about."

"Yes, Mom," Kat replied, glancing around the building. Her sister, Michelle, was slouched in the chair next to her, watching the latest episode of Chrome Cowboy on her smartpanel, an omnipresent square of smartglass that almost all company employees wore about their right eyes that gave them constant and unfettered access to their e-mail as well as entertainment and information channels.

The rest of the room was much bleaker. Dozens of nervous, low-level corporate employees occupied the remaining seats, each waiting for their turn at one of the debt counseling and consolidation booths. The walls were little more than bare concrete, with only a clock and a display indicating the ticket number and counseling booth of the next 'lucky employee.'

"I didn't even know that you were allowed to pay off your corporate ledger," Penelope continued breathily. "I mean, do I stop being a corporate employee afterward? I don't want to lose my job or anything, Kat."

"Of course you can pay off your ledger, Mom." Kat closed her eyes, wishing that her mother would lose herself in a stupid soap opera like Michelle. It would make the eternal wait that much easier. "Corporate arbitration is pretty fast and loose about many things, but it's ironclad on the questions of debt, interest, and payment of debt. It's literally easier to get away with murder than it is to default on or change the terms of a loan."

"It still just doesn't seem right." Her mom fidgeted uncomfortably. "I don't think I know anyone on our entire floor that has a positive ledger. It isn't natural."

"Calling A-89," a monotone voice cut in over the waiting room's public address system. "A-89, please report to counseling and consolidation booth A. If you do not arrive within two minutes, your appointment will be canceled and you will be billed for your counselor's time."

"Wish me luck," a man in a bright teal sweatshirt stood up, smiling nervously. "I think I have a good case to raise my weekly spending limit. My wife just had her second child and I've been working in the factory for ten years. They have to raise the limit, right?"

"Good luck," Kat said the words almost in time with her mother. After speaking, she bit her tongue. The company didn't 'have' to do anything.

Kat would wager her last credit that every employee in the building with her was heavily in debt to the company. The polite term was 'hereditary employees,' individuals indebted to the company from the moment they were charged with their birth expenses as infants. Each day after that only compounded the problem. The company provided all employees with food and housing, quietly deducting the costs from their employees paychecks.

It was unheard of for someone in the lower levels of the arcology to actually earn more in a week than they owed for their upkeep. Instead, they had to rely on their weekly spending limit, a revolving line of credit offered by the company so that employees could purchase necessities. More specifically, the little comforts that kept workers in-line and not hammering at their employer's door with torches and pitchforks.

As far as she could tell, the only real factors that went into an employee's spending limit was their debt-to-income ratio. Without changing those cold, hard facts, the hopeful man's request was denied even before he articulated it.

"Don't worry about it, Mom," Kat said as the employee walked away. "If I have anything to say about it, Michelle and you will be moving to a better floor before long, anyway. You can keep working your job if you want, but I'd prefer that you move on to something safer. After all, once your debt is paid down, you can actually apply for a new job on your own without the company vetoing it. Hell, you could probably work here at the counseling and consolidation office, if you wanted."

"About that." Penelope frowned slightly. "I'm still confused about how you got into the corporate college. I know that the top two children in your class got involved with that awful mess, having an executive killed and all that, but I don't understand how that ended up with you taking their spot at the college."

Kat grimaced. Every time she'd brought up her… other job, her mother became deeply uncomfortable. Even when Kat was only running files from one secure location to another, it had been a bit much for Penelope. Kat didn't know how her mother would react to the knowledge that she'd graduated from a courier into a full-blown infiltrator.

She knew that her mother would not react well to the actual story behind the corporate college scholarship. That her precious daughter had killed and watched her companions die in front of her in order to prevent the spoiled heir of an executive from crushing her like a bug. That, ultimately, the credits she was using to pay off her family's debt were stained with the blood of the street samurai Kat had killed to get where she was at. That the executive in question had tied Kat to her with a scholarship to the corporate college for reasons that Kat couldn't entirely decipher, and certainly didn't trust.

"I just think Belle Donnst didn't want her daughter's deposit at the college to go to waste," Kat smiled thinly, hoping that her mother would believe the bald-faced lie. "I was third in my class, and with the first two places... indisposed, I was the logical next choice. I've already talked with Belle a couple of times, and the offer appears to be completely genuine."

"To think," Penelope giggled, "my daughter talking with an executive."

"Yes." Kat rolled her eyes, shuddering slightly as she remembered Belle Donnst's calculating gaze. "I've talked with an executive."

"D-94, calling D-94," the same monotone announcement cut through their conversation. "D-94, please report to counseling and consolidation booth D. If you do not arrive within two minutes, your appointment will be canceled and you will be billed for your counselor's time."

"That's us." Kat stood up, tapping Michelle on her shoulder. The much younger girl blinked at Kat, her vision blurry as she dismissed the entertainment channel. "It's time, Michelle."

"I still don't see why you need me for this," her sister grumbled as she sat up. "Couldn't you have just done your money stuff without dragging Mom and I out here?"

Kat didn't even answer, walking across the scuffed, earth-tone carpet of the office and past the clusters of cheap chairs toward a booth marked with the letter D. Even the green paint that made up the letter was chipped and faded.

She pushed the plastic sliding door aside, struggling slightly as it caught in the poorly-maintained groove in the floor, before stepping into the booth. Inside, a slightly overweight man with a receding hairline sat at a card table, a stack of paperwork before him. His eyes glazed slightly as he looked at something on his smartpanel.

"Katherine Debs here with Penelope Debs and Michelle Debs." His voice had the rasp of a frequent smoker. "The billing for your consultation has already begun. Please begin filling out form 207-1m and hand it to me once you're done."

He thrust a sheaf of papers and a pen into Kat's hands as she took her seat, bewildered. Page after page of dense wording inquired about Kat's financial history, current earnings, and her projected advancement.

"Wouldn't it be easier to let us fill this out in the waiting room?" Kat frowned as she thumbed through the document. A fast and prepared individual might be able to fill it out in twenty minutes. "Making us wait until now to even see the forms seems like a huge waste of the company's time."

"Katherine." The man frowned slightly, his ragged voice stern. "I know that you've just graduated from school and think that you have all the answers, but you must understand. This is the way that we've always done things."

"But what if it's possible to improve the way you've been doing things?" Kat asked, narrowing her eyes as she scanned over the various invasive provisions of the document that he'd handed her. "Don't you owe it to the company to try to upgrade the process?"

"Miss Debs." The man shook his head slightly at her as Kat's mother and sister sat down in the booth next to her. "The company only does things in a certain way if there is some logic to it. Neither of us are at a level where we can or should be questioning that logic. Even if something seems inefficient, I am not going to risk my neck arguing with an executive over some procedure that they implemented. Right or wrong, I would bring unwanted attention to myself."

"It's simpler to just fill out the forms." He patted the stack of papers next to him with a grunt. "Then I can run them through the electronic rubric and inform you of the results of your application."

"Honestly." Kat set the paperwork down in front of her before reaching into the messenger bag she'd brought with her. "That all sounds like something that could just be an e-mail. Someone sends the form to me at my apartment, I fill it out and return it. The company saves money by replacing counselors with algorithms and there isn't even any need for this office space to exist."

"Ma'am." The counselor crossed his arms, unamused. "If you could return to filling out the form without insulting my work, I would appreciate it."

"That's the thing, though," Kat replied, placing three cylinders of tightly packed credit chips on the table. "That form is for an expansion of our family's weekly spending limit, but that isn't why we're here. I would like to make a deposit against each of our ledgers."

The man's eyes went wide as he looked at the stacks of credits in front of him, his mouth moving silently as he counted the chips.

"Miss Debs," he croaked, tapping the side of his smartpanel to activate some function. "That is almost ninety thousand credits. More than enough to pay off all three of your ledgers and put you well into the positive."

"Yes," Kat replied, doing her best to keep a smirk off of her face. The credits in front of her represented a substantial portion of her wealth, but it wasn't all of it.

Two months ago, the ChromeDogs, the street samurai crew that Kat had joined, collected one of the biggest bounties of the year. Between the credits she'd earned from that bounty, and her share of the salvage they'd collected from Steel and Blood, a major mercenary group that tried to stop them, Kat had more credits stashed in the cubby under her mother's sink than she'd expected to earn in her entire life.

As for the bounty, they'd managed to procure information that definitively identified Anna Donnst, a former classmate of Kat's, along with Gregory Daniels as the ringleaders behind the successful assassination of Christopher Haupt, an executive for GroCorp, the company that owned Ike Holdings, the corporation that Kat worked for.

Kat and her superior in the ChromeDogs, Xander, both strongly suspected Anna's mother, Belle Donnst, of being the driving force behind the murder. Mostly because the evidence was suspiciously complete and cleanly identified Anna, Gregory, and a classmate of Kat's, Arnold, as co-conspirators.

Somehow, despite enough evidence to convict the conspirators ten times over, there wasn't even a single mention of Belle's name. That was more than enough for both Xander and Kat to be wary of the woman. Unfortunately, Belle took their interference with her plans as a sign of competence and had more or less strong-armed them into working with her.

Even after she paid down her entire family's debt, she would have enough to set herself up comfortably at the corporate college in the Chiwaukee Megalopolis, right next to GroCorp's corporate headquarters.

"Where did you get this much money?" The counselor licked his lips, eyes glazed and twitching as his smartpanel read their micromovements. "You apparently used to be a lab tech third class before you quit your job in order to attend college."

"Actually…" He frowned. "Are you even allowed to quit your job when your ledger is in the red? Hereditary employees generally aren't allowed to decline work—"

"My contract with the lab was bought out as part of the scholarship that is sending me to college," Kat responded. "I would like to note that I have presented you with the credits needed to pay down my families' ledgers. I will report any attempt to bill me further as theft."

"But how did you get this money?" His voice became shriller. The counselor clutched his hands together, wringing them as if he were afraid to touch the credits. "Did you spread your legs for some executive? I can't think of—"

"Ninety thousand credits for sex?" Kat snorted. "I'll choose to take your accusation as a compliment regarding my appearance. Any executive that wants a night of fun could probably find it on the lower levels for a couple hundred credits. Hell, you could probably get someone selling themselves for a month or so for that much in the Shell."

"As much as I'd like to think that I'm beautiful enough to justify that kind of price tag," she rolled her eyes at him, "I'm well aware that even a fairly ordinary girl with a couple thousand credits in body mods could look like an entertainment channel star of her buyer's choice."

"Kat," her Mom hissed, unsuccessfully trying to clap her hands over Michelle's ears.

"Do you mean I could look like Jenny Silverarm from Chrome Cowboys?" the young girl interjected excitedly, dodging Penelope's grasp. "That would be soooo cool."

"No you can't, Michelle." Kat didn't even look at the girl, her glare fixed on the debt counselor. "My sponsor is Belle Donnst. If you would like to call her and ask how I earned this money, she may even give you an answer. I would not advise calling her."

"Donnst…" His voice trailed off as the portly man paled. "I don't suppose I, uh—I think I'm fine without verifying the source of the funds."

"Great." Kat smiled thinly. "Now would you mind processing the payment so we can all get on with our days?"

The man's eyes glazed over as he consulted something in his smartpanel. A second later, he winced, his expression souring.

"Good news," he replied mechanically. "Given the demonstrated increase in your income, I have been authorized to offer you a drastic increase in your weekly spending—"

"Not interested," Kat cut him off. "Please process the payment."

"The company cares for you," he continued bitterly, "and it wants you to keep your hard-earned credits. Rather than paying down your debt, wouldn't you prefer to be upgraded to a condominium on the tenth floor? You can be assured that it will have actual outward facing windows and—"

"Please process the payment." Kat crossed her arms, leaning back in the cheap chair.

"In order to handle a transaction of this magnitude," the man was sweating bullets now, "I will need to call a supervisor. Are you sure you wouldn't prefer to maintain your debt with the company, and instead receive a complimentary upgrade to your spending limit and housing?"

"I understand that the interest on my debt accrues at twenty-four percent annually?" Kat raised an eyebrow. "Is that what this is all about? Either take my money, or I will file a report."

The man groaned, reaching across the table and collecting the credits. He quickly popped open a safe and placed them inside before turning back to Kat and her family.

"Here at the debt counseling and consolidation department of Ike Holdings, a wholly-owned subsidiary of GroCorp," the counselor forced the words out through clenched teeth, "your opinions are valuable to us. Each of you has been sent a customer satisfaction survey."

"Thank you." Kat smiled sweetly at the squirming counselor. "I look forward to filling it out."

CHAPTER THREE

Kat stretched the clear strip of electrofilm across the keypad. A second later, her smartpanel buzzed, providing her with a predictive analysis of the possible passcodes based upon the wear on the keys.

The custom program helpfully flashed in red the percentage chance of each four-digit code. None of the predictions were above 15%, meaning that Kat would have had to abandon the keypad if she had any concerns about an alarm.

Luckily, the electrofilm also analyzed the keys 'unused' by the passcode for misplaced keystrokes, a telltale sign that previous users had typed the combination wrong. A smile blossomed on Kat's face as a small green light flashed in the corner of the film. It wasn't a sure thing, but there was a fairly high correlation with previous typos and a lack of alarms that would punish her for making a 'typo' of her own while trying to figure the password out.

Four combinations tapped into the keypad later, the door clicked open and she stepped into a dark room. Kat's Nightvision activated, letting her see the room in black and white as clearly as if the noon sun were high in the sky.

Her hand blurred to her waist as Kat threw three dark orbs at the glint of the walnut-sized security cameras embedded in the walls. A moment before the orbs hit, they detonated with an audible pop, turning into a spray of black ink that blanketed the cameras, blinding them.

Kat grabbed her mist-gun, little more than a water reservoir and a muscle-powered pump that would pressurize the water through a fine mesh. A couple of squeezes later, the fine fog of water settled onto the floor without revealing the tell-tale refraction of a laser alarm system.

She moved across the floor, her mind running through possible security measures that she couldn't check for. Her suit would theoretically contain her body heat enough to defeat a heat sensor so long as she kept moving. Well, an ordinarily calibrated sensor.

Short of using her magic to hover, there wasn't much she could do about pressure or tremor sensors, but they were notoriously finicky in multistory buildings. Even if the structure had a set of modern counterweights, they tended to sway and wobble ever so slightly in the wind. Their residents learned to ignore the teetering, but it was incredibly difficult to calibrate an alarm system to do the same.

In short, she should be safe from the security systems of an ordinarily paranoid gangster or corporate overlord. The countermeasures needed for an infiltrator to prepare for a real fortress would slow her down and increase the risk that a roving patrol would happen upon her, meaning that unless she had reason to believe that one of the more esoteric security systems was in use, standard operating procedure was to 'move fast and hope for the best.'

Just as she was about to open the second door, her tower-enhanced senses brought her hand to a halt. Squinting in the pitch-black, she found a small button between the doorknob and the door itself.

A quick inspection brought a frown to her face. Great. Another alarm.

If she'd opened the door without depressing the toggle, it likely would have set off a silent alarm and buried her in security guards.

She grasped the doorknob, careful to depress the button as she turned it, pushing the door open slowly. This time it opened into an office. Her target, an unsecured dataport, sat on a desk in front of Kat, calling out to her.

Her first step into the room triggered a flurry of motion. Silhouettes sprang up from behind the room's furniture as Kat let herself drop to the ground, drawing her heavy-caliber, low-velocity, silenced pistol in one smooth motion.

The gun bucked in her hand, coughing twice as she shot the first figure. Above her, the door she'd walked in from rattled as return fire sprayed it.

Kat rolled to the side, activating Levitation and Leaping at the same time to kick herself off of the ground just in time to avoid another volley of shots. She fired four shots while in the air, two striking the wall behind her second target even as the others silenced it.

Her final target adjusted their aim, sending a shot just past Kat's face even as she cut her spell and replaced it with Gravity's Grasp, jerking her body toward the ground fast enough to throw off the remainder of her enemy's fire.

Finally, one of her last two shots struck her target in the head, silencing it.

Kat stood up, wincing at the pain in her ribs. As effective as alternating Levitation and Gravity's Grasp was at throwing off enemy fire, her body paid the price. She'd needed to focus on shooting, so there hadn't been a chance for Kat to diffuse the impact of her fall, and her chest had paid the price.

She placed her shunt, the remote connection to her partner, Whippoorwill, that would let the quiet, pink-haired girl hack into the secure network, onto the unsecured port. A second later, the lights in the room turned on.

Xander walked in as Kat began reciting the incantation to Cure Wounds I. The middle-aged man glanced at the three spring-loaded metal silhouettes, each of them with a 'fatal' splatter of paint on them.

"Pretty good job, Erinyes." He nodded. "You managed to silence the cameras and defeat the alarm in time, and your reactions saved your bacon when you were ambushed by the 'gunmen.' Really, the only ding I have on your performance score is your pistol accuracy. Five of eight hits isn't bad, but those are the kind of numbers that end up with dead operatives."

"I'm not on a mission, Xan," Kat hissed as the golden light from the healing spell began to ease the bruising over her ribs. "There's no need to use my street name. Plus, you know that I would have been able to take those three in an eyeblink if you let me sneak up on them with my knife. Even with all that range time you've been forcing on me, pistols still feel bulky and unnatural to me."

"I hear you." Xander grinned, his sole gold tooth glinting. "I'm not a fan of them either. These days I mostly use what I've picked up in *The Tower of Somnus* to end fights before the other side even knows that we're scrapping. Sometimes, though, it just doesn't work. They're too far away, I'm fighting automated security, or the other side is a player with defenses of their own."

"Then," he tapped the knife at his left hip and the gun at his right, "it pays to have options. I'm not quite as into cutting people up as you are, but knives keep things quiet, and on an infiltration, that's an important factor when you can get the drop on someone. Of course, if they're more than five or six paces away…"

"Yeah," Kat agreed, straightening her back and nodding at the lack of pain in her side. "Charging someone with a drawn firearm while you're holding a knife is a great way to get shot."

"Give it some time." Xander smiled at her. "You've clearly been gaining some points in reaction in the tower. If you keep working at it, we'll turn you into a gunfighter yet."

"You do realize that the same boost to my perception and reflexes will let me close the ground between me and anyone who *hasn't* drawn their gun in a fraction of a second." Kat walked over to one of the couches that a metal silhouette had been hiding behind and flopped down in it. "Guns may be fun, but knives are a girl's best friend."

"Just keep at it." Xander waved a hand at her as he walked around the desk and moved the fake shunt off of his access port. A second later, he'd plugged in a cord that snaked around to a cranial port in the back of his head. "You're probably right that nine out of ten times, you'll be solving your problems with that knife. I'd just prefer that my protégé be ready and able to shoot someone that tenth time."

"Hey," she replied defensively, sprawled out on the couch. "You saw the footage of me trying to shoot people on my first run. Considering I can hit things without putting my gun directly up against them, I deserve some sort of 'most improved shot' award."

"How about a mission and a chance to earn some credits?" Xander raised an eyebrow at her. "I've got a juicy one on deck and it's gonna take two top-tier infiltrators. With today's results, I think you qualify."

Kat sat up, interest flashing in her eyes. Although she'd played a vital role in a handful of past missions, almost uniformly, those had ended up knee-deep in bodies. It was an unfortunate fact, but Kat was much better at killing than she was at infiltration.

Hell, even her tower-granted stealth abilities all tended toward assassination rather than sneaking into a building guarded by modern security. Constant training with Xander was helping to rectify her lack of experience with the intrusion equipment, but she was still more of a killer than an infiltrator.

Xander, on the other hand, was the whole package. She'd tried to beat his times on some of the practice courses, and it was ridiculous. The man was a ghost, flitting from one camera blind spot to another, pausing only long enough to toss a saucy wink her way as Kat monitored his progress from the command center in the warehouse Xander's gang used as a headquarters.

It didn't help when she realized that he wasn't even using his psi abilities. Like Dorrik, Xander was a psi initiate, but even without utilizing the purple energy that could boost his natural capabilities, Xander beat her two out of every three times in the sparring ring.

As far as Kat could tell, Exe, as he was known on the streets, was much more than a local name. He'd settled in the Shell, the half-destroyed collection of buildings outside the Schaumburg Arcology, in part because it was his wife's base of operations.

Nina Cromwell ran the ChromeDogs, a decently sized mercenary team of street samurais that had recently secured the top spot in the Shell. The woman herself was a skilled samurai: chromed, skilled, and significantly more dangerous than most running the streets.

She just wasn't a player. As fast and tough as Nina was, she was constrained by human limits. Kat still couldn't take her, either with a firearm or in melee combat, but given enough time in the tower, eventually she'd surpass her. Fair or not, that was the truth of their world. Entry into *The Tower of Somnus* unlocked a theoretical unlimited well of potential, and that potential came with a corresponding increase in status.

"Well, you certainly look interested." Xander's dry chuckle cut through Kat's thoughts. "How do you feel about St. Louis?"

"St. Louis?" Kat cocked her head. "Isn't it one of the few megalopolises that hasn't been completely taken over by a megacorporation? I seem to recall that most of the North American corporations have satellite offices there."

"Same with the South American corps and VodCom out of Britannia," Xander agreed. "St. Louis, Hong Kong, Milan, and Sydney are the big neutral cities. The megacorps use them to exchange goods away from anybody's home turf. If you think the Shell is bad, you haven't been to one of the neutral cities. The big players frown on open warfare, but everything else is fair game."

"That sounds chaotic." Kat frowned. "I'm assuming that we're talking about St. Louis for a reason?"

"Besides the fact that you haven't lived until you've run the streets of St. Louis?" Xander asked, a touch wistfully.

Kat just rolled her eyes.

"Fine." He chuckled. "Not to take a trip down memory lane, but once upon a time, I ran with a crew called the Cardinals out of St. Louis. I was their top infiltrator when the rest of the old guard reached their limit. We broke up so some of the older samurai could retire before their fading reflexes did them in during a firefight."

"They were a good bunch." Xander smiled off into space. "Earned my name and subscription with them, but I hadn't heard much beyond an occasional check-up and chat about old times for about five years."

"Then," he continued, "a good buddy of mine e-mails me out of the blue. She wants a ten percent cut, but she has a line on a huge score. Apparently the shareholders of a few megacorps, including GroCorp, met in St. Louis a week or so ago. A big fancy sit-down. In person with no electronics. None of them would trust the others' corporate security, so they compromised and jointly hired outside security."

"According to my friend," Xander nodded cheerfully, "the outside security made a recording of the meeting. Full audio and video of everything that took place. Maybe they just thought they needed insurance in case one of the megacorps tried to silence them, or maybe they just wanted to sell the recording to another group to make a quick credit. She didn't know, and I don't either."

Kat gasped slightly. Shareholders were more-or-less a myth. There were usually a couple in each corporate enclave, sheltered and hidden from the chaos and violence of the outside world, but a single wave of their hand could move mountains.

When they traveled, it was via motorcade with multiple tanks and armored vehicles flanking them while gunships secured the airspace overhead. Each shareholder fundamentally was the heart of a corporation, and they were protected as such.

Honestly? Kat wasn't sure whether multiple shareholders from different megacorps had ever met on neutral ground before. Maybe to put an end to the South American proxy wars or the African resource scramble, but certainly nothing that had happened in her lifetime.

"The good news," Xander steepled his fingers in front of his face, leaning forward across his desk, "is that the video and audio from that meeting are worth an insane amount of money. At least a million. The bad news is that the crew that they used for security are serious business."

"I'm assuming they're worse than Steel and Blood?" Kat asked, her mind flashing back to the gang that Anna Donnst had armed in an attempt to crush her and Xander before they could sell the information related to the woman's assassination of Christopher Haupt.

"They used the Millennium Company." Xander winced, the words dropping heavily from his lips as if they should have some sort of extra meaning for Kat.

"Who?" she asked, cocking her head. "Xan, you have to remember, for as plugged in as I am in the arcology and the Shell, I barely know what's going on in Chiwaukee. You're lucky I can even find St. Louis on a map let alone know who to be wary of."

"Millennium isn't just a St. Louis mercenary group," he replied sourly, his thunder stolen by Kat's ignorance. "They're probably the biggest non-aligned player group in *The Tower of Somnus* next to the Triads. I know you're only on the second level, but you should have run into at least some of them by now."

"I just ascended to the third, actually," Kat replied, "but I don't really spend much time with other humans. I kinda got stuck on my own after my first dungeon and a couple of aliens adopted me. I've been adventuring with them ever since."

"Stallesp?" Xander frowned. "Watch out for the moles. They're full of promises, but you can't trust the fuckers. As much as I don't like the megacorps, I'll take them over those beady-eyed assholes any and every day of the week. Every time you talk to one, you can almost see them calculating how much you'd be worth to them dead."

"No," Kat responded, "I'm teamed with a lokkel and a desoph. They aren't all that keen on the stallesp either."

"Huh." Xander leaned back in his chair. "Going to be honest, Kat, that was not the answer I was expecting."

"Probably for the best, honestly." He shrugged. "If you aren't involved with an established group, someone will eat you alive in there. I'm more or less solo right now, and finding people trustworthy enough to run a dungeon with is quite a feat. I haven't ascended a level in years."

"I could talk to my friends—" Kat began.

"I appreciate the effort," Xander cut her off with a low chuckle, "but I expect it'll be a little harder than that. I've done what I needed to in order to earn dungeon awards and ascend levels, but by the time I'd learned that the existing factions in the tower were watching and taking note, it was too late."

"I'll live with my mistakes." Xander smiled at her. "How about we leave it at that?"

"I suppose." Kat frowned. "Still, it doesn't sit right."

"And that's because you're a good person." Xander winked. "Now, how about this mission? We'll be in a strange city, sneaking into a secure facility guarded by dozens of players day and night. My contact claims she has some of the old floorplans for the facility we'll be raiding, as well as some rumors she overheard from a pair of drunk Millennium samurai."

"The actual file itself," Xander continued, "is stored separately from the facility mainframe in a much higher security vault. The plan would involve me going in first to disable the remote security while you breach the vault and secure the data. What do you say, after expenses, sixty percent me, thirty percent you, and ten percent Whippoorwill?"

"What about your friend?" Kat frowned. "I thought you said she wanted ten percent."

"She's expenses," Xander replied with a grin.

CHAPTER FOUR

The engines on their tiny, variable-thrust cargo plane screamed as they rotated in their mounts, arresting the vessel's momentum with a lurch that threw Kat into her harness before the vessel began to lower itself onto the rooftop of a large, squat building.

St. Louis was a strange sight. Near its center, gleaming office buildings jutted into the sky, many of them taller than the arcology she'd spent her entire life in, but outside of the city center, things rapidly changed.

It never quite got as bad as the Shell. Even the beat-up buildings in the city's periphery looked structurally sound, even if they were covered with garish layers of bright paint and patched up with mismatching materials. Hell, even the man guiding them in for a landing had two different colors of glow rods in his hands as he motioned their airplane down.

It settled with a jolt, and Kat hastily looked over at Whip-poorwill. The poor girl had practically turned green the moment they took off from Schaumburg, the turbulence and slapdash maintenance of the chartered plane not agreeing with her.

The landing didn't help the situation. Frantically, Whippoorwill unfastened her harness and bolted out the door. Xander chuckled at Kat as the plane's engines began to wind down.

"Newbies always ask why Frank has the landing pad painted like a bad acid trip." Xander unhooked his own harness before slinging the duffle bag that had been webbed to the wall next to him over a shoulder. "Then they experience his flying and it all makes sense. Every time a customer disagrees with his approach to flying, he has to repaint the roof."

"Sod off." A middle-aged man pulled himself out of the cockpit. Frank had close-cropped salt-and pepper hair and just a touch of softness about his gut, but he was all frowns as he limped past Xander. "You were all compliments when I said I could get you into St. Louis without the corps knowing, Exe, but now that we're here, it's nothing but gripes. You didn't pay for a luxury flight and a neck pillow. I fly fast, I fly discreet, and I fly efficient."

"Of course," Xander whispered conspiratorially to Kat as she grabbed Whippoorwill's backpack as well as her own duffle bag. "He might have just painted the rooftop while he was on a bad acid trip. Did I ever tell you the story about how he got that limp? Brickcake and I were—"

"Stuff it, Exe." Frank crossed his meaty arms, the muscles bulging slightly. "I might not be a samurai anymore, but I seem to recall kicking your ass a couple times when you got mouthy back when we were both with Cardinals. I'm not above giving that another try."

"You always were a fan of eating dinner through a straw." Xander chuckled, slapping the man on the shoulder congenially. "Is Athena downstairs? We need to talk about the job."

"Yeah," Frank grunted with a toothy smile. "She's been antsy ever since you said you were coming down. I don't think I've seen her this worked up since you guys hit that Morgan Holdings armored train."

"The good old days." Xander smiled, his gold tooth glinting in the plane's dim interior.

"Good old days." Frank shook his head as he stepped out of the plane, climbing down the ladder to the tarmac below. "I walk with a limp and can't go through a metal detector without getting reminded of the shrapnel in my shoulder and ribs because of the good old days, Exe. I don't understand how you can keep up with all of this shit. I'm perfectly happy to retire as a freelance transporter. Pay's decent and there are fewer people trying to shoot me."

"People like Erinyes keep me young," Xander replied, following Frank down the ladder. "She might not have the same technical skills as me, but she's a rising star. Give it a couple of years, and you'll be hearing her name everywhere."

Kat's chest swelled as she followed the two down to the garish rooftop below. She'd already played a key role in one of the biggest turf wars in the Shell's history, but even more than that, Xander's acknowledgement *meant* something. He was an established name, and if he said she was the real deal, that was something worth bragging about.

"Unless she ends up dead by the end of the week," Frank responded with his hefty forearms crossed once more, unimpressed. "You know better than to tangle with Millennium, Exe. I don't care how much money is involved. A samurai can't spend it if they're dead."

"Enough with the doom and gloom." Xander shook his head, smile still in place. "If I'd ever listened to you, Frank, I'd have retired five years ago. It's just not who I am."

"Plus," he continued, walking past the flight crew working to unload cargo from the small variable-thrust plane they'd taken from Schaumburg, "Athena wouldn't stick her neck out like this if it wasn't the real deal. I want to hear what she has to say before I give up on a major payday."

Kat walked over to Whippoorwill. The girl looked miserable, a puddle of bile covered in sawdust about twenty paces from her. At some point, someone had handed the poor girl a water bottle that she was haphazardly nursing in an attempt to rehydrate and remove the foul taste from her mouth.

"Hey." Kat offered the pink-haired girl her backpack. "How are you holding up? Do you need one of us to make a run to a drug store for you? Something to settle your stomach?"

"No," the girl replied quietly, taking the backpack with her hacking rig in it from Kat. "I feel a lot better now that I've had some fresh air. Still a bit weak, but I won't be the one sprinting through gunfire and jumping from rooftop to rooftop."

"Hey now," Kat stuck her tongue out at Whippoorwill, "my job is to be sneaky and avoid that sort of shit. If things go well, I won't have to do any of that."

"Just working from your track record, Erinyes." Whippoorwill smiled, her face still pale but a hint of mischief in her eyes. "I don't think I've seen you finish an infiltration mission that didn't end with you covered in someone else's blood."

Kat rolled her eyes as she walked toward the stairwell that connected the roof tarmac with the rest of the building. Whippoorwill might have a point, even if it was a bit embarrassing. So far, she'd completed all of her missions, but usually by killing all of the guards and waltzing away with her goal accomplished, rather than slipping in unseen.

The night noises of St. Louis faded away as the fire door to the roof closed behind the two of them. Dim light and cold cinderblocks hemmed Kat and Whippoorwill in, the monotony of their descent only broken up by the occasional crude graffiti, mostly anti-corporate slogans, genitalia or, in more inventive cases, both.

A minute or so later, the two of them walked into the conference room that Xander had indicated on the plane. A wiry black man with gray hair around his temples sat across from Xander while a short woman, barely five feet, paced back and forth nervously.

"Ah good!" she called out as soon as the two of them walked in. Almost immediately, Kat noticed that her green hair matched the slit, snake eye pupils of her cybereyes. "Erinyes and her partner are here, so we can begin. I'd rather get the operation underway before Millennium realizes that Frank's northbound flight to Schaumburg was anything more than his regular weekly supply run to Chiwaukee."

"Wait." Xander narrowed his eyes slightly as Kat and Whippoorwill took two of the open seats. "You plan for us to move tonight?"

"Tonight's the only window, Exe," she snapped at him, running a hand through her closely cropped hair.

"Sorry," she apologized immediately. "The stress of this all is just getting to me."

"Take it slow, Athena." Xander raised both of his hands, palms up. "Erinyes and I want to do the run, but if we're going to be taking the risk, you'll have to convince us that it's not a losing bet."

"Erinyes." Kat jolted as the short woman pointed at her across the conference room. "You have a name. How did you earn it? I need someone who can move quietly, kill, and climb. Do you have me covered on those fronts?"

"Sounds perfect, honestly." Kat pursed her lips. "I single-handedly took down a squad, mostly with a knife from the shadows, to earn my name. As for climbing? I'm a player and one of my foci is gravity magic. I can't quite fly, but I can climb almost anything."

Athena gave a pointed glance to Xander. He nodded, his gold tooth glinting as he grinned broadly.

She sighed, the tension fleeing her form as she almost slumped in front of them.

"Thank God," Athena muttered. "As good as you are, Exe, I think you're too old for the other half of the mission. The fuckers in Millennium knew that someone was onto them. They have the data stored in a vault suspended from the goddamn arch."

"*The* arch." Xander's grin disappeared. "Like the Gateway Arch?"

"Yes," Athena grumbled. "Scalpel and I," she nodded at the black man, "have been softening them up for a week now. Raids on offsite datacenters to upload them so full of worms and malware that they barely boot up. We've left some fairly nasty stuff in there that we can remotely trigger to make it look like there's another attack."

"To lure guards away?" Kat asked, drawing a nod from Scalpel.

"The last two times we went in, they've had people nearby to try to trap us," he replied, a hint of a Scottish accent to his voice. "I think we've made enough of a nuisance of ourselves to help take the heat off of your infiltration."

"The plan," Athena rubbed her hands together, "is that Exe makes it to the security mainframe at the foot of the arch and disables the pressure sensors so that Erinyes can scale it and make it to the vault. Scalpel will provide overwatch. He knows enough of the base layout that he should be able to knock out any of the cameras on your way in."

"That sounds awfully loud." Kat leaned back in her chair. "I mean, even if he's using a silencer, they're sure to notice that their cameras are going out at some point."

"Eventually," Athena grinned, "but that's why Scalpel and I are getting ten percent. The program we've uploaded into the offsite servers last week should have spread around their entire base right now. Any sensors that go offline won't trigger an alarm. They'll still be able to manually see if they've gone dark, but that's the best I'm going to be able to do."

"In short," Xander frowned as well, "even with your assistance, we're going to be racing a lit fuse and we won't even know how loud it is."

"Yes." Athena threw up her short arms helplessly as she paced nervously. "My informants say they're moving it off site next week, and if Millennium gets word that any of the local players have brought in out-of-city muscle, they're gonna clamp down vise tight. This is our best shot at this. If we wait until tomorrow, you're looking at exosuits with autocannons and miniguns at best."

The room sank into silence. Whippoorwill shifted nervously next to Kat, her fingers shaky as they went through her pink hair. Xander locked eyes with her, cocking his head slightly as if to ask a question.

She blew out a ragged breath. Athena didn't have the best plan, but it could work. It was risky, but the amount of money they were talking about was insane. If bidding would start at a million, she was looking at a quarter million easy. Enough to move her mother and sister up a couple floors at the arcology and prepay their expenses for a decade.

It would also add national acclaim to her name. Even if they didn't know Katherine Debs, everyone would know that Erinyes had been involved in the heist of the year, if they could pull this off. Kat tried to ignore the whispers of pride and greed. She needed to deal with the situation rationally, but it was hard. The survivors that eked out an existence in the Shell respected her, but soon she'd be moving to Chiwaukee for college, and that would change the game.

The gangs were harder there. The crews had access to better equipment, drugs, and more importantly, subscriptions. It wouldn't just be her knifing thugs with half-fried nervous systems, loaded down with every bit of chrome they could convince a street doc to plug into them.

This would be Steel and Blood all over again. Serious and dangerous people. If she was going to survive, the respect that came from a major gig would help immeasurably.

She nodded back at Xander. His smile sprang back to his face and he turned to Athena.

"We're in." He stood up, unlatching the compartment on the back of his neck that hid his cranial port's cord. "Now upload the base layout to me so we can get moving. The night's still young and we need to get our support into position."

Xander nodded at Scalpel and Whippoorwill as Kat stood up.

An hour later, the two of them stood in an alleyway outside the cement wall that marked the outside of Millennium's base. The Gateway Arch jutted into the night sky beyond it, over six hundred feet tall and lit up by floodlights.

For about the fifth time that night, she regretted agreeing to the run. Maybe if her high school in the arcology had focused on the history of the former United States rather than 'intermediate and advanced corporate flunky training,' she'd have known how stupid it was for her to free climb the arch.

A crunch and a tinkle of glass heralded the first of Scalpel's shots. One camera after another disappeared from the stretch of wall in front of Kat and Xander as the sniper methodically worked his way down its length. A second later, the two gun emplacements shook as their motion sensors were taken out with a pair of precise shots.

Xander tapped her on the shoulder and pointed forward, two fingers extended just before he began moving. He hit the wall at a run, his body glowing dimly purple for a second before he leapt into the air, slamming a pair of pitons into the wall roughly three-quarters of the way up. Somehow they held, and a moment later he was pulling himself upward.

At the top, Xander let go of the left piton and reached into his belt, removing a tough, but thin, dark polymer blanket and throwing it over the top of the wall. As it settled onto the razor wire that curled across the precipice of the barrier, he swung slightly to the left, grabbing hold of his piton.

He hefted himself upward, forearms glowing faintly purple as he enhanced his strength beyond human norms, and landed in a crouch on top of the blanket. Winking back at Kat, he jumped down from the wall and into the Millennium compound.

She sighed, focusing to cast Levitation on herself before sprinting across the open space between her alleyway and the barrier. No one was on the street. Hell, most people didn't even come within a city block of the fortress without a good reason, likely afraid of getting caught in the crossfire between Millennium and any other crew that might want to take a crack at them.

Just as Kat was about to hit the wall, she activated Leaping, letting the skill burn her stamina as her legs glowed red.

Then she was in the air, clearing almost all of the wall in one jump. Kat grunted as she slammed into it, her hands snagging the pitons left there by Xander.

For a second, she just hung there, a black blob in her full body suit, pressed up against the wall. Then she pulled, muscles straining against the metal spikes in the wall. Levitation did its work, and she rocketed to the top of the wall.

Careful to keep her body on top of the tough, armored blanket, Kat squirmed over the top and let herself drop into the compound. She fell slowly, almost like a leaf as her unnaturally light body drifted to the ground.

A shadow detached itself from the wall and Xander, in an infiltration suit similar to her own with only his eyes visible pointed at her and then himself before turning and moving in a crouch toward the arch.

She followed, keeping her head down as they set out. The outer layer should have been guard posts, but from the look of the unmoving boot sticking out of a nearby door, it shouldn't be a problem. She wasn't sure whether Xander or Scalpel had killed the sentry, but from there, Xander's and her path was fairly clear.

They wove in between buildings, each of them concealed by a Shadow spell cast by Kat. It was far from full invisibility, mostly just decreasing the amount of light that passed out of their immediate environment, but it was enough to let them sneak past the various barracks and residential complexes.

Judging by the sound of blaring smartglass entertainment channels and alcohol-slurred conversations, the magic might not have been necessary after all. Still, she'd prefer any drunk, sleepy, or distracted samurai glancing outside to simply see just another patch of darkness as she ran past, rather than a distinctive silhouette.

Either way, the two of them reached the security checkpoint undisturbed. A squat, one-story bunker made out of concrete with windows made of sliding, bulletproof glass, Kat frowned as she began formulating a plan to get inside.

Xander didn't wait. He slipped away from their hiding spot near the wall, walking toward the bunker at a fast clip.

"*Mind Sense.*" He glowed purple briefly as he activated a psi ability. "*Compulsion.*"

He glowed again. Kat frowned as she heard some sort of struggle inside the bunker.

"*Compulsion,*" Xander repeated himself.

She glanced from him to the bunker, unsure whether to break her cover and move toward Xander while he stood just outside the door or not. A moment later, the door opened.

A hulking samurai stepped out, a pair of metal arms gleaming in the dim light of the compound. Without speaking, the man went down on one knee in front of Xander.

In one smooth motion, Xander pulled his knife free from its sheath at his side and slammed into the unmoving man's ear. He twitched once before falling to the ground.

Kat padded across the street and joined him, a slight frown on his face.

"Help me drag him inside," Xander whispered, panting for breath. "He's a big one, so I'll need you to get his legs."

After a couple seconds of grunting exertion, the two of them wrestled the massive body inside where two corpses already occupied the ground in slowly growing pools of blood.

Kat dropped the dead man and pursed her lips at the disorder. Chairs were upended and the smartglass of the security camera displays was cracked. Apparently something large and blunt had hit it hard enough to almost shatter the resilient piece of technology.

"What the——" she began, shaking her head as she looked around the room.

"Give me a second, Erinyes," Xander gasped as he slumped down into a nearby sofa, the only piece of furniture that wasn't half destroyed. "Psi abilities burn stamina rather than mana, and carrying that lunk was a bit much after I all but emptied my reserves."

"What did you do?" Kat glanced at the bodies, noticing the

neat bullet hole between the eyes of one and the crushed ribcage and torn-out throat of the other.

"Compulsion," Xander rasped as he undid a flap on the back of his neck and fished out the cord that would allow him to directly connect with the security checkpoint's network. "It's an expensive and powerful iron tier ability, but I can directly take control of a person with a low charisma attribute. One of our friends here was a player, a footpad if I guessed right. He would have been a hard kill if he saw us coming, so I just had his friend shoot him in the head. Remember, Erinyes, almost every gun is silenced if you push it up against flesh."

"But he doesn't look like he made it," Kat replied, eyes widening as she realized what had happened. "The man that came outside—"

"Yes," Xander responded as he plugged his cord into the wall interface for the building. "I had to use compulsion a second time after the big guy killed my patsy. I can do that in *The Tower of Somnus* twice in a row without it being too awful, but the extra mana cost on Earth makes it a last ditch option. Now give me a second here, I need to disable their security systems."

Kat stood in the room, biting her lip slightly as she looked at the pile of dead bodies. She probably could have taken them, but it wouldn't have been quiet. At least one of them would have gotten a shot off, and unlike Xander and her, they weren't using silenced weapons. The entire block of the Millennium compound would have known that they were there, and that would have been the end of the mission.

As good as she was, Kat wasn't untouchable. A single slip-up and she and Xander would have been running for their lives.

She clenched her fists. There was still so much to learn, so much power to earn from *The Tower of Somnus*.

"That's dirty," Xander mumbled from the couch. "I've got the security down, but it was a lot more than just vibration sensors on the arch. They have anti-aircraft guns surrounding the thing, and the vault itself is worse."

"What do you mean, Exe?" Kat asked quietly.

"The data vault itself is about the size of a coffin," Xander continued. "Suspended by four metal cables from the arch. The problem is that they have a high voltage current running through the surface of the vault with insulators at the base of each cable. Anyone touching both the vault and the wiring at the same time gets fried like a squirrel on a power line."

"Can you disable it?" Kat questioned hopefully.

"The vault's security is completely separate." Xander shook his head. "All I can do is handle the alarms and automated guns. You'll just have to be careful up there."

"Fuck," Kat spoke the word without any real feeling.

"Fuck, indeed," Xander agreed, grunting slightly. "Okay, security is down. Good luck, Erinyes."

Taking a deep breath, Kat recast Levitation. Her wait while Xander broke into the security system gave her enough time to mostly regenerate her mana. A small boon.

She walked out of the security bunker to the base of the brightly lit arch. Kat reached into her hip-mounted pack and pulled out a pair of gloves, just as black as the rest of her outfit and covered with razor sharp barbs she could use to hook into even the narrow ridges between each segment of the giant steel structure.

Even after years without proper maintenance, it gleamed silver under the floodlights that the Millennium Company kept trained upon it. Gingerly, she approached it, slipping her hooked glove into the first narrow gap and pulling herself up.

Despite Kat's awful grip—the slit between the arch's segments wasn't really large enough for much more than her fingertips—she had more than enough levels in gravity magic to actually climb the metal beast. One hand after another, she pulled her unnaturally light body up the top side of the arch.

A couple of minutes later, she had to renew the spell, almost slipping as gravity's sudden return yanked at her tenuous hold on the gleaming structure. A second later, her weight evaporated and Kat gasped for breath.

She was only halfway up, pouring sweat inside her suit, and Kat had never felt so exposed. She didn't dare look down, but she could only hope that any samurai looking at the arch couldn't identify her as anything more than a smudge on its side. Hopefully, she'd look like nothing more than one of the many patches of rust to them.

Still, there was nothing around the arch to provide even the slightest hint of cover. Even if Millennium didn't look for her, she was probably visible to Frank and Athena back at the airfield if they'd thought to use a telescope. In short, all she could do was move faster and hope that her luck held.

Kat's arms were aching, screaming at her to stop the repetitive strain she was subjecting them to, but instead she redoubled her efforts. Each scraping claw dug into the arch pulled her further up its gleaming height and away from prying eyes.

Allegedly, there had been elevators on the inside of the arch, but Millennium had long since welded the doors shut and filled the interiors with enough detritus to make that route impossible. That didn't stop Kat from wishing that they'd given it a try. Impossible or not, any option that involved 'not climbing' was something she was willing to explore at the moment.

Her breath rasped in her ears. Thankfully, the climb was much easier near the top as the arch's angle evened out. A small blessing given how spent Kat's arms were.

Even as she reached forward, digging her fingertips into another crease in the metal in order to pull her battered torso across the rusted steel of the structure, she could tell that she would need to bathe them in ice tomorrow. Curative spells might be able to fix simple damage, but strain on this level was something else entirely.

Finally, she sat in a crouch at the top of the arch, wobbling slightly as the entire arch swayed in the wind. The metal was pitted with rust, jagged and vacant. Eroded and battered in the spots where it had once been thick with ice. Kat sighed into the night air, but she could see for miles. Miles in every direction of light, glass, and steel, St. Louis was a neon panorama beneath her.

Quietly, she recast Levitation and followed up with Pseudo-pod. Then, she closed her eyes and stepped off the edge.

Almost on its own, the tentacle of water reached out to a cable on her right, slowing Kat's gentle descent, but holding her at two arm's lengths from the strip of metal. Silently, she fell at a measured pace, her magic all that prevented her from plummeting to her death.

She opened her eyes and looked down, immediately regretting it as her vision swam. Kat slammed her eyes shut to recenter herself before opening them once more, this time focusing on the dark, metal data vault rushing up beneath her.

Finally, just shy of the vault, Kat dismissed Pseudopod, ensuring that there would be no connection between her and the cable. Then, her feet touched down.

Kat quickly went to her knees, finding the hatch that concealed the data port she'd need access to on the vault. Whatever the lock was, Kat couldn't even begin to make heads or tails of it.

She smiled in the night air. Oh well, she always had Plan B. Knife.

The blade glowed red as Kat burned through her stamina. Four precise jabs of the knife removed the hinges from the data port's armored cover.

Quietly, she picked the square of metal up and moved it to the side, replacing it with the data shunt from her pouch.

She leaned back on her heels, tapping her earpiece. They'd maintained radio silence the entire mission in order to prevent their communications from alerting Millennium, but the data stream from the shunt would be just as 'loud' to any data sniffer as a quick call.

"Whippoorwill." Kat stared off at the glittering city. "The data shunt is in place. Do your thing, but expect heavy resistance."

"Got it, Erinyes," the woman responded. "Scalpel is saying

that everything is quiet on our end. I'll let you know when I have something."

Kat sat down, stretching her back and aching arms, the vault swaying in the wind beneath her as she waited for the hacker to do her work. Above her, the stars twinkled peacefully.

She really hadn't had much time like this. Really, most of Kat's leisure had been in *The Tower of Somnus*, but even then, most of her time with her friends had been devoted to hunting and killing monsters.

Maybe once she got to college, she'd actually have some time to herself between classes. As much as she loved the adrenaline and challenge of her job as an infiltrator, she desperately needed time to herself for some reflection.

A burst of gunfire from below startled her out of her reverie. Kat sat up blinking as an alarm blared to life and lights began to snap on across the multiple city blocks of the compound.

"Erinyes!" Whippoorwill shouted into her ear, her voice panicked. "Scalpel says that Millennium samurai are moving everywhere! Oh God, I'm not even halfway—"

"Change of plans," Xander's voice cut Whippoorwill off. "Erinyes, you need to stay with the shunt until the hack is complete. No matter what, the hack *needs* to be completed. We need this data. Then you need to destroy the evidence."

Kat found herself nodding along as Xander delivered the clipped orders.

"We will meet at fallback point A in two hours. If anyone is missing, we will pick up stragglers at point B in three hours. There is no point C. Plan C is hitchhiking home."

"Good luck, Exe," Kat replied, eyes glued to the shunt in front of her.

"Good luck, Erinyes," he answered, voice softening slightly. "I'm about to break out, hopefully that will take some heat off of you. Stay safe."

CHAPTER FIVE

"Erinyes!" Whippoorwill's voice was shrill and breathy. "There are floodlights everywhere! I think they found our area of the wall by the dead cameras. I'm sure that people will be coming any second and—"

"Whip." Kat gritted her teeth, reaching into the pouch and pulling out a vacuum-sealed plastic package. "I'm going to need you to calm down and focus on my voice. Given what I had to do to get here," she popped the package open, removing the putty from inside and warming it with her hands, "the defenses on this server are going to be insane. None of us can move until you crack it and extract that data. People are going to come looking for you just like they're looking for me. Scalpel will keep you safe. You need to focus on your dive."

"But Erinyes—" Whippoorwill began.

"Movement on the street," Scalpel's clipped voice cut in on the network. "We're under some pretty heavy-duty camo tarping. I'll try not to shoot unless someone is entering either my building or Whippoorwill's, but we have a running clock here."

"Focus, Whip." Kat carefully molded a ring of the spongy high explosive around one of the insulated cable connectors, careful not to touch the metal. "You can't lose yourself like you did last time. You're better than this."

"Break it down into small pieces." Kat kept working, forming another snake out of the explosive dough as Whip-poorwill mumbled to herself. "Step by step, even the biggest problems are manageable."

"That's the spirit, Whip," she encouraged her partner, trying to avoid the tension in her shoulders as a round of shouting and gunfire exploded at the base of the arch. Xander was on the move, and all she could do was hope that he made it. "You've got this."

Below her, a building exploded. The pressure wave washed over the suspended data vault, forcing Kat to clutch its sides, the barbs on her gloves scraping against the sheer steel as she frantically tried to keep her feet from touching the conductive cables.

"Wrong building, you idiots." Xander chuckled gleefully over the comm network. "Hope the high explosives weren't too spicy for you."

A burst of gunfire punctuated his boastful statement.

"Erinyes," he continued more soberly. "That's as much attention as I can draw. I blew up the security bunker for the arch. Backup systems should be online soon. See you on the other side."

"Give 'em hell, Exe," Kat replied worriedly, carefully returning to her hands and knees even as the vault continued to rock back and forth.

Her only answer was more gunfire. From the top of the arch, she couldn't tell if it was Xander himself, someone mind-controlled by him, or just a jumpy guard firing at shadows.

Regardless, there was nothing for her to do but cautiously wrap another snake of explosives around the base of one of the cables. Either Xander would escape or he wouldn't. Same with her. All that was left was speed and luck.

"Hostiles in the street," Scalpel's voice cut in grimly. "Looks like they're going door to door. I'd say we have two minutes before they're at Whippoorwill's building and I have to start shooting. Status update please."

"Almost—" Whippoorwill's voice was clipped, distracted. "Oh, Jesus. How many connection sniffers even is that?"

She grunted.

"I'm doing fine," the young woman continued a second later. "I'd be doing better without the constant distractions, but I'm in. There's a lot of stuff in here. More than I'll be able to download and carry out."

"Erinyes," her partner's voice was serious, none of the earlier nervousness present. "I think I found the video and audio, but there's so much junk data buried in here that there's no way I'll find the encryption file. Even if I had an hour, it's just not going to happen."

"That's fine, Whip." Kat tried to keep her voice calm as she laid the last of her explosives down. "We can decrypt it later. For right now, we need you to—"

A gunshot rang out over Kat's earpiece.

"Target down," Scalpel's voice was almost a growl. She could hear the iron clank as the man worked his bolt action. "Taking shot two now."

"Grab it and go," Kat finished after the second gunshot. "Get to fallback point A with the data and we'll figure things out from there."

"I'll cover her," Scalpel offered, the metallic clank of another high velocity round being chambered audible over his live mic. "I figure I can hold their attention for a couple more minutes before I have to bug out. Give the package a proper chance to get to point A."

"Get going, Whip." Kat smiled slightly as she fished out her detonator, a small plastic rectangle with a single button and indicator light on it. "I'm about to draw a whole hell of a lot of attention myself so I'll be disposing of my communicator. I don't want anyone tracking me, after all. I'll see everyone at point A."

The last sound she heard before Kat pulled the communicator out of her ear was yet another gunshot as Scalpel brought another samurai down. Efficiently, she stuffed the earpiece into the explosive putty around one of the cables and stood up shakily.

The data vault swayed back and forth in the night wind under Kat's feet as she fished around for the last item in her pouch. A second later, she pulled out the same brand of dark and resilient, high-tensile blanket that Xander had used to defeat the razor wire earlier.

With a flick of her wrists, the square of fabric extended completely and Kat grasped its ends, forming a sort of scoop from the opaque cloth. Her grip on the right-most pair of corners was a bit tenuous in order to maintain her hold on the detonator, but there wasn't much she could do about that.

Letting out a deep, shuddering breath, Kat cast Levitation. Immediately, she could feel her body lighten.

Biting her lip, Kat jumped off the vault, sending it swinging behind her. A second later the blanket caught the waiting wind, inflating and slowing her descent further.

She floated gently, like a bit of dandelion fluff over the kicked over anthill that was the Millennium base. Floodlights swiveled, playing their light over the patchwork and poorly maintained buildings of the mercenary camp as they searched for Xander.

In the distance, she heard gunfire and screaming as the wind buffeted her. Kat smiled slightly, content to just drift quietly in the night's embrace until she neared the outside range for her detonator.

Finally, Kat shifted her thumb, pressing down on the detonator's button.

She glanced over her shoulder just in time to see the explosives go off. Three detonated correctly, balls of fire ripping the cables free from the rectangle of metal. It swung precariously in the night sky, connected to the Gateway Arch by a solitary and groaning cable.

The night seemed to hold its breath as all eyes swiveled to

the hanging, armored server as it twisted gently, buffeted by the wind.

Then, the final cable, creaking in protest under the full weight of the data vault, snapped with an audible crack. It plummeted past her, slamming into the cement below with a loud crash.

Shards of electronic debris sprayed everywhere as the vault's case shattered from the fall, the security floodlights causing them to shine and glimmer. Another alarm sounded from the center of the camp, and the dark, scurrying shapes of samurai running to and fro began to fill the streets.

Silently, Kat thanked Xander's foresight. A dark combat suit and a dark parachute against the night sky provided her with all the camouflage she needed to finish her descent unnoticed despite the hundreds of samurai on high alert.

She touched down on top of a garage, quickly wrapping the detonator in the blanket and stuffing it back in her carrying pouch. It probably wasn't necessary, but the first rule of infiltration was to provide as little evidence as possible. An infiltrator should be a ghost on the site and a name taking credit for a job on the information channels after the fact.

Nothing she stuffed into her carrying pouch had touched her skin thanks to the bodysuit, but better safe than sorry.

Objects stowed, Kat cast Shadow and used the last remaining seconds of her Levitation to scamper down the side of the garage, a mobile and unnaturally quiet chunk of night.

Activating Cat Step, she burned stamina to silence herself completely as Kat rounded the corner of the garage and approached the open bay door. A man and a woman stood under a flickering light, arguing.

"Look, Hazior." Kat froze as she heard the feminine voice. "I know that the boss sounded the all-hands-on-deck alarm, but that's for the samurais, not for us. I just finished fixing the transmission on Otto's jeep and he told me that he wants me to put a new coat of paint on it. You know how crazy that guy is. The boss isn't going to notice if we don't report to our alert posts, but Otto sure as fuck is going to notice if his jeep isn't painted."

"Otto can go polish his fancy, new chrome arm for all I care," the man responded angrily. "The alarm means that we all have to get to battle stations. I don't think either of us are going to do much with twenty-year-old rifles hiding in a crow's nest on top of the pub, but that's what the orders say."

"Fuck the orders." The woman snorted, a jangle of keys audible as she pulled something out of her pocket. "No one cares, and Otto will give me hell for months if his jeep isn't painted. You can hang out on top of the pub if you want, but you're not going to drag me into this. Now hand me the paint applicator or get out. Your choice."

Kat snuck around the corner, quietly approaching the two. The woman was walking into the garage, her back to Kat as she approached a huge red and black jeep that filled up the center of the small repair bay. Behind her, the man grunted and followed, his back to Kat as well.

"Let's just get this done, Josie." the man shook his head, tossing a shock of unruly red hair to the side. "The quicker we get the car painted, the quicker we can get to our posts. With any luck, no one will notice—"

Kat's hand slapped across his throat, the razor-sharp climbing barbs digging into his unprotected flesh before she ripped her hand away, taking a good portion of his throat with it.

He stumbled forward, hands going to his throat in surprise as he tried to process the sudden pain from Kat's strike. The woman turned, a look of confusion on her face as she tried to make sense of her companion cutting off mid-sentence.

Kat's slap literally wiped the expression from her face.

The woman stumbled backward, opening her disfigured mouth to scream only for a follow-up swipe to rip her throat out.

As the woman collapsed to the floor, Kat frowned. Both of them were mechanics, not samurai. Bystanders just trying to make ends meet in the wastes between corporate enclaves. In all likelihood, they'd started working for the Millennium Company because it was one of the more stable and profitable employers nearby.

They didn't deserve to die like this, but she didn't have a choice. Sneaking past them risked discovery, and although the entire compound was locking down, they still hadn't pinpointed her location. More importantly, Kat would need an escape route.

She sighed, removing the blood-soaked gloves and putting them into her pouch. As effective as they'd been, Kat still preferred a knife.

A moment later, Kat was rifling through the woman's pockets until she found the jeep's keys. After a couple attempts, she found the matching key on the ring and opened its surprisingly heavy door. She paused, the vehicle halfway open as she inspected the solid steel plate hidden just behind the door's upholstery.

Kat smiled as she climbed in, flicking the windshield with her index finger, drawing the hollow thud of thick bulletproof glass. It was up armored enough to ignore pistol fire, and with any luck it would be able to shrug off a decent number of rifle rounds. This might work after all.

She turned the key in the ignition. The engine turned over with a welcome thrum.

Good. Xander had only taught her the basics of driving, considering it one of many potentially useful skills that his infiltrators should know. If the vehicle had any problems, or God forbid, it was a manual, she would have been completely out of luck.

Carefully, she shifted the car into drive and tapped the gas. It lurched forward with a growl. Kat wrenched the wheel to the side, trying to avoid a hydraulic lift meant for elevating vehicles.

A second later, she was cursing herself for oversteering as the vehicle almost ended up lodged sideways in the garage door.

Foot on the brake, she shifted the car back into reverse and shimmied it back into the building.

Even as she tried to exit the building again, carefully nursing the steering wheel, she couldn't help but imagine the mercenaries in the surrounding buildings converging on her as she created a racket.

Mercifully, she managed to edge the jeep out of the garage before any unwelcome witnesses happened upon her. As soon as the vehicle was in the streets, Kat hammered the gas pedal.

The tires squealed for a second, the jeep fishtailing as their treads desperately tried to find purchase on the asphalt. Then, the vehicle kicked Kat back into her seat as it launched forward, accelerating down the narrow street of the compound.

For a second, a manic grin blossomed on her face as the jeep tore down the narrow street, scattering trash as the big vehicle's grill slammed through the cluttered and dirty streets. Then, the road curved, angling toward an exit from the compound.

In a panic, Kat switched her foot from the gas to the brakes. The car skidded, the steering all but unresponsive as the tires locked up in a futile effort to slow the jeep's momentum. At the last second, Kat remembered her lessons from Xander and released the brakes, tapping the gas.

She struggled with the wheel, failing to keep the vehicle under control as it careened sideways into a nearby building. The metal screeched as the cinderblocks of the dark and hulking structure scraped off paint and a mirror.

Kat barely managed to keep the vehicle from stalling out, accelerating away from the damaged building. Her breath came in ragged bursts, sweat filling the airtight suit. The road rumbled beneath her, but Kat's eyes couldn't help flickering to the doorways and rooftops around her.

She was more or less in command of the jeep now, but her efforts had made a lot of noise. It was only a matter of time until someone noticed that she was—

The windshield thudded as a bullet struck it, spiderwebs of

cracks springing into existence as the interior layer of glass sprayed across the passenger side seat. Kat swore.

Two nearby roofs erupted into gunfire as concealed Millennium samurai and employees opened fire with whatever weapons they had on hand. Bullets whined and cracked off of the jeep's hood even as others thumped like hail into the thick armor plates of its doors.

She ducked, windshield rattling as a spray of bullets transformed it into a cracked and cloudy mess. Squinting, Kat could barely make out the road ahead of her through the handspan of clear bulletproof glass just above the dash.

Then, she was past the emplacement. Rifles still cracked behind her, and while the occasional shot hit the back of the jeep, nothing came close to penetrating the armored vehicle.

Kat didn't have a chance to relax. Her hands were still clenched painfully tight on the steering wheel, the front of her outfit studded with glass shards from the repeated impacts on the windshield.

Ahead of her, Kat saw the steel curtain of the compound's gate, a huge man glinting with chrome and holding some sort of huge rifle standing just to the side of it. Almost in slow motion, he turned, bringing the gun to bear on her.

Kat poured mana into the air just in front of him, casting Dazzle.

The night exploded into strobes of light, visible even through her eyelids as Kat hammered her eyes shut. The man fired the massive firearm, the thunderous report half-deafening her even through the jeep's armored frame, but the spell did its work, blinding the man for a half second and sending his shot wide.

Kat's seatbelt slammed into her chest like a sledgehammer as the jeep plowed into the man.

She was spinning, all control of the jeep lost in the impact. Before Kat could even process what was happening, air bags exploded all around her, cushioning her from the sudden jolt as the vehicle slammed sideways into the fortress' gate.

A second of fuzzy fumbling later, Kat cut herself free, her black infiltration suit covered with both glass and the white powder in the airbags. Dazed, she staggered free from the jeep, trying to ignore the ringing in her ears as she assessed her circumstances.

"You slag!" an enraged baritone voice shouted behind her. "What the *fuck* did you do to my goddamn car!"

Kat whirled, eyes widening beneath the one-way mesh that covered her eyes. The man she'd hit with the jeep was still standing. Somehow.

He hadn't emerged from the crash unscathed. The huge weapon in his arms was a mangled wreck, his left leg twisted unnaturally backward, and a huge wound on his face bled freely. That said, even as Kat watched, his leg glowed red and snapped back into place with a sickening, crackling sound.

"I fucking have the Immovable perk," he looked at the destroyed cannon in his metallic arms, throwing it to the ground in disgust, "and you have the gall to hit me with my own fucking jeep?"

"I don't care whose crew you're in," he drew a hand axe from his belt, the weapon almost inconsequential in his huge grip but for the red glow of a tower-granted skill suffusing it, "I will find you and I will end you for that."

Without speaking, Kat drew her handgun, focusing mana on a Gravity Spike as she quickly sighted the weapon on him and began pulling the trigger.

He tried to dodge, but whatever skill he was using to repair his left leg hadn't quite finished its work. The limb buckled as he put weight on it, and almost half of the high-caliber bullets slammed into him.

She gritted her teeth, noticing the spark of metal on metal even when the bullets stuck his torso. The slow speeds required to silence her high caliber rounds made them almost worthless against armor, and whoever this man was, he'd had enough steel implanted under his skin to classify him as construction equipment.

"Do you know how much synth skin itches?" He growled, pulling himself back into a standing position as the slide on her pistol locked open, out of bullets. "You must, because that's all your little tantrum will cost me."

"You know," he wiped the blood from his eye with his free hand, "I'm going to cut your hands off for that. No one makes me bleed my own blood."

Kat grunted, releasing her stored mana into Gravity Spike. The gunfire and his grandstanding had kept the samurai in the same spot for the full two seconds the spell required to activate.

This time, his leg almost exploded.

For a moment, it strained as the magic pushed and pulled on the limb simultaneously, the man's pants rippling under the pressure. Then, the metal implanted under his skin gave way. Pistons and smashed electronics burst from either side of his knee as the conflicting gravitational forces ripped it apart.

She didn't wait for him to collapse, activating Levitation and Leaping simultaneously to jump onto the roof of her jeep. A moment later, her chest slammed into the gate. Kat's hands fought for purchase on the slick metal, eventually grabbing the top and pulling herself over even as the samurai screamed with impotent rage.

Kat landed in the streets outside the compound and sprinted away, casting Shadow as she vanished into the maze of urban disrepair surrounding the Millennium base. Behind her, Kat still heard scattered gunshots and shouting.

She redoubled her efforts, forcing stamina into Cat Step to increase her speed as she sprinted through the dark and empty streets of St. Louis. Ten minutes and almost two miles later, she paused, gasping for breath.

The extra point of endurance from *The Tower of Somnus* was really beginning to show its worth. Usually, she was more of a sprinter than a distance runner, but between her adrenaline and magical enhancement, Kat found herself in an alleyway between a clothing store and a smartpanel shop, exhausted but well away from Millennium pursuit.

After about three minutes, Kat stripped out of her infiltration suit, wincing as the wet fabric clung to her skin. She really needed to rehydrate.

Finally, she plopped the expensive and damp pile of polymers and armor into a nearby dumpster. She reached into the pockets of her street clothes, producing two large plastic bags of metallic powder, one silver aluminum and the other, reddish-brown iron oxide.

Efficiently, Kat spread a thick layer of the powder on the remains of her suit before removing her final piece of infiltrator gear, a simple, automated zinc firestarter on a timer. She clicked the silver and black circle twice, giving herself five minutes.

Another casting of Levitation and she was on the roof of the clothing store, darting past the rusting HVAC unit and air filtration equipment that littered its surface.

As soon as she reached the edge, Kat activated Leaping, still wreathed in Shadow, to jump to the next rooftop, repeating the process as necessary. A couple of minutes and rooftops later, she lowered herself into another alleyway and let her spells fade.

Her street clothes were rumpled and wet, but otherwise serviceable, as Kat stepped into the street just outside St. Louis's downtown. Storefronts lined the street, their doors barred shut given the time of night, but with the occasional bar, flophouse, unregulated cyberware clinic, and drug den spilling noise and light into the otherwise fairly sedate walkway.

It wasn't exactly busy, but there were enough people walking the poorly maintained streets, peering at the beat up storefronts for her to not look out of place. Most of them stood outside the handful of open buildings, smoking or drinking openly as they took care not to make eye contact with anyone on the move.

Kat smiled slightly. It was just like the Shell. Most of the time, people wouldn't bother, but curiosity could get you killed. Sometimes, it just wasn't in your best interest to remember identifying features on a dark figure hurrying alone at night.

As she drew closer to the downtown, there still weren't any streetlights, but the frequent acrid blue, green, and pink advertisements provided enough light for her to make her way even as they screamed silently at her to upgrade her smartpanel and enjoy a 'Neobeef* Barbeque at Doc Morbid's.'

Kat didn't have the first idea what neobeef was, but she knew better than to trust any restaurant that advertised itself as the 'best iguana on a stick in junktown' in follow-up ads. It just didn't seem like the sort of place someone with any other options would frequent.

Then, the street she was following turned and Kat saw downtown St. Louis for the first time. Her step faltered and she sucked in a breath as she tried to process it all.

Glass and steel buildings, covered in garish corporate logos, lined the road. The street itself was filled with a boisterous and eclectic mix of people. Most of them sported some chrome, but almost as ubiquitous were body modifications.

Whether it was metal spikes growing from a man's shoulders, or a woman's cat tail flicking back and forth in the pink and blue glow of a two-story bar wedged in between two corporate enclaves, cosmetic changes were everywhere.

She picked up her pace, hand on the knife inside her jacket and acutely aware of the empty holster on her hip. Back in the dumpster, it was melting in a thermite blaze along with the rest of her depressingly expensive infiltration gear.

Despite the waste, the chances of Millennium being able to identify her or spot Kat as she tried to leave the city were too great. Tracking people via DNA and fingerprints was hard without any sort of centralized database, but far from impossible, and from what Kat had heard about Millennium, she would prefer to only leave them with 'impossible' options.

She shouldered her way through the crowd, her smartpanel superimposing a red dot on her destination. No one bothered her, the various colorful civilians and samurai too intent on their own goals to bother.

It was refreshing, really. A combination of the Shell without the constant paranoia and threat of a gunfight mixed with the affluence of her arcology minus the slavish devotion to the company. As long as Kat ignored the massive mercenary compound in the middle of the city that she'd just escaped, she could see why Xander liked the place.

Finally, she reached her destination. Neon Taco. The pink and green displays outside lived up to its name, showing flickering images of a man shoving a taco into his face while a woman gave a thumbs up.

She pushed the door open and stepped inside, wincing as an awful jingle about the 'freshest beef, beyond belief' assaulted her ears. A quick glance around the mostly empty store located Whippoorwill sitting next to a tense-looking Xander. A table over, Athena was practically vibrating in her seat while Scalpel casually ate a burrito.

She sighed. Despite everything, it looked like the plan was still on track.

"Looks like I'm the last one here." Kat walked over with a smile, drawing relieved looks from both Xander and Athena. "Sorry about the delay, I ended up having to jog across half the city."

Now they just had to get out of St. Louis and sell their ill-gotten gains.

CHAPTER SIX

"We will start the bidding at one million." It was strange, hearing Xander's actual voice next to her even as her smart-panel displayed a smooth, metallic face repeating the same words in a heavily modulated and impossible to identify tone.

"The data is an encrypted audio and video recording of an in-person meeting between shareholders from GroCorp, NeoSyne, JB Holdings, and WMC Integrated Robotics that took place in the last ten days in St. Louis," the dual voices continued. "The information was acquired yesterday and our organization hasn't decrypted it yet. Moreover, it is laced with anti-copying protocols. The information can be moved, but doing so will delete the original."

A murmur went up in the augmented reality auction hall. Kat slowly pulled her gaze across the simulated room. Blank digital walls hemmed in a number of chairs occupied by the genderless, faceless robots that made up their buyers.

The entire display was only visible through the smartpanel over Kat's eye. In reality, Xander, Kat, and Athena were in a dingy hotel, sitting on a pair of lumpy twin beds and a folding chair respectively.

"This means," Xander ignored the interruption, "that anyone purchasing it will have the responsibility of decoding the data, but more importantly, they will be the only person other than its original owners to know the contents of the recording."

"How can anyone even know it's genuine?" one of the faceless entities asked in a blurred but feminine voice. "I'm not paying a million or so credits to watch a video of your latest vacation."

"I am displaying the metadata headers right now." Xander waved a hand at Whippoorwill. The girl nodded, her eyes blurring. "As you can see, the data was created less than two weeks ago by Millennium Company vid recorders in the St. Louis Secure Conference and Convention Center."

"St. Louis," the woman's altered voice mused. "So you were the ones responsible for the Gateway Arch raid that's been blowing up the message boards. Millennium won't even admit that it's been hit, but word on the street is that it's willing to pay a lot of money to recover something stolen from it. Interesting."

"And I'm perfectly willing to sell the data back to them." Xander smiled like a wolf as his metal avatar inclined its head at one of the robotic dolls in the auction hall that was sitting apart from the others. "I won't say how the information ended up in my hands, but I will confirm on my honor as a samurai that I haven't viewed it or been able to make a copy. If Mr. Jackson wishes to repurchase the data, he simply needs to win the auction."

"I thought this was a secure conference room, Exe." The avatar's face blurred, the smooth metal replaced by the frowning, almost emaciated face of an older black man. "I don't take kindly to being exposed like this."

Kat shifted. She knew about Mr. Jackson from her briefings on Millennium. No one really knew why he picked such an ordinary samurai name, but the CEO of the Millennium Company was one of the highest ranked players on Earth. He never admitted to a specific level, but it was well known that his class had evolved, making him at least level twelve.

"It's secure enough," Xander continued, his avatar waving a metal hand dismissively. "I just assumed that your organization would attend the auction, noticed that you were sitting separately from the rest of the guests, and verified that you were logged on from a St. Louis node. The rest was just an educated guess."

Mr. Jackson squinted at Xander's metallic avatar. "Did you just trick me into outing myself in order to convince the rest of these people that your sale was genuine?"

"Now, now, Mr. Jackson." Kat could almost see Xander's shit-eating grin on his featureless avatar. "A gentleman doesn't kiss and tell."

"I should have fucking killed you when you were a street rat, Exe." The samurai crossed his arms, leaning back into the digital seat. "Alas, here I am paying for that mistake. Your little stunt cost me good, Exe. The code says I can't retaliate unless I can prove that this is all personal. Otherwise," he continued, gravelly voice dragging itself across Kat's ears, "it's a 'regular business activity.' The code doesn't want us at each other's throats, tearing each other apart just because two crews worked opposite sides on a job, even if a couple people died."

"I've gotta say, Exe," Mr. Jackson shook his head, "this sure feels personal to me. I can't prove shit and you know it, but I have people actively looking for business that involves you. You keep this shit up, and we might be meeting up close and personal sooner than you think."

"Well," Xander replied, "I await our future business interaction with bated breath."

"We are offering discounts to prospective clients that involve you," Mr. Jackson spat the words out through gritted teeth, fire in his eyes, "and payment plans."

Kat glanced at Xander, slightly worried. Athena shifted on her bed in the dingy hotel room. Samurai code was pretty clear. If a samurai had earned a street name, usually by either killing another named individual or completing some sort of difficult and highly dangerous feat, their personal lives were protected.

All-out war was bad for everyone, and no samurai wanted to wake up to the muzzle of a gun in their mouth.

Business was business, and given how often samurai ended up shooting at each other, bad blood was inevitable. About seventy years ago, before *The Tower of Somnus* even came to Earth, all of the big crews came to an agreement. Any organization that retaliated against another for simply doing a job better than them was widely mocked and ostracized.

That didn't mean that there weren't feuds and vendettas, but for almost every samurai, their most valuable asset was their word and their name. If you got a reputation, other crews wouldn't work with you, street docs wouldn't help you, and smugglers wouldn't sell you the best gear.

Mercenaries didn't offer discounts. It simply wasn't done. It gave the impression that a crew was taking something personally. They worked a dangerous job, and the idea of accepting less money for risking their lives was anathema. Samurai didn't negotiate. That was something that corporate employees did. Either you could pay their price, or you couldn't.

Payment plans were even worse. Nine times out of ten, only the first or second credit transfers cleared. After that, clients almost always requested intercorporate arbitration which they had a tendency to win, regardless of facts.

Mr. Jackson wasn't technically breaking the code, but he was toeing the line. Honestly? If he wasn't the leader of one of the world's largest independent organizations, it would probably be enough to blacklist his entire organization. Unfortunately for Kat and Xander, there were certain privileges that came with having a lot of guns and enough chrome and players to use them.

"That is very generous of you." Xander clicked his tongue sympathetically. "I would have thought that you would be eager to devote your time and credits to fixing the flaws in your security. After all, that's what led to the data's theft. Instead, you decide to give back to the community over a business transaction gone sour. Very commendable, Mr. Jackson."

"A business transaction gone sour?" The avatar ground his teeth together. "You broke into my home, guns blazing, stole information from me and—"

"If you two are done flirting," the earlier female cut in dryly, "can we get to the auction? Mr. Jackson feels entitled to the data. Great. Let's see if he can outbid the rest of us. If he can't, all of the posturing in the world isn't going to change anything."

"One point one million credits," a male voice responded, one of the metallic avatars raising a hand.

Mr. Jackson's digital image stood up from its seat. "Now, if the august individuals present here would just show me some face and—"

"Face?" The woman sneered at him. Out of the corner of her eye, Kat spotted Xander grinning like an idiot. "The only way this footage would exist is if you had betrayed your employers. You just all but broke the code to threaten Exe and interfere with this auction. If your unhinged actions were a piece of theater by Exe to convince the rest of us that the data was a bombshell, it sure worked on me. One point two million."

Mr. Jackson sputtered, unable to respond to her.

"Plus," she continued, "You don't know who any of us are. Even if I wanted to curry favor with you, I couldn't exactly reveal my identity right now for obvious reasons. I gain *nothing* by doing you an anonymous favor."

That was Belle Donnst. Kat didn't understand where that knowledge came from, but there was no question in her mind. Even without the predatory woman's physical appearance or voice, Kat would recognize those mannerisms anywhere.

The other attendees at the auction murmured appreciatively, several of their avatars nodding while Mr. Jackson fumed.

"One point three million," a different male voice interjected.

"Too rich for my blood," a woman chuckled. A moment later, her avatar disappeared entirely, leaving only an empty seat.

"One point three five," Mr. Jackson hissed, his words almost bringing him physical pain.

"One point six," Belle responded almost lazily, her smooth metal face turning to stare down the mercenary. "You have a fair amount of money for a contractor, Mr. Jackson, but do you really think you'll be able to keep up with corporate resources?"

"This isn't over," he replied, crossing his arms. "I don't think any of you understand the depths you're swimming in right now, but I, for one, will be ecstatic when the sharks swimming just below your feet tire of your games."

The mercenary disappeared with a flourish, his avatar flashing into a spray of colored pixels before fading entirely.

For a second, no one spoke as an uneasy silence descended upon the auction. Even in their hotel room, both Whippoorwill and Athena looked very uncomfortable. The smaller woman was sweating as she sat on the end of her lumpy mattress, hands shaking as she rubbed them together.

"One point six five," a different mechanically distorted feminine voice interrupted the moment. "If Mr. Jackson is willing to risk sounding like an antagonist from Chrome Cowboys, there really must be something to this recording."

"And I'm sure there is!" Xander cut in to egg them on. "It was located in a secure data vault suspended almost five hundred feet off the ground by electrified cables with at least four 80mm anti-aircraft cannons pointed at it. I only come to the august individuals in this room with the finest of creatively sourced information, and I am sure that the data for sale today will meet your expectations."

"One point seven million credits hope you're right." The metallic avatar that Kat assumed was Belle laughed sardonically.

"One point seven." Xander whistled, his digital image giving the assembled bidders a double thumbs up. "Can anyone beat one point seven million credits?"

"One point nine million." Kat turned to look at an avatar that had remained silent and motionless until that moment. It lowered its hand almost lazily.

"Oh God," Whippoorwill whispered next to her, "that's so much money. I don't even—"

"One point nine!" Xander pointed at the avatar that had just spoken. "Can any of the gentle-beings present make that two million?"

The digital auction hall lapsed into silence with the various metallic figures glancing at each other, asking unspoken questions. Finally, the icon Kat associated with Belle chuckled.

"Unfortunately," she shrugged a pair of silver shoulders, "I'm tapped out. Enjoy your purchase, and a good night to the rest of you."

She disappeared in a flash of color, logging out of the digital auction hall.

One by one, the various other parties began to follow her lead, disappearing in bursts of multicolored pixels as they forfeited and ducked out of the auction until only the highest bidder remained.

"Well then." Xander's avatar jumped down from the podium he'd been using to address the gathered bidders. "Congratulations are in order. If I could have a drop location and a proof of escrow, we will get you your product shortly."

The figure raised a hand, pointing its palm at Xander. "First, how can I be assured that the data will reach me? I have some idea as to the identities of my competitors and none of them are known for playing fair or nice."

Behind Kat, Athena whimpered.

"A valid question." Xander waved a hand vaguely in the direction of Kat's avatar. Without a cranial jack, she was mostly immobile, only able to rotate her head and look through her smartpanel unless she purchased a controller or a joystick. "Erinyes will be handling the delivery. So long as your drop point is in Chiwaukee, we can get the product to you tonight."

"If anyone tries to stop Erinyes," Xander chuckled darkly, "she has a bit of a reputation for leaving bodies in her wake. I obviously can't promise you one hundred percent safety, but the data will be much more secure than the lives of anyone foolish enough to try to come after it."

"She was the one that took down an entire squad over in Schaumburg, right?" the man asked after a pause.

Xander and his avatar both nodded.

"That should be sufficient," the anonymous man agreed. "I am in the Oak Suite of the Royal Ambassador Hotel on Michigan Avenue. As for the money, you can contact Zurich Escrow, account number 981-B-822-J. My man is wiring the money right now. As soon as I verify the data, it's yours."

Xander motioned with a hand toward Whippoorwill. She leaned back, her eyes losing focus as she accessed Zurich Escrow's information portal to verify the man's claim. A couple of seconds later she sat up from the uncomfortable and questionably stained chair.

"It's there, Exe," her voice was quiet, almost hesitant. Kat frowned slightly as she glanced between Whippoorwill and Athena, the shorter woman rocking back and forth, mumbling something under her breath.

"Good doing business with you, Mr. Oak Suite." Xander clapped his hands together cheerfully. "Barring interference from a rival, Erinyes should be over with your data within the hour."

The avatar simply nodded before disappearing into a multi-colored sparkle as he logged out. A second later, Kat's view of the virtual space in her smartpanel disappeared as Xander dismissed it entirely.

"There!" Xander spun around, gold tooth glinting in the neon glow of the advertisements flickering outside the flophouse window. "That wasn't so bad now, was it? Whippoorwill, if you could upload directions to the Royal Ambassador Hotel into Kat's smartpanel, I would appreciate it."

Even as the hacker stood up, crossing the room toward Kat, Athena threw herself backward and screamed into her communication earpiece. "Scalpel, *now!*"

Kat's head whipped to the side a fraction of a second too

late. The window to their shared bedroom shuddered, a spiderweb of white lines appearing on it.

Then blood erupted from Whippoorwill's stomach, the girl folding over as the report from a rifle shot echoed from across the street. Kat's eyes widened as her partner collapsed in front of her.

Movement caught her eye as Kat instinctively threw herself the ground, out of sight of the damaged window. Athena was ripping a submachine gun from the lumpy pillow she'd been sitting on. It was an ugly thing, matte black rather than the usual gleaming metal, but every one of its polished angles spoke to its deadly purpose and efficiency.

Kat focused her mana, forming the spell Pseudopod even as her chest bounced off of the thinly carpeted floor of the hotel room. The breath rushed out of her with a thud, but the tentacle of water wrapped itself around the weapon, yanking it upward just as Athena pulled the trigger.

The enclosed room amplified the sound of the gunfire, practically deafening Kat as the submachine gun roared, pouring lead into the ceiling.

Plaster rained down on the three of them, filling the room with a white fog. Athena was screaming something that Kat couldn't hear through the ringing in her ears even as Xander ran to the window, his eyes burning with purple flames.

She leapt across the room, scrambling up the bed as Athena struggled with the fist-sized rope of water that held her wrist in a vise grip. Her hand landed on the smaller woman's face, hand curled into a claw as Kat struck her nose with its heel.

Blood erupted from Athena's face as her nose crumpled under the blow. Her head bounced off of the lumpy and soiled mattress as a second open-palm blow slammed into the woman's cheek. Once again, something crunched under her hand.

"*Compulsion.*" Behind her, Xander used a psi ability as Kat grabbed Athena by the wrist, twisting it so the back of the smaller woman's hand faced her.

With one smooth motion, she brought her left hand around, smashing it into Athena's elbow, shattering it with a sickening crack.

Athena screamed, dropping the submachine gun only for the pseudopod to snag it out of the air and pull the weapon into Kat's grip. She pointed it at its former owner, finger resting on the trigger.

"Stop, Kat," Xander called from the edge of the room. "It's over."

She looked up, tears blurring the corner of her vision as she took in Whippoorwill's pale form on the bedroom floor, a pool of blood surrounding her.

"Open the window." Xander's eyes flared purple as he glared at Athena. "Jump."

Across the street, Kat barely made out a silhouette throwing itself from the sixth floor of a building, arms flailing.

"Give me the gun and tend to Whippoorwill." Xander nodded toward the bleeding girl. "I've already called for a street doc, but someone needs to stabilize her before they arrive. Do you think you can handle that?"

"I…" Kat's eyes didn't leave Whippoorwill's bleeding form. Somehow her injury brought the entire situation home. The past three months of her life had been a whirlwind of ultra-violence and adrenaline as Kat killed and ran from one situation to another, but it just didn't seem real compared—

"Kat." Xander's hand was on her shoulder. "Whip needs you. You can't freeze up now. Can you take care of her until the doc arrives?"

She shook her head, clearing the cobwebs and indecision.

"I've got it, Xan," She handed him the submachine gun, crawling off of Athena and hurrying to Whippoorwill. The girl was mewling slightly, hands clutching at her bleeding stomach.

She cradled her friend's head in her lap, activating Cure Wounds I. Distantly, Kat heard her voice twist as she recited a string of eldritch phrases, her hands positioning themselves precisely to form a sequence of arcane seals. Then her hands were glowing a healthy gold as she pressed them into Whippoorwill's stomach.

"Why did you do it, Athena?" Xander stood over the bleeding and injured woman, the submachine gun trained motionlessly on her navel. "We had history and we struck a deal. If you'd wanted to do the job on your own, you didn't need to bring us in. Hell, you were about to get a hundred and ninety thousand credits for a tip and about fifteen shots taken by Scalpel. Now he's dead." Anger began to well up in Xander's voice, bubbling past his normal devil may care attitude. "And one of my girls is bleeding out on the floor. All of it is a goddamn waste, and I don't even know why, after fifteen years of friendship, you tried to pull this stunt."

Kat's breath came a little easier as the wound stopped bleeding beneath her hands. She was beginning to run low on mana, and there was still an ugly wound in Whippoorwill's stomach, but already it was beginning to visibly close under the influence of her spell.

"Nathan, he——" Athena stuttered, blood streaming down her face.

"He shot Whippoorwill, a civilian," Xander replied harshly. "He had a strong will and I only was able to control him for a second or two. Not enough time to disable him, but more than enough to force him to jump out a window."

"That bullet was meant for you Xan," Athena spat back, coughing as blood from her shattered nose and cheek began filling her mouth. "The plan was to take you down and let the girls go. This was never about them. She just stood up at the wrong time and caught your bullet."

Kat cut off her spell, completely out of mana. At some point, Whippoorwill had slipped into a restless sleep, twitching and turning but still unconscious in her lap.

"But why, Denise?" Genuine frustration filled Xander's voice. "We've known each other since before we joined the Cardinals. Hell, I remember boosting credits from corner stores while you served as a lookout when we were only thirteen. We were more than just business associates, we were fucking family."

"Family?" Athena coughed, her face a mask of blood while she cradled her broken arm. "Family wouldn't have mouthed off to Mr. Jackson and gotten a hit put on all of our heads. It's always been your fucking ego with you, Xan. You always needed the biggest and flashiest score, but you never thought about the fallout."

"Things have changed in St. Louis, Xan." Athena squeezed her eyes shut, hissing in pain. "If no one is looking, Millennium doesn't follow the code anymore. Every day, there's more of them on the street with newer and fancier equipment. They're almost a corporation of their own by now. It's only a matter of time before they force the rest of the crews in St. Louis to retire or join them."

"So what if they're a corporation?" Xander snorted, sitting on the bed, gun still pointed at Athena's petite form. "It'll just be like the good ol' days, Denise. We'll tell 'em to fuck off, steal their information, and sell it to the highest bidder. Just like we do with all of the other corporations."

"The other corporations aren't crazy." Athena opened her eyes, glaring fuzzily at Xander. "They want money. Mr. Jackson is in it for the power, and you had to go and trash his ego. I never would have done this to increase my cut, Xan." She shook her head sadly. "You heard Mr. Jackson. The only way out for Scalpel and I was to assuage his ego. That meant giving the data to him along with your body."

She sighed. "It wasn't about money. It was about survival."

For a moment she was silent, a brooding silence settling over the room.

"For what it's worth." Athena coughed again. "I'm sorry about your girl. She was never the target."

"How's she holding up, Kat?" Xander didn't bother to look back at her. "Street doc is downstairs, what does he need to know?"

"There's some physical trauma still," Kat glanced over the

hole in her friend's bloodstained hoodie, "but she isn't bleeding anymore. Whip's unconscious but her pulse is steady, so I don't think she's in shock. She still needs help, but she's doing all right."

"But how?" Athena struggled to push herself up into a sitting position with her one good arm. "Nathan was using a .308. That should have turned her insides into hamburger."

"I'm not an idiot, Denise." Xander snorted. "You go every-where with Nathan. As soon as you mentioned he wouldn't be able to make a meeting on one of the most important sales in your career, I knew something was up and requested a room with bulletproof glass windows."

"I suppose I'll have to lodge a complaint with manage-ment," he continued mirthlessly. "The windows only managed to slow his bullets, not stop them."

"Kat," she glanced up just in time to catch the coffee mug-sized portable secure hard drive that he threw to her, "I'm e-mailing you the location of the hotel in question right now. The doc is on the way and the immediate situation is handled so I need someone to make the drop."

"But—" she began, noting the flashing icon of an incoming e-mail.

"Get going, Kat," Xander cut her off. "We're in a fairly lawless area of Chiwaukee, but we've made enough noise that someone is going to check out what happened. We're going to need Whippoorwill stabilized and moved before someone shows up asking questions."

Kat gripped the hard drive tightly before grabbing her messenger bag from a nearby table and slipping it inside. She opened the door, pausing in the portal as she looked back on the three people in the room.

Exhaling, Kat closed the door behind her and began walking down the hallway. She barely made it twenty steps before the chatter of gunfire behind her stopped her.

A moment later she continued, grim determination lining her face.

CHAPTER SEVEN

The fake 'sun' of *The Tower of Somnus* beat down on Kat, its arid heat robbing her of her breath. She shielded her eyes against the light, taking in the bleached-white, multi-story buildings around her. All of them were made out of some sort of dried mud stabilized with reeds that looked like the intergalactic version of adobe or stucco.

She lurched forward as a large, scaled arm draped itself forcefully over her shoulder. Nearby, Kat heard the air 'whuff' out of Kaleek's lungs as Dorrik slapped him on the back.

"Breathe deep, Miss Kat," the lizard thrummed happily, "that's the smell of fresh gottel spices simmering in the desert heat. If the Gardeners have created a heaven, that is what it would smell like."

"Are you sure it would be this arid?" Kaleek coughed, his eyes watery and bleary. "Seriously, Dorrik, I can't understand how your people adapted to a life without any humidity. I can barely choke the air down."

"You'll get used to it." Dorrik grinned, pulling the two of them away from the Adventurer's Hall and down a cobblestone walkway. "Now come on, I'll buy the two of you a juice or something when we get to the Lokkel Enclave. Unless I miss my guess, this is Dasheera's Sands, possibly the largest oasis in this sector of the third floor."

Kat glanced back behind them. Where the Adventurer's Hall in Whiteshell on the second floor had resembled a large church made of gray stone, this building was more of a cathedral. It towered above them, at least fifteen stories tall and made of the same hardened, white mud-cement as the rest of the city.

The main building was about five stories while a tower topped with bells and a large clock filled the other ten. The tower itself was undecorated, stark white and eye-catching even at a distance. The warehouse-sized main building, on the other hand, was covered in mosaics of colored glass that shone in the harsh desert sun.

Various heroic figures were depicted fighting off swarms of enemies or legendary monsters. Some held swords high while others unleashed streams of magic, but Kat couldn't escape noticing that over half of the gleaming figures were lokkel.

"Are you sure we couldn't have stayed in Whiteshell for one more day?" Kaleek complained, his whiskers drooping and tail dragging as he allowed Dorrik to pull him down the street. "I wanted at least one more day of swimming before I let you dry my lungs out and fill my fur with sand. By the elders, I swear that shit never comes out."

"Quit being dramatic." Dorrik rolled their eyes. "We can find you a guest room at my clan's villa. The clan periodically pays a water elementalist to enchant a mist machine so whelps like you will stop whining about the lack of humidity."

"That still doesn't fix the sand." Kaleek brushed a hand through his silky fur, as if looking for some offending dust. "Once it gets beneath the outer coat, it's impossible to get out. Worse, if you try to go for a swim to get it out, it just turns into mud on you."

Dorrik boomed with laughter, shaking their head as their crest rippled with mirth.

"Come now, Kaleek." The giant lizard grinned, exposing a

muzzle full of razor sharp teeth. "We both know that your avatar resets completely the next time you fall asleep. You just pop into being with full resource pools and your bound gear. Everything else just disappears."

"It's still there spiritually," the otter grumbled. "A proper desoph can feel dirt in their undercoat even if it's just metaphorical."

Kat smiled as her friends bickered good-naturedly. Despite their eagerness to trek up to level three, Dorrik made sure to let the party take two days off so that Kaleek could swim and enjoy the refreshing coastal environment. Neither of them came out and acknowledged the situation, but Kat could tell that Dorrik was trying to slow down a bit in order to give Kaleek a break before the third floor.

"What about you, Kat?" Dorrik grinned at her as they walked past a wall guarded by a pair of russet lokkel. "Are you ready for some gottel-seasoned qat steak, still on the spit? You haven't enjoyed the Consensus until you've had a lokkel barbeque."

"Wait." Kat squinted a Dorrik, a half-smile still on her face. "Is that what we're doing today? No daring raids? No grinding skills, just a party?"

"To be fair, Kat," Kaleek interjected begrudgingly, "lokkels know how to party. They're an old race and they age incredibly slowly. Younger races like yours focus on sending people into the tower to learn how to fight, but the lokkel also invest in crafts- men, musicians, and cooks. Just like we earn skills and spells related to killing things, they gain abilities related to their art. It's quite literally a magical experience."

"That sounds great," she responded slowly, allowing Dorrik to guide her toward a three-story, domed building, "but I still don't understand why we're spending our time meeting up with your clan. Don't you spend most of each day with them?"

"I do." Dorrik chuckled. "But my clan is spread out across a number of planets, moons and orbital habitats in three different systems. We don't get a proper chance to meet and communicate in the waking world most days, especially with my off-kilter sleeping schedule."

Their arms left Kaleek and Kat's shoulders as Dorrik stepped away from them. They approached a lokkel guard covered in the same color of dusky scales. The guard was alert, eyes flicking from Dorrik to the two non-lokkel, their finely crafted, silvery armor barely making any noise as their hands touched the two sword hilts at their back.

"Dorrik of Clan Ahn approaches, requesting respite from the noon sun." The lizard spread all four of their arms akimbo, claws empty and exposed to the guard. "I have advanced to the third level and wish to enter the enclave for a period of time."

"Welcome back to Clan Ahn, Dorrik," the guard responded formally. "Is there anyone that would speak to your character so that I might grant you admittance?"

"I would request that Sikka Ahn speak for me." Dorrik brought their arms close to their chest, crossing both pairs of well-muscled limbs in front of them. "She has known me since I was but a whelp and would serve as an adequate judge of my character and mettle."

"Sikka!" The guard stepped aside, letting another dark lokkel with a strange bulge just beneath the scales of their stomach exit the compound. "This individual claims to be Dorrik of Clan Ahn, a lokkel of honor and upstanding character."

The new lokkel crossed her arms, taking on the same pose as Dorrik, a stern expression on her muzzle. Kat couldn't help but notice how quickly she had arrived. Whatever this ceremonial greeting meant, it was both expected and well-choreographed.

"This is Dorrik of Clan Ahn," she announced, her voice slightly higher pitched but otherwise very similar to what Kat had come to expect from Dorrik. "They are an honorable and virtuous child of the Clan. I ask that they be granted entrance into the enclave once again."

"Granted," the guard intoned before their muzzle broke

into a broad grin. "Good to see you again, Dorrik. You got up here faster than I expected. I'm out a couple marks thanks to you."

"It's your own fault, Basash." Dorrik chuckled. "You lose marks every time you bet against me, yet you keep doing it."

"One of these days you'll mess up, Dorrik." Basash slapped Dorrik's shoulder with one of their upper arms. "And then I will be rich. It's just a matter of time."

Kat glanced over to Kaleek. The giant otter wasn't even pretending to pay attention, instead focusing all of his attention on combing his claws through the thick fur of his arm in a vain attempt to remove some of the omnipresent sand.

"What the hell is going on?" she whispered, sauntering over to the otter.

"This is just what lokkel do." Kaleek shrugged, slightly bored. "They build enclaves on every desert floor and the first time a player reaches it, they have to formally request entrance. It's a whole thing."

"We're only going to have to deal with this each time we reach a new floor right?" Kat frowned. "I'm not sure how keen I am on a community theater production each and every time we return to town."

"Oh elders, no." Kaleek guffawed. "I suppose if the door guard didn't recognize Dorrik, they might need to re-identify themselves, but everyone at the Ahn Villa knows them. This is all just a formality. The lokkel are a stuffy people, but ultimately, they're probably one of my favorite races in the Consensus once you get past their thousand and one rituals that predate either of our species evolving opposable thumbs."

"What do desoph do at these sorts of gatherings anyway?" Kat asked, eyes on the two chatting lokkel by the entrance to the villa.

"When we meet after being away for a while?" Kaleek smiled. "Nothing too major. We swim together, eat, groom, and usually have recreational sex. Again, I apologize, but you are far too hairless and pink to participate in a proper desoph reunion."

Kat was jolted from her conversation with Kaleek by an affronted shout from the villa gate.

"And where do *you* think you're going, Dorrik!" Sikka, the female lokkel, stepped in front of her friend as they extricated themselves from Basash and began walking into the manor. "After months on D'Nai without a single letter, do you seriously think to just walk past your rearer?"

She put all four hands on her hips, staring down Dorrik sternly as she tapped a clawed foot on the eggshell-white floor.

"Sikka…" Dorrik shifted uncomfortably.

Kat squinted at them. Wait. Were they *embarrassed*?

"And not one comment about my ascension!" Sikka threw up her hands. "Here I am, no longer a rearer, finally a woman, and you can't say anything about it. I literally taught you how to hunt garr rats and hold a sword, and here you are ready to walk past me like I'm a complete stranger."

"Sikka." Dorrik's crest fluttered uncontrollably. "I have guests here. I was going to talk to you at my welcoming ceremony. Could we wait for—"

"Oh!" The lokkel's eyes locked onto Kat. "This the human, Katherine."

"Yes?" Kat responded hesitantly.

"Kraes has spoken a lot about you," Sikka practically purred, her amber eyes sparking.

"Wait," Dorrik interjected frantically, "what does Mom have to do with anything? I mean, I talked with her a little bit about what was happening in the dreamscape but—"

"Hurry along, Dorrik." Sikka waved at them dismissively. "I'll catch up with you at the welcoming ceremony. Right now I would like to get to know your Katherine, woman-to-woman."

"Dorrik's Katherine?" Kat raised an eyebrow even as a chuckling Kaleek patted her on the shoulder.

"Good luck, Kat." He walked past her, a grin stretched

across his furry face as he approached Sikka. "And good to see you again, Sikka."

"Stay out of trouble, Kaleek." The big lizard nodded at him amiably as she slipped past the desoph on her way to Kat.

For a second, she just stood there before the huge, grinning lizardwoman. Kat smiled at her weakly. Sikka was almost a head taller than Dorrik and more heavily muscled. Strapped to her back were the same twin swords that Kat had seen on every lokkel on the third floor.

"You can call me Kat, by the way." She extended a hand toward the alien. "It's what everyone calls me, anyway."

"Kat." Sikka's eyes twinkled as she savored the word, her lower hands gently taking Kat's into her own. "It's good to formally meet you. Dorrik's spoken a lot about you to their mother, and at this point, the entire extended family is fairly curious about you."

"Thanks?" Kat asked, unsure how to proceed.

"Oh, don't worry about it too much." Sikka chuckled, waving for Kat to follow her with her upper arms. "It's half that Dorrik managed to find the only non-feral human that's wandered into *The Tower of Somnus*, and half that they were actually willing to enter into a long-term partnership with a third being."

"They offered to raid a dungeon with me fairly quickly." Kat cocked her head. "Maybe they just needed someone on short notice and I happened to fit the bill?"

"That doesn't explain them changing their sleep schedule." Sikka led Kat into a small courtyard filled with flowering succulents, heavy with water. "D'Nai has a day-night schedule that is around twenty-nine of your hours. Both Kaleek and Dorrik have had to keep track of your planet's times in order to sync their times in the dreamscape up with you."

"I—" Kat blinked in surprise as the big lizard took a seat on an oversized stone bench, "I didn't know any of that. I guess we had so much going on that I just didn't think of it."

"Dorrik considers you a friend." Sikka's head bobbed.

"They don't really have any friends outside of their clutch and Kaleek. They spend all of their time training, studying, and setting records. It has made them the idol of their cohort."

"We have an entire generation of young lokkel that want to be just like Dorrik." Sikka chuckled, leaning back on the bench as she patted a spot near her for Kat to sit down. "They just don't realize how lonely Dorrik can be. Our entire quad and their cohort do what we can for Dorrik, but it's hard when they isolate themselves on a moon covered in nothing but razor-sharp crystals and lokkel-sized spiders in order to develop their abilities."

"Then why did you yell at Dorrik?" Kat asked, plopping herself down next to Sikka.

"They can get a bit stuffy." Sikka laughed. "Caught up in their own myth. I suppose succeeding at everything will do that to an entity."

"Even when they got killed in the dreamscape, Dorrik somehow turned it into a success." Sikka shook their head ruefully. "Rather than a failure, they became a hero, fighting off an entire army of stallesp and saving a probationary race from enslavement at the moles' claws."

"Every once in a while, Kraes and I will try to deflate Dorrik a little." She nudged Kat conspiratorially. "Bring them back down to ground."

"That doesn't really sound like Dorrik to me." Kat frowned slightly. "They've always been very cautious and helpful when adventuring with me. Really, the only time I've even seen a flash of arrogance was with my original partner, and honestly, Dorrik was right. The guy was a terrible match for *The Tower of Somnus.*"

"That is one of Dorrik's all too perfect traits," Sikka rolled her eyes. "They are a tremendous judge of talent. Kaleek is a skilled warrior, but more than anything, he serves as a relaxed and informal counterpoint for Dorrik. Even if they won't admit it, they realize that their mannerisms can be a bit of a weakness."

"Honestly?" Kat shrugged helplessly. "I don't know why Dorrik picked me. They watched me fight a monster without any real skills, just a knife. Then they complimented me and offered to work with me."

"What was the compliment?" Sikka folded her top pair of claws, resting her chin on them.

"They said I moved like someone who had killed before," Kat replied, slightly uncomfortably. "They, uh, complimented my lack of hesitation."

"I can see why Dorrik wanted you." Sikka nodded. "All too many of the warriors that enter *The Tower of Somnus* have trained for years, but all of it is in a gymnasium. They struggle to treat the fights like they are real and can't eke out the last little bit of effort needed to bring down a boss or an elite. Clan Ahn loses some young every year, but we make sure not to fall into that trap."

"Then why isn't Dorrik in a team of three lokkel?" Kat asked. "It seems like their siblings would be ideal partners for them."

"The word is clutchmates." The big lokkel looked away from Kat, focusing her eyes on the plump flowering plants that made up the desert garden in the center of the courtyard. "Dorrik was on a team of three, but two of his clutchmates died when a passenger liner ran into an asteroid that strayed into a hyperlane. There were some rumors that the stallesp were involved, but never enough to actually make the Consensus move."

"Oh God." Kat winced. "I'm so sorry, I didn't mean to bring it up—"

"They were my children just as much as Dorrik is." Sikka looked back at her, a sad smile on her scaly muzzle. "But Dorrik took it harder than the rest of us. As sad as our quad was, Dorrik just threw themselves completely into training only to sacrifice themself to strike back at the stallesp."

"Only now," Sikka continued, "almost two years later, is

Dorrik actually starting to open up." Her eyes gleamed as she looked directly at Kat. "Right around the time they met you."

Kat fought the desire to scoot away from the almost predatory look on the giant lizard's grinning face.

"We have an hour before the welcoming ceremony, Kat." Sikka moved closer to her, wrapping a big, scaly arm around her thin shoulders. "How could I not want to spend that time grilling someone who means so much to my child?"

CHAPTER EIGHT

Kat's throwing knife whirred through the dungeon air, burying itself up to its hilt in a fuzzy, torso-sized creature clinging to the wall. It fell to the ground, the force of the strike ripping its body from the sandstone that made up the boundaries of the room, the barbs attached to the bottom of its limbs tearing chunks from the soft stone.

It hit the ground, hissing angrily as it scuttled in a circle to face Kat. Mana pulsed through her body as she focused on the creature.

More than anything, it looked like a nightmare-sized tarantula with ten legs. There were differences, of course. Rather than a pair of fangs, the facarl, as Dorrik had dubbed it, had a proboscis that dripped acid, pitting the dungeon floor. Two of its six eyes, equidistantly arranged around its oval torso, blinked at her angrily. Perhaps most importantly—

She swore, dancing backward as the facarl angrily rubbed its oversized forelimbs together, generating a cloud of black dust as its fur shredded itself into a cloud of toxic and borderline microscopic blades.

Dehydrate struck the monster, leeching the last moisture from its bleeding body. Its legs curled under itself as it crumpled and fell to the rocky floor. Kat didn't move any closer, keeping her eyes warily on the barely visible mist hanging over the creature's body.

She'd made the mistake of approaching a facarl corpse too quickly and breathing in the microfilaments exactly once. Twenty minutes of coughing up her lung lining, hands glowing as she expended almost all of her mana on Cure Wounds I while struggling with a poison-induced fever had taught her the error of her ways.

Apparently, the creatures used the microfur of their legs to blind and disable prey before injecting them with the acid they needed to turn their innards into a slurry that could be consumed with their proboscis. It had only been a matter of luck that Kat's eyes were closed when she stepped into the cloud of fur mist. As useful as Cure Wounds I was, Kat didn't think it packed enough punch to prevent full-on blinding.

Nearby, Kaleek cut one of the facarls in half. He looked ridiculous in the goggles that Dorrik had bought for him, but between his natural desoph ability to hold his breath for up to a half hour at a time and the glass eye coverings, he was the scuttling monsters' natural enemy.

Kaleek simply ignored another puff of the toxic dust as the final facarl dropped from the ceiling behind him.

"Kaleek!" Dorrik shouted, their hands opening and closing, filled with nervous energy. Unfortunately, the big lizard's psi abilities only worked on sapient creatures. That meant that they could boost their own abilities, but none of their ranged attacks would even scratch the facarls.

The otter whirled, his greatsword cutting the creature in half as it fell. With a quiet thud, the bisected portions of its body landed on the sandstone floor on either side of Kaleek. He grinned, turning toward Kat and Dorrik as he took a step toward them.

"No." Dorrik crossed their arms as they shook their head.

"You're positively covered in facarl dust. Stay where you are while Kat washes you down."

"Isn't there a more dignified way of doing this?" Kaleek whined even as he stepped away from the bodies and braced himself against a dungeon wall. "I mean, I get the point of it, but it's both humiliating and cold. At least teach Kat how to warm the water up first."

"Unfortunately, we do not have a spare fire skill stone for Kat." Dorrik shook their head slowly. "So the water will not be warm anytime soon. As for whether we could find a more dignified way of washing you down...?"

"Probably." Dorrik's muzzle broke into a grin. "But the humor of this method outweighs your discomfort."

"Wait." Kaleek's eyes widened under his goggles. "That's some—"

Kat finished casting Water Jet, the spell slamming Kaleek into the wall as it unloaded a small swimming pool's worth of water on the otter. The magic didn't do any damage, having been designed to knock targets off balance and to the ground, but it did buffet and almost trip the sputtering desoph.

A second or two later, he whirled on the two of them, glaring, his fur drenched. Kaleek reached up, whipping off his goggles and stuffing them into a belt pouch.

"All clean now," Kat said cheerfully. "Unless the microfibers made it into your inner coat, you should be washed down well enough to join civilized company."

"Don't worry, Kat," he grumbled, shaking his entire body in an effort to dry himself off. "Your water magic has leveled up enough that the spell made it all the way to my inner coat. Even if some of that damnable fur managed to work its way deep, you managed to wash it out. Thanks. I guess."

"You should look at yourself," Dorrik barely choked the words out in between peals of laughter. "You look like a soaked dune rat. I never thought I'd see a desoph look so despondent from nothing more than water."

"Yeah, yeah." Kaleek fought to keep a smile off of his face

as he brushed the remaining water off of his oily, waterproof fur. "Keep laughing. Next time we have to wade into some water, you're coming with me. You'll see how funny it is to be soaked when you're flailing around neck deep in water."

"Come now, Kaleek." Dorrik struggled to bring theirself under control. "I only suggest the optimal ways to overcome opponents. My clan's records indicated that this dungeon could be conquered fairly easily if the party had a fighter without exposed mucus membranes. Of course I thought of you: it was only logical for us to let the individual that doesn't need to breathe take point."

"Speaking of your clan." Kaleek grinned. "What did Sikka want to talk about, Kat? She pulled you aside for quite a while before the welcoming ceremony."

"You shouldn't feel obligated to respond to that." Dorrik shifted slightly. "Sikka is just a friendly lokkel. I'm sure her conversation with you was very ordinary and nothing that either Kaleek or myself need to know about."

"She mostly wanted to talk about you, Dorrik." Kat smiled, wiping the grime off of one of her knives as the big lizard stiffened. "Something about how you had a lonely childhood without too many friends and how glad she was that you'd finally found another playmate."

"Oooh!" Kaleek splashed over, leaving wet pawprints in the white sandstone floor of the dungeon. "They—" He gritted his teeth. "Sorry, she. I first met her before she moved on from rearer to female," he muttered apologetically.

"Anyway." the grin was back on the sopping otter's face. "That was more or less the speech I got. We talked for a little bit about who I was and my family, and once Sikka was satisfied, the rest of the meeting was talking about her poor little Dorrik and how they didn't have any lokkel friends because they pushed themselves too hard."

"Did she show you the paintings of Dorrik as a whelp?" Kat's eyes lit up mischievously. "Their tail was so stubby and cute as they were scuttling down the sand dunes!"

"My favorite was the painting of Dorrik at their clutch's first induction into the dreamscape," Kaleek replied. "They were maybe as high as my shoulder, and so eager. Whoever the artist was, they really captured the expression in Dorrik's eyes as their father granted them their first subscription."

Dorrik simply groaned, burying their face in their upper pair of arms. Kat's smile only grew wider. Dorrik was a friend, but Sikka was right. They spent too much time focusing on training and research. Every once in a while, they needed a gentle needle poke to take some of the wind out of their sails.

"Why didn't you tell us how good of an artist you were, Dorrik?" Kat asked. "Sikka showed me some of the abstract paintings you made from your first tower climb. I really like the way you used color to really pull the viewer into the scene."

Dorrik turned their gaze on Kaleek and Kat and she burst out laughing. Their expression said everything, a combination of mournful, pleading, and utterly bedraggled.

"Fine." She slid the now-clean throwing knife into her bandoleer. "That's enough for now, but I really do want to learn more about you. Kaleek can't shut up about his siblings, blitzball scores, bars, and meals, but everything with you is a mystery. Maybe it's a human thing, but I want to learn a bit more about that mystery."

"That's fair enough." Dorrik nodded slowly, their expression brightening. "As much as I find your race interesting in a fairly horrifying sort of way—"

"It is kinda like seeing a reactor fire," Kaleek interjected agreeably. "You know you should look away but you just can't."

She cocked her head at the otter, shooting him a slightly confused look. Obviously human society wasn't great, but there were plenty of good people in it. Her family, Whippoorwill, Xander, Xander's wife Nina. All of them were doing the best they could with a bad situation. None of them had the spare wealth and power to be saints, but there was a certain honor born in the gutter.

Some of the people Kat grew up with were feral, nothing

more than animals just looking for a chance to betray her, but for enough of them, their name was all they had. Their lives were still a constant struggle for their next meal, a constant race to try to claw their way up the next rung of the societal ladder, but they at least recognized that the world was already miserable enough without tearing each other down for no reason.

Kat opened her mouth to defend her people, but Dorrik just continued speaking.

"I am more interested in you, Kat." The big lizard nodded at her. "You are a survivor. Where solitude and pride have driven me to try to perfect my craft, you exist in a constant state of crisis, growing to stay one step ahead of a never-ending stream of disasters that dog your footsteps."

"That…" She frowned slightly, unsure how exactly to respond. "I'm not sure that's *wrong*, Dorrik, but it still feels a bit strange to boil my entire life down to me sprinting from one disaster to another."

"But that is what you do, Kat." Dorrik inclined their head slightly, crest fluttering. "I understand that you are making efforts to free yourself from the chains of your masters, but for right now, what I'm interested in is what makes you tick. What makes you struggle against forces outside of your control even as you perfect yourself?"

"Wouldn't anyone?" Kat shrugged uncomfortably. "I didn't exactly have many choices, but given the options of slavery or struggle, who wouldn't struggle?"

"That's a good question." Kaleek shrugged. "One that I've been trying to understand for years. As long as you don't call it slavery, all too many entities are willing to let their rights be eroded away piece by piece."

"Kaleek has the right of it." Dorrik nodded. "You could have had an uncomfortable but stable existence, but even before you had entered *The Tower of Somnus*, you had been struggling against the status quo. You've risked your life and freedom to better your situation in some small way, and that has given you the skills you've needed to thrive here."

"I suppose." Kat shrugged uncomfortably. "Still, it's starting to work. I start college tomorrow, and that's the first step toward actually having people listen to me."

"College?" Kaleek asked. "That's what your race does for higher education right? I still don't understand why your leaders wouldn't make that free. Even from a purely utilitarian perspective, having a trained workforce means having a productive workforce."

"They pushed us hard enough during our mandatory schooling to make sure we can work in the farms, factories, and laboratories," Kat responded, slightly bitterly. "College is more about other things. Managing workforces, negotiating with other departments, attending networking parties, and etiquette. As far as I can tell, everything from here on out is how to navigate the complex social minefields that come with working in management. Useful things to be sure, but hardly something that needs a full four years of schooling."

"I don't think I understand." Dorrik frowned. "If you're going to sacrifice four years of your life going to this advanced school, that is logical to me, but to learn nothing over that time..."

"The school is a stand in." Kat shrugged. "Many of the advanced jobs won't even look at you unless you've attended college, and they make college into something impossible for the average worker to attend. Ostensibly, the process is fair and meritocratic, but the end result is that the same people that were in power continue to stay in power in the future."

Dorrik's crest fluttered in distress. "But what about people like you? Those who manage to succeed despite the odds. Wouldn't your race be throwing away your potential by only looking to a narrow pool of applicants for their positions of power?"

"Yes." Kat sighed. "But that's beside the point. Most humans I know have a narrow circle of people that matter. Beyond their family and friends, no one else really seems real. You can recognize that they're people, but when trouble rears its head, they just seem abstract and different. It's hard to care about a stranger's troubles when you can't feed your kids or your best friend doesn't have access to the healthcare they'd need to cure a basic but life-threatening illness."

"The rich are like that too." She crossed her arms in front of her chest. "Their problems might be bigger than mine, but they're struggling for their lives as well. Hell, half of my other job is to help them tear each other apart. Really, I don't think anyone has the time to care about the species as a whole. It's all just about surviving another day."

"Well." Kaleek nodded cheerfully. "That was bleak as hell, but I'm dry and ready for the next fight. What do we have on deck?"

"The dungeon boss shouldn't be a challenge with the right party makeup," Dorrik replied affably. "It's a parasitic organism known as a blood pearl, about as big around as my torso and immobile. All it can really do is fire bolts of psi energy and try to control the minds of anyone near it. Generally, it takes over the mind of the party member with the lowest charisma and turns them against their companions."

"Fuck," Kaleek grumbled, kicking a chunk of sandstone that had been loosened from the ground by a facarl's dripping acid.

"That means Kat and I will go in while you hang back," Dorrik nodded to her. "Kat can trade ranged attacks with it, distracting it while I walk close enough to stab it. The good news is that blood pearls don't have that many hit points. They're just a nasty surprise for unprepared parties."

"So," Kat responded, checking the knives attached to her armor, "just run around the outside of the chamber peppering it with attacks while I try to avoid getting hit? I think I can handle that."

"Very good." Dorrik opened the door into the dungeon's final chamber, motioning for her to go first. "Kaleek, if you could hang back outside of the monster's range, I would appreciate it."

"Yeah, yeah." Kaleek twitched his whiskers at them deject-edly. "I'll stick it out back here with all of the facarl corpses. That sounds super fun."

Kat stepped into the room. The entire space was at an upward angle, maybe twenty degrees, with a pedestal at the center well above her. On that pedestal, a large lump of reddish pink flesh grew around the dungeon altar.

Almost immediately, a purple nimbus appeared around it before it spat out a bolt of energy. Kat threw herself to the side, feeling all of the hair on her body stand straight on end as it crackled and fizzled into the wall where she had just been standing.

She activated Cat Step, stamina draining from her as she sprinted around the outside of the room. Her first thrown dagger missed the creature entirely, but even as the mana welled inside of her for a Gravity Spike, the second dug into its side.

A strange energy tried to claw at her. For a fraction of a second, Kat just felt an ill-defined pressure around her skull before her emotions began to run haywire. At first she was angry, then she was just as sad as she'd been at her father's funeral. Above everything, a sickly sweet scent began to fill the room.

She shook her head, concentrating on the face of her mother and sister even as she forced the Gravity Spike into being. One side of the pearl erupted, spraying gore as the forces under her control twisted it, pulling and shoving the entity at the same time.

Distantly, she heard a voice screaming something indeci-pherable and the pressure began to subside. Another bolt of purple energy crashed into the stone in front of her, forcing Kat to skid to a stop.

Then, as it built energy for another attack, Dorrik's swords cut through its pulsing flesh, one after another, hacking deep grooves in the immobile monster. It deflated, orange ichor pouring from the wound as the psychic assault abruptly cut off.

Kat frowned, looking around the chamber at the skeletons

from previous avatars that had failed. "That... was under-whelming."

Dorrik brushed some of the creature's dead flesh away from the altar. "That is the power of a scouting report. Any player with three charisma would have been taken over almost imme-diately. For most parties, they would be spending too much time fighting each other to actually make any progress toward the boss. Same with the facarls. While you can fight them and Kaleek excels against them, I am almost useless. It is simply a matter of having and using the right tool for each job."

"Kaleek," Dorrik shouted, "we're done here, but be ready for tomorrow. Sikka let me know that there is a superb dungeon with semi-aquatic elements."

"At least I won't have to deal with this hot and dry air that much longer," the otter grumbled, sauntering into the room as Dorrik disappeared in a rainbow cocoon of light. He nodded at Kat. "Go on, you fought the thing, you're next."

She approached the altar, trying to avoid as much of the pearl's gore as possible before placing her hand on it

Congratulations Adventurer!
You have completed the Wood Tier Level Three Dungeon, Skittering Ruins.
Three of three party members surviving. Good job!
Assigning awards:

+1 Strength

She sighed as the cocoon of light surrounded her. Tomorrow was move-in to the college, and as harrowing as meeting the scions of wealth and privilege that would be her classmates for the first time would be, her mother would be worse. She would want to know how big her room was, what classes she was taking and, worst of all, whether there were any cute boys.

CHAPTER NINE

"Here." Xander threw Kat a package. Really nothing more than a large plastic bag taped shut. She caught it, cocking her head to the side and raising an eyebrow in an unspoken question.

"I, uh…" He blushed slightly scratching the back of his neck. "I promised to buy you a new winter jacket as part of that last mission you did as a runner back in Schaumburg. I guess we all got so caught up in the Haupt business that I forgot. So, happy first day of college, I guess?"

"Thanks," she replied, flashing a smile at him. "Better late than never."

"Quit rubbing it in, Kat." He chuckled in embarrassment. "Now try it on, I want to see if it fits. I'll be heading back to Schaumburg tonight and I want to know if I'll need to get it resized first."

A smile still on her face, Kat ripped open the plastic bag before pulling out the knee-length jacket. The outside was a slick dark green, well made and hopefully at least slightly water-proof. She slipped her arms into the sleeves before buttoning the jacket up, taking note of the GroCorp College logo printed on the upper-right chest.

"Did you get this from the college store?" Kat asked, a teasing note in her voice. "I've seen the prices on those. What will the kids in the Shell think of me now? Wrapped up in fancy branded apparel?"

"You're gonna stick out enough as is," Xander grumbled, his cheeks still flushed. "I just thought it would be nice for you to have something from the college so that you'll fit in. Chiwaukee is a rough enough place without having to worry about looking like an outsider."

"Thanks!" Kat laughed, skipping forward to throw her arms around his neck. "You didn't have to, but I love it anyway."

"Check the pocket." His voice was gruff with emotion as he struggled to get the words out. "I owed you the jacket, but it didn't feel right to send you off without an actual present."

Kat's hands dove deep into each pocket, the fingers of her right closing around a glossy cardboard box. Quickly she pulled it out into the dingy flophouse's weak fluorescent lighting. After the incident with Athena, Xander had negotiated their way into a larger 'suite,' leaning on the failure of the bulletproof glass.

"This is the latest smartpanel model." Kat turned the box over in her hands. "Short of a cranial jack, this is the most advanced personal organizer and computing device on the market. It must have cost a fortune."

"It did." Xander grinned. "But I think you forgot how rich both of us are now. Plus, now that you're rubbing shoulders with the elite, you're going to need to look the part. Even with all of our newfound wealth, you're going to have a hard time fitting in."

"Your birth might be a step above a slumrat like me," he continued, shaking his head, "but to the managers and executives that actually run things, that makes you a gerbil. We're both rodents. The only difference is that one of us is feral."

Kat removed her current smartpanel, carefully pulling out the earpiece and pulling the cold metal contacts off the side of her head. Even if it wasn't as nice as the new one, it was always useful to have a spare.

Maybe the truly rich could just afford to throw the expensive piece of equipment aside, but Kat knew better. Partly due to her 'night job,' she was a bit rough on electronics. Maybe it was a childhood of hand-me-downs and repurposed products, but she refused to simply get rid of something valuable just because she no longer needed it.

"I just wish Whip were here." Kat sighed, bittersweet emotions filling her as she tapped the initialization sequence into the smartpanel's earpiece. "It doesn't feel right for us to sit around celebrating while she's stuck in the hospital."

"She'll be fine, Kat." Xander walked over and rested a hand on the shoulder of her new jacket. "The bulletproof glass might not have stopped the rifle shot, but it slowed it down enough that your healing skill was able to do most of the work. She's gonna itch like crazy and have to take immunosuppressants for a couple of weeks to acclimate to her new vat-grown intestines, but it's not the end of the world. If you work this job long enough, it's bound to happen. Hell, I think half of my body originated in a factory or a lab at this point."

"I'd prefer to avoid that, honestly." Kat grinned easily back at him. "Getting shot doesn't seem like much fun to me. I'd like to opt out of that."

"Oh, shush you." Xander blinked, his eyes slightly misty. "That's why you're the smart girl, heading off to college while the rest of us schlubs muck about in the gutters trying to make an honest credit."

"An honest credit?" Kat asked, shaking her head slightly as she chuckled. "Didn't you just make about a million credits? You're richer than most mid-level managers and we both know it."

"Well, so are you." He smiled warmly back at her, his golden tooth glinting faintly. "Now get a move on. Enrollment starts at ten o'clock, and you wouldn't want to be late on your first day."

Kat chuckled, extricating herself from Xander as she walked over to the lighter spring jacket she'd worn to the flophouse. Drawing her knife from the hidden internal sheathe and setting it on a nearby counter, Kat folded it and packed it away in her suitcase along with the rest of her meager belongings.

Finally, she picked up her knife, lovingly maintained and razor sharp. She glanced at Xander, confusion on her face.

"There's a sheath inside the jacket, just under your left arm." He nodded at the jacket. "Nina had one of her boys install it. He took out a good chunk of the insulation and replaced it with a weave of lead, aluminum, and some sort of proprietary fabric he pinched from a NeoSyne shipment. It won't be as warm, but the knife or anything else you try to smuggle in the sheath shouldn't show up on a basic scan."

"It's a shame that Nina couldn't be here," Kat commented as she slid the knife into its new home. "I know that the ChromeDogs needed someone to hold down the fort in Schaumburg, but I'd like a chance to thank her in person."

"She knows." Xander chuckled. "Feel free to write an e-mail if you want, but you really need to get going, Kat."

With a wave of her hand and a roll of her eyes, Kat buttoned up her jacket and grabbed the luggage before leaving the room. The hallway was bare concrete, barely broken up with faded paintings and limp and half-dead flowers. The sounds of a domestic disturbance and a blaring entertainment channel followed her into the elevator as it 'dinged' shut behind her.

The elevator jolted and stuttered on its way to the ground floor even as Kat triggered her brand new smartpanel and called for a cab. Theoretically, Kat had enough money that she could buy herself a car, but she'd learned her lesson in St. Louis.

Life in the arcology had given her a very specific set of skills and, despite her recent efforts, firearms and automobiles really weren't part of those abilities. Given what she'd heard about

Chiwaukee traffic, she'd rather trust an AI driver than her own rudimentary skills.

She walked through the building's atrium, ignoring the bored clerk and the trio of sex workers smoking cigarettes just inside the door, unwilling to brave the late winter cold. One of them eyed her tiredly, but Kat just shook her head, leaving them to kill time as she stepped out onto the street.

Even in daytime, the glowing neon advertisements were an eyesore. Men and women in heavy coats hurried up and down the snowy street, body modifications and weapons plainly visible.

More than one eyed her, but they largely kept their distance, the GroCorp College logo on her jacket out of place, but marking her as a troublesome target to any restive street toughs. Finally, a cab skidded to a halt in front of her just as her smart-panel pinged to let her know of its arrival.

Its door opened upward with a shriek of tortured metal, and Kat pulled herself inside. Instantly, her nose was assaulted by the chemical 'evergreen' smell of the air fresheners hanging from the taxi's roof. She shifted slightly to put her seatbelt on, trying as hard as she could not to think of the way that her brand new jacket stuck to the seat.

The smartpanel read her pupils as Kat flicked them back and forth, selecting her destination and authorizing payment. Then the car took off, screeching into traffic as it cut off a truck.

Kat's heart leapt into her throat as the vehicle accelerated, swerving into another lane, accompanied by a symphony of horns. Then the seatbelt bit into her chest as the taxi slammed on its brakes, a limousine weaving through traffic in front of them.

Adrenaline coursed through her body, her fingers digging into the sticky fabric. Out of the corner of her eyes, Kat could barely make out a man and a woman in the back seat of the limo, eating and laughing together, completely unperturbed as their vehicle accelerated past her.

Then they were gone, and Kat's taxi was on two tires as it

screamed onto a side street as her smartpanel flashed the word 'recalculating' like that was supposed to make the vehicle's sins against the laws of physics acceptable.

Five minutes later, she staggered out of the cab, short of breath and struggling to keep her stomach settled. Next to her, a car calmly came to a halt, disgorging a young woman in a fashionable blazer that glanced worriedly at her before ascending the massive marble steps toward the twenty-story stone building that was the combined dormitory and college.

Finally, Kat took a hesitant step, her rubber legs almost betraying her. A second and a quick breath of the brisk, chilly air later, and she began making her way up the staircase.

Before long, she found herself at the back of a short line just outside of the large glass doors to the college.

Ahead, a pair of figures wearing heavy body armor directed the line, one running a metal-detecting wand over the students while the other held a rifle in a casual, low-slung grip and directed the teens to run their luggage through a large x-ray apparatus.

"Remember," the figure without the metal detector shouted, her feminine voice clear and crisp over the sounds of traffic and honking horns. "Firearms, schedule two recreational drugs, and explosives are strictly prohibited. Muscle-powered weapons that correspond to recognized Tower skills are permitted, but you need to register them before entering the building."

For a second, Kat considered testing the effectiveness of the scanner shielding on her jacket, but then she crushed the instinctive urge. She wasn't on the streets anymore. There was no reason to tempt fate by concealing the knife.

Many of the students had the power and backing to be players, and it would be strange for an institution such as the GroCorp College to neglect the tower side of their development. In fact, 'archaic weapon combat' was one of the more common electives at the college. Not only could she have the knife, bringing it into the dorms wouldn't even raise an eyebrow.

"Are you from an arcology too?" Kat looked up into the smiling face of the girl that had exited her car in front of her. "I'm just asking because I think most of the Chiwaukee students checked in before us. Everyone around here looks lost."

Kat nodded.

"Great." She reached out a hand and took Kat's in her own. "My name is Emma Tiller. I'm from the Crystal Lake Arcology where my dad is a senior manager. It's good to meet someone just as lost and confused in the big city as me."

"I'm from Schaumburg, actually." Kat smiled weakly back at the girl. "My mom's an employee, but I was third in my class when the top two got disqualified."

"Schaumburg..." Emma trailed off for a second before brightening. "That was the Haupt murder! You went to school with Anna Donnst and Arnold Jacques! Oh my God," the girl squealed, her eyes widening as her grip tightened on Kat's hand. "You have to tell me *everything*. That scandal was on *every* gossip channel back home."

"Err." Kat glanced around nervously, noticing that more than one new student was listening in to their conversation. "Maybe when we get inside? I'm in room 2107."

"Great," Emma replied cheerfully. "I'm in 2214, it's in a different wing but on the same floor. We can meet up to study together and talk about what happened. I'm so excited to get the inside scoop."

Kat cocked her head slightly at the girl. Her instincts should have lit up like a Christmas tree screaming warnings at her, but they weren't. She struggled to think of anyone who'd approached her so casually in her entire life, simply wanting to talk with nothing in return.

Really, only conversations with her family were this free. For a while, Arnold had been the same, but he'd revealed his true colors eventually.

She struggled to stop herself from making a face. Well, he'd always been showing her true colors. It was more that she noticed them eventually.

"That sounds fun." Kat smiled at the girl, trying to keep her expression natural. "I'd love to have a study partner. I actually used to practice for my exams with Arnold Jacques, but... You know."

"You were friends with Arnold." Emma's eyes widened. "I need to call Stephanie as soon as possible, she'll just die if I—"

"Move along," the armored man with the wand interrupted them. "You're up next, lady. You can keep chatting once you get inside."

Kat watched, bemused, as Emma practically buzzed forward, placing her suitcase in the scanner before letting the man run the wand over her. It whirred angrily as it passed over her smartpanel, but the guard didn't seem to take any special note of it. A couple of seconds later, he was approaching Kat.

"Okay, ma'am." The armored figure pointed the wand at Kat. "You walk like you've been in the tower. Do you have any weapons to declare before we begin?"

"Just a knife," she responded, pulling the weapon smoothly from its hidden sheath before flipping it in her hand and offering the hilt to the guard.

She could almost see him raise an eyebrow under his faceplate as he took the weapon from her. The wand whirred gently as it passed over her body. Finished, the man handed her the dagger back.

"Enhanced agility and a skill related to knives or bladed weapons?" he asked, stepping to the side to let Kat pass.

"A lady never tells," Kat replied, winking at him as she walked by to retrieve her luggage from the detector.

Just as she picked it up, a young man, well-built and a head taller than her, approached Kat, the easy smile on his face barely concealing a bad case of nerves. He kept cracking his hands at his side, feet shuffling anxiously even as he beamed at her.

"Miss Katherine Debs?" he asked, thrusting his hand into hers. Despite the practiced strength and firmness of his grip, she could feel the clamminess of his palm as it slapped against her own.

"Yes?" She shook his hand, glancing from him to where her luggage was waiting at the end of the scanning tray.

"Don't worry about it." He waved with his other hand and a man in a suit hurried past the two of them to grab it. "My man Davis has it handled."

"Okay?" she responded, retrieving her hand and crossing her arms across her chest while eyeing him up expectantly.

"Oh, right." The easy grin returned to his face despite a slight clench of his jaw. "My name is Jasper. I overheard your name when you were talking to the young lady over there and I couldn't help but think that we might have something in common."

"And what is that?" Kat's eyes followed the servant as he began walking with her luggage in the rough direction of her room.

"I may have looked into your background a little bit." His eyes didn't even flicker as he admitted it. "And it appears that we have some mutual acquaintances. I was wondering if you'd be willing to accompany me to my quarters so that we could catch up on old times."

Around them, the buzz of conversation swelled as the various students reacted to his statement. Apparently it was quite scandalous, but Kat could barely bring herself to care. All she knew was that he was triggering the warning bells that Emma had avoided. Maybe it was his practiced facial expressions or the obvious nervous tension filling his body, but everything about Jasper seemed off.

"I'm afraid I'll have to decline." Kat tried to smile as graciously as possible. Following a nervous rich man to his room without witnesses? She'd watched Chrome Cowboys. That's how you ended up in pieces in Lake Michigan.

"I don't think you understand who I am." His pleasant smile faded somewhat.

The buzz turned ugly. The whispers weren't friendly

anymore and she was sure that at least some of the rubber-neckers were taking pictures or uploading the scene he was creating onto the gossip channels.

Kat tried to make the movement casual as she slipped her right hand into her jacket to brush her fingers across the hilt of her knife.

"Is this the part where you give some long-winded speech about how I should be grateful for your intentions?" she asked sarcastically. "About how I might escape you today, but you and your family will make me suffer for rejecting you?"

"What?" He took a step back, blinking at her as genuine bewilderment flashed across his face. "Oh God, is that what you thought? No. A thousand times, no. Let's start over." He closed his eyes, exhaling as he splayed his right hand out on his chest. "My name is Jasper Haupt. You were friends with two of the people who conspired to kill my father. Even if no one will admit it, I *know* that there is more to the case, but you're the first lead I've had in months."

"Please." He fixed his blue eyes on her, begging. "I need to talk to you about the death of Christopher Haupt."

CHAPTER TEN

"It doesn't feel right fighting a yeti in the middle of the desert."
Kat wiped the foul gray ichor off of her knives while she stared
at the hulking, white-furred corpse in the center of the
dungeon's boss chamber.

"Yeti?" Kaleek asked as he used a belt knife to begin
removing the monster's pelt, his breath fogging the cold air.

"A fictional creature from Earth." Kat sheathed her knives,
finally satisfied with their cleanliness. She began walking toward
Kaleek, struggling to maintain her footing in the unstable and
bitterly cold sand that made up the floor. "Some people still
claimed that they existed in some of the untouched wilderness
areas well into the 21st century. Now? The megacorporations
have been everywhere and exploited every natural resource that
could possibly have turned a profit. You can be sure that if there
were yetis, they'd have captured them and turned them into
either a luxury good or a theme park by now."

"And what doesn't feel right about it, Miss Kat?" Dorrik
asked, squinting at the light reflected from the cavern's icy walls
as they returned from looting the marks from the quartet of ice
sculptures that they'd defeated during the boss fight. "Although

The Tower of Somnus draws upon some creatures from strange or forgotten worlds, it is not terribly uncommon for it to select an entity from myth or to invent a creature entirely."

"I guess." Kat shrugged, looking down at Kaleek as the otter carefully worked his knife under the body's pelt. "It's just that yetis were always associated with cold areas and I always thought of deserts as warm."

"But plenty of deserts are cold?" Dorrik cocked their head curiously. "There are entire expanses on Lokkel near the mountains that only see snow once a year. The most beautiful sand and rock as far as the eye can see, but they never get above freezing."

The big lizard paused, nodding slightly, their crest fluttering as they smiled wistfully.

Dorrik looked back at her. "Once your race is no longer under probationary status, Miss Kat, then you can travel out to Lokkel and hike the Aguatt Plateau with me. It's chilly, but a dozen days hiking the freezing sands does wonders to clear the mind and put things in perspective."

"That..." She stopped the pithy response stuck on the tip of her tongue. "That actually sounds really nice. It'd be nice to spend some time with Kaleek and you while we're all awake."

"Not at the Aguatt Plateau you won't." The otter stood up, folding the heavy fur pelt from the dungeon boss. "Desoph evolved on a tropical archipelago. I'm sure you've noticed from my constant and vocal complaints, but I need a certain amount of humidity or I will be absolutely miserable. Combine that with ice-cold temperatures? I'd literally need an oxygen tank to prevent lung damage from exposure." Kaleek shivered theatrically. "Maybe if you can convince the lokkel to crash a couple of comets into their planet, up the humidity a little, then I'd be on board."

"Just something to think about." Dorrik smiled at Kat before glancing at the pelt in Kaleek's arms. "Did you collect all of the drops from the boss fight?"

Kaleek wrinkled his nose, whiskers rippling in the cold air.

"The boggrun's fat can be rendered into tallow that's fairly useful as a base for potions and oils," Kaleek replied. "I'm pretty sure they used it in those warmth potions you had me use for the underwater portions of the dungeon." The big otter shrugged. "Unfortunately, I didn't bring any wax paper or containers for something so… goopy."

"Then we've collected everything we need?" Kat asked.

"Time to go," Kaleek agreed. "At least it'll be warmer once we get to the surface."

Kat checked her status as the otter made his way over to the dungeon altar.

Name: Katherine Debs
Class: Elementalist Initiate
Max Level: 3
742 Marks

HP: 22
MP: 33
STA: 25

Dodge: Insignificant
Damage Mitigation: Insignificant

Strength: 4
Agility: 4
Fortitude: 3
Endurance: 4
Mind: 5
Reaction: 5
Charisma: 4
Spirit: 3

Spells Known:
Gravity's Grasp
Levitation

Pseudopod
Dehydrate
Dazzle
Shadow
Water Jet
Gravity Spike

Skills Known:
Knife I - 8, 96%
Gravity I - 7, 59%
Water I - 8, 21%
Cat Step - 5, 74%
Light I - 5, 61%
Cure Wounds I - 5, 11%
Penetrate

Perks:
Nightvision
Leaping

"Why the introspection, Miss Kat?" Dorrik asked, walking up next to her as she stared off into space. "It hasn't shown in combat, but you've seemed a little withdrawn today."

"There's just been a lot going on in the real world," she replied, shaking her head to dismiss the status screen. "The last couple of days, I've been tied up in a fairly major job, and I wouldn't exactly say it went wrong, but it certainly got complicated."

"Complicated?" Dorrik's crest fluttered in amusement. "You don't seem like the type of individual to get bothered by complicated."

"Well, it was three things really." Kat shrugged uncomfortably. "My boss might have pissed off someone he shouldn't have. It led to a lot of threats from someone who was in a position to do some damage. Xan says he has it under control, and who knows, maybe he does."

"That wasn't the worst of it." A sigh dragged itself from her throat. "Our partner on the operation got antsy and tried to double-cross Xan and I. A friend got shot, and I had to take down someone I thought was an ally. It all happened in a split second and…"

Kat closed her eyes, taking in a deep, shuddering breath.

"That certainly sounds like emotional whiplash to me," Dorrik agreed. "The excitement of battle can conceal trauma in the moment, but those sorts of events tend to leave wounds that healing magic can't fix."

"God." The tears were ice cold on Kat's face. "I almost forgot about the two people I killed retrieving the data. I thought they were samurai, and I needed a vehicle that they had in order to get myself to safety, but they couldn't even fight back."

"Miss Kat." Dorrik placed one of their hands on her shoulder.

"I'm sorry, Dorrik." She smiled at him weakly, wiping off her face before the tears froze. "It just all hit me suddenly. I've been in fight-or-flight mode day in and day out for so long that it just never registered until now. Then suddenly, their faces were flashing in front of me."

She took a moment to center herself. The last week had been a race, everything moving at a breakneck pace. One burst of adrenaline fading into another.

"Don't worry, Miss Kat." Dorrik's grip tightened on her. "Mistakes happen. Challenges happen. We must simply do what we can to become better people. Move past them. And in the meantime? Kaleek and I are always here to talk."

"There are plenty of monsters to fight in *The Tower of Somnus*," Dorrik continued, releasing her shoulder. "But most players don't spend every night delving in dungeons or improving their skills. For many, the dreamscape is a place to meet with old friends and absorb new cultures while relaxing. Maybe we should look into slowing our pace a bit. Give you a chance to relax. There will be plenty of time to level later."

"Thank you, but no." Kat smiled at the big lizard. "I know how badly Kaleek and you want to get back to your former levels. I... think I just needed to let all of that out. You being here to listen was already a lot."

"Then go ahead, Miss Kat." Dorrik smiled. "Kaleek has already teleported out of the dungeon, so the altar is free."

With a quick nod, she approached the obsidian structure next to the boggrun's skinned corpse. A moment later, her hand was on its smooth surface and a rainbow of light and energy wrapped her in its embrace.

Congratulations Adventurer!
You have completed the Wood Tier Level Three Dungeon, Ice Flow.
Three of three party members surviving. Good job!
Assigning awards:

+1 Spirit

Kat gasped at the sudden heat and light as she burst out of the dungeon and onto the third floor of the tower. Kaleek stood nearby, a contemplative look on his face and the boggrun pelt at his feet as he looked out into the desert.

She blinked, shading her eyes from the overly bright, fake sun that *The Tower of Somnus* used to make the unending deserts of the third floor feel authentic. Kaleek turned to her, frowning slightly.

"You should probably put on that hat Dorrik got you, Kat." He shifted slightly on the rocky spur that jutted out of the desert, hosting the portal into the dungeon. "I'm doomed to be miserable regardless, but Dorrik was very proud about looking up human physiology. Apparently the hat will prevent ultraviolet damage to your skin and hopefully help keep you cool."

"Are you sure this will work?" Kat asked, fishing the gauzy white hat out of her pack and slipping it on her head. She had to admit that the mist netting that covered her upper shoulders felt nice, taking some of the immediate sting of the light off of her, but it still felt ridiculous.

"I don't really know." Kaleek shrugged, flashing teeth as he smiled at her. "But Dorrik was incredibly proud of researching that factoid, so I vote you wear it to keep them happy."

"This has nothing to do with you snickering at me while I look ridiculous?" She planted her hands on her hips as she stared the grinning otter down.

"Honestly?" Kaleek's whiskers wiggled mischievously. "It actually makes you look a bit better. It's almost like a mask covering up all of that hideously smooth, pink skin."

Before Kat could retort, Dorrik appeared in a shower of light, stumbling slightly as they exited the dungeon. Smaller rocks tumbled down the outcropping as Dorrik fought briefly for their balance after the disorientation of the teleportation.

A minute or two later, the pelt was on Dorrik's back as they began the trek back to town. Theoretically, they could just sit around the dungeon waiting to wake up and save themselves a trek across the desert. When they returned to the dreamscape, they would respawn in the Adventurer's Hall like always, but all of the monster parts they collected would be gone.

The only exception to the rule was dungeons. Apparently the Tower didn't want people to be able to exit without paying for a return stone. If you woke up while in one, you simply returned to the beginning with all monsters respawned the next time you entered the dreamscape. Apparently, it was a good way to annoy other players as it would lock down the dungeon for the entire time that the player was in it, regardless of whether they were active in the Tower or not.

"So," Kaleek gasped, panting to keep cool under the beating light, "Kat, how was your first day of that new educational program you're in?"

"Really?" she asked him incredulously.

"Yes, really," he practically snapped back. "It's too hot and too dry. I am absolutely miserable. If I tried to talk to Dorrik, I would end up with a lecture on the mating practices of Antaran

Devil Wasps or something. Therefore, it is your responsibility to handle small talk."

She glanced at Dorrik and the big lizard shrugged.

"I may have tried to explain the unique facets of the reproductive habits of Antaran Devil Wasps to Kaleek several times," they replied without a hint of hesitation. "In my defense, it was relevant to an upcoming encounter with Devil Wasps. One that likely would have gone much smoother if Kaleek had bothered to listen to what I had to say."

"As I said." Kaleek rolled his eyes. "How was school?"

"Yesterday was just orientation." Kat tried to suppress a chuckle. "They showed us to our housing, helped us select classes, and I met a couple of people. Unfortunately for me, one of them was a boy. As soon as Mom found out, she would *not* shut up about it. I ended up having to talk about him for like an hour."

"Ah, yes." Dorrik nodded sagely. "Humans come into sexual maturity early. Biologically, it is almost your prime period to find a mate."

"No." Kat glared at them, trying to ignore Kaleek failing to stifle his laughter.

"You are eighteen years old, correct?" Dorrik glanced at her in confusion. "The textbooks that the expedition copied down seemed to be very clear that—"

"I get enough of this from my Mom," Kat cut them off, glad that the hat's veil covered her growing blush. "I am not going to 'mate' with Jasper. For all I know, he's just trying to lure me to his room so he can torture secrets out of me."

"Some people still might consider that part of the mating process." Kaleek winked at her.

"Dorrik might be oblivious, but I know *you* know better." Kat glared at the giggling otter. "Seriously though, I'm not sure what Jasper knows, but he's managed to figure out that I know something about his father's murder and now he wants to talk to me about it."

"Huh." Kaleek frowned. "That isn't nearly as sexy as I

imagined it. I mean, did you have anything to do with his father's death?"

"After a fashion?" Kat shrugged. "I was part of the team that investigated his death, even if Jasper doesn't know that. The only problem is that we couldn't properly identify everyone involved. Three people stood trial, and I strongly suspect that four were involved. I feel for the guy, both him and the fourth person are incredibly rich and powerful. I just don't want to have anything to do with the entire situation if I can help it."

"Certainly, you didn't actually agree to meet this man alone?" Dorrik frowned at her.

"Of course not." She sighed. "I agreed to meet up with him for a coffee. It'll be in public and ostensibly we're going to be discussing school as well as his investigation, but I still don't feel all that comfortab—"

"Heads up," Kaleek called out, lifting up his sword. "We have company."

Kat looked up, frowning. Cresting the dune in front of them stood a team of three humans, all men armed with swords and spears. Behind the warriors, a trio of hairless, black, man-sized moles shuffled their way to the top as well.

"Stallesp." Dorrik almost spat the word, dropping the pelt to the sand. "Working with humans despite the embargo."

"Yeaaaah." Kaleek cracked his neck. "Get ready, Kat, this is about to get ugly."

"Lokkel!" Kat's head whipped up as one of the hunched mole creatures pointed at the three of them with a heavily muscled claw. "Leave no survivors!"

Dorrik's voice left no room for backtalk "Kaleek, you handle the three humans. They look like idiots that can't handle their weapons, but they made it to the third level, so who knows."

"Kat," they continued, drawing their blades, "you're the fastest. Try to get to the stallesp and bring them down. They have the look of support casters, and I would prefer you to at least distract them enough that they don't end up peppering us with arcane bolts. I will provide support to both of you as needed."

She just nodded at Dorrik before activating Cat Step and sprinting up the side of the dune, struggling against the shifting sand that tried to pull her off balance as she made her way up.

Behind her, Kat heard a clash of steel on steel as Kaleek began his fight with the humans, but her attention was focused on the three aliens. One of them chanted, forming various eldritch seals with their hands as they began to harness mana for some unknown spell. Another drew both of their paws above their head, mumbling slightly as a golden light began to encompass them. The final mole stepped in front of the other two, their claws glowing purple with the telltale light of an activated psi ability.

Her first knife found the psi initiate's forearm even as Kat gathered her mana to cast Water Jet. The spell wouldn't deal any damage, but that wasn't even the point. She might not recognize the specifics, but Kat had enough experience to recognize arcane and curse magic.

If any of the three stallesp got their spells off, the rest of the party was in trouble. Depending upon the school of arcane magic, it could do anything from directly harm her friends to hinder them enough that the advancing humans could finish them off. As for the curse? One might not be enough to turn the tide of the battle, but they tended to last for hours and if the enemy healer got a chance to stack a couple more on, Kaleek and Dorrik would be in trouble.

The water hit the three moles, knocking the wizard entirely off of their feet and sending them sprawling and stumbling to the edge of the dune before they tripped and began sliding down the sandy incline.

As for the other two stallesp, it knocked the healer's hands out of position enough to disrupt their curse, but the spell did little more than knock the psi initiate back a step. Apparently that first ability had been some manner of body reinforcement.

"*Ego Shard*," the mole snarled. Kat tried to dodge, but her left foot sunk into the sand just as the bolt of violet energy slammed into her.

Her vision flashed purple and blurred. For a brief moment, the entire tower was silent and blanketed in a lavender fog.

Then, on instinct, Kat threw herself to the sand as a massive claw passed through where her chest had just been, the stallesp psi initiate having closed the distance between them in a fraction of a second.

"Hold still, girlie." The alien's voice was a combination of a bass tone, almost a foghorn, with a reedy whistling voice warbling the words over the top. "I'll make this quick if you stop this nonsense."

The sand hit her chest and face, a red warning indicator in the corner of her vision indicating damage. Kat wasn't sure if it had started flashing when she'd taken the *Ego Shard* to the chest, or if the fall did it, but she didn't have time to care.

Her response came in the form of casting Levitation on the stallesp even as she grabbed its ankle and yanked it toward her.

It gave a startled squawk, and began falling in slow motion, giving Kat just enough time to scramble to her feet and throw the alien as hard as she could, her hands still wrapped around its leg.

Even with the spell, the stallesp still weighed a fair amount, but her newly enhanced strength was up to the task, flinging it far enough that there would be no way for it to avoid a tumble of its own down the dune.

She cut the spell at the apex of its arc through the air, drawing another throwing dagger and turning to the healer just in time to feel a golden glow surround her. Suddenly, it felt like she was under the influence of Gravity's Grasp. Every step was duller, heavier. Even the colors seemed less bright.

With a grunt, she threw the knife in her hand. Frantically, the stallesp healer brought up a claw to block. A clang and a flash of sparks later and the blade hit the sand at the alien's feet.

It was some small comfort to Kat that the alien looked just as surprised as her to see that it had actually successfully blocked the throw. Either it was bad luck, or Kaleek was entirely on point with his intense distaste toward healers that specialized in curses.

Either way, Kat activated Cat Step once again, gathering her mana as she charged the slowly backpedaling alien. Before the healer could gather enough mana for another curse, Kat beat them to the punch, shielding her face just as she cast Dazzle and cut to the side.

Even through her eyelids, the flashes of light generated huge bursts of orange and purple. The false 'daytime sun' of the desert level halved the effectiveness of the spell, but it was enough.

Kat's knife slipped under the alien's arm, tearing into the side of its chest as the alien clawed at its face. It stepped backward, squealing as cyan blood leaked from the wound only for Kat to follow, stabbing it in the chest twice before stumbling backward, the curse and damp sand robbing her of her usual grace.

The stallesp raised a claw, panic in its beady eyes as it began to recite the words to Cure Wounds I.

Kat slid forward, her kick connecting with its lower thigh rather than the knee she was aiming for. Still, it was enough to startle the alien long enough for her to stab it again, this time her heavy combat knife cutting its forearm open.

Then, her opponent tripped, obviously not used to the rigors of frontline combat as the being's legs got tangled up with each other and it tumbled backward.

Kat pounced, noting her stamina dropping under half as she activated Penetrate just in time to punch her dagger through the alien's forehead. It shuddered once before going still. A moment later, she felt her strength return as the creature's death broke the curse.

She pulled herself to her feet, yanking the knife from her opponent's skull. A quick glance revealed that the wizard from the beginning of the fight was now standing at the bottom of the dune, eyes glowing slightly as they stared up at her, casting some sort of spell.

With a quick wave, she turned and scurried down the other side of the dune, breaking line of sight with the alien. Although it would still be able to cast the spell, it was very hard to hit a target you couldn't see.

A moment later, an explosion shoved Kat forward a step as an evocation spell detonated at the top of the dune behind her. For a second, she frantically tried to regain her footing as she stumbled down the sandy incline toward where Kaleek fought the two remaining humans.

She caught herself just as Dorrik finished off the psi initiate she'd sent sailing toward her two companions, one blade severing the mole person's arm while the other ran it through entirely.

Kat began casting another spell as she jogged toward Kaleek and the humans. He was holding his own, but the big otter bled from a sword wound down his side and a deep spear wound in his thigh. Even as she watched, the spear wielder shifted into Kaleek's blind spot and brought his weapon back for another strike.

She shifted her spell, encasing the human's head in the area of effect of Dehydrate. It wasn't nearly as powerful of a spell as Gravity Spike, but in the dry desert air, there wasn't much moisture for it to attack, and Kat almost winced as the man dropped his weapon and clutched his eyes, almost certainly blinded by the spell.

Kaleek took advantage of the distraction to surge forward, slamming the other human's sword aside before his own blade glowed red and reversed course with impossible quickness, taking the person's head.

Less than a breath later, he pirouetted and slashed his blinded opponent's stomach open, hip to hip.

Then, Kaleek stumbled, falling to one knee with his sword planted point first in the sand.

"Heal, please," he croaked, eyes still on the living but disemboweled human in front of him.

"Watch out for the arcane caster," she shouted at Dorrik as she ran over to Kaleek. "I only knocked them down. I don't know if they've taken any damage yet, and I'm about to be occupied."

Dorrik simply nodded at Kat before turning their gaze to the ridge where the entire attack originated.

Kat didn't have time to look back, instead mumbling the words to Cure Wounds I as she grabbed Kaleek by the shoulders and forced him to lay down. The spear wound in his thigh was deeper than expected, bright red arterial blood bubbling steadily out of it.

She put her hands over the injury, trying to ignore the sticky warmth under them as the spell took hold and they began to glow gold. In the corner of her vision, she watched her already partially depleted mana reserves tick down.

Finally, when she was down to only seven mana remaining, blood stopped actively flowing from the wound. Kaleek grabbed her by the shoulder, smiling tightly at her before he indicated the dune where she'd been fighting earlier with his eyes.

Kat followed his gaze, frowning as she saw the sole remaining stallesp standing there, far enough away that neither side could really attack each other.

She stood up, reaching for a knife on her bandoleer and taking a stride forward to join Dorrik as the big lizard glared at the alien.

The stallesp turned from them and began jogging away. Kat stepped forward, but Dorrik put out a hand to stop her.

"Enough." They shook their head. "I doubt we will be able to catch them with Kaleek's injury, and even if we do, they'll be able to see us coming. Arcane magic is slow to cast, but from a distance and with clear lines of sight, it has the potential to cripple or kill one of us if we aren't careful."

Almost as if sensing that the battle was over, a dialogue box popped into Kat's vision.

You have reached Level 9 in the skill Knife I. You have received the following reward:

+3.3% speed and damage with knives (total +26.4%).

"But we just can't let them get away after what they did to Kaleek," she protested, turning a worried glance at where the otter was breathing heavily on his back, covered in dry blood as he baked in the false sun.

"It is sufficient, Miss Kat." Dorrik shook their head once more. "We will need your mana to finish healing Kaleek, and after this surprise, I do not think it is a good idea for any of us to venture off alone."

They smiled gently at her. "You did a very good job with your portion of the fight. You managed to kill their healer first. Always a good strategy in large engagements."

"A target of opportunity." She sighed, relaxing her grip on the throwing knife slightly. "The healer couldn't defend themselves properly and it didn't seem like a good idea to let them rain curses on the two of you from afar."

"Good." Dorrik nodded. "Now our job is to make it back to town, where we can report to my clan that some of the humans and the stallesp are cooperating. Otherwise, my only other option is via courier, and my physical form is currently... in a remote location. That would likely take weeks."

CHAPTER ELEVEN

"This is just coffee, right?" Kat asked, glancing at the uniformed man standing behind Jasper as they sat down in the small cafe built into the college. "No strings attached?"

From the well-pressed dress shirt and slacks that Jasper wore, to the perfect part of his hair, nothing about him looked casual. His eyes bored into her intensely from behind a top-of-the-line smartpanel, a watch worth more than every item her entire family had owned before she started working for Xander hanging casually from his wrist.

She'd done some research, and so far their meeting was proceeding almost exactly how she'd expected. Every aspect of Jasper Haupt's persona was purposeful. He was rich and in command of almost every situation he found himself in, and he knew it. Luckily, unlike many scions of wealth, Jasper at least made a show of egalitarianism. Kat was still concerned about coercion—the man was destined to be an executive, after all—but he would at least make an effort to not be caught explicitly extorting her.

"Nothing to worry about, Katherine." He pulled a chair out from the beautifully varnished wooden table and sat down. "I do want to know more about my father and what happened in the Schaumburg Arcology leading up to his death, but I'm also interested in you. It's not every day that I get an opportunity to talk to an actual rank-and-file employee."

"What about…?" Kat motioned toward the servant standing behind him, her brow furrowing slightly. The man didn't react in the slightest.

"Davis doesn't count." Jasper waved a hand dismissively. "He's always there."

Kat looked at Davis, the frown still on her face as she tried to find a non-offensive way to respond to Jasper's statement.

"Look." Jasper swiveled in his seat, turning to the servant. "You didn't take offense to me saying you don't count, right, Davis?"

"None at all, sir." The middle-aged man inclined his head slightly to Jasper. Kat couldn't help but notice the difference in age. That a grown man was forced to respond so carefully and deferentially to the casual dismissal of someone just out of boyhood.

"Great." Jasper smiled. "Can you get me a Twenty of the Colombian dark roast, nonfat, with two pumps of sweetener, and—"

He turned to her, his motions cheerful and vigorous. "What do you want, Katherine?"

"Just a normal coffee?" she responded, struggling to make sense of the string of jargon. "What the heck is a Twenty anyway?"

"Two Colombian's then. Thank you, Davis." he nodded to the servant before turning back to Kat. "It's a large coffee. I thought it was because it was twenty ounces of liquid, but there are only sixteen. Honestly? No one really knows."

"I guess?" Kat tried to smile as she shrugged. "Anyway, here we are meeting in public. What do you want to know?"

Jasper leaned forward, both of his elbows on the polished wood of the table as he steepled his hands in front of his face.

"You knew Anna Donnst and Arnold Jacques, right?" His

expression was unsettling. He stared at her intently, like a housecat enraptured by the birds flitting about just outside a window.

"After a fashion." Kat hesitantly picked the words for her response. "I was pretty good friends with Arnold until he decided to date Anna. He pretty much stopped talking to me after that. Apparently, she thought I was some kind of threat, but I barely knew her beyond brushing shoulders with her from time to time at school."

"But you also moonlighted as a runner for the independent contractor crew that took Donnst down," Jasper stated rather than asked as he accepted a coffee from Davis. "The Chrome Wolves or something."

"The ChromeDogs, sir." Davis handed Kat her coffee. It was warm, with an earthy scent that she didn't usually associate with the overly chemical brands of instant coffee that she normally consumed. "A mid-sized independent contracting firm with high marks in infiltration and data retrieval. That rating is subject to revision as they've recently been associated with a very high profile job, but the quality and value of the information retrieved is still under review."

Kat stiffened. They only mentioned her history as a runner, but—

"The ChromeDogs!" Jasper snapped his fingers, coffee sitting untouched in front of him. "I don't know exactly what happened in Schaumburg, but shortly after the ChromeDogs received the bounty from my family, your entire family paid off their debts, so I'm hoping that you'll be able to fill me in."

Nervous energy ran through Kat's body. She could barely feel the heat of the coffee through its paper cup as it singed her hand. Frantically, her eyes searched Jasper's trying to figure out what he knew. What he suspected, but only turning up blanks.

Clearly, he knew a bit about her situation, but just as obviously he was leaving what he knew open-ended in an effort to get her to overplay her hand. It was a bluff, but without any way of knowing the extent of the bluff, she was acting blind.

"I was on a run, pulling data out of the arcology," Kat answered, taking a sip of the coffee to buy herself time. "Things got dicey a couple of times, and I apparently went above and beyond the call of duty enough to get a bonus."

Half-truths are better than whole lies. Xander repeated the phrase to the point that it might as well be a motto, but he was the one at home in situations like this. Sometimes she would swear that he preferred the adrenaline and intrigue of negotiating with a high-end corporate client more than the actual operation itself.

"Holy shit, this is good!" Kat exclaimed, looking at the understated paper cup in her hand. "I don't know what a Colombian roast is, but this is better than anything Java Bounty serves."

"Java Bounty is trash." Jasper smirked. "Unfortunately, GroCorp has struggled to develop a cold-resistant strain of coffee beans that's worth a damn. For all of our technical prowess, Great Lakes Coffee tastes like dirty dishwater. We have to trade with JB Holdings out of South America if we want anything worth drinking."

"Wait." Kat frowned slightly as she blew across the top of the cup to cool it. "Doesn't Java Bounty advertise Great Lakes Coffee as 'local and delicious, keeping jobs in our communities,' or something like that?"

"Cafe-chan," Jasper laughed. "One of Dad's greatest inventions. Great Lakes Coffee is cheap and it has great profit margins. It's just hard to sell to anyone that has actually had real coffee. Fools think the point of business is to create a better product. The real purpose is to convince consumers there is no better product than what you've created."

"I can see why you wouldn't want people knowing about this." Kat took another sip. "It's phenomenal."

He winked. "Well, let's just keep it our little secret then."

She took another drink, savoring the rich earthiness of the coffee. Fighting Jasper would only raise his suspicion, and so far the corporate scion had only been friendly with her. Better to cooperate as much as possible. Jasper Haupt might never consider himself a 'friend' to someone with Kat's background, but it was imperative that he not decide she was an enemy.

"So." She set the cup down. "What do you want to know about Arnold and Anna? I was Arnold's tutor for school, and we were sort of close, but honestly I don't know how much he had to do with everything. I doubt he was even fully in control of his own life, let alone capable of serving as some sort of criminal mastermind."

"They were both idiots." Jasper waved a hand dismissively. "I had them investigated before the execution, and neither of them knew what they were doing. Arnold was completely lost, and Anna was barely competent enough to pay someone to perform the hit."

"Honestly?" Jasper frowned for the first time, pensive furrows lining his face. "All of the evidence was too neat. No offense, but we shouldn't have needed to hire mercenaries if the people who killed my father were foolish enough to keep such specific and in-depth logs of their sensitive dealings. The more I look at it, the entire affair smells funny. My father was too great of a man to be brought down by this circus of incompetents. There must be another actor."

Kat's stomach dropped. She focused on regulating her breathing, trying not to think about the final raid on the Steel and Blood headquarters. How Belle Donnst had not quite revealed her role in the entire affair while explaining that the evidence they were retrieving pointed squarely at her daughter. It did, and Jasper was right. The entire case was far too neat.

"It sure as hell wasn't Gregory Daniels." Jasper slumped in the hardwood chair. "I looked into him. The guy is a schmuck. As dumb as Anna Donnst was, she legitimately led him around by the nose. I believe the evidence was doctored, but that man wasn't the brains behind it."

"You tell me, Katherine." He glanced up at her, frustration in his voice. "My dad is dead. Did Arnold and Anna kill him alone, or did they have help?"

She chewed on her lip, weighing her options. She didn't know anything for sure, and getting entangled with Jasper wasn't a decision for her to make, but at the same time, stonewalling him was a good way to court trouble. More than anything, Kat needed some breathing room to work things out.

She smiled at him, trying to put the brooding young man at ease. "First of all, call me Kat. Everyone does. Second," Kat ran a hand through her hair, trying to pick her words carefully. "ChromeDogs would only report information to you that they were sure of. With the exception of Arnold, Gregory Daniels and Anna Donnst were both guilty as hell. As for crews? Steel and Blood were almost certainly the group that handled that hit. They were getting a lot of money from Anna Donnst and specialized in assassinations. Christopher Haupt wasn't the only person they killed to fuel Gregory Daniels' ambitions."

"But," she let the word drag out before continuing, "that doesn't mean that everything got reported to you. Hypothetically, if there were other people we thought were involved, but we couldn't prove it? That wouldn't make it into a report to a client. Loose ends like that aren't productive, they just make the person highlighting them a target."

"What do you mean?" Jasper perked up, leaning forward and almost knocking his cooling coffee over.

"Look." Kat took another sip of her drink. "I don't have authorization to talk about this, but like you, I walked away with suspicions. I just don't feel safe—"

"I'll protect you," Jasper hissed, his eyes flashing. "Whatever it is you need, I'll make sure you're safe. That your family is safe. My dad is rotting in a grave, half-avenged. I *need* this information."

"Jasper." Kat shook her head. "All I have are suspicions, but if they're right, we're talking about the person who successfully killed Christopher Haupt and escaped all consequences. Do you really think I can trust you to keep me safe from them?"

"I..." He deflated, slumping back into his chair. "I understand, Katherine. If there are any hints you can provide, I'd be happy to hear them. I know it isn't just about credits, but I am prepared to offer a subscription to *The Tower of Somnus*, free and clear, if you can provide me with information that I can act on."

"I can talk to my handler with the ChromeDogs the next time I visit the arcology," Kat replied, trying to hide her distress. The last thing she needed was Jasper to realize that she didn't need a subscription. Still, it wasn't something that anyone in her position would turn down without serious thought. At a minimum, she needed a plausible excuse.

"That sounds great." Jasper perked up slightly. "Hell, tomorrow is Saturday and none of us have any homework. It's the perfect time for you to go home for a visit already."

"What—" Kat blinked, feeling the conversation suddenly slipping out of her control.

"Davis can get you maglev tickets to the arcology for tonight." Jasper smiled at her, standing up and leaving his cold and untouched coffee behind. "First class, my treat."

Before she could respond, Jasper was already making his way toward the exit of the coffee shop. Kat simply blinked as the door closed behind him, abandoning her to the wood paneling and soft music of the cafe.

"Madame." Davis coughed, drawing her attention. He removed himself from the nearby wall and approached her, tapping his smartpanel. A moment later, a dialogue box popped into her vision asking Kat if she wanted to accept a contact request from Davis Stoller.

"Hello." She accepted the request, standing up and offering her hand to the uniformed man. "I'm sorry that Jasper and I just talked over you like that."

"It is not a problem," he replied stuffily. "Is the eight o'clock maglev acceptable?"

Kat accessed her personal planner, paging through her schedule for the afternoon before nodding to Davis. "That should be fine, thank you."

A moment later, her inbox lit up as Davis transferred a purchased ticket to her.

"Thank you again, Mr. Stoller." She smiled at the older man. "Will there be anything else?"

"Yes, Miss Debs." Davis shifted nervously. "Do you mind if I call you Kat?"

She nodded slowly, picking up her coffee as she stood up so that she could look at the slightly taller man more or less eye to eye.

"Kat." Worry crinkled the corner of his eyes. "Jasper is a good boy. He respected and looked up to his father, but the man wasn't in his life as much as either of us would have liked. I've been with him for a long time, and I've tried to instill a sense of honor in him."

She clutched the coffee to her chest, unsure where Davis was going.

"What I'm trying to say," Davis closed his eyes, sighing, "is that you should try not to think too badly of him. Jasper is a romantic. He wants to find out what happened to his father in a world where most children would simply delight in an early inheritance. You don't seem like the type to take advantage of him. In fact, you seem like you want to be anywhere but here. A sensible response."

"You seem like a reasonable girl, Kat." He looked at her once more, his gray eyes as sharp as steel. "Simply deal fairly with him. Don't string Jasper along with empty promises and we won't have a problem."

"What happens if we have a problem?" Kat didn't move an inch, her gaze hardening to match the older man's.

Davis looked her up and down before responding. "You don't move like someone who is just a runner, Kat. I saw you register a weapon during intake. You're a predator."

"I don't mean that as an insult." Davis shook his head. "Far from it, I respect who you are, what you represent, and what you've obviously done to get where you are. I just want you to know that even if Jasper may resemble prey to someone like you, there will be repercussions. I don't think I need to spell this out. You got into this institution without parental help. You're a smart girl."

"I'm not a fan of being threatened." Kat frowned at him, her feet almost unconsciously spreading into a combat stance.

"Oh, don't worry," he chuckled, the dangerous look fading from his eyes. "I don't intend to back you into a corner. I can respect another professional. I just want to make sure you know where my line is drawn in the sand."

"The maglev will arrive at eight o'clock, Kat." Davis inclined his head slightly before he turned to leave. "Hopefully your trip back home will help jog your memory."

Thirty seconds later, she was alone in the coffee shop, Jasper's untouched and now cold coffee her only companion. Kat finished her own drink and sighed, the quiet music already beginning to grate on her nerves.

Disposing of both of the cups, Kat returned to her room, shooting an e-mail to both her mother and Xander letting them know that she'd be visiting home for the weekend. A couple changes of clothes and some snacks in a duffle bag later, she was ready to head to the maglev station.

This time, rather than a cab, Kat decided to walk. She had a couple of hours to kill, and she wasn't terribly keen to relive the string of near death experiences that could charitably be called her ride to college.

Chiwaukee itself was fairly pleasant in the early afternoon light. Corporate security patrolled the streets beneath towering edifices of steel and glass, nodding at the GroCorp logo on her jacket even as they kept their eye on clusters of more mundane employees.

The people all reminded her of her time in the Schaumburg arcology, albeit wearing slightly different color schemes. Company workers either hurrying to work second shift or lounging around local bodegas drinking overpriced neon fizzy drinks.

Not one of them looked like a samurai. There weren't any visible physical augmentations, and none of the people carried themselves with the swagger and menace she'd come to associate with the professional freelance soldiers that lived their life on the edge.

It was safe, but the entire ward felt... boring. There was no vibrancy here, the streets didn't carry any of the life she'd come to associate with the abject poverty of the Shell, the garish neon of St. Louis, and the seedy hustle of the neighborhood where Xander had rented the flophouse.

She felt like she was in a tiny room on a hot summer day. The air was stale and felt flat in her lungs. Even when she made it to the maglev station and presented her ticket via smartpanel, she still just felt lethargic.

There were other people in the station, waiting to take the nightly commuter train to Schaumburg, but Kat didn't bother to approach any of them. Most were managers or corporate security, neither a group she had a natural rapport with. Luckily, no one cared that she just stood in the corner letting the entertainment streams melt her brain rather than socializing.

The train was on time, and the actual trip out to Schaumburg was comfortable and only took a couple of minutes. Really, the maglevs were a modern miracle, one that allegedly had its origins in material science advances that could be traced back to *The Tower of Somnus*.

Kat wasn't entirely sure how the tower had influenced the magnetically hovering high speed trains. As far as she could tell, their technology predated humanity's introduction to the tower, but it sounded like studies of the abilities humans had brought out of the tower had allowed scientists to optimize the advancement.

The train slowed to a halt, magnets grabbing the vessel and arresting its momentum soundlessly, and minutes later, Kat was walking out onto the tenth floor station of the arcology.

She smiled to herself as she stood in line at the security kiosk, waiting for her turn to present her credentials to the overworked company employee inside. Kat couldn't help but find it funny that boarding and disembarking the maglev probably took more time than the actual trip.

Finally, she was in front of the harried clerk, and with a tap of her smartpanel she sent the poor woman a copy of her ticket, employment status, and trip itinerary. A glance to the side transformed her quiet amusement into pensive brooding.

Alongside the usual Ike Holdings corporate security officers stood a pair of samurai. They were wearing well-fit and expensive clothing, but that was like putting a bowtie on a tiger. Chrome limbs and the steel glint of cybereyes were only the most obvious of clues. Everything about the men, from the custom weapons at their sides to their posture, and the way they surveyed the maglev station like they owned the place, rang alarm bells in Kat's head.

Whoever they were, corporate security didn't carry themselves with the casual arrogance that practically dripped off of the samurai. That was something earned through struggle and blood in forgotten gutters and alleys. A couple months of firearm and crowd control training at a security academy just couldn't.

"Thank you, ma'am." Kat blinked, looking back at the frazzled clerk. The twenty-something woman smiled at her wearily. "Your paperwork all checks out. Thank you for coming back to visit the Schaumburg arcology."

Kat smiled at her and began walking toward the elevator, doing her best to keep her breathing and posture natural as she passed the two samurai, heart pounding. Even if she didn't know who they were, Kat knew better than to believe in coincidences. The samurai might not be there for her, but their presence was almost certainly an ill omen.

If they noticed anything amiss about her, neither commented on it, and there was no way Kat could turn to observe them without giving up the charade. Only when the elevator closed behind her with a ding did she finally exhale, slumping up against the wall. A low-level manager glanced at her in confusion, but Kat just ignored her, content on riding the lift down to her mother's apartment.

A brief check-in with her younger sister to ensure that the girl was actually studying and not watching Chrome Cowboys, and Kat was on her way to the ground floor. She made her way through the giant open-air market that was the first floor of the arcology and out onto the streets of the Shell.

Her steps faltered slightly as she took in the half-deserted streets of the shantytown that surrounded the arcology. Scavengers in human form peered out at her from busted windows before going on their way, recognizing someone that was more trouble than they were worth.

It was a hellscape strewn with decades old garbage and burned out cars, but at least in the Shell, you knew your place. If you weren't careful, you'd die. No one even bothered with the fake smiles and niceties of corporate life. They were either in your crew and family, or they were a rival.

She set out toward the ChromeDogs' headquarters, hand on the hilt of the knife in her jacket. Although Kat felt eyes in between her shoulder blades, keeping tabs on her movements and sizing her up, no one bothered her and she arrived at the warehouse that Xander and the ChromeDogs used without much trouble only for a frown to blossom on her face.

The formerly nondescript building had been updated since their raid on Steel and Blood. Machine gun nests roosted on each corner of the warehouse, and defenses, both manned and automated, occupied many of the allegedly abandoned buildings dotting the street running up to the headquarters.

New, however, were the trio of armored transports parked just outside the half-disabled armored fighting vehicle that the ChromeDogs had salvaged from their war with Steel and Blood and pressed into service as a fortified road block.

All three of the heavy cars were brand new, painted in GroCorp colors and guarded by a quartet of corporate security officers that actually looked like they knew how to shoot their heavy rifles at something other than rioting factory workers. All four of them wore heavy exosuits covered in armor, and their visored helmets snapped up as soon as Kat stepped into view.

A ChromeDog samurai she vaguely recognized hurried over to talk to the four soldiers as Kat approached, and other than the gooseflesh on the back of her neck, she was able to enter the warehouse unmolested. Quietly, the samurai that let her in directed Kat to the first floor conference room rather than the second story office suite usually used for the organization's meeting and planning.

She frowned as she approached the door. Honestly? She hadn't even been in the conference room since her time as a runner. As soon as she joined up with Xander, every meeting had taken place deeper in the building. Really, the conference room was only used for clients and trusted outsiders.

Kat pushed the door open and stepped inside, her pensive expression immediately dissolving into one of shock. Xander sat at the large cheap table that filled most of the room, a worried look on his face. Next to him bristled Nina Cromwell, his wife and the actual head of the ChromeDogs military operations.

"It's good to meet you in person, Katherine." Belle Donnst stood at the other end of the room, her suit immaculate and probably worth enough to feed a large family for a month. She smiled at Kat, a cheerless display of perfectly straight and white teeth. "Why don't you take a seat? We have a lot to discuss."

CHAPTER TWELVE

Kat glanced uncertainly to Xander only for him to wave her inside, an unhappy expression on his face. She closed the door behind her, eyes taking in both Belle and the massive and heavily chromed bodyguard standing beside her as she took her seat next to Xander.

"Thank you for joining us, Kat." Ice water trickled down her veins as Belle addressed her. There was just something off about the older woman. No matter the expression on her face, her eyes were as lifeless as a shark circling its prey. "Do give Jasper my best when you return to Chiwaukee."

"Jasper Haupt?" Kat's breath caught in her throat. "You know Jasper?"

"Of course, dear." Belle's mouth opened into a smile that showed slightly too many teeth. "It was a shame about his father, after all. I couldn't make it to his funeral, so I made sure to send a fruit basket. There's no real reason to be impolite over a minor personal disagreement."

"You killed—" Kat began, her mind flicking to the conversation with Jasper and the boy's earnest desperation.

"I allegedly allowed Christopher Haupt to die," Belle interjected. "But that's hardly why I'm here. As I'm sure you noticed, security has changed at the Schaumburg arcology."

"The new goons have been giving my runners some trouble," Xander agreed. "They don't really take bribes, and they're fairly good at plugging security holes that have existed for decades. Nothing major has happened yet, but they're certainly cutting into my bottom line."

"I would agree that they are a hindrance." Belle inclined her head. "Unfortunately, it appears that they are peacekeepers hired by GroCorp from the Millennium Company."

"Shit." Nina glared at Xander. "Look at where your grandstanding got us. I know it must have made you feel like a big man to mouth off to Mr. Jackson given what he'd done to you, but now here we are. Stuck out here while his thugs sniff around, waiting for an excuse to jump one of my boys."

"You overlook the point, Miss Cromwell," Belle responded. "Even given Mr. Jackson's dispute with Xander, there isn't much he could do without GroCorp's invitation. At some point, GroCorp has decided that the security of Ike Holdings, a wholly owned subsidiary of GroCorp, was insufficient."

"This is troublesome in two major ways." Belle pursed her lips. "First, it creates an extra layer of security that is much harder to... come to an understanding with. Given how much of corporate work requires these sorts of understandings, I am sure you can understand why a genuinely independent and incorruptible layer of law enforcement would be considered a negative factor."

"Of course" Xander nodded in response, his voice thoughtful.

"More importantly." Kat shivered as all pretense of amiability disappeared from Belle's voice. "Millennium couldn't be here without a contract. Even at a discount, their services cost money, and that means someone in the corporate hierarchy was willing to pay and pay a lot."

"Do you know why?" she asked, matching Belle's steely glare for a second before the older woman smiled.

"Not at the moment." Belle chuckled without any real warmth. "And I will admit that the lack of knowledge irks me. I've managed to trace the contract to a GroCorp shareholder, and as overinflated of an opinion as I might have of myself, I know that a shareholder is out of my reach."

"A shareholder?" Kat asked, confusion wrinkling her brow. "Honestly, why would they even care? I mean, I get it if a share-holder would intervene to replace the CEO of Ike Holdings—"

"—a wholly owned subsidiary of GroCorp," Donnst spoke over her. "Come now, Miss Debs, we must be precise about these things."

"Right," she continued, slightly rattled by the older woman's interjection, "but the idea of directly taking charge of Schaum-burg arcology's security just doesn't seem right. They only get involved when something major is happening, like a division being spun off, being traded to another company, or needing a restructure due to being unprofitable."

"We are quite profitable." Belle smiled thinly. "No need to worry about that. Given our position just outside the Chiwaukee headquarters, I would be surprised if Ike Holdings, a wholly owned subsidiary of GroCorp, is being sold or spun off. Allowing another corporation this close would be a security liability."

"Honestly?" Belle began, raising an eyebrow.

"For once?" Xander asked, leaning back in his chair, a smug smile on his face.

"Very droll." She turned the full weight of her gaze on the slouching man, glaring at him until he wilted in his seat like a cut flower left for a week without water.

"Honestly," Belle continued, as if the previous exchange had never happened, "Millennium's presence concerns me. It speaks to a lack of trust and a potential need to have indepen-dent forces on hand in order to remove a major player in the area. As a major player in Schaumburg, I would rest easier knowing why Millennium was here."

"I don't know." Kat glanced at Xander. "I think tangling

with Millennium once was more than enough for me. Even with a plan, preparation, and surprise, we barely got in and out of St. Louis."

After a swift elbow from Nina, Xander nodded in agreement. "Sorry, Mrs. Donnst, we just finished a fairly big job and it's probably for the best if our organization lays low for a little while. We have some pretty hefty cash reserves now, and Nina was thinking of upgrading our defenses—"

"Don't worry." Belle smiled mirthlessly. "This is nothing for the ChromeDogs. I agree with Miss Cromwell's assessment. Much of North America has its eyes on your organization right now, and it would be for the best if it did not draw any more attention. After all, how can I use the ChromeDogs in the future if a megacorp decides that you're idealists and takes it upon themselves to crush you?"

"Idealists?" Kat asked.

"The ChromeDogs aren't worth destroying if they're a normal mercenary company," Belle lectured. "If the companies think that you are just looking out for your profit margins, the ChromeDogs are just another tool. Attacking an independent contractor is illogical. After all, why would you destroy a tool when you could crush the hand holding it?"

"On the other hand," the older woman continued, gracing Kat with a chilly smile. "If companies become convinced that you are an idealist, your little band is no longer a tool. Once you start picking and choosing your contracts, a mercenary company becomes a player in its own right. At that point, if there's a pattern to your activities, such as a vendetta against GroCorp, you become fair game. Where GroCorp might not care about a random company making a living, they certainly will take efforts to stomp out someone who actively means them harm."

"Never mind that." Nina crossed her arms, glaring at Donnst and her bodyguard. "If you didn't come here to hire the ChromeDogs, why the hell did you come here? I'm assuming this wasn't some sort of casual social call."

"I didn't just swing by to grab a coffee." Belle gave Kat a knowing wink. "I've already done some research into the shareholder in question. Elise Williamson. Fourth generation GroCorp, living primarily in Chiwaukee."

"More importantly." The older woman's gaze settled on Kat. "Her primary lieutenant is Thomas Franklin, a vice president with GroCorp and the current Dean of GroCorp College. I happen to know that he lives on campus, meaning that anyone who happened to be attending that school would have fairly easy access to him."

Kat stood up, chair scraping beneath her. At the other end of the table, Donnst's heavily chromed guard's hand blurred toward a holster at his hip only for Belle to bring him to a stop with a wave of her hand.

"No, no, no!" Kat backed away from the table. "I barely know my way around the campus. Security is everywhere, the college isn't some two-bit data repository in the middle of nowhere. They designed that place to protect some very rich and powerful students. It's practically a fortress."

"It's a good thing we have a person on the inside," Belle countered smoothly. "Don't worry, Katherine, all I want is some data from his personal desk computer. In fact, I would actively be upset if you handled this your usual way and simply killed everyone. While imposing, that isn't the goal. I would prefer that this little fact-finding mission take place unnoticed."

"This sounds like an amazing way to get caught and poof," Kat blew out a puff of air as she paced back and forth past the table, "disappear."

"Now, now, dear," Donnst replied. "I've seen your work, and I believe in you. It might take you a little while to prepare, but at the moment there isn't any rush."

"Maybe." Kat exhaled frantically, trying to think of a way to get out of the situation. "But this still seems like a bad idea. I already feel like I have a target on my back from the Millennium raid."

"I don't need the money." Kat stopped pacing. "I can help

someone get in, but right now the most important thing is letting things blow over."

"Come now, Katherine." Belle clicked her tongue disapprovingly. "I thought you were smarter than this. Please don't make me get crude. We both know that there are more matters than just 'money' at play here."

"Kat." Xander reached out and touched her wrist. She looked down at him. A hint of worry touched the corner of both his eyes as he shook his head slightly.

She sighed and sat down next to him. There were any number of reasons why going after Dean Franklin was a bad idea, but at the end of the day, her entire family lived in the arcology where Belle was an executive. As long as Kat was useful to the older woman, they would be looked after, but that didn't mean that they weren't all but hostages.

"How much are we talking about?" Xander asked, his hand still covering Kat's wrist, almost protectively, while he made eye contact with Belle. "Look, Kat is going to need a support team. That means my side of the operation, if not Nina's, and that means we have an entire team to pay. You might be able to strongarm us into taking a mission, but by God, you're going to pay market rate for our work. Extortion is one thing, but we aren't a charity."

"I wouldn't dream of it," Belle replied. "Twenty-five thousand credits. Ten thousand up front and fifteen upon delivery. In addition, you can keep a copy of the data. Exclusivity isn't important to me, and I think you'll be almost as interested in learning Millennium's role in the area. After all, they're hardly just *my* problem."

"What do you think, Kat?" Xander turned to her. "The rate of pay is fair and this time we'll be doing the pre-mission scouting in house. Though I'd still prefer to lay low, Belle's right. We do need to learn what's going on with Millennium in the area. It clearly isn't a coincidence, and that's the sort of ignorance that could get all of us killed if we aren't careful."

She nodded. Too angry at herself to trust her voice. Angry

because she let Belle wind her up until she wasn't thinking clearly. Angry because she let Belle maneuver her into a corner and force her to do something dangerous. Angry that there wasn't really a way out of the situation.

"We'll be in touch, Belle." Xander nodded to the woman. "But for now, Nina will walk you and your associate out."

Next to them, Nina unfolded, easily as tall as the huge body-guard standing next to Belle. From personal experience, she knew that the huge woman had almost as much chrome as the guard, just tactfully hidden beneath artificially tough synthetic skin.

Nina nodded wordlessly at Belle and led the two of them out of the conference room. For a couple of seconds, they sat in silence, Xander brooding as he stared off into space. Finally, he turned back to Kat as she stewed, trying to overcome her frustration with the status quo.

"It's just like programming, you know." Xander smiled slightly.

"What?" she replied, confused by the sudden digression.

"Sometimes solving one bug means you find two more." He shrugged. "I guess I was never in a corporation, but when I was young, I grew up on the streets of St. Louis and things were pretty grim."

"I don't know what it's like to be owned by a company from birth." Xander sighed. "But I did have my share of hungry nights and bruises from bigger kids taking food from me."

"The proudest day of my life," he stared up at the ceiling wistfully, "was when I joined the Cardinals. They weren't the biggest crew in the city, but suddenly I had a roof over my head, a gun at my side and some cyberware in the back of my head."

"You should have seen me." Xander chuckled slightly, his eyes still on the crumbling panels above the two of them. "I thought I was hot shit. Just a thug, barely even a samurai. Definitely no name of my own, strutting around my old neighborhood and bragging about having a backing."

"For about two weeks, everything was perfect." A flicker of

a grimace flashed across his face. "Then I had to go on a mission with two other guys. One of them died, fell out of the getaway car on a highway and a truck flattened him. The other?"

Xander looked back at her, his eyes serious. "He was like your teammate, Smits. He froze up, but he survived. Couldn't hack the job and ended up retiring to desk work."

"At that point," he continued, "it hit me. I was getting all of this money and power, but it wasn't freedom. It came with responsibilities and duties. I wasn't hungry anymore, but I was tied to my crew, and I ended up having to do some things I didn't like."

"A full six months undercover in Millennium." Xander shook his head. "Mr. Jackson gave me my subscription himself. Hell, Athena was my handler. It was the toughest job of my life, but I got through it, burning a bunch of bridges on my way out."

"I guess deep down I knew that Athena was up to something." Xander grimaced. "But she was almost family."

"I couldn't just act on a gut feeling with her, Kat." He stared at her, teeth grit. "I needed to give her one last chance to not go through with it. I just thought that it would be me taking the bullet rather than Whip if the window couldn't handle it."

"I think I understand." Kat frowned slightly. "I just don't get what that has to do with programming?"

"Oh." He chuckled. "Sorry, I was woolgathering for a bit there. What I meant is that, in this world, freedom is more or less an illusion. If you ever think you've solved a problem, something new is going to pop up."

"You got rid of your debt slavery and the threats to your day-to-day life." Xander shrugged. "Only to get stuck working for someone like Donnst. Our kind don't get to retire often. We exist because we're useful to those with actual power, and once that ends, well. You'd better have an exit plan or things get ugly."

"That's... pretty grim, actually." Kat shook her head, smiling tepidly at Xander.

"Sorry," Xander replied. "Athena's betrayal has had me feeling pretty morose. She always called it 'wearing a golden collar.' You could get a fancier one or something that fit better, but at the end of the day, you're still a rich person's dog."

"Anyway," He shook his head. "We should probably talk about how you're gonna steal these files from your dean."

"I'm going to need Whippoorwill." Kat slumped in her chair. "At a minimum, we'll have to wait until she's feeling up to it."

Xander flashed her a quick grin, his golden tooth glinting. "First things first, I want a better setup than a flophouse. I've been thinking, the ChromeDogs need a branch office in Chiwaukee. Now that we've got the money, it's time to set up a base of operations and a safehouse out there."

"Is that just for me?" Kat raised an eyebrow, confusion in her voice. "I know we have more money now, but this just seems extravagant."

"Sort of." Xander chuckled. "It makes sense that I have a base of operations for my best agent, and it helps that you'll be based in the financial hub of the upper Midwest. Plus, this is my retirement plan, after a fashion."

"One of these days I'm going to have to retire and pass all of these headaches on to you." He winked at her. "Having a safe house I can retire to where no one recognizes my face, well, that just sounds nice."

"Retire." Kat rolled her eyes at him. "Don't pretend to go senile on me. I know you're having too much fun to give any of this up."

"You never know." Xander stood up. "I'm thinking of taking up whittling. It seems... wholesome."

CHAPTER THIRTEEN

"Kat!" Sikka shouted, elbowing past Dorrik as they walked alongside Kaleek. "Have you been keeping Dorrik out of trouble? I heard they got into a tussle with the moles out on the dunes."

"Sikka." Dorrik turned to the older lokkel, crest flaring in frustration. "I'm right here."

"Never mind them." Sikka waved Dorrik aside with her upper limbs while the lower pair grasped the crook of Kat's arm. "Dorrik is just being grumpy because the enclave is on lockdown while we try to figure out what's going on."

"Lockdown?" Kat cocked her head, looking at the bustling crowds of four-armed lizard people buzzing about the white stone enclave. "Things still look pretty lively around here to me."

"The stallesp won't do anything in the city." Sikka led her through the winding hallways of the compound, weaving Kat through the crowds of lokkel with ease born of experience. "The Clan has a couple scouts coming down from the upper levels to figure out what the stallesp are up to. Once they give us the heads up, the adventuring types will leave the compound to do whatever it is you danger junkies like to do with your time. Then things will finally be quiet enough that the rest of us can actually finish some of our crafting orders."

"I don't understand why we're waiting on the scouts?" Kat shrugged. "Aren't most of the people here warriors? Why don't you just send out the teams on hand to figure out what's happening?"

Sikka chuckled, taking a seat on the garden bench. Kat joined her, shifting slightly to find a comfortable position on the stone seat while the fake sun beat down on her.

Sikka leaned back, closing her eyes as she basked in the light and heat. "While your courage is laudable, there's no promise that the stallesp won't have sent their own ringers. The last thing we need is our hunting parties getting ambushed by moles with evolved classes. None of you would even stand a chance."

Kat shuddered, thinking back to her fight with Anna Donnst where the girl had used an iron tier skill. Anna didn't have the stats to make the most of the evolved ability, and it was only one field of magic, but even then it was enough to push Kat to her limit. The idea of fighting an enemy that had evolved all of their skills to iron didn't exactly appeal to her.

"What do we do then?" Kat shrugged. "Are there any jobs to do around town, or am I just cooling my heels until the scouts can give the all clear?"

"There probably are some jobs." Sikka chuckled, her eyes still closed. "But don't worry about it too much. The three of you have been working too hard. You can get back to fighting eldritch horrors in dungeons in a couple of days. Until then, everyone should just relax. Have some food. Catch up with friends. Upgrade your gear. None of this is worth anything if you crack from stress and get killed in some wood tier dungeon in the middle of nowhere."

"I guess." Kat blew out a sigh, glancing at the relaxing lizard out of the corner of her eyes. "I just don't like sitting still. Back on Earth, living is like swimming. If you stop treading water, you end up under the surface."

"There's a reason your planet was blockaded, dear." Sikka chuckled, shifting slightly so that a new set of scales would be exposed to the tower's fake sun. "A proper society encourages and nourishes its citizens. There's no need to coddle layabouts, but any number of sociological studies have shown that constant anxiety over economic and social status is counterproductive."

Sikka opened her eyes, stretching both pairs of arms with audible pops. "Plus, lokkel don't swim. The idea of voluntarily diving into that much collected water is enough to turn my scales inside out."

"If you don't mind me asking," Kat turned to face Sikka, "what do you do in water dungeons or on levels of the dreamscape that are mostly water? I can understand not enjoying swimming, but it seems like a glaring weakness given the difficulty of *The Tower of Somnus.*"

"I pay for help." Sikka grinned at her. "Not everyone enters the dreamscape solely to throw themselves into mortal danger. Maybe that's how things are with your race, but among the lokkel, it's common wisdom that a clan should have three to four support players for each adventurer. After all, you're only going to be able to clear low level dungeons without advanced gear. Fairly soon, even with a talon as seasoned as yours, you're going to start struggling without upgrading."

"That makes sense." Kat nodded slowly. "Wait, what in the hell is a talon?"

Sikka tilted her head to the side, staring semi-blankly at Kat before chuckling.

"I forgot that you were new to the dreamscape." Sikka held up a hand, displaying three of her clawed fingers. "Combat groups recognized by the tower come in two sizes. Talons are three players."

"Claws," Sikka continued, opening her hand so that all six of its fingers were visible, "are six individuals. The whole hand. Generally talons are used for resource gathering—more groups means more ground covered, after all—while claws aim for dungeons and floor guardians. Only a couple crazy groups like yours seek to ascend the tower as a talon. The free attribute points from beating floor guardians as a talon add up, but it generally isn't worth the people we lose over time."

Kat nodded as Sikka's explanation sank in. "Well, if leveling up with a three person team is so dangerous, what exactly should we be looking for in equipment and how do we go about getting it?" She chuckled bleakly. "Unlike the rest of you, I don't get another shot at this if I die out here. I don't really have any friends on Earth that would give me a new subscription."

Briefly her mind flashed back to Jasper. He wasn't exactly a friend, and the subscription would come with enough strings attached to weave a net, but she wasn't completely without options.

Sikka smiled. "Oh, never mind that. I could hardly let Dorrik, Kaleek, and you run around with this drab gear. I'll talk to some of the other crafters and we'll outfit you at cost. That still means that the three of you will need to supply the materials, but we should be able to provide you with lists for what you will need and where the monsters in question have their lairs."

"Do any of the monsters in question live close enough that we can sneak out and start gathering components despite the lockdown?" Kat asked hopefully.

"I'll see what I can do." Sikka laughed. "Someone will track you down to take measurements and let you know about pricing. Now run along." She made a shooing motion with both of her upper hands. "I'm sure Dorrik is like you, vibrating with frustration at being locked down, and Kaleek? Well, he's probably in a bar somewhere, harassing a musician into singing an off-color drinking song."

Kat thanked Sikka for her time before wandering off into the lokkel enclave. The whitewashed hallways were bustling with the large, dark lizard people, many of whom threw her curious looks. Every once in a while, a different species of alien would walk by with a lokkel chaperone before noticing Kat and whispering to their companions. None of them approached her or acted impolitely, but it was clear she was out of place.

About ten minutes later, with some directions from a helpful lokkel after she accidentally barged into what appeared to be their art studio, Kat found her way to Dorrik. They were sparring with their clutchmate, Basash, the two of them a whirling and clanging storm as they tore into each other.

The fight went on for almost a minute, both of the lokkel matching each other stroke for stroke, each blow turned aside by a parry or an expert riposte. Then the riot of noise and movement stopped as Basash staggered backward with a grunt, a long cut on their forearm.

"Of course, Dorrik." The injured lokkel's chuckle ended in a wince as they cradled their arm. "I spent months training and I have four dungeons on you, but I still can't even get a single slash in."

"Kat, would you mind?" Dorrik nodded at her and indicated Basash's wound. She approached Basash, the lizard nodding in thanks as she began casting Cure Wounds I.

"You are getting better, Basash," Dorrik tried to cheer their sibling up as they sheathed the two swords. "Your defensive form is strong, if a bit overly orthodox. It left you rigid, and I only had to slow my last couple of strikes to disrupt your rhythm and slip through."

"You tell me, Katherine." Basash turned to Kat, flinching as her hands touched their injury, wrapped in the golden light of the spell. "Has Dorrik ever been anything but orthodox? I swear, from the egg, every problem was solved by research, extensive planning, and then sticking to that plan."

"That does sound like Dorrik." Kat chuckled, eyes on the injury as Basash's scales knitted together under the spell's influence. "It's a good thing, too. On our own, Kaleek and I would probably rush headlong into a fight we weren't suited for and get killed by something that we could have just breezed by with a little bit of preparation."

"I enjoy planning." Dorrik crossed their arms huffily. "But

I'm not going to let it become a weakness. One of the first rules of combat is to improvise if you think your opponent has foreseen your next step. Basash had clearly trained to counter my preferred sword style. The answer was obviously to alter my sword style."

"And that's why we win fights," Kat agreed, stepping away from Basash as the lokkel flexed their newly healed arm. "Kaleek and I have the right instincts, but Dorrik always takes it a step beyond us."

"Thank you, Kat." Dorrik nodded at her, a brief smile on their muzzle.

"Oh, don't mind me." Basash chuckled. "It's just a bit frustrating to be the second fastest lokkel in Clan Ahn to hit level four only for Dorrik to still outperform me. I won't disagree that they're a better swordsperson than me, but honestly, Dorrik, would it kill you to let me get a slash in just once?"

"You've made it to level four?" Kat asked, stepping back to give the lokkel some personal space.

"Yes." Basash preened, their crest fluttering slightly. "Having to fight the floor guardian to get back was a hassle. You don't even get any drops." They shuddered. "But the fourth floor was awful. I know that there are some planets that are mostly ocean, but that isn't a proper place for lokkel. I'd rather spend some time down here on guard duty, earning enough marks to buy upgraded equipment from the crafters that spend their time on the third floor."

"About that." Kat turned to Dorrik. "Sikka mentioned that she would get you, Kaleek, and I outfitted with gear so long as we provided the materials. She said that they'd have some people down to take our measurements shortly."

"Good luck gathering the materials." Basash shook their head. "I'm a level ahead of the sand wastes and I'm not all that enthused by the prospect of trying to solo some of the more valuable creatures out there. Even without the stallesp threat, it's a lot easier to let dedicated hunting parties handle missions like that."

"That's us, I suppose." Dorrik nodded. "A dedicated hunting party. I will have to thank Sikka. Upgrading our armor and weapons would be a great boon. Some of the enchantments available to the more skilled crafters in the enclave are truly amazing. It will depend upon what materials we can bring back, but this could easily serve as a force multiplier for the three of us."

"The only problem," Kat smiled mischievously, "is that Sikka said that the enclave will be on lockdown for the next couple of days. That means we're stuck training and cooling our heels, while Kaleek gets himself into trouble."

"It is unfortunate," Dorrik agreed. "But training is always helpful. It might not help the skills granted to us by the dreamscape, but those abilities are only useful when combined with actual combat experience. A couple weeks of sparring would serve all of us well."

Kat clapped a hand on their shoulder. "Or... once we get the lists, we start making plans. I want to be ready to start hitting the lairs of the monsters we need as soon as the scouts give us the all clear."

"That..." Dorrik paused thoughtfully. "That is certainly something we could do. Still, it would be a waste for us to not take advantage of our access to a proper gymnasium. Your bladework is already quite good Kat, but with a couple nights of intense training, I'm sure we could polish it into something truly spectacular."

Dorrik beamed at her, drawing a pained smile from Kat. They were a relentless and talented drillmaster. She was sure that the lokkel would push her to her limits, and she was equally sure that they would help her train her Cure Wounds I skill almost as much as her knife play.

"Oh, I apologize." Dorrik turned to Basash. "We were just sparring. Obviously I can continue training with you, Basash, I don't want you to—"

"No worries." The other lokkel chuckled as they exited the room to a groan from Kat. "I just wanted a single match to see how my abilities stacked up. Apparently, I still have some distance to go, but to be fair, I probably should have already known that. Good luck, Katherine." Basash disappeared out the door with a wink tossed over their shoulder.

"Fine, Dorrik." Kat sighed and drew her long knife from its sheath before settling into a fighting stance, knees bent slightly with the weight on the balls of her feet. "We can train, but you have to promise that as soon as the lockdown drops, we'll be out there gathering material for our gear the next day."

"Of course, Kat." They smiled, all sharp teeth as their crest fluttered. "I, too, am excited to upgrade my swords. I have no reason to delay the process."

"Now," the huge lizard swooped forward, their right blade forcing her to bend to the side while her knife barely deflected the left, almost knocking Kat to the ground. "Your stance is all about explosive bursts of energy, lunging and stabbing a distracted or unsuspecting foe."

Kat rolled with the force of Dorrik's attack, tucking her shoulder and planting it into the ground as she tried to position herself in the lokkel's blind spot.

A taloned foot, careful not to slash her with its wicked claws, slammed into her ribs, throwing Kat into the air and knocking the wind out of her.

She stood up with a wince to see Dorrik standing in the same spot, a grin still on their face as they held both of their blades in a loose guard, not even breathing heavily.

"As you can see, Miss Kat," they flicked a blade toward themselves, motioning for her to attack again, "your abilities are fine-tuned, but only against a foe that you outclass or have caught by surprise. For now, your magic is enough to create the openings you need to thrive, but that won't always be the case."

Kat frowned, rushing toward Dorrik, ducking under one sword slash and bringing her knife up in a double-handed thrust toward their scaled stomach only to abort the attack and throw herself to the right.

A fraction of a second later, Dorrik's elbow passed through the air where her head would have been if she hadn't moved.

"Good, Miss Kat." Dorrik let her scramble to safety. "Now we need to work on a more sustainable fighting style for you. Something that takes advantage of your agility to let you fight toe to toe with an enemy with a more traditional weapon."

"Lower your stance slightly." The lokkel motioned downward with their sword. "It will give me less of a target, and a lower center of gravity will help both your ability to dodge and those throws you are so fond of."

She followed Dorrik's directions, stalking forward with her knees bent, knife in a low guard. As soon as she got within range of her opponent, first one sword and then another whipped through the air toward her, one horizontal across her chest while Dorrik's upper pair of arms brought the other down in an overhand blow aimed at her collarbone.

Kat hopped backward, letting both slashes whistle past her before stepping into the gap in Dorrik's defenses created by the attacks.

Pain exploded in the back of her head, and the entire room wobbled as the pummel of one of Dorrik's swords slammed into her. She dropped to her hands and knees as the world spun.

"Better," Dorrik continued, stepping back to give her some space. "But still too aggressive. The goal is for you to develop a style that can keep you in a fight long enough to take advantage of your opponent's mistakes. The first step to achieving that end is to ensure that you can recognize a genuine error as opposed to a feint."

"I don't know if anyone but you can recover from a slash that fast, Dorrik." Kat's eyes were locked on the floor as she tried to steady her vision. "That would have been a perfect counter on my part except for the fact that you apparently have superhuman reflexes."

"Correct," Dorrik agreed cheerfully. "Unfortunately, in *The Tower of Somnus* superhuman abilities are more the norm than an exception. You can no longer judge your opponent based upon your common understanding of how fast a body can move or how agile a person's joints should be."

She stood up, walking backward to open up some more distance between the two of them before turning around and glaring at the lokkel.

"To fight a player, you must first be able to judge your opponent's abilities," they continued. "At our level, someone who has achieved level thirty or forty will move faster than either of us can see. Your current style counts on your reflexes being as fast or faster than your opponent. It may work at lower levels, but the three of us won't be stopping here. Against more powerful players, your instincts will only hinder you, make you an easy target for feints and traps."

Kat grunted, rubbing the bruising on her rib with her free hand while she kept her eyes on Dorrik. They seemed to be having altogether too much fun with the moment.

"The next week or so is going to be absolutely miserable, isn't it?" she asked rhetorically.

"But of course, Miss Kat." Dorrik grinned back at her. "It is only through repetition and suffering that we can truly learn from our mistakes. I respect you far too much to skimp out on either."

CHAPTER FOURTEEN

"Still doing homework, I see," Emma's lunch tray clattered onto the marble tabletop next to Kat. "I don't see why. You're so far ahead of the rest of the class in biology that it's pretty much cheating."

Kat blinked, dismissing the notes projected onto her smart-panel, replacing the fizz of pixels with Emma's bright smile. The other woman cheerfully tore into the salad and grilled chicken that she'd ordered from one of the upscale restaurants that served the college 'cafeteria.'

"They focused on biology in my arcology." Kat smiled back, trying to stifle a yawn. The past ten days were a blur of pushing her limits as a student to uncover more information about the Dean and training with Dorrik in *The Tower of Somnus*. Even if she was sleeping, the big lizard pushed her so hard that Kat kept waking up feeling like she'd run a marathon.

"Rhetoric and human resources?" She shrugged helplessly at the other girl. "I guess they just never expected that I'd need to know them."

Kat took a bite out of her sandwich, noting Jasper and his servant's approach out of the corner of her eye. The turkey, avocado, and bacon sandwich was far from the most expensive thing on the college deli's menu, but it served as yet another casual reminder of how far she'd come.

It was all real. The turkey and bacon came from actual animals that lived and died on a farm within a twenty minute maglev of Chiwaukee, and the avocado grew on an honest-to-God tree before it was refrigerated and shipped to the deli. Before meeting Xander, Kat was lucky to have one meal a month that didn't originate entirely in a lab.

Marketing teams did their best to make SynthMeat, Kale Flakes, SoyMeal, and Seaweed Mesh sound appealing, but even the poorest of employees never truly fell for it. No matter how much corn syrup, oil, and salt they drenched the vat-grown food with, it never tasted quite right. Still, it was cheap and didn't involve having to trade with other megacorporations, and that was what really mattered for the powers that be.

Of course, that didn't stop those same powers that be from dining like royalty, Kat mused as she swallowed her mouthful of turkey and bread. Lab food might be an affordable substitute for others, but almost every executive she'd met would never deign to touch the stuff.

"Ugh, that sounds awful." Emma frowned at her. "I don't have it as rough as you on that front; my parents made sure to hire tutors on rhetoric and personnel management."

She paused, tapping a well-manicured, wine-red nail against her cheek. "Now that I think of it," Emma continued, "almost everyone I knew in the management and executive classes hired those tutors. I guess that was just a 'thing' everyone did outside of public schooling to make sure that we would all have an edge on the testing."

"That checks out." Kat laughed, trying to defuse the tension behind the sudden unhappy look on Emma's face.

"But it isn't fair," the other woman replied, frowning at her. "School is supposed to give everyone a fair shot at career advancement. I mean, those with more money can afford extra study aids, there's no way to get around that. Wealth is always going to have some advantages, but if essential classes aren't being taught, that means the core of our entire system isn't meritocratic."

"It would mean that," Kat agreed before hastily trying to change the subject. "How are the rest of your classes going?"

"Fine, I guess." The other woman shrugged, still frowning slightly down into her bowl of salad. "For some reason, the aptitude testing decided that I would be good at accounting, so now I'm taking like three different classes on bookkeeping and auditing. The test wasn't wrong. I am good at it, it's just boring as hell."

"*Auditing: Preventative Measures* with Professor Barnes?" Emma jumped at the question as Jasper sat down next to the three of them. His servant, Davis, stood a couple of paces back, alert as always. "I haven't seen you in that class, Miss Tiller," Jasper continued.

"Emma, please," she stuttered, drawing an eye roll from Kat. "and no, *Investigative Auditing: Basic Principles* with Professor Lanzer."

"Professor Lanzer's a brilliant woman." Jasper nodded sagely. "We use her best practices guide in our concealment and obfuscation labs. Let me tell you, she doesn't make it easy to redirect contract payments into personal accounts."

"Wait," Kat interjected, trying her hardest to suppress a chuckle as she set her sandwich down and turned to Jasper. "Emma's taking a class on accounting and you're literally taking a course on embezzlement."

"It's not embezzlement." Jasper's brow furrowed. "The class is on creative reapplication of wealth. Everyone at the division chair level and above does it. The rule is just to make sure that you aren't so greedy or obvious as to get caught."

"Yeah," Emma agreed. "You get fined and put on an improvement plan if you get caught, but only dumb people get caught. The entire auditing guidebook is available on the information channels, and if an auditor doesn't follow procedure, they will be the one fined instead. It's meaningless to know that someone is appropriating money if you can't prove it through proper channels."

"I wouldn't say meaningless," Jasper responded through a mouthful of food. "You can submit a Financially Incentivized Discontinuation of Prosecution Request Form if you find irregularities outside of procedural guidelines. The target won't get punished and the auditor gets a little bit of extra money. Everyone wins."

"We haven't gotten to FIDP yet," Emma replied excitedly, her earlier bashfulness around the executive forgotten as she gushed about her classes. "I'm really excited to learn about the process. Our class syllabus says that over sixty percent of managers that have been promoted to executive positions did so via FIDP payments."

"Financially Incentivized..." Kat cocked her head at the two of them. "Are you two just talking about straight up bribery?"

"No, no, no." Emma shook her head, stretching out to put a hand on Kat's wrist, her salad all but forgotten. "Bribery is unregulated and illegal. FIDP has a formalized process, as well as a schedule for payments that's published quarterly. It's all very legitimate and above-board."

"If you say so." Kat took a bite out of her sandwich to avoid saying anything she'd regret. Emma wasn't a bad person. In fact, the girl was very sweet. It was just that she strolled through life without an ounce of self-awareness. At some point, she would encounter a true challenge and wake up to the reality of their world. Despite everything, Kat couldn't help but hope that Emma's introduction to the brutal unpleasantness of corporate strife didn't harm the girl too much.

It was inevitable that someone would take advantage of the naive woman at some point. She was too easy of a mark for anything else to happen. When it happened, Kat wanted it to only be a wakeup call. Not a life ruining iteration as the fall person for someone richer and more powerful.

She didn't have much sympathy for Arnold despite growing

up with the boy; he lacked empathy on an almost sociopathic level. Still—she looked briefly at Jasper—the way he died didn't exactly sit right with her. Arnold had done plenty of things wrong, and he deserved to be punished for all of them, but he had little, if anything, to do with Christopher Haupt's death.

Jasper perked up, reading some sort of import into her look. He nodded at her, agreeing with whatever he'd erroneously interpreted her furtive glance to mean.

He smiled at the other girl. "Emma, I think we're boring Kat. Do you mind if I steal her for a second? We'll be back in just a minute."

"Of course." Emma blushed, winking at Kat. "Take all the time you need."

Kat frowned, opening her mouth to correct the other woman's misconception when Jasper made things worse by putting his hand lightly on her elbow and guiding her away from the table. She tensed, hand flexing as Kat fought the instinctive urge to go for her knife.

Not here. She wasn't in the Shell.

The faces of the two mechanics from St. Louis flashed in front of her eyes. That was what happened when she defaulted to violence. Maybe they weren't innocent, but she could have taken them down quietly and without lethal force.

She unclenched her jaw, releasing her clenched fist and relaxing her taut muscles. Out of the corner of her eye, she caught Davis stiffened into a state of vigilant readiness, his vision locked on her. Whoever the man really was, he'd been perceptive enough to note her reaction.

"Come on, Kat." Jasper smiled congenially, unaware of the moment's subtext. "Let's go grab a booth so we can talk."

Kat tried to ignore Emma as the woman called a couple of her friends over, loudly whispering to the two newcomers and pointing at her and Jasper as they walked away.

She tried and failed to gently pull her arm from Jasper, not wanting to cause offense.

"Look, Kat." Jasper leaned over to whisper to her as they

walked, his shoulder brushing hers and drawing a round of giggles from behind them. "I know that you're worried about trusting me. Davis says you probably have your reasons, but I want to show you that I'm on your side."

"This isn't about sides," Kat whispered back, watching as Jasper ran his corporate ID over a lock on a privacy booth, depositing fifteen credits and opening the soundproof room for the two of them. "This is about survival for me. You tell me what happens if I make an accusation against a powerful person without proof. You know GroCorp law better than me on that point."

"You don't have to make it public," he responded, sealing the door after her with Davis waiting just outside. "But that's hardly the point. Davis has had some people keeping an eye on you, and they've reported that you've been wandering around the faculty levels of the college. It almost looks like you're searching for something."

"Keeping an eye on me?" Kat squinted at him. "Are you trying to blackmail me or something?"

Nothing he'd said had been menacing or threatening. Rather, as best she could tell, Jasper was eager to please. After the debacle with Arthur, she was hardly in any position to market herself as an expert on interpersonal dynamics, but Jasper honestly sounded like he just wanted to be her friend.

"God, no." He flinched backward as if stung. "Why do you always assume I'm some sort of monster? I just wanted to send you a copy of the college's schematics and see if there was anything I could do to help."

Her smartpanel pinged, indicating an incoming e-mail.

"Look." Kat ran a hand through her hair, oddly affected by the hurt look on Jasper's face. "I'm on my own in a world that has it in for me. I think your servant, Davis—"

"Majordomo," Jasper corrected. "He's like an executive assistant crossed with a bodyguard. Technically I employ him, but he's much more than just a servant to me."

"And that respect for him does you credit," Kat nodded her

acceptance, "but you're asking me to trust you, and on the street, trust isn't something you give lightly. Even friends you've known for years will betray you for enough money."

"Right now I'm not asking you to do anything." He shook his head earnestly. "I will admit that I'm trying to prove myself worthy of your trust, but everything I'm giving you is free and clear of any connections."

"Not everyone in the higher levels of GroCorp is evil, Kat," Jasper continued, an urgent, almost puppy dog look in his eyes. "There are groups of us that are trying to undo the harm inflicted by our parents from within. In a couple of years, it will be our cohort that will be executives and shareholders. Then we can actually begin to change things."

"I appreciate the sentiment." Kat took a deep breath, closing her eyes for a second as she tried to center herself. "But you're asking me to go above and beyond the code, Jaspar. I can do jobs for money, and I can turn over my information and observations, but the minute I start speculating or working for a friend, that's when I become a player, and players without backing tend to die quick and brutal deaths."

"Look." She smiled weakly at him, brushing a stray hair from her face. "I know you're just trying to be friendly, but the information you're looking for could easily get both of us killed. If you act on it, not only would it be my head, it would be my entire crew's."

"I'm not going to lie and say I don't want to know who was behind my father's death." Jasper grimaced. "But I understand and accept your reluctance. Davis has explained some of the samurai code to me, and I don't think I completely understand it, but I can at least comprehend its importance."

"Thank you," Kat replied gratefully.

"Although I would appreciate it if you'd be willing to meet with some like-minded friends of mine." Jasper beamed at her. "It's nothing too serious, we just have biweekly meetings to talk over current events, politics, and economic theory. Everyone is super excited to meet an honest-to-God employee."

"Of course." She could feel her face falling at the prospect of being presented like an exotic pet.

Five minutes later, they rejoined Emma and her friends. Twenty minutes of pleasant but meaningless conversation about classes and the entertainment and gossip channels later, Kat was finally able to extricate herself from the constant chatter.

That night, before bed, she went over the floor plans with Xander and Whippoorwill. Her casual exploration and review of visible security systems over the past week had helped paint a picture of what they were up against, but the documents from Jasper filled in all the gaps.

Unlike her forced casual sojourns, the blueprints covered the entirety of the college's upper floors. More importantly, they contained a complete map of the HVAC tubing and maintenance access stairwells.

Ostensibly, Jasper's documents even had a diagram detailing the electrical and security systems, but Kat knew better than to put too much weight on the reported locations. Given the prevalence of promotions via assassination and blackmail, no executive would report any 'custom work' done to ensure their personal security.

Still, it was enough for Xander to green light the infiltration for the following night. Kat would need to be careful. Murders in the college would trigger an investigation that would almost certainly reveal her 'strolls.' No, this would need to be something that she'd always struggled with: a quiet job.

She packed her infiltration gear into a duffle bag and returned to the dorms. It registered as nothing more than clothing and electronics to the cursory scan at the door, and an hour later she was in bed, her equipment stashed under her bed while Kat tried to calm down enough to sleep and enter the tower.

Closing her eyes, Kat began to go over the infiltration in her head, trying to think of new ways to make it through the hallways of the penthouse where the dean lived without triggering the overlapping cameras. Finally, her thoughts began to grow fuzzy and sleep washed over her, quieting her anxiety.

"Finally, Miss Kat!" One of Dorrik's clawed hands slapped her on the shoulder before she was fully oriented.

She blinked in confusion at her teammate as the buzz and bustle of the Adventurer's Hall assaulted her senses, demanding her attention.

"The scouts have confirmed that there were abnormal numbers of high level stallesp in the area, but they've moved on," Kaleek supplied helpfully, his whiskers twitching in amusement as he leaned against a nearby stone pillar. "Dorrik is excited."

"Of course I am," Dorrik replied with a toothy smile. "We can finally acquire new equipment. I, for one, am looking forward to armor that can actually take a blow from a boss-level monster."

"I'm not going to turn down that concussive force enchantment that Sikka was hyping up," Kaleek agreed. "It might not do a whole lot of extra damage, but the stunning or staggering of enemies at a key moment would add a lot to my arsenal."

"More importantly," Kat interjected, grinning back, "we actually get to go and fight monsters. No offense, Dorrik, but I was starting to go crazy. I don't know how you train at that intensity day in and day out, but I'd be gibbering to myself if I tried to follow your schedule indefinitely."

"Me too," Kaleek barked out a quick laugh, "but that's why Dorrik is a generational talent and the rest of us are just 'really good.' I used to try to compete with them until I realized that there was no way that I could match that day in and day out intensity. Now I just settle for being their dashing and debonair sidekick."

Dorrik ignored the otter, patting Kat on the shoulder.

"Don't get too comfortable, Miss Kat," they continued, "I will still be watching your form and we will need to redouble your training if I catch you backsliding, but until then, the enclave has cleared us to hunt sand sharks."

Kat cocked her head, raising a single eyebrow as she looked at Kaleek, waiting for the desoph to explain the situation in more manageable terms.

"Armored burrowing carnivores." The otter winked at her. "Their scales are a key component in a lot of lower tier magical armor and their fangs can be used for smaller enchanted blades. A good first start if we're actually going to improve the party's gear."

"Fill your waterskins." Dorrik began walking toward the exit of the hall. "We have a bit of a hike ahead of us, and we'll need to hurry. Sand sharks are one of the top targets for resource gathering teams. If we don't get moving, other teams might hunt all of them and force us to wait for tomorrow's respawn."

Kat followed, making sure to fill her waterskin and wet down her sun hat at one of the communal wells before they left the city. The damp fabric would only help her keep cool for an hour or so before the moisture evaporated, but that was still one more pleasant hour than she'd otherwise experience in the 'sun' and dry heat of the third floor.

An hour and a half later, her fears were confirmed. The hat and veil kept the worst of the sun off of her, but the dry air was sawing at her throat as they trekked across the unending dunes, Dorrik occasionally pausing to compare their location to a map they carried with them.

Kat had no idea what they were looking at. As far as she could tell, the entire level might as well be nothing more than small rolling hills composed of fine, tan sand.

"Dorrik," Kaleek rasped miserably, staring at the empty waterskin in his paws. "We'd better find a sand shark over the next dune or I'm turning around and coming back tomorrow. I will be the laughingstock of my pod if I have to start over from level one due to dehydration and heat stroke."

"Just a short while longer," Dorrik agreed amiably, preening comfortably in the hot air. "If we don't see anything in the next ten to twenty minutes, you might be right about coming back tomorrow. We will just need to make sure that we leave early enough that the sand sharks aren't over-hunted by the time we arrive at their breeding grounds."

"I probably won't be on time tomorrow," Kat responded ruefully. "I have to do some late night skulking. I might not even make it to the Tower at all depending upon how things go."

"Are you sure we're in the right spot?" Kaleek complained, more or less ignoring her. "Dorrik, you keep talking about how we have to beat other hunters to the punch, but I'm going to be honest: I haven't seen a single other team in our entire time out here."

Kat brushed some of the netting aside to scratch at the clammy back of her neck. "Now that you mention it, we haven't seen a single player or monster since we left the city."

For a couple of seconds, no one responded. Kat shielded her eyes against the glare as she stared out across the dunes, taking in a lot more of the barren nothingness that had plagued their party for the entire expedition.

"Sometimes a hunt is simply unsuccessful," Dorrik began unconvincingly before pausing and craning their neck at a tiny dark blob in the distance. "Wait, there are two people now."

Kat squinted her eyes, trying and failing to make out any details distant individuals.

"If you say so," she replied with a shrug. "I still don't see how that changes things. We came here for sand sharks, and instead we found strangers."

"Let's check to see if they've seen anything," Kaleek grumbled, "or at a minimum if they have any spare water we can trade for."

"I could always just hose you down with Water Jet," Kat supplied helpfully, winking at the bedraggled otter. "Just make sure to point the open spigot of your water skin at me when I finish the spell. We wouldn't want to waste any of it."

Kaleek glared at her, but it was hard to take him seriously given the bleariness in his eyes and the slump of his shoulders. Kat grinned back, the sun veils of her hat hiding her expression. He practically snarled at her, letting Kat know that her intent had been received regardless.

"Maybe if things get desperate," Kaleek conceded grudgingly.

"I don't entirely know if approaching strangers is a good idea right—" Dorrik interjected before pausing with a frown. "Well, they've seen us and they're on their way over right now."

Kaleek glared at the two of them before walking to Dorrik's side and plopping down in the sliver of shade provided by the towering lizard. Wisely, neither of them commented on his behavior as Kat suspected the desoph had another diatribe ready to go if provoked.

"Kaleek." Kat winced as Dorrik put one of their claws on his shoulder. "It's time to go."

Kat glanced over at the lokkel as their gentle shaking of the slumping otter grew in urgency.

"What, Dorrik?" Kaleek snapped back. "Did you seriously have to wait until I was finally comfortable just to bother me?"

Dorrik's entire body was tense, their crest flared in distress.

"The newcomers are stallesp," they hissed, "and one of them has some sort of floating orb. I think it's a spell focus."

Kaleek's face screwed tight in confusion, his whiskers twitching as he looked up at the two of them.

"But that would mean—" he began, only for a jagged crackling bolt of red arcane energy to slam into the dune about fifteen paces from them, flash fusing it into glass.

"What in the *fuck* was that!" Kat yelled, grabbing onto one of Dorrik's lower arms to maintain her balance as the sand heaved and shook under her.

"An iron tier offensive skill," they responded grimly. A moment later, a crossbow bolt wreathed in flames struck nearby, burying itself almost up to the fletching before the magical fire guttered out.

"The good news is that we're out of their effective range." Dorrik pulled Kaleek to his feet as they pushed Kat gently to force her into movement. "The bad news is that *arcane lightning* at that level would rip any of us in half. Whatever their levels, that isn't a brand-new ability. We need to move. Now."

"I thought there weren't supposed to be any stallesp out here!" Kat shouted, sliding and running down the loose sand of the dune.

"I'm sure our friends will be happy to field your complaints," Kaleek replied, skidding down the dune on his armored back as a storm of acid from some unknown spell sprayed the dune where they were just standing.

Dorrik joined the two of them at the bottom of the sand hill, grimacing as they beat at a hissing hole in their armor where a droplet of the acid had caught them in their retreat. For a second or two, they just stood there, breathing heavily as they contemplated their situation.

"Unless they can shoot directly through the sand dune, the stallesp can't see us," Kat shrugged. "What now?"

"They can if they have silver tier abilities," Kaleek spat out a mouthful of sand, "but at that point, we might as well start planning out our next avatar's build."

"So we're running then." Kat pursed her lips. She was already worn out from the sun, heat, and lack of water. A headlong flight across the desert sounded miserable, if not quite impossible. "Any idea as to where?"

"Here," Dorrik interjected, an upper claw stabbing at a point on a map held by their two lower hands. "Stinging Mist Dungeon. We're only about a ten minute hike or a five minute panicked sprint from it."

"I'm not sure we're ready to take on a dungeon." Kat glanced worriedly at Kaleek. "Plus, we don't know if it's a good match for our skill sets. There had to be a reason why the Ahn Enclave didn't recommend that we raid it."

The dune next to them shook as another spell struck it, sending a spray of molten glass into the air above them, the droplets tinkling and cracking as they froze and shattered in the air.

"Five minutes it is," Kaleek exhaled before taking off.

A moment later Kat and Dorrik caught up to him with Dorrik's long quick strides letting the lizard take the lead. The stallesp pursued them, steadily gaining ground as they lobbed spells and elementally charged crossbow bolts at them every time the trio crested a dune and popped into sight.

By the time they reached the dungeon portal, the stallesp were close enough for Kat to roughly make out their features. Worse, as they drew closer, their aim improved. One of Dorrik's arms hung limp at their side and Kaleek's fur was a smoking patchwork of acid burns.

As for herself, Kat's ears were ringing and her vision blurred, signs of a likely concussion. Perhaps more importantly, the same *arcane lightning* near miss that rattled her had sprayed her entire left side with molten glass. Kat's armor had protected her from the worst of it but her hair, face, and hand were riddled with third degree burns.

Every step sent another jolt of pain through her injured body, but Kat forced herself to scramble up the small rock face toward the dungeon entrance. Behind her, the stallesp yelled something incoherent but menacing.

Dorrik touched the gate, activating it for them even as they turned and faced down their pursuit.

"*Arrest Momentum,*" Dorrik's words were almost as comforting as a blast of air conditioned air. A field of purple energy crackled into being around one of the two stallesp, forcing the other to pause and turn to help their companion.

Kaleek jumped through the portal, disappearing in a crackle of rainbow light.

The purple field of psi energy slowing the angry mole person shattered, forcing a grunt from Dorrik as they slumped from the strain of maintaining the ability against a more powerful foe.

"Go, Miss Kat!" the exhausted lokkel shouted at her. "I will close the portal behind you, but you must go now!"

A brief backward glance at the stallesp wizard casting a new spell brought a frown to her face, but dutifully Kat touched the energy field of the portal, disappearing in her own multihued burst of energy.

Seconds later, she staggered out into a wood-paneled room. Kat blinked. A cool fog wreathed everything, preventing her from seeing more than a couple of paces. She sighed in relief, enjoying the feel of the chilled air against the jagged heat of her burns.

A quick survey of the room revealed Kaleek, half collapsed nearby, heaving for breath. He waved at her weakly, features obscured by the thick mist. Before she could approach him, a spray of prismatic light filled the room, reflecting off of the fog and practically blinding her.

Dorrik stumbled forward a step or two, appearing from nothingness only to fall forward and reveal a massive hole in the armor and scales on their back.

Kat wheeled around, immediately beginning the incantation to Cure Wounds I as she propped her friend up onto their side. Moments later, the golden glow of healing light encompassed her good hand.

"That was a bit closer than I'd like." Dorrik chuckled weakly, the flesh and scales of their back slowly knitting together under Kat's magic. "But we should be safe for now."

"Safe." Kat rolled her eyes as she pushed her hands deeper into the lokkel's wound, practically touching one of their shoulder blades. "We're stuck in a dungeon without return stones and I'd be surprised if your hit points are in double digits. I struggle to find anything 'safe' about the current situation."

"The stallesp know that this area is being patrolled by Clan Ahn forces." Dorrik gritted their teeth against the pain. "They won't be able to wait outside the dungeon forever, and they can't follow us in. We just need to leave the dreamscape. Tomorrow, we'll reappear here at the start with full health and no infirmities."

"Then we just have to complete a dungeon we know nothing about and with half of our gear lost or destroyed in our retreat." Kat sighed, slumping back with a wince as she ran out of mana.

"Well," Kaleek replied from the corner, at least partially restored by the humid air of the dungeon, "at least it'll be interesting."

CHAPTER FIFTEEN

Kat worked her knife under the access panel, popping up the plate of plastic that was designed to look like wood paneling. A quick glance behind her revealed that the night guard patrolling the hallway was nowhere nearby.

She crawled inside the cramped space before pulling the faux wood shut behind her. It sealed with a pop, leaving her in the claustrophobic shaft. Her Nightvision perk revealed a tunnel lined with water pipes and electrical wiring.

Kat reached out to touch one of the pipes, pulling back from the heat before she burned her fingers on the blistering metal. The blueprints marked what she was in as a maintenance shaft, designed to provide access to the master breakers, wiring, and water pumps for each floor. At the very minimum, now she'd know where to go if she ran out of hot water during a shower.

Pausing to check the map uploaded to her smartpanel, Kat made note of her location and began crawling to the left. The access tunnels were thick with dust to the point that she might have had problems with the air quality if it wasn't for the rudimentary filter built into her infiltration suit. Apparently, maintenance wasn't the highest concern for the powers that ran the college.

After about five minutes, the narrow tunnel opened up into a cramped room lined with circuit breakers and valves. She ignored them, instead gripping one handhold after another as Kat climbed past bundles of cables and pipes almost as big around as her waist en route to the next floor.

A brief review of her smartpanel later and Kat was on her hands and knees in another access tunnel, wincing at the way her shuffling movements echoed in the silent passageway. Minutes later, she was at another hidden panel, ear pressed against it and listening for the footsteps of one of the patrolling guards.

After a minute of hearing nothing, she popped the slab of plastic from the wall, just enough for her to peer over the edge. In the distance, she saw the bobbing glow of a flashlight as someone walked away, abandoning the hallway entirely.

Hastily, she slipped out of the tunnel, replacing the covert panel. A moment of focus and mana later, she cast Shadow, letting the light flow past her as she faded into the dark hallway.

The spell wasn't perfect. Someone looking closely could still see her, and a direct light would reveal a cloud of murky air, but it was more than enough to hide her from casual observers.

Kat crept forward through the second year's dorms. Following the blueprints, she cautiously worked her way to another hidden access point. A few moments of knife work later, and she was in another set of undersized tunnels, smearing her expensive infiltration suit with even more dust as she crawled through the dark toward her next maintenance ladder.

By the time she reached the fourth floor, Kat could feel her sweat beading the inside of the suit as her breath came in short, even bursts. Really, the exertion wasn't too bad. Climbing and crawling were a bit of a workout, but nothing too serious. It was more the tension of the moment when she opened each panel onto the dorm hallways. Each and every time, it wore at her nerves, not knowing whether or not a particularly quiet guard might be waiting on the other side.

Quietly, she picked her way past dorm rooms, careful not to wake the fourth years. One or two rooms still had light peeking out from under their doors, and Kat had long since refreshed Shadow to minimize the chance that a student opening their door for some reason would catch sight of her.

Her heart rate jolted even as Kat told herself how impossible that would be. Despite being dorms, each room was a small suite complete with a kitchenette and bathroom. Frankly, despite the constant complaints from her classmates, it was nicer than the apartment she'd grown up in. Even if there wasn't a curfew 'for their security,' barring a fire alarm or a risky late night tryst between classmates, there wasn't any reason for a student to leave their dorms after ten.

Kat stopped, the unworried and steady footfalls of another person alerting her just before the guard rounded the corner. Her movements unnaturally silent due to Cat Step, she sprinted to the protruding vestibule for the floor's recycling bins and trash incinerator, pressing her body in the small corner made by the doorway jutting out into the hallway.

A woman wearing a simple GroCorp tactical vest walked into view, flashlight held listlessly in her hand. Kat held her breath as the woman walked by, her eyes locked on the heavy flashlight as it bobbed and swayed in the guard's hands.

It never strayed. Despite Kat's heart hammering in her chest, the security officer walked her beat without interruption.

As soon as she was past, Kat slipped away, using Cat Step to silence her steps as she made her way through the dorm's twisting hallways. Finally, she reached the locked metal door to the next floor.

Unfortunately, it only made sense that the college wouldn't have one interconnected set of maintenance shafts traveling all the way to the top level. Clearly, the tunnels were a security risk. Even in the much lower security of the dorms, they would only travel up one level at a time. Now that she was attempting to breach the more secure labs and classrooms en route to the penthouse, Kat was all out of easy avenues of ingress.

From here on out, there wouldn't be any hidden access tunnels, just locked fire escapes and elevators. Unfortunately, the interior of the elevators were riddled with electronic monitoring equipment, so it would be manual stairs for her.

Of course, it wasn't like the fire escapes didn't have their own security. Cameras and fingerprint scanners were what was indicated on the blueprints, and Kat would bet her bottom credit that college security had added something else in the meantime.

A quick glance over her shoulder assured her that the floor's patrolling guard was still walking her route. With practiced efficiency, Kat pulled a strip of electrofilm and stretched it over the thumbprint scanner that locked the door.

The film glowed a dim blue as the mini-LEDs built into it illuminated the oil residue on the security device so that the electrofilm could analyze and replicate them. The scanner flashed red, indicating an unsuccessful attempt to open the lock as it registered the light from Kat's intrusion device.

Moments later, her smartpanel pinged, updated by the advanced strip of clear material. Kat flicked her eyes to the side, the subtle movement picked up by the smartpanel and translated into a request to open the alert from the electrofilm.

The images of three different thumbprints popped up, one only a partial print but the other two full-sized and photorealistic. Focusing her attention on the far right picture was all it took. Seconds later, the electrofilm glowed again, the tiny LEDs in its densely packed structure reproducing the thumbprint.

The door flashed green, opening with a click. Kat quickly grabbed its handle, pulling it halfway open before she peeled off the electrofilm and stepped into the stairwell, letting the heavy metal fire door close behind her.

Inside the cement and steel landing, she spotted a security camera. Without hesitation, Kat stepped directly under it before any operator could notice her presence. Even if they were watching, likely all they'd see is the door opening and a blur of shadow stepping through.

Kat placed the electrofilm into its padded ceramic case as she used her eyes to page through the mission notes and pull up the building's blueprints once more. Four stories via the fire escape, and then she'd have access to the first of the college's security nodes.

Clinging close to the wall, she began climbing, her vision scanning back and forth as she watched for any surprises. She didn't think that any of the guards would venture into the stair-well—they had access to the elevators, after all—but it was better to be alert and prepared than to let something unfortunate happen due to a lapse in vigilance.

Kat counted the landings as she passed them, anything to break the monotony of unadorned concrete walls and steps. Even then, each new floor wasn't anything special. Just a metal door, unlocked from the inside, and a solitary security camera trained on it.

In all likelihood, the metal fire doors would unlock if an alarm sounded, letting anyone on the upper floors escape the building without the risk of the elevators seizing up on them. Still, it didn't look like the stairs were patrolled often. They weren't exactly dusty, but from the dull and chipped paint on the doors and the occasional scuffs on the walls, the entire stair-well gave off almost the same ambience as the abandoned buildings of the Shell.

A line of red light flashed into Kat's vision. Her foot stopped in the air, hovering for a second before she stepped back. Just about chest height, a ruby string of light trailed across the shroud cast by Shadow, bending and twisting crazily as it entered the area altered by her light magic.

She squinted, inspecting the cold, unpainted concrete to her left. Sure enough, the tiny lens of a laser was hidden in a crack. Next to it, a slight discoloration in the cement gave away where something had been buried in the wall.

Carefully, Kat took another step back, inspecting the rest of the wall. There weren't any other tell tales, but Kat shuddered anyway. She wasn't sure whether the new cement hid a shotgun or a bomb, but either way, that explained the lack of guard activity. GroCorp didn't offer much security to its employees, but even for them, directing someone to walk into an active and lethal booby trap was frowned upon.

She ducked low under the laser before continuing, much more slowly. Where there was one trap, there easily could be more.

A minute later, she was hopping over a stair whose concrete surface had recently been replaced and onto the fourth landing. It was possible that the resurfacing was completely innocent, a simple replacement for the crumbling, under-maintained step, but Kat wasn't willing to take the risk. Knowing her luck, the entire step would explode or trigger an alarm that would bring every guard in the building down on top of her head.

She refreshed Shadow, noting grimly the steady drain on her mana caused by keeping the spell active in the real world. Kat would need to stop soon to allow her mana to recharge, or risk running out at an inopportune moment.

Leaning forward, she placed her ear against the metal door, straining to hear footsteps or conversation on the other side, anything to alert her that a patrol was nearby.

Nothing.

Kat grimaced. The absence of noise didn't mean she was alone. It could just mean that the security officer was being quiet. She could either sit here listening for a guard that might very well not be there, the dark smudge of her magic square in the center of the security camera, or she could push the door open and hope for the best. Either way, she was taking a risk.

Biting her lower lip, Kat opened the door and slipped through, almost choking when she spotted a guard about twenty paces away. Her hand darted silently toward her knife only to stop at the last second.

The man's back was to her, his foot tapping impatiently as

he stared off into nothingness. A couple furtive steps later, and she had a better view of him. In the darkness, the bright flashes of light from his smartpanel display lit up the guard's face in oranges and reds.

Kat felt her shoulders relax, and a half smile creep onto her face. She always told Michelle that the entertainment channels would rot her brain, and here was the perfect example. It was awfully hard to successfully watch for intruders if your attention was held by the mindless amusement pumped out by the mega-corps to keep employees docile.

Sure, the ninth floor of the GroCorp college was hardly the number one target for thieves or assassins, but on the other hand, here Kat was. She padded noiselessly past the insensible man. Whatever show he was watching or game he was playing drew enough of his attention to let her pass entirely unnoticed.

Finally, after passing any number of low security labs and research facilities, Kat reached the node. Little more than a glorified break room for the guards except for a weapons locker and a bank of closed circuit projection screens displaying the contents of the various cameras placed about the building.

Kat reached into her pouch, pulling out a trio of metal disks. One by one, she depressed a tab in the center of them before slipping them under the door.

Then she began counting to one hundred and twenty. The security node would almost certainly be lit and manned. There was no way she would be able to raid it without being noticed. Xander's solution had been ZZ3 gas.

Originally, ZZ3 had been manufactured for crowd control purposes during the South American Resource Wars. Colorless and odorless, it would knock someone out for about five minutes. Long enough for riot officers to disarm and zip tie anyone involved.

The ChromeDogs had liberated a fairly sizable supply when they took over the Steel and Blood headquarters. Apparently the Urban Area Denial vehicles they'd seized from the rival mercenary group had been fitted to launch fist-sized grenades of the substance out of belt-fed launchers.

Unfortunately, ZZ3 wasn't the answer to every question. As effective as it was, a simple filter like the one built into Kat's suit or most exoarmors was more than sufficient to neutralize it entirely. Still, for a bored guard flipping between security and entertainment feeds in an enclosed space?

A thump from behind the door answered Kat's rhetorical question. She opened the door and entered the node. The duty guard had fallen out of his chair, a half-finished microwaved meal and lit cigarette on the table before him, lit by the flickering light of dozens of security cameras.

Kat hurried over, fishing a hypodermic needle from her satchel and injecting it into the skinny man's neck. He twitched slightly in his sleep before his breathing slowed further.

The ZZ3 might be enough to put him down for a couple of minutes, but the sedatives used by GroCorp scientists to keep bioengineered cattle calm would be more than enough to knock him out for at least an hour.

She pushed his dinner to the side, finding the data jack that someone would use if they had a cranial interface. Kat pulled a shunt out of her satchel and seated it on the jack.

Finally, Kat exhaled slowly, letting most of the tension drain from her. The hard part was over. After pulling the unconscious guard back up into a sitting position in his chair and cleaning up the ZZ3 dispenser, Kat found an overstuffed faux-leather couch and sat down.

"I'm in." Whippoorwill's voice startled Kat as it broke the complete silence almost three minutes later...

"That was fast." Kat chuckled, shaking her head as she tried to calm her racing heart.

"They weren't expecting anyone," Whippoorwill replied disdainfully. "Seriously, I've run into better security on vending machines."

"Tell me what we're looking at, then." Kat stood up from

the couch and began sorting through the items in her satchel as she prepared to head out once more.

"As bad as the security is," Whippoorwill grumbled, "they weren't quite dumb enough to put the dean's personal files on the same network."

"One of these days we'll find someone stupid enough to make it easy for us, Whip," Kat chuckled.

"Where would the fun be in that?" Whippoorwill sniffed. "You'd just sneak in, and then ten minutes later you'd have the information you needed and you'd leave. No suspense, no fights. It'd just be boring."

"I'm fine with boring." Kat shook her head, smiling under the mesh facemask of the infiltration suit. "You're not the one getting shot at when things get exciting."

"It still sounds asinine to me," the pink haired hacker groused.

"Your objection to my safety is noted," Kat replied, rolling her eyes. "Now tell me what the situation is with regard to security."

"I have complete control of their system." Whippoorwill's whining disappeared as she switched to a matter of fact situation report. "While we were talking, I removed the footage of you sneaking your way up to the ninth floor. The good news is that from here on out, I should be able to let you know the location of the guards and traps on your way up. Better, I have enough control that you should be able to use the elevators freely."

"That is good news," Kat responded cautiously. "Now what's the bad news?"

"Dean Franklin is still awake," Whippoorwill answered uncomfortably. "He's in his living quarters rather than his office, so you should still be able to sneak in and set up the shunt, but—"

"I remember the blueprints." Kat sighed, clenching her jaw in frustration. "His office and living quarters are connected.

There will be an intervening wall between us, but that wall has a door in it."

"Yeah," the hacker muttered. "Still, the back door we have into their security network should last for a good twenty minutes. Once you get what we came for, you'll just be able to take the elevator back down to your dorm room and get a good night's sleep with no one the wiser."

"Thanks," Kat replied wryly, "but I'm still not over 'breaking into a secure network without getting noticed by someone in the other room.' That put a bit of a damper on my mood."

"The coast is clear, for what it's worth," Whippoorwill replied, almost apologetically.

Kat left the node, following her guide's directions to the elevator before hitting the button that signified the fortieth floor. The lift pulled down on her, whirring as it traveled upward before slowing to a stop. The metal doors opened on a darkened hallway dominated by the empty reception desk of the Dean's secretary.

"Straight and to the left," Whippoorwill's voice pulled Kat back into the present, "it will be the third door."

She followed the instructions, the entire floor quiet other than a single male voice. Kat couldn't quite make it out—there were multiple walls and doors between her and the speaker—but she did note that it became louder and clearer once she opened the door to the dean's office.

Once inside, it wasn't hard to find the spot for her shunt. It clearly wasn't the waiting area, and there was nothing but massive wooden bookcases filled with antique paper tomes in the study.

The dean's workspace, on the other hand, had a full wall smartglass projector and a massive walnut desk with a jack built into it. After all of the work and risks it took to get to the penthouse, it seemed anticlimactic to just drop the shunt on the jack and let Whippoorwill do her thing, but that seemed to be how things were shaking out.

With an internal shrug, Kat snuck over to the side door that connected the office to Dean Franklin's living quarters. She'd have at least a couple of minutes before Whippoorwill finished downloading the files that Belle would need, and it only made sense to stay as on top of potential threats as possible.

The voice she'd heard from the hallway became clearer, and by the time she pressed her ear against the door, she was actually able to make out one side of the conversation.

"I wasn't the one to okay the raid," the man said angrily, his voice a raspy tenor. "I know it was a fucking disaster, I could have told you that. Schaumburg is one of our most independent subsidiaries, of course they'd kick up a stink. It didn't help that you used a bunch of trigger happy mercenaries."

The hair on the back of Kat's neck stood up straight.

"Of course you didn't find any evidence," he continued, chastising the unknown party. "They aren't fucking idiots over there. Even if you turned the entire arcology on its head and shook, we would just end up having to pay out a ton of money in arbitration. They have access to their own shareholders."

She unclenched her fists, focusing on slowing her breathing. The silence stretched on. Whoever was on the other end of the conversation just kept talking.

"No," the man said again, finality in his voice. "I don't care what your 'friends in orbit' have to say. So long as they can't land and replace the shareholders, we're going to tread carefully. Intelligence and support in the tower are great, but they aren't going to stop us from getting dragged before a tribunal if anyone catches wind of what's happen—"

"The files are downloaded," Whippoorwill's voice drowned out the speaker, "I'm ready to get you out of there whenever you want, but uh, try to make that 'whenever' in the next couple of minutes. The system looks like it's going to reset itself soon and that will be the end of my backdoor access."

Reluctantly, Kat pulled her ear away from the door, concern sending ice water down her spine as she went back to pick up the shunt. In the distance, she could still hear the man, now shouting incoherently at his conversation partner.

As the door to the elevator closed behind her, Kat pressed the button for the second floor. She still needed to visit *The Tower of Somnus* tonight, but it was probably about time she called her mother. Just in case.

CHAPTER SIXTEEN

Kat opened her eyes to the dungeon's clinging mist. Nothing about their surroundings had changed since last night. The initial spawning room, safe until they passed its threshold, was still featureless and packed with dense fog that limited her visibility, even when she tried to switch to Nightvision to account for the lack of light. Whatever the substance was made of, *The Tower of Somnus* wasn't going to let her sidestep the hazard it posed that easily.

Dorrik and Kaleek were sitting back to back, eyes closed. Then Dorrik spoke.

"B10 to D12, my Lancer has taken your fortress, and your Hive Queen is now under threat."

Kaleek grunted, shifting slightly as a grimace rippled across his fur. Kat coughed, clearing her throat to draw the attention of her teammates.

"Kat's here!" The otter sprang to his feet, sour expression clearing from his face. "Time for us to clear the dungeon."

Dorrik stood up in a more dignified manner, rocking forward and then almost unfolding until they towered over the rest of the party, crest fluttering in amusement as they contemplated the excitable desoph.

"What was that anyway?" Kat asked, eyes on Dorrik but inclining her head toward Kaleek as their companion scrambled over to where his sword had been leaning against the dungeon's wall.

"Raknok chess," her companion replied smugly. "A fine way to pass time and keep your mind sharp simultaneously. Kaleek was about to lose his third match when your presence saved him."

"Who even cares about that nerd stuff?" Kaleek retorted, walking back over to the two of them with his massive sword balanced on his shoulder. "We have a dungeon to raid."

"Kaleek," Dorrik shook their head, crest fluttering once more, "you are literally a physicist. I've read your thesis on using gravity magic to compress cargo on freighters and it was an inspired work. Preliminary studies have shown that your work has spurred a flurry of innovation that could decrease bulk transportation costs between one and two percent."

The otter looked away, his fur fluffing out in the desoph equivalent of a blush. "Well, that's in the real world. Here in the dreamscape, I like to hit things hard with a sword. The bigger the sword, the better. It's cathartic after wracking my brain going over extrapolated math all day."

"I can relate." Kat cracked a smile at the distressed desoph. "My day job for a while there was a lab assistant training to be scientist. Nothing glamorous, mostly just monitoring cell cultures to see how they reacted to modifications to their code so that shareholders could eke out an extra percent or two of profit from crops that we made disease or cold resistant."

"After a day of that," she shrugged, "I wanted to get into the tower to stab things too. Your reaction seems pretty natural to me."

"I have moved to a jungle moon populated almost entirely by huge predators in order to properly test myself," Dorrik replied, drawing bemused glances from both Kaleek and Kat.

"For me, the dreamscape is an opportunity to spend time with my family and catch up on the latest political events. It is a welcome respite from the constant life or death struggles that characterize my everyday life."

"Oookay." Kaleek chuckled, shaking his head. "Maybe that's why you beat me every time we spar. I spend my days developing civilian applications for the gravity drive while you throw yourself into daily fights to the death."

"Speaking of which." Kat turned to Kaleek, a twinkle of curiosity in her eyes. "Tell me more about gravity drives? Are they related to the 'extrapolated math' you were talking about earlier? That sounds fascinating to me."

"Sorry, Miss Kat." Dorrik patted her gently on the shoulder. "Kaleek and I may be able to convince people to trade with you in the tower, but we can't get around the embargo on your planet. Any visits or technological transfers would result in extreme punishments, and unfortunately, talking about the gravity drive could very easily be interpreted as an attempt by us to transfer a technology to humanity that your race isn't ready for."

"Actually…" Kat paused, recalling her raid on the Dean's office. "Would it break the embargo for a member of the Consensus to park a ship in orbit or to help certain factions in a probationary race?"

Dorrik froze, turning to her, their face displaying equal parts uncertainty and concern.

"Not explicitly," their clawed fingers drummed against the top of another scaled arm, "but that sounds like someone is skirting the rules. Technically, laws of embargo ban direct contact with a restricted race, but in practice that means that the Consensus simply avoids that race's planet. As for the helping a faction? There are vague rules, yet to be tested in court, that prohibit interfering with the natural development of a race that hasn't fully joined the Consensus."

Kat nodded slowly. "In short, something is probably up, but

I'll need more information before we can act on it. The story of my life."

"What is happening, Miss Kat?" Dorrik asked, concern in their voice. "Is there something Kaleek and I can do to help?"

"I overheard someone powerful talking about political matters on Earth," Kat replied. "He mentioned 'their friends in orbit' providing aid in the tower. Given that we're trapped in a dungeon due to stallesp marauders, I think we can infer what he was talking about even if we don't know the full details."

She didn't mention the raid on the Schaumburg arcology. Xander had only heard fragmented accounts—that Millennium samurai had gone through the upper levels of the building with the delicacy of a bowling ball smashing into a plate glass window.

It didn't sound like her family was impacted by whatever political game had led to the attack, but Kat wouldn't know until she got a chance to call them tomorrow morning. Until then, she was too far from Schaumburg to actually change anything. All Kat could do was clamp down on her anxiety and hope for the best.

"I will let my Clan know." Dorrik nodded soberly. "Obviously, we cannot directly intervene, but if the stallesp are going to push the rules to their breaking point, there is no reason we can't counter them in kind."

"Thank you." Kat still felt some worry over her family fluttering in her chest as she smiled at her companions. "I would appreciate any assistance you could provide humanity. Things aren't exactly great on Earth at the moment."

"First things first." Kaleek took a step toward the door that sealed them in the relative safety of the spawning area. "We're going to have to beat this dungeon. I don't suppose we have any information on what to expect?"

Dorrik shrugged, drawing both of their swords and walking toward the desoph as they spoke.

"Not much that we couldn't infer from the name. There will primarily be water-based and partially aquatic foes, some of whom have access to minor poisons." Dorrik paused for a second before continuing wryly. "Of course, I could always wait a week for a ship to pull into orbit with a full analysis of the dungeon. I'm sure at some point a lokkel team has explored it."

"Decreased visibility, venom, and getting wet it is." Kaleek paused just in front of the door. "Sounds like a blast to me. Is everyone else in?"

Kat nodded as Dorrik's crest rippled in amusement. Seeing their responses, the big otter grinned and pushed the door open.

Immediately, more mist poured into the room, as thick as soup and almost as opaque. Kat could almost taste the heavy earth scent of decaying plant matter as the gray fog flowed past her, cutting her visibility down to maybe two arm's lengths.

A deep, resonant moan filled the hallway, sending a shiver down Kat's spine. The mist billowed around her, curling and seemingly reaching toward her with tendrils of vapor that trailed across her skin, raising gooseflesh on the exposed skin of her arms.

"That can't be good," she muttered, knife at the ready as she squinted into the thick fog, trying to make out the shape of her unknown opponent.

Wind buffeted her, startling Kat into jumping backward. Something passed through the space she'd been standing in, completely invisible except for the trail it left in the swirling mist.

Dorrik grunted in pain, the whistle of their swords passing through empty air coming a moment later, prompting Kat to scurry to the side and put her back against one of the dungeon's walls. With visibility as low as it was, there wasn't really any way to know where the rest of her team was fighting. A distracted ally's sword would leave her just as dead as a monster's claws.

"Smoke wraiths," Dorrik shouted, their voice clipped with pain. "Use Dazzle, Miss Kat, they're susceptible to light magic!"

She began channeling the magic, only to grunt as pain spiked into her side. She swung her dagger downward, meeting resistance as it passed through... something.

The pain turned ice cold, a needle of frost jammed in between her ribs that threatened to take Kat's breath away and muddle the flow of mana that was coalescing into a spell. She staggered to the side, swinging her knife once more to ward off her assailant.

In the moment of the creature's attack on her, Kat's attention had wavered. The mana she'd been gathering to form Dazzle had fractured, releasing strands of the warm energy throughout her body.

Biting down on her lip, she focused herself entirely on finishing the spell. More mana swirled up from her depths, connecting with the frayed streams she'd already summoned.

She twirled to the side, barely avoiding a disturbance in the mist as an otherwise unseen attack thumped into the wall of the dungeon. Her forehead furrowed as the muscles in her face and neck tensed from concentration. More glowing bridges of mana appeared in her mind as the shards of the spell came together like a puzzle.

Once more she ducked as another pair of ripples slashed through the fog. Whatever this wraith was that Kat was fighting, it was fast; barely a second had passed since it had first struck her and this was already its third attack.

Then Kat screwed her eyes shut as Dazzle erupted in a brilliant strobe of light. A moment later, blinking against the glare from her spell, she could barely make out a trio of amorphous shadowy forms attacking her companions.

Her enemies were mere blobs, barely visible as darker patches in the omnipresent mist, their silhouettes little more than undulating spheres with spikes and threads swirling about them. The wraith in front of her swayed wildly, slashing out with a collection of limbs that it freely detached from its main body.

Only one even came near Kat, the other five tendrils flailing about the mist aimlessly. Ducking under the blow, a smile blossomed on Kat's face despite the frigid wound in her side.

It couldn't see her. The monster was attacking blind.

Her knife came up, stabbing deep into the spasming wraith. Her blade and wrists sank into the creature, passing through a damp outer membrane and into a frigid substance with the consistency of soup.

Then, the dagger hit something hard. Almost without thinking, Kat activated Penetrate, feeling her stamina drain as the warmth of the ability flowed into her hand, counteracting the chill of the wraith.

The resistance disappeared, and her knife sank up to its hilt. The creature shuddered, dissipating into the mist and only leaving behind a fist-sized chunk of ice impaled on her weapon.

Kat looked up, prepared to help her companions, but the fog had returned to its previous opaque state, the effects of Dazzle fading in the seconds after she cast it. She could still hear them, grunting as they struggled against the wraiths, but Kat was unable to see how much, if any, progress they'd made with their opponents.

For a moment, she contemplated healing the wound in her side. The icy cold was fading with the death of its creator, and the raw ache of the injury was beginning to wear at her, but at the same time, her companions were fighting blind. Kaleek and Dorrik were skilled, but even they had no way of fighting a monster that they couldn't see.

Kat shrugged internally as she summoned the mana for another casting of Dazzle, a throwing knife in her hand. Dorrik probably could. If she could see the trails in the mist made by the attacking wraiths, the giant lizard could probably pinpoint the monster's cores and tell what they'd had for supper the day before.

"Eyes closed!" she shouted, following her own advice as she fired off another brilliant strobe of light.

A moment later, a pair of knives were in flight, passing through the sloppy body of the wraith assaulting Kaleek. The otter staggered backward, using the reprieve from her spell to gasp for breath. She couldn't see any wounds on his silhouette —even the reflected light from Dazzle wasn't quite enough to penetrate the fog in its entirety—but from the way the desoph warrior moved, it was clear that he had been hit several times.

A third throwing dagger left Kat's hand as she took in Dorrik's opponent in the fading light. It was much smaller than she remembered, flailing miserably as even blinded Dorrik fought evenly with it. As she watched, the lokkel's blades shaved off another chunk of its body, diminishing it further.

She was already gathering mana for another casting of Dazzle as her final dagger struck something deep inside Kaleek's opponent. It howled mournfully as it dissolved, leaving the desoph to recover against the wall.

The final casting of Dazzle was all it took for Dorrik to finish off their foe. Their blades formed an 'x' as they passed through its body, one of them clipping the ice core of the wraith.

Suddenly, Kat became aware of her own ragged breathing as well as the wound on her side. Blood soaked her armor and her status proclaimed that she'd lost five hit points from the attack.

Now that the monsters were dead, the visibility in the room increased.

She let the alien words to Cure Wounds I fall from her lips as she made her way over to Kaleek, briefly healing herself long enough to stop the bleeding and the immediate threat before treating her teammate.

"Thanks," Kaleek said, relief filling his voice. "I would have been the laughingstock of my pod if I was done in by smoke wraiths on the third level."

"They are simply a bad matchup," Dorrik interjected, their scales infuriatingly unblemished as they approached. "Miss Kat has the agility to fight them, but her weapons are too short to fight them safely. I have long enough weapons to kill the wraiths, but they are too fast. Without the help of Miss Kat's magic to identify their main bodies and disrupt their attacks, I probably could have finished my opponent off, but it likely would have taken a half hour."

Dorrik took in Kaleek's injuries, a slightly sour look on their face. "As for you, you are better suited for a larger foe where your heavy sword can do some serious damage. Against wraiths, even if you were a couple levels higher, you'd struggle to even fend off their attacks."

Kaleek stood up, stretching the kinks out of his battered body. He frowned, trying to brush out some of the blood staining his fur.

"This is going to mat," he grumbled, his efforts doing little more than smearing his blood around. "Seriously, as soon as the blood starts clotting, my fur is going to be an absolute mess."

"If I weren't trying to conserve mana," Kat responded helpfully, drawing a scowl from the otter, "I could spray you down with Water Jet. That would get rid of the blood in fairly short order."

"Well get on conserving." Kaleek glared at her. "The sooner we can clear out the rest of the dungeon, the quicker I can get back to town and have a shower."

Rolling her eyes, Kat folded her legs under herself and sat down, her eyes half closed as she began to wait for her mana to return. She'd need to heal herself before they continued, and if she'd learned any lesson from the first encounter, it was that having enough spare mana to let her spam spells was vitally important.

Twenty minutes later, she stood up, nodding to her companions. With a sigh, Kaleek stopped scratching his clumpy fur and walked to the end of the second room, the fog almost swallowing him up before Dorrik and Kat began to follow.

The otter pushed open another door. Thankfully, this time they weren't drowned by the thickening mist as they walked down a short hallway and into another room. Still, Kat had a hard time making out the walls of the room. She assumed that they were the same nondescript stone as the rest of the structure, but—

Something hissed, prompting Kat to whirl around and stand back to back with Dorrik, her knife in hand as she scanned the room. She stepped slightly to the side, allowing Kaleek to step into their formation as the three of them formed a triangle of glinting steel while they squinted into the swirling darkness of the dungeon. Even with Darkvision, all Kat saw was a black and white tableau of an empty room.

The sticky 'pop pop pop' of suction cups pulling themselves off the dungeon stone echoed throughout the room. Kat tensed as Kaleek shifted next to her, but he was only bringing his greatsword up into a guard position.

The noises stopped. For a moment, the entire room held its breath.

"Do you think it's—" Kaleek began, only for Kat to cut him off.

"Don't you *dare* finish that sentence," she hissed angrily. "The second you say it's safe, something horrifying jumps out of the shadows and we get attacked by surprise."

"That's silly," Dorrik scoffed. "Maybe in your human entertainment things happen in such a fashion, but—"

They all ducked as an earsplitting screech filled the room, followed a moment later a spray of cool liquid that coated all three of them. Before Kat could react, a long, spongy pink tongue darted out from the mist before splatting wetly against the flat of Kaleek's sword.

Then, the liquid coating her hair and face began to burn. It started as an itch, but the sensation quickly morphed into an inferno of agony. She almost didn't notice Kaleek's sword being ripped from his hands and pulled into the mist.

Something wet and soft wrapped around Kat's ankle, yanking her from her feet. Her back hit the ground, knocking the wind out of her and sending her knife clattering off into the mist.

The fleshy appendage gripped tight around her leg, jerking her away from the rest of her party. Her foot erupted into the same itching, burning pain of her shoulders and scalp as Kat was dragged across the dungeon floor, her back thumping and scraping against the hard stone.

She slapped her hand onto her chest, patting around for one of her spare throwing knives by feel even as she began gathering her mana for a Gravity Spike. As soon as her hand closed over the knife, she drew it and turned all of her focus toward fighting off the pain in her face and ankle and the disorientation from being pulled across the ground.

Then it was in front of her, an eight-legged lizard, slightly bigger than a large dog. Its scales were a mottled blue and gray that seamlessly blended with the mist and stone of the dungeon. Even as she watched, the colors rippled slightly, its coloration adapting to its surroundings as it unstuck its sucker-covered foot from the ground and took a step toward her.

Kat ignored the red icon blinking in the corner of her vision as she released her Gravity Spike square in the center of the monster's body. The creature's torso blurred and contorted as the forces of gravity tried to rip it apart.

It released her ankle, tongue going slack as it bleated in pain. Quickly, Kat rolled over, gritting her teeth against the omnipresent burn, and activated Penetrate. The smaller throwing dagger slammed through the monster's tongue and lodged itself in the dungeon floor.

The monster tried unsuccessfully to jerk backward, blue-green blood flowing from its open mouth.

Kat rolled to her knees, lunging once again with another throwing dagger in her hand. It attempted to jerk its head to the side, frantic fear in its eyes, but the knife in its tongue held fast long enough for Kat to find her quarry.

Once again, Penetrate empowered her knife, but this time it punched through the creature's skull, lodging up to its hilt in the struggling monster's brain. It shuddered once and went still, the combination of her spell and the two daggers enough to finish the ambush predator off.

Kat stood up, careful not to put too much weight on her still-burning ankle. One of the monsters lay bisected at Dorrik's feet while another tried to pull itself away from them, missing three of its eight legs. As for Kaleek, even weaponless, the desoph had managed to clamber onto one of the monsters' backs. As she watched, he gripped either side of its head, corded muscles straining and twisting.

With a pop, the creature went limp and Kaleek rolled tiredly off of it and onto his feet. Kat frowned slightly at his upper torso. Most of the fur was missing, replaced by his greyish skin which was covered in a web of scars, likely from the same acid that had been sprayed on her.

Kat drew her third throwing knife, prepared to help Dorrik only for the monster to fire its tongue at them. The lokkel's four arms blurred, and a moment later the severed tongue fell to the dungeon floor, oozing blood.

Before the creature could retreat, Dorrik lunged forward, blades opening either side of the monster's neck. It croaked, oxygen whistling out of its severed windpipe, and tried to open the distance between itself and Dorrik once more.

This time, the lokkel let it, watching like a hawk as the creature rapidly bled out on the dungeon floor. Little more than twenty seconds after they had cut its throat, Dorrik nodded in satisfaction and sheathed their swords as the light left its eyes.

"You look like crap." Kaleek smiled at her, almost all of the thick and lustrous fur burned off of his face by the surprise attack.

"You too." Kat chuckled. "But on the plus side, I don't think you'll have to worry about your fur getting matted anymore. You need to have fur to worry about that."

"Very funny." Kaleek rolled his eyes. "Anyway, what in the name of the elders were those, Dorrik? I know we're flying blind here, but I've never seen anything like them."

Kat began casting Cure Wounds I. By the look of things, she was about to run her mana dry healing Kaleek and herself.

"How should I know?" Dorrik asked with a shrug, his uncharacteristic ignorance startling Kat badly enough that she lost the flow of her spell. "All I know is that one of them was on the ceiling above us. It spit something at the two of you and then tried to drop on me."

"Wait," Kat sputtered. "We just encountered a monster that you don't know anything about? You? The walking encyclopedia of dungeon lore?"

"What?" Dorrik replied, glancing with surprise at a nodding Kaleek. "Is it really that surprising that I wouldn't know a creature that we're fighting? I'm knowledgeable, but far from all-knowing."

"Honestly," Kaleek scratched at his raw and damaged skin, "yeah. Up until now, you've basically known how to win every fight before we wandered into it. This is kinda new."

"Get used to it." Dorrik shrugged again. "As we climb, we're going to find ourselves fighting more and more esoteric monsters. Sometimes there's nothing to do but throw yourself into a fight and hope that your skillset is well-rounded enough to handle whatever blows the monster strikes back with."

CHAPTER SEVENTEEN

"How is your mana, Miss Kat?" Dorrik stood next to her, back against the wall as they watched Kaleek and her through the mist.

"Almost up to full," she replied after checking her status. "That last round of healing took a lot out of me."

"Indeed." Dorrik nodded. "Between the cliff frogs and the troglodytes, all three of us took a fair number of severe blows. The cliff frogs in particular were worrying. None of us were properly ready for their hallucinogenic mucus. I will have to talk to Sikka about equipment that will protect us from poisons and intoxicants when we get back to the enclave."

Kaleek stepped closer to the two of them, his face and neck almost completely hairless and covered in burns. Kat winced even though she knew that she didn't look much better. After all, Cure Wounds I was only a wood tier ability. It could restore the hit points lost to the acid, but it couldn't touch any true disfigurement or disability.

"Just so long as we can easily take off the equipment in question." Kaleek grinned, the expression turning his face into a nightmare of bubbly skin and taut scar tissue. "Some of us want to be able to have a couple of drinks to unwind when we're back in town."

Dorrik stepped away from the wall and put a single claw on the desoph's scarred and bare shoulder. "Kaleek, I love you like a clutchmate, but please do not smile until your avatar is refreshed. Already you've managed to turn both of my stomachs."

"Pssshhh." Kaleek blew out a breath dismissively through his acid pocked lips. "You were always a softy, Dorrik. If it's really that big of a deal, I say we spring for a skill stone for Kat to learn a better healing ability."

Kat turned to the deformed otter incredulously. "Did you seriously just accuse Dorrik of being soft?" she asked, struggling to believe her ears. "Dorrik, the warrior-monk fighting gigantic jungle predators day and night? That Dorrik?"

"They're squeamish about injuries." Kaleek winked grotesquely at her. "It comes from being a good enough fighter that they almost never get hit. One day they'll realize that females dig the scars."

"Not this female." Kat snorted, rolling her eyes.

"Indeed." Dorrik nodded thankfully in her direction. "When looking for satisfactory genetic material, why would a female look to the warrior so bad at fighting that they keep on getting hit? Obviously, the superior option is the fighter strong enough to emerge from battle unscathed."

"Hey now." Kaleek frowned, squinting at Dorrik.

"*Anyway.*" Kat stepped in between the two of them, ignoring the smirk on the giant lizard's face. "My mana is back at full. If the two of you are done with your posturing, I'm as ready to tackle the boss as I'm ever going to be."

"Fine." Kaleek grinned, drawing a flinch from the lokkel. "Let's go kill a giant lizard or something."

The three of them approached the final door, Kaleek taking his usual spot in the lead and pushing the door open. Kat followed the partially bald otter into the final room and frowned. The center of the boss chamber was a lake with the dungeon altar at the center. Other than that, it was completely empty. Even the mist was gone.

"That's new," she mumbled, scanning the room and ceiling with Nightvision. Kat's frown deepened as her search failed to reveal any sort of hidden monster.

Dorrik followed her in, a frown sprouting in their face as they surveyed the room as well.

"Have you ever heard of a dungeon altar without a boss to protect it?" she asked, her eyes still flitting about the room, trying to discover how and where she was missing their foe.

"No," the lokkel responded simply, their crest flaring with distress.

"I would make some sort of quip about us being lucky," Kaleek sighed, "but the last time I did that, the monster sprayed me with acid from above. Nothing about this entire dungeon has been lucky."

"On that, we are agreed," Dorrik replied, drawing both of their swords. "We should fan out enough that an area attack won't catch all of us at once while staying close enough to aid the rest of the team if we are attacked."

Kat nodded, gripping her knife as she slipped to the left, letting Kaleek continue in his role as the point of their team while Dorrik worked their way to the right. Once all three of them were in position, fifteen to twenty feet apart, they began moving cautiously toward the lake.

Still, no matter how closely she inspected the dripping stone walls of the boss chamber, Kat couldn't spot anything. If there actually was a boss monster in there with them, the only conclusion she could come to was that it was invisible and stalking them, hardly a pleasant possibility.

The tension only built as they traveled the entire distance to the lake without incident. Each step, Kat kept expecting a monster to burst from hiding and attack them. By the time they reached the lake, she was ready to stab anything that moved.

"Do you see anything, Miss Kat?" Dorrik's question startled her into jumping, slightly.

Silently, Kat checked their surroundings once more before shaking her head. It was almost madness on her part. She didn't know if this was the thirtieth or the hundredth time she'd checked for foes only to turn up empty.

"Maybe we're just lucky?" Kaleek asked flippantly, stepping into the lake to begin wading toward the altar.

After a moment of chewing on her lower lip and exchanging worried looks with Dorrik, Kat followed him. A dozen steps later, the water was up to her waist, and Kat was staring down at the murky liquid and contemplating her options.

They were barely a quarter of the way to the altar, and at this rate they would have to swim. Kaleek and her would be fine, but she had no idea if Dorrik had ever even learned, given his dislike for large bodies of water.

Something brushed her leg.

"Guys." Kat's knife was in her hand as her eyes glued themselves to the surface of the dark water, looking for any sign of a disturbance. "There's something alive in here."

"That's your imagination," Kaleek responded, not even turning to look at her.

A soft, spongy substance tickled past her other calf.

"Something just moved past my leg." She whipped around, trying to spot anything in the direction she'd felt the object moving.

"Hold on," Dorrik interjected, concern on their face. "I think I felt something too."

Before Kat could respond, a fist-sized tentacle wrapped itself around her ankle, whipping her up into the air.

Her head snapped back, teeth clacking shut as it swung her side to side. Distantly, Kat heard Kaleek and Dorrik screaming as she clenched her eyes shut in an attempt to fight the world's sudden tilt and spin.

She marshaled her mana, trying to tune out the abuse the rest of her body was going through while concentrating on Gravity's Grasp. No matter how powerful the monster was, the laws of physics and biology were fairly simple. It could only pack so much muscle into a tentacle.

The spell snapped into place, almost tripling Kat's weight in a fraction of a second. For a moment, the tentacle around her ankle held on, bowing as it tried to keep her suspended in the air.

Then, she slipped through its slimy grasp, tumbling downward toward the beast itself.

Almost immediately, Kat regretted her decision. Kaleek was trying to fight back another pair of the tentacles, his big sword removing large chunks of flesh whenever they approached him. About ten paces to the otter's side, Dorrik glowed purple with the power of their psi abilities, swords blurring as they opened deep gashes in the monster's main body.

As for the main body? Kat frantically cut her mana to Gravity's Grasp, instead focusing her attention on Levitation. Its body was spherical, a slimy hemisphere of mottled grayish flesh dotted with short eyestalks around a large circular central mouth. Specifically, a central mouth lined with forearm-length teeth that she was falling directly toward.

Kat spread her arms out as Levitation finished casting, increasing her surface area and air resistance. The remains of the clothing under her armor flapped wildly as her rate of descent slowed dramatically.

It wasn't enough.

She clenched her jaw, eyes on the gnashing blender of teeth below her as she began channeling her mana into Pseudopod. She was still falling too fast, the spell wouldn't finish in time for her to pull—

Kat's world flashed purple, and suddenly, with the force of a crashing car, she *stopped*. She almost lost hold of her spell, her sudden jerking halt taking her by surprise, but with a grunt and a burst of mana she managed to smooth over the flaws her distraction introduced into the spell.

A moment later, the purple glow disappeared, and a tentacle of water reached out from Kat and gripped onto one of the monster's nearby fleshy appendages. With a pulse of her will, Kat dragged herself to it, shooting a quick smile of thanks at Dorrik for the save.

As soon as Kat touched the creature's slippery tubular limb, Kat jammed her knife into it up to the hilt and ripped downward. The blade parted its spongy flesh like paper, drawing a gush of hot blood before Kat kicked off of it, aiming toward the monster's main body, her Pseudopod still wrapped around the tentacle to guide her descent.

Even with her decreased weight, Kat felt her foot sink into the monster's soft flesh. She glanced around at the various tentacles sprouting from the creature's massive spherical body. All of them were occupied with the rest of the party.

Setting her jaw, Kat dismissed Pseudopod. As soon as her second spell was gone, she began casting Gravity Spike, aiming the dangerous ability deep into the toothy pit that was the monster's mouth.

A tense second or so later, it activated, sending a burst of magic into the creature's fleshy depths. Its skin rumbled under Kat, and a number of its hand-sized eyestalks swiveled to look at her.

She activated Cat Step, taking advantage of her decreased weight to blaze across the monster's slimy skin as she began casting Gravity Spike once again. "Well, that got its attention."

She planted a foot in its springy flesh, jumping backward just before one of the tentacles slammed into the monster in front of her. Another five blurred steps in the other direction, she crouched, only to use every ounce of energy in her body to leap over a second tentacle that whipped horizontally at chest level through the space she had just occupied.

At the apex of her jump, she released the second Gravity Spike, utilizing her vantage point to watch a chunk of flesh deep in its gullet twist and pull before dissolving into a mess of blood and mangled meat.

It shuddered once again, drawing a muffled curse from Kat as *all* of its tentacles shifted to her, ignoring the rest of her party entirely. The moment she landed, her world devolved into a deadly ballet of sprinting and careful twisting dodges as the tentacles whistled past her.

She didn't have the time or focus to work on another spell, but Levitation kept doing its work, keeping her body light enough that she could outrun and out jump the fleshy tapestry of spongy appendages that sought to slam her off of the monster and into the water.

The monster shuddered again, the careful weave of the attacking tendrils disrupted by a keening wail of pain from below her feet. A quick glance revealed Kaleek, a grotesque smile on his scarred face, unmolested by the monster as he hacked through its blubbery flesh with great, brutal slashes.

Kat ducked under a clumsy swipe that carried enough force behind it to cave in her skull. She couldn't see Dorrik, but that only meant that the lokkel was on the other side of the monster, hidden from her by its bulk as they carved their own way deep into the slimy abomination.

The fight only lasted a minute longer, but by that point, Kat was almost out of stamina from her constant use of Cat Step. She collapsed backward in exhaustion, not even caring that her back was soaked in a combination of the boss monster's stinking blood and the oily mucus that covered its skin.

Kaleek climbed up next to her, his mottled skin and sparse fur covered from whiskers to tail in blood. He wrinkled his button nose at her before reaching down and offering her a hand.

"Don't tell Dorrik," he whispered cheerfully, "but I think I'm okay with them picking out the dungeons from here on out. That was absolutely awful."

She grabbed his hand, groaning as she let the otter pull her to her feet.

"I think we're on the same page." Kat flashed him a grin. "I don't want Dorrik to get insufferable, but if we could avoid this sort of disaster in the future, I'd be ecstatic."

"What are the two of you chatting about?" Dorrik called

out from the small island with the dungeon's altar. "I thought you'd be excited to get out of this humidity and into the refreshing heat of the desert."

Kaleek groaned, drawing a giggle from Kat.

"We'll be with you in a second," Kat called out, stretching her back as the two of them walked along the huge floating corpse of the boss monster. Dorrik placed one of their claws on the altar before disappearing in a rainbow flash of light.

"You know…" Kat stopped just before jumping into the water at the edge of the monster.

Kaleek dove into the water, acrobatically spinning around to face her while treading water, a single singed-off eyebrow raised quizzically.

Kat chuckled, rubbing a hand over her partially bare scalp, the puckered ridges of her own acid scars sensitive under her questing fingers. "As painful and awful as all of that was, it was kind of fun. There's really something about being thrown into the unknown and having to figure out how to overcome a challenge on the spot that really gets the heart pumping."

"I know." Kaleek grinned back, the expression straining his scarred face. "All of us are like that. Dorrik might not show it, but they're the same way. That's the core of what this party is. Competence and absolutely loving the challenge and thrill of throwing yourself into danger as you seek to get stronger."

"A year ago," Kat nodded thoughtfully, "I would've said that you're full of shit. That I only risked myself because I had to. Now? I think you're right. As dumb as it is, I love these dungeon dives."

"Then I'm glad I met you now rather than a year ago." Kaleek dove into the water, quickly working his way to the island in the center of the lake, leaving a thoughtful Kat behind.

Only after he activated the altar and disappeared did she set out on her own. A short, almost leisurely swim later, she climbed up onto the small pile of dirt and approached the altar. Without hesitating, she put her hand on it.

Congratulations, Adventurer!
You have completed the Wood Tier Level Three Dungeon,
Stinging Mist.
Three of three party members surviving. Good job!
Assigning awards:

+1 Agility

In a flash of light, the desert appeared around her, the stallesp raiders that had chased them into the dungeon long since gone. For a moment, she took in the smiling faces of her friends, exultant after their triumph over the dungeon and their escape from the alien marauders.

Name: Katherine Debs
Class: Elementalist Initiate
Max Level: 3
812 Marks

HP: 22
MP: 33
STA: 26

Dodge: Poor
Damage Mitigation: Insignificant

Strength: 4
Agility: 6
Fortitude: 3
Endurance: 4
Mind: 5
Reaction: 5
Charisma: 4
Spirit: 3

Spells Known:

Gravity's Grasp
Levitation
Pseudopod
Dehydrate
Dazzle
Shadow
Water Jet
Gravity Spike

Skills Known:
Knife I - 9, 21%
Gravity I - 7, 95%
Water I - 8, 42%
Cat Step - 6, 29%
Light I - 6, 29%
Cure Wounds I - 6, 68%
Penetrate

Perks:
Nightvision
Leaping

Between her skills and her attributes, Kat's abilities were improving steadily. Even without her magic, Kat could feel that her body was stronger, lighter, and significantly more responsive. She still had a long way to go, but it finally felt like things were starting to move on the right track.

CHAPTER EIGHTEEN

Kat exited the maglev into what looked like a military checkpoint. Security wearing GroCorp armor guarded every exit, and an armored waypoint made of reinforced concrete sat next to the customs station.

A frown worked its way onto Kat's face as she took in the machine gun nest on top of the checkpoint, manned by a Millennium samurai. He scanned the timid crowd with chromed out cybereyes, alert and more than ready to open fire at a moment's notice.

In fact, the more she watched, Kat began to pick up on a sort of electric tension that permeated the station. The GroCorp security with their matching uniforms and submachine guns spent almost as much time watching the motley collection of heavily armed Millennium samurai as they did the quiet and nervous crowd.

As for the mercenaries? Only three were visible, clustered tightly around the squat armored building, but Kat could see at least two more rifle muzzles poking from gun slits in the side of the bunker. It was clear from Millennium's heavier weapons and the casual disregard with which they swept the guns over the corporate guards that there was no love lost between the groups.

She shuffled forward, lifting her arms so that a nervous woman in an Ike Holdings, a wholly owned subsidiary of GroCorp, uniform could run a metal detecting wand over her. Just behind the woman, an imposing figure in GroCorp colors, face and body invisible behind the ceramic trauma plates attached to their powered exoskeleton, watched impassively.

The wand fizzed and hummed slightly as it passed over the sensor camouflaged pocket in her jacket, but the woman didn't appear to notice. More importantly, the security goon's weapon didn't move, still in the figure's hands and ready, but pointed safely at the ground.

A minute or so later, another Ike Holdings, a wholly owned subsidiary of GroCorp, employee was checking her travel pass as Kat struggled to keep her impatience under wraps. The pass was another recent imposition for anyone trying to enter the arcology. Now, visitors were required to go through screening and submit an itinerary before they would be allowed to enter or leave the massive tower via the corporate-owned maglev.

The only real explanation Kat received regarding the new requirement was a vaguely worded e-mail about the 'unprecedented events' and the 'security crisis' gripping Schaumburg. Luckily, Belle had been able to smooth over the requirement, having someone issue her an evergreen pass that didn't require her to justify her comings and goings.

Kat couldn't make herself feel grateful toward the older woman. Belle had the personal warmth and emotional depth of a viper. The pass was just one more way to tie her and Xander down. One more favor that they'd need to pay back if they ever wanted to slip out from under Belle's thumb.

One elevator ride under the watchful eye of a GroCorp guard later, Kat was back on her home floor and walking through unnaturally subdued streets toward her mother's apartment. There still a couple teenagers out, hurrying to and from classes, but the pairs of GroCorp and Ike officers, patrolling the streets with shotguns and pistols visible, put a damper on the usual bustle of the arcology's lower levels.

More than anything, it reminded her of her times in the Shell. Kat could feel eyes on her back from the various stores and apartment complexes as she walked home, but no one made any effort to flag her down or call out to her.

Finally, Kat found herself in the elevator of her family's apartment building. The solitary bulb lighting the cage of metal sputtered as the lift jerked to a halt with a squeal, drawing a frown. The apartment complex had never been particularly luxurious, but at least it was usually clean and in good repair.

The doors opened, revealing a trash strewn hallway, scuff marks on the wall where the paint had been chipped back, revealing bare concrete underneath. Kat hurried down the corridor, her sour expression deepening until she reached the door to her family's suite. A quick swipe of her identity lanyard and the door opened.

Michelle sat on the couch, her day's homework hopefully done as she watched an episode of Chrome Cowboys on the massive smartglass screen that occupied half of the wall. Kat closed the door behind her, waiting until the lock clicked into place before turning back to her sister.

The girl was still watching the smartglass, eyes glazed over as a cybercow blew up, throwing a woman into the air, only for her to fall down a yawning mineshaft. Kat cleared her throat.

"Wha—*Kat!*" Michelle sprang up and threw herself across the room. Kat smiled, teeth peeking out from behind her lips as a pair of skinny arms wrapped themselves around her neck.

She swung her sister around, tower-enhanced strength letting her lift the girl high enough for her bare feet to clear the apartment's floor. With a whoofing exhalation of her breath, Kat set Michelle back down.

"When did you get back?" Michelle gushed, scrambling back a couple of steps. "Everyone at school is still talking about you. Delaney, the girl whose dad is a manager, is super jealous of you, but everyone else is excited about you attending college."

"Slow down." Kat chuckled. "I wanted to surprise the two of you so I didn't message ahead, but I just came from the maglev. I have to head out to meet some people this afternoon, but I'll be home all weekend. We'll have plenty of time to catch up."

"Mom is getting off of her shift in an hour." Her sister was practically hopping with excitement. "You can tell me all about Chiwaukee over dinner."

She paused, her tiny face scrunching into a look of concern and then a frown. Finally, Michelle forced a smile, worry still wrinkling the corners of her eyes.

"It'll be fine, probably." Her sister's eyes flickered as she used her smart panel to rapidly type out an e-mail. "I'll let Mom know, and we'll figure something out."

"What's wrong?" Kat asked, crossing her arms as she looked down at her sister. "Seriously, Michelle, don't try to weasel out of this. I can tell when you're pulling a fast one."

The younger girl squirmed for a second, obviously at war with herself as she debated how much to tell Kat. Finally, Michelle gave up with a sigh.

"Ever since the new guards showed up, things have changed." Her sister shifted unhappily. "Not everyone is working. GroCorp announced that they only wanted people leaving their houses to do necessary work. A lot of people have been sent home with their weekly spending limit cut by two-thirds."

Michelle shrugged, a defeated look on her face. "Even if you can afford to buy things, food is rationed. I'm sure we'll be able to work something out, but dinner will be a bit tight."

"Things didn't look good out there," Kat responded, mind whirring. "But no one gave me any trouble after I made it through customs at the maglev station."

Michelle rolled her eyes, "Of course, you're wearing a GroCorp College jacket. That means you have connections. Plus, there aren't any official rules against walking the streets.

You just hear stories about people who aren't going to or from work being questioned. Worse, every once in a while there are whispers about someone not making it home. It might all be urban legends, but no one I know is willing to take the risk."

"Well." Kat smiled reassuringly at her sister. "Don't let Mom worry about it. I need to go out for a business meeting anyway, and I'll be sure to come back with proper food."

"Are you sure?" Michelle asked, concern warring with excitement on her face. "We've been stuck eating kelp wafers on everything, but still. Even if someone didn't stop you this time, that doesn't mean you're completely safe. They'll probably leave you alone, Kat, but every time you go outside they might pick you up for questioning."

She reached out, ruffling her younger sister's hair. At some point, Michelle had grown. The top of her head was at eye level now. It seemed like yesterday that her sister hadn't even cleared Kat's shoulder.

Her breath caught slightly as a pang of regret tightened Kat's lungs. It hadn't been like this before when it was just Mom, Michelle, and her. They lived their lives and Kat had been in the thick of it, there for every event, good or bad. Mom's birthday, Michelle's first day of school, the first time she'd kissed a boy, she'd been there for all of them. There was no period of acclimatization, no sudden realization that her kid sister was growing up.

"I'd just like to see them try and catch me." Kat winked at Michelle, trying to ignore the wave of melancholy. "I was running circles around local security for years before these new guys showed up. They won't even know which crawl space I've used to make it past them."

Kat stepped away from Michelle, dropping a hand to each of the younger woman's shoulders. She'd just have to get used to the feeling of coming back to changes. Subtle differences marking the passage of time and the development of her family in Kat's absence. One more price she would need to pay in order to get ahead.

Kat unslung the duffle bag containing her gear and clothing, putting it just inside the apartment's door. "I'll leave my things here, but I have to run to that meeting. Tell Mom that I'll be back for dinner, okay?"

"Be careful, okay?" Michelle asked, a hint of a frown on her face.

Kat just winked and stepped back outside. Immediately, the cheerful expression fell from her face as she began composing an e-mail to Xander. If anyone had black market food in Schaumburg, it would be him, but at the same time, that didn't solve the problem.

The dean had mentioned something about the arcology, but the crackdown was much worse than expected. If she hadn't already been meeting with Xander and Belle Donnst to debrief from the mission, she would have been calling for a sit down of her own.

Something was wrong, and it was more than the normal corporate infighting. Executives blackmailed, extorted, and sidelined each other all the time. Expecting them to behave any differently was the height of folly.

That said, shutting down most of a profitable corporation's operations wasn't business as usual. Disrupting the company's profits was the one cardinal sin that no executive could get away with. By all rights, whoever launched the operation should have been torn apart by their fellow executives and shareholders for shredding the bottom line, but instead, it only looked like things were getting worse.

Her journey to the first floor was almost as harrowing as her usual trips through the Shell. Patrols eyed her, and at least one changed its regular course to follow her all the way to the elevator. The man checking her papers, to verify that she was cleared to travel to the ground floor, took much longer than usual, the pair of guards eyeing her the entire time.

Eventually, her pass checked out and Kat was back in the wreckage of the Shell. Quartets of samurai, all heavily armed and wearing Millennium colors, marched openly past the burned out and half-destroyed buildings, forcing her into the poorly lit back alleys on her way to the ChromeDogs warehouse.

When she arrived, the building's security was even stronger than before. New faces manned additional guns mounted on the building's roof, and almost every surrounding structure had a pair of windows sprouting rifle muzzles.

Kat's expression slipped into a scowl as she surveyed the headquarters of the gang that had taken her in. The street out front had a deep crater in it, and a burned out armored car had been pushed into a nearby alleyway. A closer inspection revealed lines of bullet holes stitched into the steel and concrete walls lining the road just outside the entrance.

One of the guards waved her through, tapping his smart-panel to send word ahead of her arrival. A minute or so later, she'd made her way past the training mats and into the second story rooms reserved for senior members of the gang.

Nina and Xander were already there, along with a couple of the more senior samurai, waiting for Kat's arrival. Nina nodded, a short professional jerk of her head before she turned back to her subordinates, continuing her former conversation in a hushed voice.

"Kat!" Xander called out cheerfully, slipping past one of the samurai and clapping a hand onto her shoulder. "I got your e-mail. I've talked with the quartermaster and we have a fair amount of food on hand. Hell, over the last couple of weeks, we've been making more money off of smuggling luxury food into the arcology than information drops."

"Can we set something up so my family gets regular deliveries?" she asked, a hint of sourness pinching the corners of her mouth. "It sounds like they're living off of kelp right now, and I can't help but feel like I'm being a terrible daughter if I don't set something up for them."

"You certainly are rich enough now," he replied with a chuckle. "I'll set something up with one of our runners to make sure your mother is getting some extra food weekly."

Xander stopped for a second, the quiet conversation between Nina and the ChromeDog combat leaders filling the void. He smiled wistfully.

"None of them are quite as good as you, though." Xander shrugged. "We have this whole new crop of starry-eyed kids ready to learn how to run, climb, and fight, and all I can think when I see them is that none of them had half the raw talent you did."

"Talent?" Kat rolled her eyes. "When you first brought me out here, I was shaking. I thought I'd made the biggest mistake of my life in coming to the Shell. I was sure you were going to sell me off to some organ harvesting operation."

"That is the thing, Kat." Xander ran a hand through his salt and pepper hair. "You were terrified and it was obvious, but I don't think I've ever seen someone work harder. Every day, from the minute you got off your part time job, you were skipping sleep to slip out to the Shell and run obstacle courses or do self-defense training."

"Or maybe I'm just getting nostalgic," he hurriedly finished, the words falling flat after his brief burst of sentimentality.

A red indicator flashed from a partially disassembled pile of electronic equipment in the center of the conference table. Xander had assured her that it was a secure uplink in the past, but she'd always been doubtful of the pile of metal and exposed wires.

"Game faces, people," Nina's voice reverberated around the room. "Donnst is on the line."

Quietly, everyone but Xander made their way to the seats around the table. Nina and the combat arm of the Chrome-Dogs on the right, and Kat taking the seat next to Xander's while the older man plugged his cranial jack into the projector.

Briefly, Kat took in the two empty seats next to her. Right now, Xander and her represented the totality of the group's intelligence gathering wing. Originally there had been two other infiltrators, but Elise had died in the raid on the Steel and Blood headquarters.

The other infiltrator, Smits, had frozen up under fire. His panic had put the entire team at risk. Kat hadn't given the nervous boy a hard time. It was obvious that he was beating himself up over what happened to Elise, until one day he just... stopped showing up at the warehouse.

No one really said anything about it, but they didn't need to. Smits had been a nice boy, but it was clear that he wasn't cut out for the life of a samurai.

The smartglass screen occupying the far wall flared to life, displaying an image of Belle Donnst glaring at the room in the same manner that the ball pythons in the company lab stared at rats.

"Exe." Belle frowned, a hiss of static blurring her feed. "Please tell me that this connection is secure on your end. We are under too much scrutiny to make a mistake right now, and when I tried to interface with your network, the protocols felt a bit... dodgy."

"It might not be designed to look pretty, but it's a custom build. More secure than any corporate uplink you've ever used." Xander patted the pile of exposed wires and metal boxes appreciatively, causing the audio to shriek and Belle's image to blur and stutter.

"If you say so." She folded her hands in front of her. "Just be aware that my enemies aren't the sort for half measures. They will destroy my allies as swiftly and thoroughly as they would me."

"Jasper?" Kat asked despite herself, struggling to square Belle's words with her vision of the man. Maybe Davis, but—

"The Haupt boy?" Belle raised an eyebrow. "He isn't a threat. Little more than a pup, really. No, if the data you've relayed to me is to be believed, GroCorp has a whole lot more trouble than some whelp playing the avenger of justice."

"Does this have anything to do with what Kat overheard during her run?" Xander asked, leaning forward with his elbow on the conference table. "I'd think that 'friends in orbit' could have the potential to shake things up a bit."

"Possibly," she responded, a perfectly manicured nail clicking against the marble countertop on her end of the transmission. "But there are no references to the stallesp. Instead, the problems are of a much more terrestrial and mundane nature. The data retrieved from Franklin's office describes a coalition of shareholders and senior executives that are conspiring to take over GroCorp and drastically rework its subsidiaries."

"That's why the arcology is under lockdown right now." The steady tattoo of her finger against the table served as a metronome, underscoring Belle's words. "Franklin's allies generated fake evidence that Ike Holdings, a wholly owned subsidiary of GroCorp, was conspiring with NeoSyne to spin off into its own company. Really, it was an excuse to try to put a handful of active senior executives and myself under close surveillance."

Tak. Belle stopped speaking for a moment. *Tak*. Her finger kept tapping the same beat against the stone.

"We are under surveillance," she continued grimly, "but they haven't found anything. I know because the data you provided made it clear that they were looking for something, but I still don't know what. The good news is that even now, our allies amongst the shareholders are screaming about lost profits, and it's just a matter of time before they let up. The only problem is that I don't know if it will be enough. The data contained two important factors that I am struggling to find a counter to."

"First." Belle's finger clacked against the counter, punctuating the word. "Our enemies appear to have a fairly comprehensive plan to bribe, blackmail, extort, or simply murder those that might oppose them. While they may play by the rules at first, I doubt that things will remain that way for long."

"Second." She leaned back in her chair. "They have a list of 'inventions,' all ready to go but hidden from the public, that they repeatedly refer to as their funding source."

"The stallesp," Kat whispered, lips pursed.

"Quite." Belle nodded. "Franklin's benefactor, Elaine Williamson, has been quite vocal about setting up an alliance with the stallesp. I have always advised against such an agreement, as I know that any treaty with the aliens would lead to the entire corporation being exploited like a common employee."

"Unfortunately," she finished, "Elaine is a shareholder. Well beyond my reach. If we don't stop her, it's only a matter of months before she has all of us framed or killed."

"How do you want us to stop her then?" Nina asked, worry in her voice.

Belle just shrugged.

"Honestly," the executive sighed, "I haven't the slightest clue. If you have any suggestions, I'm all ears."

CHAPTER NINETEEN

"So your faction is in the middle of a power struggle?" Sikka asked, adjusting the new bandoleer strapped across Kat's chest. "Be a dear and tighten the buckles on your armor, the enchantments won't work unless all of the interior stitching is in contact with your skin."

"That part's hardly new," Kat responded, reaching across her body to feed more of her leather straps through the meta buckles. "It's hard to go a week on Earth without some group extorting, maneuvering against, or betraying another. The real issue is that we think that the stallesp are involved with one of the factions. It isn't absolute, but it sure looks like they're providing support outside of the tower."

"Wait." Kat frowned. "What do you mean the interior stitching needs to be touching my skin?"

"Enchanted clothing and armor use magical reagents woven into their fabric," Dorrik chimed in helpfully from the other side of the room where they were taking experimental swings with a new pair of swords. "Unless the enchantment is going to be powered by mana batteries, it will need to connect to the person wearing it. Given that mana batteries need to be recharged by an artificer at great cost, most enchanters build leads into their works so that they can directly absorb power from their wielder's skin."

"Unsurprisingly, Dorrik is right." Sikka rolled her eyes. "When your armor was commissioned, the artisan evenly distributed connections into the stomach and back of the outfit so that it could draw mana from you without any serious discomfort."

Kat stopped moving, her hands still holding on to the various straps and buckles of the ivory-inlaid leather armor.

"But I wear clothing under my armor?" she asked hesitantly, the hint of a blush rising up on her face. "Wouldn't that interfere with the connections?"

"Of course." Sikka cocked her head to the side, crest flaring in amusement. "Why do you wear underclothing? It can't be a matter of comfort. We pad the interior of all low tier armor with the inner fur from a stone ram in order to imbue it with some electrical resistance. I've tested your cushioning myself, Kat, and it should be plenty soft, even on that fragile pink skin of yours."

"Wait." The lizard's head resumed its normal position. "This isn't about you getting cold, is it? Hasn't your race invented some form of temperature control? Really, even if you haven't, the third level of the dreamscape is on the warmer end of things. Much more comfortable than the rest of the dreamscape. The place can get a bit drafty."

"Well yes, but—" Kat began, struggling to answer the barrage of questions. The big lizard had a point. Fashion and social norms on Earth meant nothing in *The Tower of Somnus*. The only thing holding her back was her own hang-ups.

"Sikka." Dorrik sighed with exasperation, sheathing their own swords. "Kat's race has nudity taboos. It's fascinating, actually. There's an entire culture based around modesty, but at the same time revealing enough of your body to attract a mate. Our xenologists are still trying to figure out exactly how the belief came about from a deep study into human informational and entertainment programming."

"Of course," they frowned, a single claw tapping their scaled chin, "it might be a simple matter of embarrassment. Most of the humans in entertainment programming are taller than Miss Kat, and their proportions—"

"That's enough of this conversation," Kat cut in. "I'd rather this not turn into a surprise makeover reality program."

"Reality programming?" Dorrik asked hopefully. "I've seen some references to it in the cultural studies of your people, but the xenologists couldn't make heads or tails of it. As far as they could tell, it was just like normal entertainment programs except noticeably cheaper and more chaotic."

Kat snorted. "Don't try to make sense of it. It'll rot your brain."

She took a breath in, closing her eyes for a moment to center herself. Even in the brief moment of darkness, she could almost feel Sikka's amusement, Kaleek goofing off in the corner, and Dorrik leaning in close, unable to abandon a nugget of information that eluded him.

She rolled her eyes at Dorrik. Just as she predicted, they were crowding toward her with excitement in their eyes. "Look, we're getting distracted here. If I need skin contact with my armor, I'm a big girl and I can handle it. I was just wondering if I could have a private room to change in? I know it's a stupid hang-up, but I'd still prefer to avoid going nude if I can help it."

"Please!" Kaleek shouted from the corner of the room where he was adjusting the fit on a new pair of bracers made out of a dark metal while a lokkel artisan watched on. "The last thing we need around here is more of Kat's disgusting pink skin. Anything that involves covering it up is a plus, as far as I'm concerned."

"Quiet, or I'll have you shaved!" Sikka thundered back, drawing a startled flinch from the usually saucy otter. She turned to Kat with a sweet smile on her muzzle. "By all means, dear. Our private fitting rooms are normally used for warriors outside of the clan that don't want to reveal all of their secrets, but I don't see why we can't let you use one."

Fifteen minutes later, Kat was back in the main sales room for the Ahn Enclave, jumping up and down on the balls of her feet experimentally as she tried to get the feel for the new equipment. Even her new long knife felt different. Theoretically, it had the same dimensions and balance as the one Kat was used to, but it just felt wrong.

The rest of her equipment had the same slight sense of wrongness. It was slightly heavier than her old set, but given the increases to her strength attribute, the extra weight shouldn't have been too much of a problem.

Deep down, Kat knew that it was sentimentality. From her first week in the tower, she'd used the same starting gear with an occasional consumable potion or ointment thrown in. She could feel the almost electric thrill from the dormant magic in her new knife and armor. It was clearly superior, but at the same time, it didn't feel like it was *hers*.

Of course, that was completely foolish. The three of them had spent weeks killing monsters to gather the materials needed for the equipment. Even then, she'd had to pay almost half of her marks for the various ingredients that couldn't be sourced on the third floor of the tower.

At least that had led to a pleasant reunion with Gasoot. The merchant had followed them to the third floor, taking advantage of their connection to Dorrik and the lokkel in the area to establish themselves in the massive desert.

Still, Kat couldn't quite shake her unease over the new equipment. Neither Sikka nor Dorrik had talked about it, but Gasoot was impressed when she brought the armor up. Apparently, Clan Ahn's custom armor and weapons fetched a premium in the tower. Ordinarily, a player trying to purchase a set would be expected to furnish both the ingredients and at least five thousand marks to compensate the skilled lokkel artisans for their time and expertise.

In short, it was a massive gift, and that didn't make her

comfortable. She trusted Dorrik and liked Sikka, but the sums of money involved were insane. Maybe it was the hunted street rat in her, but outside of family, no one would spend that on a friend. As powerful as the enchanted armor and knife were, they felt like shackles restricting her and binding her to Dorrik's family.

Even Xander, the man that had all but become her father after the accident that left the actual position open, would only loan her money without interest. Of course, on the streets, an interest-free loan with no set end date was an act of incredible generosity.

The entire situation left her feeling lost and anxious. On Earth, Kat had the context to know what she was getting into. Any deal had certain unspoken provisions and norms that all of the players simply knew about. Samurai didn't take jobs personally. Even if captured, you didn't turn on an employer. No lunch was truly free.

In the tower? She'd stepped into a community entirely outside of her understanding. True, everyone talked about how enlightened they were and the importance of being trustworthy, but just below the surface, the stallesp sounded like they would be at home in any megacorp boardroom back on Earth.

"Snap out of it, Kat." Kaleek clapped her on the shoulder. She felt the weight of his blow and a tingle as the enchantments in her ivory and enamel inlaid leather armor redirected its force, but little else. "Dorrik was just saying that they found the perfect dungeon for us to try out all the new equipment."

"Oh?" She shifted the bandoleer across her chest slightly, repositioning it into a slightly more comfortable spot. "Did they say what the dungeon's theme would be?"

"Sarvash," Dorrik responded, walking up to the two of them. "Originally nomads from the ice deserts of Sarv. They're pack hunters covered in chitinous armor. Four legs around a central core that has two arms. They traditionally use bronze weapons and overwhelming numbers to bring down prey. Since entering the tower, they've managed to acquire some healers and elementalists focusing on earth and air magic. Luckily, they haven't gotten the hang of any other spellcasting classes."

"I'm not sure we should just be diving right into combat," Kat replied with a frown. "I understand what the new gear does in principle, but I'd prefer to experiment under controlled conditions a bit longer before I actually use it in the field. I'd hate to have an enchantment give out on me at the last second or for me to miss a throw with a knife because the new ones have a slightly different balance."

She shifted uncomfortably, acutely aware that both of her teammates were looking right at her. "I mean, it's one thing to know that my armor uses my mana to decrease damage dealt to me as well as air resistance. I can intellectually understand that the sheaths in my bandoleer automatically coat anything put in them with a paralytic poison, but that doesn't mean I know how to integrate all of that into a fight."

Kat sighed, closing her eyes for a second to compose herself. "Ok," she continued. "My combat knife, for example. It's enchanted to be sharper than normal and to leave a minor curse behind in any wounds in order to fight magical healing and coagulation. If I stop and stare an enemy down, I can figure out how to use those abilities effectively, but no one in their right mind will hold still long enough for me to think everything through."

"Just stab them," Kaleek suggested with a shrug. "Once we get past level twelve and have to upgrade our gear again, then we'll start using more unique abilities. At that point, we will need to find someplace secluded to figure out attack patterns. Until then? Pretty much everything you're equipped with is just an enhanced version of itself. Your armor is better at protecting you and your knife slashes things better. Just fight how you normally do and you'll figure out the little details as you go."

"But how much damage can my armor take?" she asked, frustration in her voice. "How much force do I need to put behind a knife strike now that it's sharper? There's a careful balance to these things, and I could overextend myself if I put too much force into a blow."

"It'll be fine, Kat." Kaleek tossed a wink her way. "Now that we have actual armor, we won't die from an unlucky blow. Even if there are some growing pains, we'll be alright."

Dorrik nodded gravely, their crest fluttering slightly.

"Ordinarily," they shrugged, "I'd agree with Miss Kat. Unfortunately, her reports about the power struggle on her homeworld has me worried. If the stallesp are willing to risk breaking the embargo for a probationary race, even if only by proxy, Miss Kat will need all of the help she can get."

Kat opened her mouth to respond and stopped. Her mind flashed over the events of the last month or so.

"Crap." She sighed, running her fingers through her hair. "You're right. For someone that should be spending her time in school, I've been sneaking and fighting for my life a whole lot more than I should be. A couple more dungeon awards would probably help."

She winced, the image of the two mechanics from St. Louis seared into her memory. Kat was growing stronger in order to survive, but she needed to make sure that the process didn't change her. Fighting people that wanted to hurt her and hers was all well and good, but at the same time, Kat didn't want to end up as what she hated. Powerful, but callous to the impact of her actions.

"Then let's get going." Kaleek grinned, walking toward the courtyard's exit. "Once you hit level six, you'll get the opportunity to evolve one of your skills to the next tier. You might not be able to take over your world or anything like that, but with an iron tier elemental skill, you should be able to keep yourself safe."

"So level six is the goal." Kat nodded slowly, digesting the otter's words as she followed him and Dorrik out of the compound. "That seems surprisingly achievable."

"The goal has always been level 144." Dorrik handed her a pair of waterskins from their pack before passing a trio of the containers to Kaleek. "Every step along the way is another chance to grow stronger. Level six grants access to iron tier skills, but classes evolve at level twelve. Then at level eighteen, you can begin earning silver tier skills, with another class evolution at level twenty-four. The process follows the same pattern until master-tiered skills become available at level sixty-eight, followed by your terminal class becoming available at seventy-two."

"Wow," Kat stopped, blinking against the faux sun of the tower for a moment when she stepped out of the compound before lowering her veil over her face. "I don't think any humans have even made it to level twenty. What happens after level seventy-two, though? Do you just collect dungeon awards until the end of time?"

"None of the warriors at that level talk about it much," Dorrik responded, frustrated. "Some have given hints, but most scholars consider them to be disinformation, intended to throw off their rivals. Given that each avatar over level seventy-two is more or less a strategic asset for the faction they're aligned with, I cannot discount that possibility."

"Either that," Kaleek grinned at her, "or the scientists were too scared to ask details of an entity that could rip a moon apart with magic."

"Eidrass only did that once, and it was to prove a point," Dorrik snapped. "It ended the Gliese trade dispute before it had any real chance to get started."

"Plus," Dorrik muttered defensively, "the moon was smaller and in a decaying orbit anyway. It was either magic or use a battlecruiser to tow it into a nearby star."

They walked outside the city walls in silence, the bleached white cobblestones giving way to burning and shifting sand as Kat ruminated over her companions' exchange.

"So," Kat ignored Dorrik testily crossing their lower arms as she spoke up. "A moon? Like, a big ball of rock in orbit?"

"Yep." Kaleek's reply was smug. "Eidrass Ahn. Dorrik doesn't like to brag about it, he's their grandfather. He's one of the two dozen lokkel rankers, a huge name in Consensus politics, and a large part of why the other races treat the lokkel with respect."

"You're right," Dorrik grumbled, "I'd prefer to not talk about Eidrass. Everyone either compares me to him or acts like he dotes on me and that's why I've achieved so much. The fact of the matter is, I've never met the man. Once he made it past level seventy-two, he received many breeding offers from established triads. He may be my grandfather, but almost a quarter of Clan Ahn young can say the same."

"Fine." Kat's smile was hidden behind her veil, but she was sure the other two could hear it. "We'll stop teasing you about it."

"Speak for yourself," Kaleek grumbled, only for Kat to soak him with a spray from Water Jet, almost tipping the heavily armored desoph face first into the sand.

"What in the name of the elders was that!" he sputtered, glaring at Kat in indignation. She only grinned in reply and kept walking.

About a half an hour later, the three of them had lapsed into wary silence as they kept watch for desert predators. Under her veil, sweat was streaming down Kat's face as they crested another dune only for Dorrik to raise a hand, halting their party.

As soon as Kat's perception wasn't focused on the sound of her feet shuffling against the sand, she heard it as well. The clash of metal combined with distant shouting that could only mean a battle.

The three of them shared a glance. Kaleek and Kat nodded at the unspoken question, and a moment later they were skidding down the dune, running toward the echoing noises of combat.

Two dunes later, Kat's breath was coming in short gasps and sweat was pouring down her face, but their quarry was in sight. A human man and woman stood back to back in the valley between the great mounds of sand, struggling against six opponents. Namely, a trio of humans and a trio of stallesp.

Before she could say anything, a blast of fire from one of the stallesp caught the male defender in the leg, dropping him to the sand with a scream.

"*Ego Shard*!" Dorrik's shout was a starting pistol, sending Kat scrambling down the sandy embankment as the pink bolt of energy hit one of the three humans.

The man froze, stunned as the psi energy clouded his mind long enough for one of Kat's thrown daggers to catch him in the stomach. Her fears about the new weapons' balance proved unfounded as the blade sank in up to its hilt, pumping paralytic venom into him. A moment later, she finished casting Dehydrate and unleashed the spell.

He collapsed, the trio of sudden attacks overwhelming his avatar.

A soldier standing next to him shouted something, causing one of the stallesp to point at Dorrik. The lokkel was glowing with crackling purple energy as they ran into the fray, their already bulging muscles enhanced further by the psi skill.

The five remaining assailants began to run away, one of the stallesp stopping long enough to summon a wall of flames to stop direct pursuit. Kat didn't even bother. She might have the speed to catch up to the attackers, but without Dorrik and Kaleek's support, she suspected that chasing them down wouldn't be the best idea that she'd had.

Instead she ran over to the injured man, casting Cure Wounds I in between her ragged breaths. Already, his blood was beginning to stain the sand, and if she didn't hurry, Kat ran the risk of shock setting in.

Crouching down next to him, she pressed her golden glowing hands to the wound, drawing a hiss of pain from her patient. His body stiffened, only to relax as the healing energy flowed into him.

"Oh, thank God," the woman standing next to her babbled,

her excited words a bit hard to make out through a thick English accent. "Is he going to be all right?"

"Probably," Kat grunted back. "My skill is pretty low level, but I've managed to stop the bleeding status effect, so the tower should let him wake himself up."

"Good." The woman ran a hand through her hair. "I don't think I could pay Rick Moreno back for this without Dave's help."

"Rick?" Dorrik asked, frowning as they took in the disturbed sand of the battle sight.

"The fucker said he found a dungeon that he wanted to tackle with six people." The survivor spat on the ground. "I figured that since we were both with VodCom that there was no way he'd try anything funny, but as soon as we got out here, three of those mole things jumped out of the side of a sand dune and everyone attacked us."

Kat looked up from the injured man. Her mana was beginning to run low, but he was breathing easily. "VodCom?" she asked. "Out of Britannia? If you both worked for the same company, why would he ambush you?"

"Yeah," the woman nodded, "Britannia. As for why he did it? I don't know. Maybe for our marks? Maybe because his boss and mine are in the middle of a turf war. Whatever it was," she muttered grimly, "I'm killing the wanker as soon as he respawns tomorrow. I don't rightly care if it gets me kicked out of the city."

The woman paused for a second, closing her eyes and shaking like a leaf as she tried to process her anger and betrayal.

"Don't mind me," she continued with a weak smile. "I'm grateful that you saved Blake. I'll remember it if the three of you are ever in a spot of trouble, but for now, I think the two of us should make ourselves scarce and wake up. I don't mean to insult my saviors and all, but I'm about out of trust at the moment, and the three of you look like you could turn our team into diced meat on our best days."

She stepped past Kat, slipping the mostly healed man's arm over her shoulder. He nodded gratefully to her before leaning on his companion. Together, the two of them limped away, occasionally casting furtive looks at the three of them.

Silence reigned in the sandy valley. Dorrik glanced back and forth between Kat and Kaleek, a worried expression on their face.

"As soon as Miss Kat's mana has returned," they began, their voice downcast, "we should hurry to our next dungeon. It looks like our fears about the stallesp remaining active and involved in human politics have been realized. We will need to let the rest of the clan know first thing tomorrow."

Kat could only nod unhappily.

CHAPTER TWENTY

Congratulations, Adventurer!
You have completed the Wood Tier Level Three Dungeon, Ice Sands.
Three of three party members surviving. Good job!
Assigning awards:

+1 Mind

Kat dismissed the award. The dungeon hadn't been easy, but with Dorrik's guidance, they'd moved through it cautiously and safely. The insect-like enemies were smarter than the usual foes provided by the tower, laying ambushes and protecting spellcasters, but ultimately their primitive weapons weren't a match for the well-crafted lokkel equipment.

Even if she had been using her original equipment, Kat's armor would have turned away many of the strikes from the bronze scimitars favored by the sarvash. So long as the three of them avoided the traps set by the sarvash, she could have danced circles around the angry, skittering monsters. Given their opponents' limited ranged options, Kat could pepper the insectoid warriors with spells that slowed and hindered while Dorrik eliminated their spellcasters and Kaleek finished their weakened foes off.

With their new equipment, it was barely even a challenge. Her knife almost cut straight through the sarvash blades, and the one time she was surprised and shot by a hidden archer, it only shaved off one hit point and two points of mana. The blow barely even staggered her, and she simply returned the favor by planting a poisoned throwing dagger into the surprised warrior's throat before it could react.

The encounter reinforced her concerns about owing Clan Ahn. The cost and difficulty of gathering the components for the armor were one thing, but actually seeing it in action just drove the point home: whether Clan Ahn was too polite to bring it up or not, she owed them, and she owed them a lot. A feeling she was less than comfortable with.

"Did you see me take down that tribal patriarch?" Kaleek was grinning ear to ear despite the beating light and heat of the tower's pseudo-sun. "He tried to tag me with his venom spikes, but I just dodged one and cut the other off. Then Kat blasted him to keep him off balance, and I cut off enough of his legs that the stupid thing couldn't stand anymore."

"Now that," he slapped her on the shoulder cheerfully, "was a good fight. A little bit of challenge, but mostly a chance for us to hone our craft in a proper combat setting. See, Kat? The new equipment worked perfectly. Nothing to worry about."

"It was a bit more fun than expected." Kat shook off her worry to smile back at the exuberant otter.

"Be prepared for another dungeon tomorrow." Dorrik walked up to the two of them, one of their upper claws shielding their eyes against the fake light. "I've spent some time researching our available options, and I think I have pinpointed our final candidate. One more dungeon and, so long as we're careful, we should be on the fourth floor in a couple of days."

"Good." Kaleek stretched, his sleek fur rustling in the desert wind. "I'm sick of this dry heat. The sooner we can get to someplace with proper oceans and other desoph, the happier I'll be."

"What does the final dungeon look like?" Kat asked, rolling her eyes at Kaleek. "I thought we were running low on dungeons that our team was optimized for?"

"We are far from optimized for it," Dorrik replied ruefully. "It is an acidic swamp full of blood-sucking quasi-amphibians that lurk in the water. The good news is that there is almost never a wait to gain admittance, and with the use of proper consumables such as oils of acid resistance and powders of clotting, the actual dungeon will be fairly easy. The bad news is that raids on it are invariably disgusting and miserable."

"Sounds like fun." Kaleek chuckled. "As long as it will get us to the fourth floor quickly, I'll manage."

Dorrik inclined their head toward Kat, as if asking a question.

"I'm in." She flashed him a quick smile. "As awful as this sounds, I just wanted to thank both of you for accelerating our climb like this. I know that Dorrik especially wanted to spend a couple more weeks on the third floor, and that without you I'd be stuck here for months, if not years, trying to figure out my own way up."

She shifted, trying to find the words to explain herself. It wasn't often that Kat was at a loss, but on the other hand, it wasn't often that she opened up to people. Emotional vulnerability on Earth was just one more weakness to be exploited, but here in the tower amongst her friends…

"We understand." Dorrik reached out and gripped her forearm, a pleasant smile on their muzzle. "You have helped Kaleek and I a great deal, it would only be right to return the favor. And even if it weren't, you are a friend, Miss Kat. That alone is enough reason to help."

"Even if you are pink and weird." Kaleek nodded, a mischievous grin still on his face. "I'm always happy to lend a hand."

"Thanks." Kat's chest felt tight, as she struggled to process the moment. "I mean it."

"We do too." Dorrik gave her arm a squeeze. "Now it's probably time for us to wake up so we can reconvene tomorrow. After all, I have a date with a feral canopy skulker before I can return to the dreamscape."

"Lucky you." Kaleek winked. "I only have a date with two females. Nothing so fun as a life and death sword fight, but by the elders, you should see the way their fur glistens in the sun."

He leaned close to Kat, eyes gleaming conspiratorially before he whispered, "They're sisters."

Kat smiled back weakly. "It must be different among the desoph, but that would be pretty dang weird on Earth. Anything involving siblings is taboo, kind of like humanity's issues with nudity."

"Oh no." Dorrik shook their head. "It's still plenty strange among the desoph."

They began to fade, a smile still on their muzzle as Dorrik willed themselves out of the dreamscape and into wakefulness.

"They're just jealous because they haven't reached sexual maturity yet." Kaleek winked at her. "Don't worry, if we get you some emergency hair growth formula to cover all of that pink stuff, I'm sure I could find you a pair of strapping desoph brothers. Just say the word."

Kat stared at the otter blankly as he faded as well. Finally alone, she shook her head, chuckling quietly to herself. She cast one last lingering glance around the empty desert before closing her eyes and willing herself awake.

The sound of some bustle in the hallway roused Kat from her comfortable bed. She pushed down the genuine goose feather comforter before standing up. Although technically her dorm room was a single room or 'efficiency,' that room was easily bigger than the entire living room and kitchenette of the two bedroom apartment she'd lived in with her mother and sister.

She ignored the sound of a woman's voice shouting in the

hallway as one of her classmates began arguing with someone, instead making her way to the small bathroom attached to her room. The water from her faucet drowned out the raised voices as Kat washed her face before brushing her teeth and hair.

After dressing herself in a nondescript GroCorp button-down shirt and pair of slacks, Kat stepped out into the hallway. Iris, the daughter of a senior executive, was red in the face, her long brunette hair streaming behind her as she screamed at her maid. Each angry word was punctuated by her shaking a blue ribbon clutched in her perfectly manicured hand just beneath the terrified servant's nose.

"I asked for a *cerulean* bow, Jane!" Kat hurried past her irate classmate. "This is *cobalt*! Cerulean brings out my eyes, but cobalt mutes them. *Do you want me to be muted, Jane*?!"

Kat winced, silencing the snarky voice deep inside her that wanted to blurt out 'yes please.' Luckily, she managed to work her way to the end of the hallway without any further trouble where she found Emma waiting, probably for her.

"Kat!" The other woman bounced down the hallway, grasping both of Kat's hands in her own.

She flinched. Everything inside of her demanded that she pull her hands back, to clear enough space between her and the person approaching her so that Kat could draw her knife or cast a spell.

Intellectually, she knew that her knife was tucked safely under her pillow, and that Emma was the furthest thing from a threat to her physical safety, but at the same time, her hands shook as she forcibly suppressed her reflexes.

Kat licked her lips nervously before smiling weakly at the other girl. She wouldn't let St. Louis happen again. She couldn't lose herself to the constant violence that was beginning to consume her life. There were other ways to deal with things than a bared blade.

"Are you ready for your presentation on human resources?" Emma didn't seem to notice her hesitance, but then again, the bubbly girl never did.

"I think so." Kat barely managed to face calm as her voice cracked. "Some of the performance metrics still confuse me, but I think I've managed to figure out most of the standard methods of task flow optimization."

"That's great," Emma gushed, releasing Kat's hands and walking toward the elevator with her. "I'm sure you'll do great, Kat. You were already so smart, but then you go and study all the time."

"That's because I don't have any friends." She quirked a half-smile at Emma. "Other than you, nobody really bothers to spend any time with me."

"But that's not true." Emma cocked her head, giggling. "Jasper Haupt is friends with you too. Pretty much every time you go home for the weekend, he shows up in the girls wing asking about you. He looks like a kicked puppy when I tell him you aren't around."

She leaned closer to Kat, a twinkle in her eye and a hand on her upper arm. Kat's skin crawled, uncomfortable with the other girl's proximity.

"I think he likes you," Emma whispered. "He's awfully cute."

"Maybe." Kat's memory immediately flashed back to Davis' watchful glare every time that they met. "But I've recently had a fairly bad experience with boys. I think it might be best that I remain single for a while in order to center myself emotionally."

"You go girl." Emma nodded firmly. "I did the same thing for two weeks after I caught my last boyfriend hooking up with that snake Brianna Ray. There's something empowering about—"

"Wait." Her eyes widened. "Is this bad experience you're talking about Arnold Jacques?"

Kat grimaced at hearing his name, nodding slowly. The boy had been a petty, self-centered asshole, but at the end of the day, he hadn't deserved what had happened to him. She still felt occasional pangs of guilt over her role in the asshole's demise, but those usually faded when she remembered that he'd sent thugs after Michelle.

"*OhmyGod*," Emma squealed. "Your last boyfriend killed your current boyfriend's parents? This is like the second arc of Chrome Cowboys where Jenny—"

"I don't have a boyfriend," Kat responded firmly. "And I've never had one. It was just bad luck with the men in my life that's making me cautious now. Nothing more."

"What's this about a boyfriend?" Jasper's smooth voice interrupted from behind them, drawing a wince from Kat. "I didn't know you were dating anyone?"

Emma squealed again. Kat swore she could almost make out the wisps of steam escaping the other girl as she emulated a tea kettle.

"I'm not." She turned back to look at Jasper, a slightly forced smile on her face. Behind him, Davis was his usual self. Glowering at her as he watched her every move.

"I was wondering what you're doing after your test in Management Methods and Practice?" Everything about him was casual. Like there couldn't be anything more natural than what he was doing at any given moment, as if the world needed to adapt to him, rather than the other way around.

"Nothing too much," Kat answered slowly. "I don't have any afternoon classes, so I was going to get started on my advanced biology coursework, but I don't suppose that's something that *needs* to happen today."

"Great!" Jasper clapped his hands together before taking a step back. "It's decided. The Worker's Liberation Vanguard is meeting today, and I'd love to introduce you to them. I'll have someone pick you up after the exam."

Kat did her best to ignore Emma as the girl practically vibrated with excitement next to her. Almost worse than the idea of spending an afternoon with a room full of wealthy strangers convinced that they were 'helping her' was the prospect of answering Emma's barrage of questions afterward.

"This doesn't have anything to do with you trying to drag a guess out of me on the—" she began, locking eyes with Jasper.

"No." He returned her gaze with a confident smile. "You said that you weren't comfortable, and that's good enough for me. I'm sure that given enough time, you'll change your mind, but for now there are no ulterior motives. I just want to introduce you to a group of like-minded people."

"Fine," Kat replied, partially against her will. "I'll meet up with you after the exam, but for now I need to get going. Management Methods and Practices is the course that I'm the least confident in, and showing up late and harried to my first major test is hardly how I want to establish myself."

"Of course." Jasper gave her a dazzling smile of perfect, almost certainly augmented, straight white teeth. "You'll knock it out of the park, Kat. I believe in you."

She smiled back weakly as Jasper and Davis walked away. As soon as they were out of sight, both of Emma's hands gripped hers.

"Seeeeeee," the other girl drew the word out knowingly. "I think he liiiiikes you."

"That'll be tough for him, then." Kat rolled her eyes as she began walking toward her Management classroom. "Come on, we're both going to be late if you keep mooning over my nonexistent love life."

The exam itself went fairly quickly. Kat was absolutely sure of her multiple choice answers, but some of the essay questions left a fair amount up for interpretation. All of it covered material she was confident in, but she knew better than to count on a specific grade when subjective standards were going to be applied to her answer.

Emma was still working on her answers, clearly struggling, when Kat stepped out of the classroom. Pairs and trios of her fellow students milled about outside, anxiously discussing their answers with each other or panicking over questions that they had missed.

A man with straight blond hair in his mid-twenties, wearing a conservative suit, and a pleasant smile approached her.

"Katherine Debs?" he asked, inclining his head slightly.

"Yes?" she responded, stepping out of the classroom's doorway to let a hurriedly whispering man and woman pass.

"Mister Haupt sent me to fetch you for the Worker's Vanguard meeting." He leaned to the side to let a woman, tears streaming down her face, sprint out of the classroom toward the nearby bathroom. Without remarking on the disturbance, he continued speaking smoothly. "The meeting place is offsite and in a restricted area. You won't be able to reach it with an automated taxi, so Mister Haupt thought it best that I drive you there."

"By all means lead the way, Mister...?" She waved him onward with her right hand, quirking an eyebrow at the last second as she inquired about his name.

"Andrew is fine, Miss Debs," he replied without missing a beat. "Now if you'll follow me, the car is waiting."

Several more attempts to talk with Andrew on the way down to the ground floor of the college were courteously rebuffed. By the time they got into the sleek car, Kat was pretty sure that the polite young man knew nothing and had no opinions on any subject. Likely a useful skill when dealing with the opinionated scions of wealth that made up most of the college.

The drive itself was surprisingly sedate. Chiwaukee traffic was, as per usual, about as calm as lit fireworks in a running dryer. Andrew just handled it with a deftness and grace that Kat found surprising. Honestly, by the fifth time he smoothly merged the car into an opening in traffic that was only a hair's breadth bigger than the vehicle itself, Kat was beginning to suspect that he was a player. His agility and reactions were just inhuman.

About twenty minutes later, they were pulling through a gate in front of a mansion on the outskirts of the megalopolis. A pair of guards, armed with assault rifles with grenade launchers mounted beneath the barrels, waved them through after Andrew flashed his lanyard.

He parked the car smoothly, and before Kat could open the door on her own, Andrew was there, ushering her out with a smile.

She frowned at the building. It towered above her, at least four stories, supported by massive stone pillars encased in ivy. It had none of the placards or logos that would mark it as a GroCorp property.

"Is this," she began hesitantly, "a private residence?"

"The Leander Estate," Andrew replied. "Now if you would follow me, Miss Debs, I'll guide you to the door where one of the Leander servants can take over and lead you to wherever the Worker's Vanguard is meeting."

"But isn't the Worker's Vanguard a club associated with the college?" she asked, confused. "When you said that we would be meeting off campus, I thought they might be meeting some-place secretive to avoid monitoring, but this doesn't even make sense. A mansion this size surely has operatives and informants crawling through it. There's no way that whatever is happening in there is actually being concealed from corporate intelligence."

"Davis said you were a smart one." Andrew broke character for a brief second, flashing her a roguish grin before his previous expression of placid neutrality returned. "But I'm sure I have no idea what you're talking about, Miss Debs."

He stepped away from the vehicle, and with a sigh, she followed him to the mansion's massive doors.

CHAPTER TWENTY-ONE

A woman in a demure dress led her through a wood-paneled hallway toward the parlor where the Worker's Liberation Vanguard was meeting. Lining the passage were paintings, oil on canvas, most of which predated GroCorp's founding by at least fifty years. Kat did her best not to think about how much more each and every piece of art she was walking past was worth than the entirety of her family's possessions.

Finally, the servant opened a mahogany door inlaid with hundreds of gilt flowers. Inside, heavy velvet and cloth curtains obscured the walls, muffling the sounds of a woman speaking. Kat's eyes immediately fixated on the soft wall coverings, estimating the dozen places she could easily hide a recording device from the room full of amateurs.

A number of faces turned to look at Kat the moment the door opened. She recognized all of them from school. The main area of the parlor seated about two dozen young men and women in overstuffed chairs or regal leather couches. To the left, just out of sight, there was some sort of raised platform, obscured by the gaudy drapes hanging about the cavernous room.

The speaker's voice stuttered to a halt.

The students stared at her with confusion on their faces as they unabashedly looked her up and down. A couple seemed to recognize her, squinting as they tried to place where they knew Kat from, but the rest simply stared blankly. She shifted uncomfortably, looking for Jasper amongst their number.

The angry click of high heels on hardwood drew her attention away from the milling crowd. A woman in a blue dress, a matching blue ribbon tying her hair into a ponytail, stalked toward Kat and the servant, her face a rumbling storm cloud of rage.

"Annabelle," she hissed at the woman standing next to Kat. Out of the corner of her eye, Kat watched the maid begin to shake. "Would you care to tell me why you interrupted my speech with a newcomer? I believe I specifically said *no* interruptions and *no* visitors. Especially people I don't know."

"Iris?" Kat cocked her head, finally placing the woman and the blue ribbon. "Iris Leander? I'm Kat Debs. I live across the hall from you at college."

She cocked her head, glaring at Kat, clearly upset by her interruption, but before she could say anything, Jasper hurried across the parlor floor, a huge smile on his face.

"Kat!" He stepped past Iris and reached out to grab her shoulder.

Once again, she found herself fighting the urge to pull back from his sudden movement.

"This is who I was talking about, Iris!" He pulled her away from the entrance, leaving Iris next to the servant that was wilting with relief. "Kat was born an employee but managed to work her way into the company college. She's sure to bring a unique perspective to our organization!"

Now that Kat was in the parlor, she could see the raised dais where Iris had been speaking. There were three chairs on either side of a podium, half of them occupied.

"Jasper." Iris' voice was low, dangerous. "Can we talk for a minute about this before you bring an unvetted newcomer into our midst? For all we know, she's an informant for GroCorp and she'll be reporting back to the authorities as soon as she leaves this meeting."

"She's right," a man sitting on the dais called out. "Allowing someone to attend one of our meetings requires a vote of the Executive Council. Even then, that vote is only supposed to happen after the candidate has been vetted and received a recommendation from the Membership Committee, with over-sight and consultation from the Security Committee and the Revolutionary Aims and Ethics Committee."

"Well, I'm the Co-chair of the Executive Council and the Chair of the Security Committee," Jasper responded, letting go of Kat's shoulder long enough to cross his arms. "I had Davis investigate her. He literally laughed at me when I asked if she had connections to GroCorp. Kat's safe, and she's our only real connection to the workers we're trying to connect with."

"As the Chair of the Direct Action Committee," a woman on the dais stood up and addressed Jasper, "I must disagree with your statement. After several months, our anonymous e-mail campaign has started receiving replies from employees. Right now, we suspect that half of them are genuine workers with the rest being corporate disinformation. We're only a month or so of screening those contacts from opening a genuine and mean-ingful discourse with members of the working class."

Kat felt the eyes of the entire parlor burning in between her shoulders. Behind her, the rest of the chamber began whis-pering excitedly.

"I can leave if this is a problem?" Kat asked hopefully. She was only at the meeting because Jasper had forced the issue. She'd gladly use an internal dispute as an excuse to duck out of the proceedings.

"It isn't a problem." Jasper glared at the two speakers on the dais. "Kat isn't a security risk, and she can meaningfully contribute to the meeting. I say that she stays."

"You can't just make a decision like this unilaterally." Iris walked up to the two of them, the staccato click of her high heels marking each step of her approach. "Both Jason and Amanda haven't been in school for the last week, and when I e-mailed them, I got an auto-reply saying that they were busy. The company is watching us, Jasper. We can't be too careful right now."

Kat put both of her hands up. "Wait, are you saying that people have been disappearing? I literally don't know what you guys do here. Jasper just said that I should show up and I didn't want to be impolite, but if the company is actually moving against you guys, I don't want to have any part in it."

"We don't know that the corporation is targeting us," Jasper said stubbornly, glaring at Iris. "Everything we are doing is above-board. There's no reason we can't talk to workers and discuss their grievances with management. It's all perfectly legal within the GroCorp bylaws."

"Fine," Iris spat out. "Let's have a vote. Everyone on the Executive Council in favor of suspending rules and admitting Jasper's friend as an observer, say 'aye.'"

"Aye," Jasper and two of the people on the dais, including the man that had initially backed Iris' complaint, said simultaneously.

The woman glared at the man that had voiced support of her earlier.

"Sorry." He shrugged, no real apology on his face. "Jasper has a point. The new girl doesn't seem to be some sort of super spy, and if Davis cleared her, it means she's clean as a whistle. We all know that Davis has been as keen as a hawk since…"

He trailed off awkwardly, glancing at Jasper. To the Haupt boy's credit, he managed to keep his face calm as his peers spoke rather casually about his father's death.

"Then seat the girl so we can get back to our regularly scheduled business." Iris clattered past them, climbing the dais and resuming her position at the podium. The minute her hands rested on either side of the wooden lectern, she glared meaningfully at Jasper and Kat.

Jasper flashed a rueful smile at her before motioning with

his hand toward the dais. Kat's throat bobbed as he walked past her, taking one of the two unoccupied seats. He leaned over and patted the armrest of the remaining chair.

She sighed and followed him, her skin crawling as dozens of students stared at her with expressions that ranged between curiosity and anger. Ascending the carpeted steps to the raised platform, Kat turned around and took her seat, eyes boring into her every movement.

They looked at her with the same curiosity she used when observing the effects of a newly unlocked gene or chemical supplement on a mouse. She recognized each and every one of them, having walked past them in the hallways of the college dozens of times without acknowledgement or comment. Now they tried to strip off her clothes and skin with their eyes, to dissect her, to break Kat down into her component parts and see what made her work.

She'd rather fight a floor guardian or a street samurai.

"Thank you." Iris' visible anger was gone, only tension in her shoulders hinting at her barely contained agitation as she smoothly addressed the parlor once again. "As I was saying before our unfortunate interruption, our outreach campaigns have been a smashing success. At the suggestion of the Worker Safety and Standards Committee, we've started contacting the managers of factories owned by GroCorp subsidiaries. A full ten percent of the individuals we've contacted have written back to say that they will take our demands 'under advisement' and thanked us for our concern."

The room erupted into polite clapping. Iris paused, letting the sound wash over her with an exultant grin on her face.

"Soon," she continued once the noise died down, "we will be ready to move on to phase two. The dropping of anonymous pamphlets regarding the unsafe conditions in GroCorp-owned factories and farms. Once the employees are made aware of the danger their jobs pose to them, we can begin mutually supporting each other against the profit-driven vultures that are wrecking our society."

Kat bit her lip to try staving off a frown. An occasional cheer punctuated the applause. A quick glance to Jasper revealed his rapt attention to Iris' speech.

Iris stepped to the side of the podium. "Without further ado, I would like to call Comrade Alicia Gartt, Chairperson of the Direct Action Committee, to speak on the preparations for phase two."

On the other side of the dais, the woman that had previously spoken out in support of Iris stood up and approached the podium.

"Thank you, Co-chair Leander." Alicia placed a hand on either side of the lectern as she began her speech. "I would like to point out that the Exploratory Committee on Class Consciousness has openings if anyone in general membership would like to apply, but I would like to motion for a commendation to the Committee for the great work they've been doing understaffed."

"Seconded," Iris called out from her seat a fraction of a second later.

"By unanimous consent?" Kat almost jumped when Jasper responded within moments of Iris, his voice practiced as he repeated the formulaic words.

A chorus of ayes came from the crowd, followed a moment later by silence.

"Hearing no dissent, the motion is passed. You may continue, Alicia." Jasper nodded to the woman.

"Thank you Jasper, Iris," Alicia said pleasantly, inclining her head once to each of them. "As I was saying, the Exploratory Committee on Class Consciousness has been trying to brainstorm ideas on connecting with employees. Some of their most productive work has been a collaboration with the Committee on Outreach and Communication. Next meeting, they will be circulating a memo detailing their proposal for educating the working class as to the manifest unfairness of their pay and working conditions. I am hopeful that we can move into breakout groups at that time and workshop possible topics for the anonymous pamphlets that we will be distributing to the employees."

Kat dug her nails into her hands as the crowd clapped again. She was used to two-faced corporate speak, but it almost seemed like these people believed what they were saying. Somehow, they honestly believed that hereditary employees were simply content to work in miserable and dangerous conditions for literally negative pay because they 'didn't know any better.'

"We also have a preliminary design for the posters mentioned at the last meeting," Alicia continued. "Proofs have been circulated, but we are hopeful that people will respond to our 'fifty-hour work week now' campaign. Iris and Jasper have put a general membership vote on the calendar for next week's meeting, so if all of you could look over the proposal, with any luck we will be able to put the posters into production as early as the first of next month."

She paused, allowing another round of polite but meaningless applause wash over her as Kat stared on incredulously.

"Thank you." Alicia nodded to the students sitting in the parlor, the back of her outfit shifting and bunching with the motion. "With that, I yield the floor to Co-chair Haupt of the Security Committee."

Jasper stood up and approached the podium, leaving Kat on her own as Alicia returned to her seat. He put his hands on either side of the stand, leaning forward slightly until he looked like a bird of prey, hunched and ready to strike.

"Thank you, Co-Chair Leander and Committee Chair Gartt," he began pleasantly. "As I'm sure you're all aware, there have been concerns with disappearances from our organization. The Security Committee took the possibility of a breach seriously, and we've investigated the situation. So far, we've found nothing to indicate that either of the missing individuals have actually been picked up by GroCorp or any of its subsidiaries. It is very possible that both individuals' parents found out about their membership in this organization and are punishing them accordingly, a risk that we all were aware of when we agreed to join the Worker's Liberation Vanguard."

A quiet murmuring filled the parlor.

"What the Security Committee has discovered," Jasper continued, "is that the disappearances aren't isolated to members of the Vanguard. It looks like some major actors, perhaps even shareholders, are in the midst of a power play far above our level. It's very possible that we are in the middle of a purge."

The whispers erupted into a furor. One or two of the students even sprang up from their seats, arms pumping excitedly.

Jasper shrugged. "Unfortunately, if there's a purge, there isn't much we can do but hunker down and try to figure out the causes. With any luck, the factions our various families are affiliated with will come out victorious."

"In the meantime," he turned back to Kat with a grin that made her blood turn cold, "I propose we have Miss Katherine Debs take the floor for a question and answer session. It isn't often that we have a bona fide employee here, and I'm sure all of you have plenty of questions about the working and living conditions that our fellow men and women labor under."

The polite applause hammered into Kat like a hailstorm as Jasper stepped to the side, offering the podium to her.

She stood up, trying to force her gritted teeth into something that could be mistaken for a smile. Jasper patted her on the back in a 'comforting' fashion on his way back to his chair. The entire time Kat ascended the single step to the raised lectern, she imagined the dozen ways she could murder the man before security could intervene.

"Hello, I guess?" Kat spoke hesitantly, microphones in the stand in front of her picking up her words and projecting them about the parlor.

The crowd stared at her expectantly, hungrily. Finally, one of them raised a hand.

The next half hour was an absolute blur. After a couple of

minutes, she wasn't even sure who was speaking. Each question was a delicate balance of casual condescension toward the workers that the group claimed to support combined with elements that demonstrated how phenomenally out of touch the speaker was.

Eventually, the session ended and Iris called an end to the meeting. At that point, snacks and drinks were served, but Kat made a polite exit, exhausted after her ordeal.

As she was walking out to the car that Andrew had waiting, her e-mail pinged. A flick of her eyes later, Kat was frowning as an e-mail from Xander scrolled across her smartpanel.

She sat herself down in the car's heated leather seat and fastened the seatbelt. Andrew opened the front door of the vehicle and buckled himself in before turning the ignition. He twisted his body around the driver's seat and looked back at her.

"Back to the dorms, Miss Debs?" he asked politely.

Kat blinked, dismissing the e-mail. "Actually, can you take me to the 1000 block of Galt Avenue? There's something I need to do first."

"This time of day that means the Nozick Tollway," Andrew mused out loud, "but I have a GroCorp EZ Pass installed in this vehicle. Barring some sort of accident, I can have you there in fifteen minutes."

"Thanks," Kat replied, the car's acceleration already pushing her back into the cushion of the seat.

CHAPTER TWENTY-TWO

"I wasn't followed here," Kat responded, slowly. "I had my driver drop me off one street up and two streets down, and I made sure that he left before I started moving. The only way the Haupts would know where I am is if they tracked me via satellite, and even then I made sure to cut through a couple of stores to try to lose any sort of overhead observation."

"Fine," Xander muttered. "You're probably clean."

He paced back and forth, a nervous, almost manic energy animating his quick, jerky movements as he wore a hole in the safehouse's cheap carpet. Off to the side, Whippoorwill was perched on top of a pile of duffle bags filled with their gear, eyes flickering as she played some game on an entertainment channel.

"I know you're not comfortable with wet work, Kat." Xander stopped walking, reaching his hand into the breast pocket of his dress shirt only to frown. "Damn, I quit smoking years ago, but it still gets me sometimes."

"What's wet work?" Whippoorwill asked, still leaning back on the pile of equipment, eyes unfocused as she fiddled with her smartpanel.

"An infiltration job where the goal is a human asset," Kat replied carefully, gaze never leaving Xander. "Sometimes it's assassination, sometimes it's a kidnapping, sometimes it's torture, but it's almost always messy."

Whippoorwill sat up straight, blinking away whatever she was doing on the small computer as a look of concern blossomed on her face.

"We just need information." Xander sighed, running a hand through his hair. "Belle doesn't think that Williamson will trust it to a computer, and I'm inclined to agree. We're going to extract and interrogate someone important. Pull out their secrets the old-fashioned way."

He smiled weakly. "You know, along with their fingernails."

"Gross." Kat frowned at him. "At least tell me that we aren't going after someone I know and like. A job is a job, but there are some lines I'm not willing to cross."

"It's Tom Franklin." Xander's hand reached for his breast pocket again, only to stop halfway there. He patted his chest nervously.

"The dean?" Kat asked incredulously. "But we just hit him. I think Whippoorwill covered my tracks, but if we do something drastic, they'll be looking over his security with a fine-toothed comb. This is exactly the sort of shit that gets infiltrators caught."

"It is in fact the sort of amateur mistake I drill you on avoiding," he replied, sighing.

"Then why in the chrome-plated hell would you be telling me to do it?" Kat threw her hands up in the air, frustration and stress straining her voice.

"Because we don't have another choice, Kat." Xander was quiet, all of the anxiety and his usual bluster drained out of him. "Things are getting really bad in Schaumburg. Like, people disappearing even when they aren't out past curfew bad. No one can go to work, so no one is making money, and Millennium is sweeping the entire arcology floor by floor. They're looking for someone and something, and they aren't afraid of stepping on toes to get it. Belle and a couple of the senior executives have called for a shareholder meeting and Williamson has called in every favor imaginable to get it delayed for a couple of months."

"The shareholder meeting is our only hope." He grimaced. "Schaumburg isn't turning a profit, and they're already starting to run low on food. God damn, do I need a smoke."

Kat frowned, worry for her mom and sister flashing through her. "If Ike Holdings isn't turning a profit, even a shareholder is going to catch hell for basically destroying a profitable subsidiary. I don't get it. As soon as the shareholder meeting happens, Williamson is going to get slagged. She might be able to delay it, but there's no way she can put off the meeting forever."

"The two problems with what you are saying is that it's completely true, and Elaine Williamson knows it better than you or I." Xander's hand reached for his breast pocket once more, shaking slightly. "God damn, I need a cigarette."

"What's her endgame then?" Whippoorwill chirped up. "If her visible moves look like suicide, that means that there's something else going on."

"And that," Xander pointed at Whippoorwill, "is why Belle wants Franklin and I want a cigarette. Something's going on, and we don't know what the hell it is."

"I'll admit," he continued grimly, "the situation has me spooked. Hell, I think even Belle's scared. There are certain things that an executive just doesn't do to another executive, and the last couple of weeks have seen almost every unspoken rule in the book get broken."

"It's that bad?" Kat asked.

Xander leaned back, running both of his hands through his hair. "Look, you're the only one that can pull this off, and I wouldn't be asking you if I didn't think it was necessary. Belle can burn for all I care, I'm just worried about your family and the crew in the Shell."

"When are we doing it?" she responded, resigned. Xander

was almost a father to her. Admittedly a parent with a fairly mercenary attitude toward money and repaying debts, but he was family nonetheless. If this were business, he'd be talking money. This was Steel and Blood all over again. It was survival.

"Are we changing the plan from last time, or are we just going to try to repeat the previous run?" Kat continued, crossing her arms.

Xander stepped forward, swiping one of his arms through the empty boxes of fried rice and delivered food, clearing the room's single ratty coffee table. He reached up, spinning his smartpanel around and pointing the projector at the now clear surface.

"Tomorrow night," he began, tapping his smartpanel to activate its high performance mode. A second later, a blue-and-white mockup of the college flickered into being on the chipped and stained table. "We're mostly following the plan from last time, but there will be some modifications, especially on your egress."

Xander's voice washed over her, and all of Kat's anxieties and concerns from the pointless meeting earlier in the day evaporated. As much as she tried to fit in at school and live a normal life, deep down, this was who she really was.

The woman that leaned over a battered coffee table as Xander projected a floor plan of the college—complete with the patrol routes observed in their previous run—was the real Kat. Her eyes were practically aglow as Whippoorwill leaned closer, pointing out an alternative route from the third to the fourth floor, one that would avoid all guard contact.

During the day, she had the time to fret and worry about what she was becoming, how the magic coursing through her from the tower was changing her, but here and now? It was just so easy to slip back into her days in the Shell. All of her focus locked in on the plan and how to tweak it to take advantage of her strengths.

In moments of self-reflection, Kat might kick and scream. She might insist that violence wasn't the only way to solve problems, but in moments like this, she had to admit to herself: after all of the false smiles while dealing with Jasper's idiotic friends and simpering like an obedient puppy before Belle Donnst, there was something satisfying about taking the straightforward approach. Hit fast, hard, and silent.

They broke up the meeting without fanfare, the plan firmly lodged in Kat's mind as she accepted a duffle bag with her gear in it. She walked a couple of blocks from the safe house, glares driving back locals covered in chrome inlaid with neon lights. Finally, once she was far enough away, Kat physically hailed a cab and paid cash, not wanting to leave an electronic record of her location.

Once she reached the dorms, Kat walked through the security screening, her equipment registering as little more than new clothes and cosmetics, and went straight to bed.

After the events of the day, she found herself in *The Tower of Somnus* almost the moment she closed her eyes.

"There she is." Kaleek clapped Kat on the back before she could even register the bustle of the marketplace around the city's spawn point.

"Dorrik was worried that you'd leave us hanging, that you'd forgotten the plan for the day." He winked at her before giving an overexaggerated shake of his head toward the massive lizard.

"He literally spent the last thirty minutes pacing back and forth." Dorrik shook their head, bemused. "I'm half surprised Kaleek didn't wear a rut in the cobblestones while we waited for you. I'm not sure I share all of his enthusiasm, but it's a much bigger day for him than me."

"What was the plan for today?" Kat asked innocently, struggling to keep a smile from creeping onto her face.

"*Oh, for the love of the ancients, she did forget!*" Kaleek threw his hands up in the air, shouting into the cathedral's rafters and drawing the attention of a dozen or so of the aliens surrounding them.

Kat's face broke for a second, half of a snicker slipping out of her mouth before she was able to resume her look of overly earnest confusion.

"Calm down." Dorrik fluttered their crest in amusement. "She's just trying to torment you."

Kaleek wheeled around, peering closely at Kat as he shoved his furry face in close, whiskers twitching. She just blinked at him without flinching as the otter invaded her personal space, feigning innocence.

She cracked.

"Sorry." Kat giggled as Kaleek opened and closed his mouth wordlessly. "The waking part of today was awful and I just couldn't stop myself."

"Come on, Dorrik!" The otter wheeled around toward their companion. They were starting to draw a bit of a crowd. "How come she gets to make fun of me! She's the newbie, I'm supposed to be the one hazing her."

Dorrik glanced around before letting out a long suffering sigh.

"The two of you children are making a scene." Dorrik shook their head. "Come on, Kaleek and I already grabbed all of the equipment. We should probably leave before every information broker in town knows exactly where we're going."

"Fair enough." Kat made a face. "I've had enough unwelcome truths for one day. Engaging in some extreme violence to release stress sounds pretty nice right now."

"Well said, Kat." Kaleek brightened immediately. "No sense dallying around here any longer. There are monsters and frustrations that need slaying!"

Dorrik simply chuffed in amusement and led the way out of the stone Adventurer's Hall and out into the desert where they would be challenging the floor guardian. As they walked over the shifting dunes, Kat went over what she knew about the monster they would be fighting.

The sand lurker was a fairly straightforward if formidable foe. Functionally, it was an eight-legged antlion, an armored ambush predator that would wait just outside the door to the fourth floor stairwell. It didn't have any real ranged attacks other than its ability to burrow.

If anyone tried to hang back and pepper it with spells, the monster would simply dive beneath the sand and wait for its enemies to either leave or draw closer. Given that a party couldn't really avoid the monster if they wanted to use the stairwell it guarded, lying in wait was an annoyingly effective strategy. Even if you knew exactly where it was, you still had to fight it.

Of the three guardians within a day's travel, Dorrik believed that the sand lurker would be the easiest target. Although it was heavily armored, her gravity and water magics would largely ignore its chitin, and if things didn't go well, it probably wouldn't pursue them. Considering their other options were a heat mirage that drained mana and hit points from its victims magically and a twelve-legged monstrosity with heat magic that skated like a hockey player across the glass dunes created by its spells, Kat was inclined to agree.

Finally, the three of them found themselves standing atop the dune nearest the bleached white stone pillar of the stairwell. No monsters were in sight, but a keen observer would notice that a ridge of sand ringed the tower, forming a basin with a slightly deeper depression right in front of the doorway itself.

From the distance, Kat could barely make out the white specks of bone in the sand ringing the stairwell, the last remnants of explorers less wary or prepared than their group.

"Are you ready?" Dorrik asked, eyes closed as they soaked in the fake sun of the tower. "We don't need to try to beat the guardian with only three people. If you want, we could always go back for another team."

"Nice try." Kaleek flashed an easy grin at the two of them, his armor gleaming and clinking as he began to descend the mound of sand. "I know you just want to avoid the fourth floor. No such luck, old friend."

Kat cocked her head quizzically at Dorrik but the lizard just shook their head.

"Stick to the plan then." Dorrik stepped off the crest of the dune, skidding down after Kaleek. "The two of us keep it distracted while Miss Kat serves as the armor cracker. If you see a weak spot, go for it, but otherwise, we're mostly there to keep it off balance."

Kaleek sped up, stopping just outside the edge of the depression that marked the edge of the sand lurker's burrow. Kat began her own descent as Kaleek drew his sword and planted it point first in the sand. A moment later, he unclipped a sack from his belt and pulled out a large shank of bloody meat. With a smooth motion, he threw the steak into the center of the sandy pit before immediately drawing his sword from the sand.

The moment the steak hit the sand, the depression exploded. A pair of ochre mandibles, each slightly bigger than Kat's forearm, burst out of the ground, slashing through the meat in a spray of blood.

Kaleek darted forward, his two-handed sword glowing red as he swung it with deceptive speed, bouncing it off of the lurker's chitinous shell.

Sand flew everywhere as the guardian launched itself from the ground with a shriek. It snapped wildly at Kaleek only for the otter to dance back nimbly, his entire body glowing red as he burned stamina.

The sand lurker was over three times longer than it was tall, each of its body's five segments covered in thick, orange armored plates. Kat focused on the dead center of the huge monster and began casting Gravity Spike.

Just as it was about to close its snapping jaws on the otter, Dorrik's two swords, both flickering purple, struck together on one the lurker's legs, carving a 'v' and meeting almost a handspan deep within the creature's heavy armor. An anemic trickle of black blood welled up from the cut as a triangular chunk of armor with a small amount of the lurker's flesh fell to the sand with a thud.

It whirled around, eager to try its luck with the new foe that had actually managed to punch through its shell, only for

Kaleek to step forward into its blind spot, swinging his two handed sword overhead in a crushing downward swipe.

The sand lurker stumbled as the blow slammed into the side of its head, crumpling armor and mashing the flesh beneath.

Kat's spell went off and gravity went haywire in the monster's third body segment. Competing forces pushed and pulled against each other, turning the guardian's massive bulk and heavy armor into a liability.

It squirmed, thrashing against the internal pain but unable to defend itself as its body tore itself apart from the inside out.

She smirked, already preparing a second iteration of the spell. Kaleek and Dorrik took advantage of her attack, darting in under the creature's manic flailing to chip away at its armor, looking for an exploitable weakness.

Just as Kat was about to finish her next Gravity Spike, the lurker reared back, and bellowed, an angry dissonant rumble that caused the hair on the back of her neck to stand on end. It vomited a gout of sand, steaming with stomach acid.

She released her spell just as the lurker veiled itself in the damp and biting sand, causing her to lose sight of the monster and her companions completely. It shrieked once more, hopefully indicating that her ability had hit, but Kat was left biting her lip and unable to assess the spell's damage.

The sand swirled at the center of the basin, hissing and spitting out billows of yellow gray smoke where the potent acid encountered sand. Kat couldn't see anything.

Mouth set in a grim line, she drew her dagger, the new weapon still a bit unfamiliar in her hand, but its weight comforting enough as she activated Cat Step and blurred across the basin toward the vortex of acid-soaked grit.

Kaleek flew past her, his fur sizzling and a huge green blemish covering most of the front of his formerly pristine armor. For a second, she pondered healing him, but the otter was back on his feet before she could slow down.

Instead, she dove into the tempest. Immediately, a red indicator began flashing in the lower left of her vision as the sand choked wind burned and wore at her exposed skin. She squinted against the pain and pulled out two potions, one less than she could safely drink at her current level, and downed them one after another.

Immediately, a pleasant warmth filled her body as they did their work, steadily restoring her damaged hit points and depleted mana.

Feeling slightly more confident, Kat waded forward through the biting sand, squinting her eyes for some hint of the floor guardian's bulk.

A leg the size of a light pole slammed into the ground in front of her as the monster shifted its weight. Distantly, Kat heard the dull thwack of Dorrik's swords taking another chunk out of their foe.

She froze, dagger in hand, and began casting Gravity Spike for a third time at the hazy outline of the lurker's shifting thorax. The leg moved to her left, and she followed, using Cat Step to remain undetected through the obscuring sand. Then it stumbled toward her, and Kat had to use every point of her enhanced reaction and agility to avoid getting trampled as she backpedaled.

Finally, it planted the leg, its entire body rumbling ominously as it did... something. Kat finished her spell, acutely aware of the red icon in the corner of her vision as the monster's stinging aura of acid and sand damaged her faster than the potion could recover.

Gravity Spike tore into the lurker, competing planes of force shattering armor and pulping the flesh beneath. It shuddered, and the thrumming noise it was making reached a crescendo, ending in a deep bass tone that rattled the very air in her lungs.

Before Kat could properly start investing mana in another spell, the ground opened up under her. One minute, she was weaving back and forth on the sand in a delicate dance to keep its leg close enough to her for an attack, but not so close as to risk impalement on the sharp spear of chitin. The next, she was almost knee deep in the sand as it abruptly began sucking her in rather than supporting her weight.

She switched her spell, opting for Levitation instead of Gravity Spike. The much simpler ability activated in a fraction of a second, stopping her descent long enough for Kat to cast Pseudopod.

The tentacle of water reached out from her chest, grabbing onto the Lurker's leg and almost throwing her into the air as she pulled herself toward the floor guardian's limb.

A second later, she was scrambling up the leg, a flash of purple and a scream of frustration from Kaleek her only indication as to the rest of her team's progress.

Her Pseudopod reached out, grabbing onto a shard of the lurker's armor where Gravity Spike had savaged it, and yanking her toward it.

As soon as Kat felt the surprisingly warm and rough surface of the chitin under her hands, she began slamming downward with her dagger. With each blow, she could feel a sliver of her mana flowing into the knife. In exchange, each slash removed ribbons of armor and flesh.

The monster bucked, trying to remove her from its back, but Kat's Pseudopod was already curled around its thorax. Instead she just grunted, slamming her dagger into it once more.

She was rewarded with a geyser of steaming black blood as her blade stripped the last vestiges of armor from the lurker. It shuddered under her as Kat leaned forward, practically crawling into the hole she'd carved in its chitin.

Inside its body, a fleshy purple organ, the size of a watermelon, pulsed slowly, expanding and contracting about one time per second. With a mental shrug, Kat stabbed her knife into it, sinking the blade up to its hilt.

The lurker shuddered, listing to the right for half of a second before Kat felt herself in freefall.

She kicked off of the floor guardian, letting Levitation carry her far from its bulk as the monster slammed sideways into the ground, its veil of acid soaked sand fading away as it twitched.

Near the front of the monster, Dorrik stood heaving, both of their blades covered in black ichor and blood leaking from any number of cracks between their scales. The front of the lurker, on the other hand, was covered in cuts where Dorrik had done a number on it.

Most of the slashes weren't all that deep, barely making it through the floor guardian's armor, but there were dozens of them, and at least a couple were serious. A blow had taken one of the creature's four eyes, and another had opened up a major artery at the base of its head.

Kaleek, on the other hand?

"What in the name of every patriarch, matriarch, elder, and ancient was that?!" he screamed from where he was trapped, buried chest deep in the sand. "Can someone explain to me how we went from 'it doesn't have any special abilities' to 'it's a full blown earth elementalist' while they *dig me out of the blasted sand?*"

"What happened is that we learned an important lesson about putting too much weight on intelligence reports." Dorrik nodded solemnly as they wiped off and sheathed their swords. "The tower changes, and overreliance on what has happened in previous fights can be more harmful than going into a battle completely blind."

The lizard glanced at Kaleek struggling to free his arms from the sand. Their crest fluttered.

"We also learned an important lesson about paying attention to our surroundings." Dorrik nodded in Kaleek's direction. "With the proper presence of mind and reflexes, your current situation—"

She burst out laughing. Kat was covered head to toe in the monster's thick black blood, and she still hadn't recovered from the damaging aura, but she felt more alive than she had in days back on Earth. There was just something about coming down from an adrenaline high after killing an overpowered monster with her friends that erased all of the fretting and anxiety from home.

There wasn't any need to worry about political complications, about saying 'yes' to the wrong person or no to the right one. There wasn't any looming threat, pushing her and her family into a corner. It was just her, her friends, a knife, magic, and something to kill.

The lurker shuddered, and its breathing stopped.

Congratulations, Adventurer!
You have defeated the Sand Lurker and ascended to the fourth floor!
For achieving this feat with three or fewer players, a bonus attribute point has been awarded. Assign it wisely!
For ascending a level as an Elementalist Initiate, you gain the following benefits:

+2 Mana
+1 Stamina
+1 Unassigned Attribute Point

Keep climbing! Your answers and the Gardeners await you at the top!

CHAPTER TWENTY-THREE

Maybe an extra point in agility and reaction was overkill, Kat mused as she hopped over a trapped step in her college's stairwell. Still, until she learned magic that would let her stop bullets, simply 'not being where the bad guys were shooting' seemed like a valid plan B.

Dorrik had grumbled about how charisma, mind, and spirit were a spellcaster's greatest tools, but as often as the big lizard gave good advice, it wasn't like they were sneaking through a stairwell at two a.m., dodging guards with shotguns.

She pushed the fire door open and froze. Shadow was active, but barely ten steps in front of her, a corporate security officer was slouched against the wall. Her hand inched toward the knife strapped to her infiltration suit's belt.

The guard pushed himself off of the wall with a grunt and began walking away, never turning to check behind him.

Kat's hand returned to her side as his footfalls faded away, a slight frown on her face. The security officer was gone, but something deep inside of her screamed that he was a combatant, that she should tie up loose ends here and now.

It didn't sit right.

Even if the officer might be a threat, even if the decision might come back to haunt her, Kat couldn't bring herself to kill someone that wasn't a threat to her at the moment. The guard could have just as easily been one of her school friends or one of the people she met in the ChromeDogs.

She wouldn't hesitate to bring the man down if he spotted her or became a threat—a job was a job—but she *wanted* and *needed* to be a better person than she'd been in St. Louis.

With a sigh, she kept moving, creeping toward the security office. Kat took the lack of alarms and armed guards looking for her as a sign that she'd made it once again to the observation room without getting spotted.

She slipped another two disks of ZZ3 under the door and began counting. Halfway through, she heard a thud from inside. With a shrug, she waited five more seconds and tried the door.

A Hispanic woman in a guard uniform lay on her side in the middle of the room, pistol still in her holster. She looked peaceful. Almost like she was sleeping.

Kat closed the door behind her, locking it just in case the man patrolling the hallway wandered past. Efficiently, she put the shunt on the computer input, letting Whippoorwill have her way with the college's antiquated security system while Kat found a length of extension cord to tie the woman's hands and feet.

Technically, the plan called for the guard to be terminated, but Kat had three ampules of sedative. One for the dean, and two backups just in case.

She placed the applicator against the bound woman's neck. It hissed as the pressurized gases inside the tube of plastic forced the drugs through her captive's skin and into her carotid artery.

"Are you sure about this, Erinyes?" Xander's voice in her ear almost made Kat jump. "If someone finds the guard, it could scuttle the entire operation, and you already left the patrolling guard on his feet. This seems like asking for trouble."

Kat took a deep breath, closing her eyes behind the opaque mesh of her infiltration suit. Xander was right, but at the same time—

"If they become a threat to the mission…" Her voice came out a little harsher than she expected, but maybe that was for the best. "I've been resolving too many problems with my knife, Exe. You know I won't hesitate to bring down an actual threat, but given where I grew up, I could have ended up as any one of these guards. Hell, it would have made more sense than what I'm doing right now."

For a moment, there was only silence over their communication channel.

"I understand, Erinyes," Xander replied. Even with the crackle of the poor transmitter he was using from the roof of a high rise across the street, she could hear the stress in his voice. More than that, he sounded bone tired. "We all have lines that we don't like to cross. Just don't be shy about crossing them if you have to. This isn't a business for strict morals and clean hands."

"My hands are already pretty dirty." She chuckled. "A little more blood won't change things all that much, but I'm not going to kill someone that I could just as easily spare. The world is already a shit enough place without me making it a little worse. I understand that I'm a grain of sand in a beach here, but—"

"I have him," Whippoorwill interrupted the two of them. "Security has some minor updates, but nothing that slowed me down. Franklin is in his penthouse suite, reviewing something on his smartpanel. He has a secretary and a guard up there with him, but everyone else has been sent home."

"How do I get past them, Whip?" Kat checked her knife, pistol, and supply kit as she walked toward the security room's door.

"I don't think you do." The other woman sighed. "The secretary is working at a desk that has a plain view of the elevator. She's going to hear you coming up and be watching."

"I'm sorry, Erinyes," Whippoorwill continued, genuine emotion in her voice. "The girl is just a bystander, but she has access to a hardwired alarm. I can spoof an e-mail making her think that there's some sort of late night security sweep of the penthouse, but I can't stop her from tripping the siren. You're going to have to bring her down fast and hard."

Kat closed her eyes, gritting her teeth to avoid letting loose the scream burbling up inside of her.

"It's for the mission," Kat replied woodenly a moment later, trying not to think about the mechanics from St. Louis. She kept repeating to herself that this was different, this was necessary. Even as the elevator doors hissed shut behind her, the words rang hollow.

Gravity pulled at her as the lift accelerated upward. She drew a throwing dagger and frowned at it. It might be her weapon of choice, but it was a slow weapon. Knives killed by cutting tendons and ligaments to disable, and arteries and veins to bleed their target out. A precise enough throw would do the trick—the secretary couldn't press a button if Kat disabled her hand—but that was hardly something she could count on with the entire mission on the line.

With a sigh, Kat sheathed the weapon and drew her pistol. It was squat and ugly, but it was quiet. High caliber, and low speed, the silencer screwed onto the front would reduce its report to a quiet cough, and the subsonic ammunition would eliminate the telltale crack of the sound barrier.

The elevator began to slow as it approached its destination. Kat closed her eyes and began channeling mana.

The doors opened with a 'ding' and Kat unleashed Dazzle on the waiting area beyond their metal embrace. Even through the mesh and her eyelids, Kat saw the brilliant white and orange strobes as the spell fired a dissonant burst of extremely bright light into the opening.

A woman let out a strangled scream of shock as Kat opened her eyes and stepped out of the elevator into the richly appointed reception area of the penthouse.

The secretary was beautiful. Like if someone had tricked Whippoorwill into dyeing her hair blonde and wearing an expensive, low-cut dress.

Kat's eyes didn't soften as the pistol jumped in her hand.

The first shot took the secretary in the shoulder, its momentum spinning the woman in her rotating chair. The second shot missed entirely, punching a hole in the elegant wood paneling behind the woman. The third hit her in the back of the head.

Kat didn't bother to confirm the kill, the spatter of viscera on the wall behind the secretary evidence enough of her lucky shot.

"Christa!" a male voice shouted from the main area of the suite. "Are you all right? I thought I heard you shouting."

Jogging footsteps announced the imminent arrival of another individual as Kat put her back to the wall a mere step from the entryway to the reception area.

A man in a suit, several inches taller than Kat and with short, cropped dark hair stepped through the opening. She could almost see his eyes widening as he took in the mess at the secretary's desk as she pulled the trigger.

The gun coughed twice, and he staggered, but rather than blood, Kat saw a hint of chrome shining through the holes in his blazer.

Subdermal armor. Silently, she cursed herself for only carrying the bulky silenced pistol. Its big and slow bullets were about as effective as tennis balls against the guard's armor. Unless she managed to hit exposed flesh, the pistol might as well be a paperweight.

The man grunted, swinging a backhand at her head with his left hand as he tried to bring his gun around.

Kat ducked, her tower-enhanced reflexes more than a match for the poorly telegraphed blow. Only as his fist was passing over her head did she make out the two inch metal spurs jutting out from each knuckle.

"Assassin!" he shouted, the word devolving into a scream of

pain as her throwing knife punched through the palm of his right hand, forcing him to drop the submachine gun.

He tried to kick her, but Kat flowed to the side seamlessly, drawing her actual fighting knife. She tensed her body, ready to spring into action at a moment's notice.

The man's eyes flickered back toward the office suite, looking for support.

Kat used that moment of distraction to dart in, slipping past the guard and activating Penetrate as he drew her dagger across the back of his thigh.

The skill wasn't necessary. Whatever armor he had covering his torso, it didn't extend to his legs. His eyes widened and the security officer collapsed as her knife cut through his hamstring.

Before he could hit the ground, Kat pulled her knife free from his leg and drew the blade across the inside of his forearm, slicing open tendons and opening his brachial artery.

He swung a bleeding limb at her, trying to fend Kat off, but it only bought him a second as she simply leaned backward and let his bladed fist swish past her face.

She leaned forward, dagger in hand, ready to finish him when Xander's voice shouted in her ear.

"Use your gun!" She blinked down at the man, as he stared up at her in fear. "Your knife work is getting too distinctive, and the other side isn't playing by the rules. We can't afford to leave a calling card."

The guard lunged for his submachine gun, awkwardly trying to grab the weapon with his still functional left hand, but a quick burn of stamina, and she Cat Stepped past him in a blur and kicked the gun away.

Keeping an eye on the injured guard. Kat ducked down and picked up her pistol from where she'd discarded it earlier in the fight. The man slid backward on the ground, his blood smearing everywhere.

"You don't have to do this," he whimpered, eyes fixed on the handgun. "I won't tell anyone I saw you, I swear. I'll quit my job tomorrow, say my mom is sick and move away. Just don't—"

The gun coughed and his head jerked back. If his head had subdermal armor, it wasn't thick enough to stop the pistol's oversized bullets. A second shot missed.

Kat stepped closer and fired twice more, each time taking careful aim to ensure that her shots hit him in the face.

Hands shaking slightly, she ejected her magazine and stowed it in her hip-mounted kit, replacing it with one of the two spares. She racked a fresh round into the pistol's chamber.

"Good job," Xander cut in, "but stay on your toes. Franklin probably heard the guard's warning, and we don't have any idea what he's capable—"

A metal sphere clinked off of the floor, bouncing once on the threshold of the entryway to the reception area before sailing further in.

Kat didn't think, she reacted. Cat Step active, she blurred forward, committing every iota of stamina and tower-granted speed to throwing herself into the hallway leading toward Dean Franklin's suites.

The reception area erupted into an inferno, the pressure wave from the expanding ball of flame punching Kat in the back and throwing her further down the hallway. She hit the ground shoulder first, turning her momentum into a roll that returned her to her feet.

Standing about ten feet away was a middle aged man in a bathrobe and holding a massive silver handgun. Despite his apparel, he looked every inch a corporate executive. He was tall but not too tall, with salt and pepper hair, and a square, statuesque jaw that was agape as he stared at Kat.

She began sprinting toward him, serpentining through the hallway with Cat Step active as she began pouring mana into Gravity's Grasp.

Time seemed to move in slow motion as he raised the pistol, the golden links of the spell forming in her mind as Kat closed on him. Just before she reached him, Gravity's Grasp snapped into place, the magic dragging down the barrel of his pistol a moment before he pulled the trigger.

Rather than a bullet, a bolt of lightning sprang from the revolver's barrel, causing all of the hair on the left side of her body to stand on end as it seared the wall. Then Kat's shoulder hit his waist and her arm snaked around his leg, pulling it out from under him and spilling him to the ground. He hit with bone-jarring force, the enhanced gravity from her spell snapping the back of his head into the floor.

She landed on top of him, the breath rushing from his body as her elbow slammed into his solar plexus. Before he could recover, she straddled him, slamming her hand down on his temple. His eyes rolled back up into his head.

Kat checked his pulse and took note of the man's steady breathing before pulling out one of the applicators and pressing it to his neck.

She stood up wearily, surveying the wreckage of the hallway and reception area.

"This is Erinyes," Kat said as she pulled a pair of zip ties out of her kit and began trussing up the dean's hands and legs. "Please confirm that the penthouse is secure. Please also tell me what in the fuck just happened."

"Uh." Whip paused for a second. "I don't see anything on the cameras but it doesn't look like the fire alarms or sprinklers are working. It looks like the dean had them disabled because he was afraid of them being used for some sort of gas attack."

"For heaven's sake," Kat mumbled to herself as she walked back toward the reception area, mustering her mana to cast Water Jet.

"As for what happened?" Xander's voice was grim. "Franklin is a player. An artificer initiate, from the looks of things. That grenade and handgun were magical constructs. To anyone but him, they're nothing more than lumps of metal. It's one of the more uncommon classes from *The Tower of Somnus*."

"Shit." Kat frowned. "Is it safe for us to kidnap him? Without knowing exactly what abilities he's hiding, how in the hell are we going to keep him secure?"

"Leave that to me," Xander replied. "If you can deliver him to me unconscious, I can take care of the rest. As for you? Get your secondary shunt onto the terminal in his study. We're going to need to activate the delta contingency plan."

"Delta?" Kat asked, spraying down the last of the fires with magically generated water. "You want to fake a defection? How in the hell are we going to sell a false betrayal when half of the penthouse is burned down and his support staff is shot to death?"

"With whose gun?" Xander replied smugly as Kat uncovered the computer terminal and inserted her second shunt so that Whippoorwill could have access to the system. "The weapon you're using is untraceable and doesn't have any prints on it. All we need to do is mash it into Franklin's hand and it'll look like something he picked up on the black market."

"Hell," he continued, "the fire works to our advantage. Originally ,I was going to make you drag their bodies to the kitchen and stuff them in an oven to erase the evidence of the knife wounds, but this is better. The fire was started with Franklin's magic, and if all that's left is bones with bullet holes in them, they won't even know that a knife was used."

"That could work," she agreed grudgingly. "At least for the means of death."

"Exe and I have put together some false bank records that show him embezzling funds," Whippoorwill supplied helpfully, "and I'm already working on crudely erasing the security footage to make it look like an amateur is trying to cover their tracks."

Kat nodded slowly. "And if you erase everything, anyone investigating what happened won't know to look specifically for the records involving my dorm. Even if they could reconstruct the surveillance logs, the investigators won't know where to look."

She glanced at the unmoving dean and sighed.

"It's a bit rushed, but let's do it." Kat reached into her hip pack and began unfurling a lightweight parachute. "Tell me when you're done, Whip. I have to get sleeping beauty ready to jump out of a building with me."

CHAPTER TWENTY-FOUR

Kat soared through the sky, Levitation active as she steered her parachute toward the brightly lit neon street below. She pulled one of the cords, slightly redirecting her descent. Strapped to Kat's back was the unconscious form of Dean Franklin, hopefully covered by the same casting of Shadow that she used to hide herself.

Despite the late hour, dozens of cars honked and jockeyed for position, marking the road as a technicolor ribbon of light as it stretched into the city proper. Kat squinted against the darkness, willing Nightvision to activate so that she could make out her landing zone, a squat three story building where Xander and Whippoorwill would be waiting.

Her vision shifted into black and white and sharpened, letting Kat make out the tarp that Xander had spread on the rooftop for her arrival. She adjusted her course once more before closing her eyes and simply enjoying the feeling of the wind against her infiltration suit.

For a moment, her world was nothing more than the sound of traffic and the flapping of her parachute, a welcome release after the recent mission. All too soon, a gust washed over her, forcing Kat to reopen her eyes and change directions once more.

Less than a minute later, the rooftop rushed up to meet her feet as Kat thumped into the building, barely able to keep herself from tumbling over with the advantage of her magic and enhanced agility.

As she was trying to slow herself, Xander leapt up, grabbing the straps to her mini-parachute and pulling the camouflaged fabric from the night sky. Efficiently, he beat the air from the chute before crushing it into a ball and stowing it in a backpack so that it could be folded and reused later.

Kat reached up, pulling the dean's arms from around her neck and laying the man down gently on the tarp before undoing the industrial Velcro she'd glued to his shorts from the connectors attached to her infiltration suit.

She stepped away from the unconscious man, glad to finally have him be someone else's problem. Xander nodded to her and began rolling the man up in the tarp as Whippoorwill began rapidly blinking her glazed eyes, finally stirring from her spot next to the haphazard pile of equipment she claimed was her hacking rig.

"How'd it go?" Kat asked quietly, crouching next to her partner as the pink-haired girl reoriented herself.

"I've downloaded everything and scrubbed the surveillance system." She smiled back at Kat, unplugging her cranial jack from the computer. "There shouldn't be any electronic records on the network for the last couple of days. I made sure to get the entry and exit logs too. That way no one will be able to call you out for showing up tomorrow morning."

Kat nodded slowly, her heart still fluttering with adrenaline as a million nightmare scenarios flitted through her skull.

"And I made sure it would look clumsy, but not too clumsy. Anyone looking into Franklin's private files will see records of him embezzling money for the last five years, along with some e-mails to a headhunter about defecting."

"So we're clear?" Kat unzipped Whippoorwill's duffle bag as the other girl began loading her equipment into it.

"I even triggered the self-immolation trigger on the shunt," Whippoorwill replied as she shoved most of the rig into the bag with a grunt. "All they'll find in the security room is burn marks and scrap metal. It'll look like Franklin tried to melt the control panel down to hide his tracks on the way out."

"I just can't help but feel like things have gone too smoothly." Kat shuffled uncomfortably as Whippoorwill loaded the last of her peripherals into the duffle bag before zipping it shut. "There was a fight in the penthouse, but other than that... nothing. It just doesn't feel right getting in and out of a place this smoothly."

"You almost got shot and blown up," Xander chimed in, the dean's limp form covered in a tarp and draped over his shoulder. "I really think we need to have a talk about what you consider to be a successful infiltration. It isn't supposed to always involve explosions and shooting. Those usually mean you've done something wrong."

"Thanks for the lecture, Dad." Kat rolled her eyes. "Now how the hell do we get down from here? I'm still antsy about being this close to the college with someone as important as the dean."

"If you will, Whip." Xander grunted, nodding toward a corner of the building. "If you could get the car started, I have to load our luggage in the trunk."

Kat let herself smile despite the situation as Whippoorwill practically skipped to the edge of the building before grabbing a coil of rope that was looped over a steel piton and jumping over the edge. She followed the hacker to the edge and glanced over. Half a floor down was a padded mat placed in the center of a rickety metal fire escape. Whip was looking up at her, a grin on her face as she looped the rope around her arm.

With a shrug, she vaulted the side of the building, landing in a crouch next to Whippoorwill. The other girl tied the rope off with a knot before padding gently down a couple of the steps of the fire escape before turning back.

"I'll get the car," she whispered. "You grab the padding once Exe is through, and cover the rear. Remember, there are apartments in this building. We have to be quiet."

"Come on." Kat grinned at Whippoorwill. "I'm an infiltrator."

"I've seen your infiltrations." Whippoorwill began walking down the metal stairs. "Remember to be quiet, Erinyes."

Kat chuckled quietly only to whip around, knife out as Xander landed on the mat next to her. He grinned, golden tooth gleaming in the dim light, and set out after Whippoorwill.

Grumbling, Kat rolled up the padding and slung it over her shoulder before following Xander down to the street level. By the time she caught up with her teammates, Xander was slamming the trunk of a polished sportscar, the dean's body conspicuously absent from his shoulder.

She walked up to the car, noting that Whip was already in the front seat before opening the back door and shoving the padding inside. As Kat was buckling in, Xander started the vehicle, sending a quiet thrum through the leather seats.

The car purred before Xander tapped the accelerator, edging the vehicle out into traffic. Immediately, the blood left Kat's face as she gripped frantically at her armrest.

Xander didn't drive with Andrew's quiet and machine-like efficiency. Instead, he marked a line between point A and point B, and woe upon any car in his way. Landmarks blurred past, neon and chrome, while lasers projected advertisements into the low hanging clouds, but all that Kat noticed was the honking of horns as vehicles swerved out of their way.

Finally their car took a two-wheeled turn down a seedy side street, past a technicolor sign bragging about the loosest slots and escorts in Chiwaukee. Xander pulled up to a three story cement parking ramp and swiped some sort of passcard before bringing the car inside and parking it.

Kat exited the vehicle shakily, frowning at a large painting

depicting a male android placing a credit chip in what she charitably decided was an unclothed female android's navel. Whippoorwill walked past her, opening the trunk to retrieve her rig
from where it sat atop Franklin's tarp-clad body.

"Wait," Kat began hesitantly. "Are we in—"

"Yeah." The pink-haired girl wrinkled her nose in distaste as
she hoisted the duffle bag over her shoulder. "We're in the Neon
Dream's parking structure. Xander paid for a couple rooms to
be built into the foundation, off the record and only accessible
via a service stairwell."

"A low-rent casino and brothel is the perfect cover." Xander
pulled the tarp-clad body from the trunk. "There are so many
people from all walks of life coming and going at all times, so no
one will think anything of us being here."

"And does Nina have an opinion on this?" Kat asked, taking
the mask off of her infiltration suit and raising an eyebrow
at him.

Xander paused, a flash of panic on his face rapidly replaced
by his trademark cocky smirk.

"We could sit here all day bantering—" he slung Franklin's
body over his shoulder "—but we have a busy night in front of
us. Jumper cables to hook up to a car battery and whatnot."

Whippoorwill glanced at Kat worriedly, but all she could do
was shrug. Xander sounded like he was joking, but he was also
the sort of person that would tell a joke during a firefight. You
just never knew when the humor was genuine or an attempt to
defray tension right before he dropped something serious
on you.

They followed him past a reeling drunk in the process of
pissing on a pillar and his own feet, en route to a stairwell
marked 'employees only.' Xander used his free hand to swipe a
card through an old-fashioned magnetic reader, and a couple of
seconds later, they were descending into the cool concrete
depths of the building.

Xander led them through a small kitchen and a bedroom
lined with bunks that folded into the wall before pushing his

way through a metal doorway and into a storage room. Whip-poorwill flipped on the lights, igniting two large directional lamps aimed at a metal chair placed in the center of the room, just behind a prominently positioned drain.

Whistling cheerfully to himself, Xander placed the tarp next to the metal chair. He began unrolling it, spreading the water-proof blue fabric on the concrete floor of the room, only pausing to pick up the metal chair and put it on top of the now-unfurled tarp.

Xander stepped back and surveyed the scene, nodding to himself before he drew a knife and cut a hole in it, just above the room's drain.

"Waste not, want not," he grunted at the two of them with a wink as he wrestled the dean's body into the chair. "We have a perfectly good tarp just sitting here. Might as well put it to good use before we have to burn it after the mission is over."

Kat rolled her eyes. It would take more than a little blood to make her squeamish. She might not want to involve civilians in her raids, but that didn't mean that she would bat a single eyelash for people like the dean. Every antique painting and length of opulent hardwood decorating his penthouse office was earned by dirtying his hands.

She didn't pretend to have the moral high ground. That was a mistake some samurai made, but it was nothing more than a gentle hypocrisy to help them sleep at night. Kat might not be a major player, but the ChromeDogs were a business, and working for a business meant getting your hands dirty. It was true that she was doing this to protect her family, but at the end of the day, she couldn't hide from the truth of her existence.

Xander finished shackling the dean to the chair and stepped back for a moment to admire his handiwork. Clapping his hands together, he walked over to a nearby shelf and opened a briefcase.

Kat leaned against the room's cool concrete walls as she watched Xander put on a pair of elbow-length black rubber gloves and remove a thin-bladed knife and a needle from the case. He walked back to the prisoner, tapping the needle to clear out any bubbles before he inserted it into the man's neck.

"Whutha?" The dean jerked forward in his chair, lurching against the handcuffs that chained him to his seat.

"Thomas Franklin," Xander savored each word as he smiled ghoulishly at the man. "It's good to finally meet you."

The handcuffed man blinked up at Xander, his eyes still dilated from the drug that had kept him unconscious. He leaned forward, his movement arrested once again by the rattle and clank of his bonds.

"If this is about money," Franklin slurred, shaking his head as he tried to clear it.

"I have plenty of money." Xander crouched in front of the man tapping the flat of the thin blade against the palm of his hand. "What I don't have is answers."

"Ah, fuck." The dean blinked up at Xander, trying and failing to make out his features through the intense backlighting that illuminated the room. "I don't suppose that it would do me any good to say that I'm a GroCorp executive?"

Xander shook his head, extinguishing the hopeful note in the dean's voice.

"Sorry, friend," Xander replied mournfully. "The people that hired me are GroCorp executives too. I'm truly working in rarefied heights this time."

"So, it's going to be like that, isn't it?" Franklin's eyes were glued to the knife in Xander's hand.

"It's going to be like that." Xander stood up. "I'm sure you know the rules for this sort of thing. I'm going to ask you questions. We already know the answers to some of the questions. If you refuse to answer, or you answer wrong, things are going to get painful. If things go well, we drug you and drop you off in a park with a splitting headache and no memory of what happened here. If things don't go well, you disappear into the night, another casualty of the corporate battlefield."

Their captive's Adam's apple bobbed soundlessly as he squinted at Xander.

"First question." Xander leaned forward, reaching forward to place the tip of the knife against Franklin's cheek. "Do you work for Elaine Williamson?"

He nodded slowly, careful not to cut himself on the razor-sharp knife pressed into his skin.

"Good answer," Xander continued, grinning at the man. "Next question. Did Elaine order the occupation of the Schaumburg arcology?"

"Wait." Franklin frowned. "This is about Schaumburg?"

He screamed, blood flowing down his cheek as Xander put pressure on the dagger's hilt, pushing it until its tip struck the dean's cheekbone.

"That," Xander said nonchalantly, "was a bad answer. I am the one asking questions, and I would appreciate an answer. Once again, did Elaine order the occupation?"

"Fuck!" Franklin rocked back in his chair, trying to get away from Xander. "If you're asking about Schaumburg, I'm not answering anything. You can do what you want to do, but it won't be any worse than what Elaine would do to me if she found out I narced on her. Hell, for all I know, this kidnapping is all some sort of complicated loyalty test on her part."

"I can assure you, it is not," Xander responded, crossing his arms in front of his chest as his knife slowly dripped blood onto the tarp below. "Are you sure about this? It's your final chance to walk away from this without it getting very ugly."

Kat shifted slightly against the wall, her lips pressed bloodlessly together. On the other side of the room, Whippoorwill simply turned and walked out.

Part of Kat wanted to follow her, but at the same time, that would be turning her back on the ugly reality of her job. Eventually, as much as she wanted to avoid it, she would need to interrogate a target, too. It might be easier to play the part of a wilting violet and run away from the ugliness inherent to being an infiltrator, but ultimately, she needed to face the unpleasant parts of the job head on.

"Elaine will find me." Franklin spat some of the blood that

had trickled down his face onto the floor. "She will reward my silence. You won't get anything out of me. At the end of the day, I'll have a promotion, and you'll be dead. Just another street thug, face down and without a name in a gutter."

"I don't enjoy this you know," Xander mused out loud as he walked over to the briefcase and fished around in it. "I know some people get a rush out of torturing corporate execs. They act like it's some sort of nihilistic blow for the 'class struggle.'"

Xander pulled out another syringe and held it up before nodding at it.

"You and I, Tom," he continued as he walked back toward their prisoner. "I can call you Tom, right?"

The dean just glared at him, blood streaming from the deep cut down his face.

"We know how foolish those beliefs are." Xander crouched in front of the captive, careful to ensure that the room's lighting was behind him so that Franklin couldn't make out his face. "There is no class struggle. The rich won decades ago. People like me? We're just trying to survive. There's no real point in raging against the wealthy."

Xander reached out, grabbing Franklin's wrist and slipping the needle into it. The dean stiffened as the needle hissed, depositing its payload into his veins.

"These interrogations are just so *boring*." Xander stood up and sighed. "The target always starts by bargaining. Then they threaten me. When both of those don't work, they brag about how I'll never get any information from them. It's like all of you corporate types are reading from a bad script or something."

"Whatha?" Franklin tried to answer, his eyes dilating under the floodlights. "Whath are you doin' to me?"

"I'm putting you into a suggestible state so I can get some answers," Xander replied calmly. "*Compulsion*."

"Now, let's try this again." Xander's gold tooth glinted as he smiled. "Thomas Franklin, did Elaine Williamson order the occupation of the Schaumburg Arcology."

"Yes." The dean's voice was dead, emotionless.

"Why did she order the occupation?" Xander towered above the board-stiff captive, staring into his glazed eyes.

"Millennium contacted her." Kat shuddered as she listened to the dean speaking. They were getting answers, but looking at his face and eyes, there was nothing there. "The recordings from the Starfall planning meeting had gone missing. The mercenaries tracked them to an Ike Holdings, a wholly owned Subsidiary of GroCorp, executive in Schaumburg. Elaine ordered the occupation to try and flush him—"

"What do you mean by 'Starfall'?" Xander asked, interrupting the man with a frown.

"Starfall is the operating name given by the cabal of executives working with the stallesp for their plan to stage coordinated hostile takeovers in every megacorporation simultaneously."

The room lapsed into silence. Xander turned back to Kat, shooting her a worried look. She stepped forward, stopping just behind the floodlights.

"Who is the executive that had the recordings?" Kat asked.

"Please answer the lady's question," Xander followed up with a grateful nod in her direction.

"Colyn Raster." As soon as she heard the dean's response, Kat frantically began flipping through the Ike Holdings management and executive directory downloaded onto her smartpanel. She hadn't opened the thing since she bought the smartpanel, but corporate bylaws mandated that all electronics sold in the arcology have the directory. Usually it was a minor annoyance, little more than a waste of system memory, but today it was a godsend.

Raster's profile popped up on the display. Her eyes flickered across the screen as she began reading about him. Senior Vice President of Finance and Trust Management. She scrolled down until his picture popped up.

Kat's gut tightened. Middle-aged with hints of white around his temples, it was the man from the oak suite. This was all about the recording she'd stolen from St. Louis.

If the recording detailed the Starfall planning meeting, Belle and the ChromeDogs needed a copy. It would be proof that Elaine and a number of other shareholders were planning on betraying the entire planet and, more importantly, their employers. More than enough to unseat them and buy everyone involved a little breathing room as they tried to find a way to stave off the stallesp's predatory designs.

"Has Mr. Raster been apprehended?" Kat barely heard Xander's follow up question. The entire room was spinning.

"Yesterday." Her head whipped around at Franklin's bland voice. "We haven't been able to find the recording, but Colyn is being shipped to the Beloit Detainment Center for questioning."

Her heart almost stopped. Everyone knew about Beloit, even though no one dared talk about it above a whisper. The place was a hellhole of crime, torture, and starvation. Once the company officials got what they needed out of Colyn, they'd dump him in the general population where he'd be lucky to last a week. People of interest that went to Beloit didn't return.

"Tell me about the transportation arrangements," Kat commanded the captive, hoping against all logic that Colyn would be in some sort of intermediate facility where they could rescue him.

"An armored van containing Raster and some malcontents from Chiwaukee left downtown at midnight," the dean said woodenly, without any inflection or emotion. "I was tasked with monitoring them from my office when your team grabbed me. They should already be there."

"*Compulsion.*" Xander renewed the spell grimly before turning to one of the storage shelves and rustling through the material there.

A moment later, he pulled out a bottle of thirty year old scotch and began splashing it on Franklin's clothes. He put the bottle to the robotic man's lips and tipped it back.

"Drink." For a second there wasn't any sound but the glug

of the dean's Adam's apple working. Then Xander pulled the bottle away and corked it.

"Such a waste," he muttered with a sad shake of his head. "That one bottle was as expensive as some of the chrome I've seen the boys sporting."

Xander leaned close to the dean, whispering something in his ear while his hands swiftly unlocked the handcuffs. Franklin stood shakily, almost stumbling as he took his first hesitant step. Then, with Xander leading the man, he wobbled robotically toward the door and out of the room.

As soon as the door closed behind him, Kat whirled to face Xander, confusion on her face.

"After all of that," she hissed, "we're just letting him go?"

"Go?" Xander quirked an eyebrow. "Oh, God no. He's seen far too much, and it would completely blow the cover story about embezzlement if he survived long enough to answer questions."

"No." He shook his head, mouth set into a grim line. "Drunk driving is a clean and understandable way to go. That was his car we took here and we'll need another way back. After all, he's about to drunkenly drive it off of an overpass at something like three times the speed limit without a seat belt on."

"That's the thing, Kat." Xander patted her gently on the shoulder. "None of our cover stories will hold up under prolonged investigation. Sure, we made it look like he was embezzling money, but it's not like Whip and I knew enough about GroCorp's inner workings to make the evidence ironclad. What we need are neat and easy explanations."

"If you give a corporate detective a mystery," he continued, "they'll spend the next three months lifting up every rock to see what's under it. If you give them a simple story of corporate greed where the 'bad guy' is already beyond punishment? There aren't any promotions to be earned digging for the truth there. Just more paperwork."

"I really shouldn't be surprised or depressed by that." Kat furrowed her brow. "And yet I am."

"Come on, let's get you back to school," Xander replied with a chuckle. "We'll figure out how we're breaking into Beloit and fill you in once we have a plan."

The drive to the college was a good deal more sedate. Xander still wove in and out of traffic like an absolute madman, cutting other vehicles off with abandon, but for some reason it didn't faze Kat nearly as much.

Security barely checked her on the way in, and Kat made it to her floor in a fog, her mind awhirl with the implications and adrenaline afterglow of the night.

Just as she was reaching down to swipe her lanyard past the electronic locking system to her dorm room, a hand landed on Kat's shoulder.

Without even thinking, Kat dropped her card and grabbed the wrist of the hand gripping her shoulder, rotating the person's arm until their elbow was locked and they were bent over at the waist staring at the floor.

A gasp up the hallway drew her gaze to a vaguely familiar girl. The girl's hands began moving as she muttered strange words, clearly some sort of tower-granted spell or ability.

The person in the arm lock struggled against Kat's grip, causing Kat to plant her free hand into their shoulder, pushing their body closer to the ground as their arm twisted unnaturally. Kat began summoning Pseudopod as the person beneath her let out a feminine gasp of pain.

Before the other girl up the hallway could finish her spell, Kat's water tentacle grabbed her by the ankle and yanked, spilling her to the ground and knocking both the mana and the breath out of her.

Then pre-dawn silence descended on the hallway. The girl in Kat's grip lurched to the side, an attempt to escape that Kat easily thwarted by putting more pressure on her shoulder. The person on the ground groaned, rolling onto her side and clutching her head in both of her hands.

"God, I knew it," the woman struggling beneath her hissed. "Jasper goes missing the same day I catch you sneaking into the college after hours and you're a fucking high-level *player*. It all makes sense now."

Kat frowned, squinting at the woman she was holding.

"Iris Leander?" she asked incredulously, releasing her victim.

CHAPTER TWENTY-FIVE

The other woman staggered back, massaging her wrist as she glared at Kat. Iris glanced at her friend on the ground before scowling at Kat once again.

"You said something about Jasper disappearing?" Kat asked, trying to ignore the other party's animosity.

"Yes." Iris reached down to help the other girl up. "Alicia and I are in a book club with him. We were going to meet to discuss Thorstein Veblen, but he never showed up. When we tried calling his estate, they hadn't seen him either."

"Did you contact Davis?" Kat struggled to suppress the flash of impatience that ran through her.

Kat's head was whirring as she tried to make sense of the chaotic thoughts rushing through her. Schaumburg was under siege and Jasper was gone all at the same time. He must have been picked up in the purge Franklin mentioned, but for the life of her, she couldn't figure out how Jasper had been targeted.

"No," Iris replied defiantly. "You showed up at that meeting, and I knew you were trying to get your claws into Jasper. I thought it was just gold digging at first, but then you disappeared all night right after he went missing. I could put two and two together. You're working for the capitalists to try to under-mine the worker's struggle."

"Are you fucking kidding me?" Kat muttered to herself, feeling her control beginning to fray as Iris puffed out her head in triumph, as if her nonsense declaration meant anything.

"*Everyone* works for capitalists, Iris!" She cut herself off for a second before continuing quietly, but with the same intensity. "I admire what Jasper and you are trying to do, but I'm just looking to survive. I don't have the luxury of high-minded polit-ical philosophy, but I will say unequivocally that I did not do anything to Jasper."

The woman behind Iris, Alicia, shuffled back, nervously licking her lips as she tried to avoid notice.

"And that is the attitude of a revanchist and counter-revolu-tionary," Iris crowed triumphantly, pointing a finger at Kat.

"I barely know what that means, and I care even less." Kat shook her head. "Now can we stop accusing each other of being ogres in the hallway and take this to a room? We're going to wake up the rest of the girls, and I don't think either of us want that."

"Fine," Iris relented, folding her arms in front of her. "We'll meet in Alicia's room."

The other woman's head snapped up, startled.

"Why me?" she asked, a hint of a whine in her voice. "This is between you and Katherine. You just wanted me here to drop a curse if things didn't go our way, and you saw how that worked out. She went through both of us quicker than a middle manager with an open-ended budget. Honestly, I'm not sure I want to be alone in a room with her."

Kat grinned at Alicia, triggering a flinch from the discon-tented woman.

"Just open the door, Alicia." Iris didn't even turn around, still glaring at Kat with her arms crossed.

They walked two rooms down where Alicia opened the door hurriedly, her hands shaking slightly as she ran her ID over the scanner. As soon as the lock clicked, the three of them filed in,

Kat casting a hasty glance over her shoulder to make sure that no one else was watching them.

She stepped into Alicia's room and sighed. Kat knew she shouldn't be surprised that an executive's daughter had a suite almost three times the size of hers, but somehow it still took her aback.

The walls were covered in massive, signed posters from entertainment channel stars and singing groups. More than one of the heart-throbs had scrawled a phone number or e-mail address beneath their signatures. Kat quirked an eyebrow at Alicia and the girl blushed.

"My daddy paid for the suite upgrade, and uh—" Alicia shuffled her feet slightly. "I like musicians. I would pay extra for backstage passes to meet them, and uhm, talk about their mus—"

"We don't care about who you're sleeping with," Iris cut the girl off. "We're here to figure out what Katherine did to Jasper."

"*I didn't sleep with all of them!*" Alicia squealed indignantly, her face beet red.

"Sure," Iris replied unconvincingly while her friend sputtered. "It's counter-revolutionary for me to care about you being a slut, so I don't, naturally. After all, the only struggle is class struggle."

"I didn't touch Jasper." Kat massaged her own temples as she repeated herself. "But I was out looking into another disappearance last night. We need to call Davis, because I think he's being sent to Beloit."

Both of the other girls paled. The keycard Alicia had been playing with dropped from her hand.

"Beloit," Iris whispered shakily. "But that isn't possible. His family are executives, Jasper should have been isolated and fined, not..."

"Do you actually think this has anything to do with your little club?" Kat asked incredulously. "The entire Schaumburg arcology is on lockdown, and shareholders are making power plays. We literally could be in the middle of a hostile takeover right now, and the two of you think that corporate leadership cares in the slightest about your efforts?"

"Lockdown?" Alicia whimpered, licking her lips nervously. "Why haven't we heard anything about that? Daddy has interests in Schaumberg's bio-research division. He should have heard something about it by now."

"Lockdown usually means interrupting communications," Kat replied, trying and failing to be patient with the distraught girl. "Unless someone was able to make it past the guards and bring information directly to your father, he'd have no way of knowing."

"Then how did—" Alicia began, only for Kat to silence her with a condescending glare.

Iris worked her mouth, looking like nothing more than a fish gasping on a riverbank as she tried to process Kat's eruption.

"Oh for God's sake," Kat grumbled. "I need to get back into *The Tower of Somnus*. Someone call Davis and tell him I said I have information about Jasper, but that we'll need to move fast. We can meet at the restaurant across the street from the college at six o'clock. Tell him I'll bring one of my friends from Schaumburg."

"What are your friends going to do to fix this?" Iris blurted out, practically hyperventilating. "If we need to get into Beloit, we'll need a merc company. I can talk to my mom. She doesn't approve of the Vanguard, but if I tell her that there's the potential for a hostile takeover—"

"We can work that out with Davis." Kat cut her off with a decisive movement of her hand.

"But you don't understand." Iris just kept talking, cheeks flushed as she rattled on at a feverish pace. "This isn't the sort of thing that our personal guards can handle. We're going to need to hire some independent contractors. My mom has a fixer, someone who can set us up with some samurai. It might take a couple of days, but—"

"Holy shit," Kat interrupted, failing to contain a chuckle despite the severity of the situation. "You seriously didn't even do a background check on me before you tried to jump me? That's absolutely priceless."

"What's that supposed to mean?" Iris asked, finally jolted out of her monologue by Kat's laughter.

"Ask Davis before you decide on whether to attend the meeting tomorrow." Kat turned to leave, waving at the two of them over her shoulder.

She closed the door to Alicia's room behind herself, ignoring the urgent questions from the other two girls as she made her way back to her room. A minute later, her head was on the pillow. Kat closed her eyes and let herself float off to sleep.

Kat stumbled as Kaleek slapped her on the shoulder.

"Another long night, Kat?" The otter chortled as she staggered and shot him a playful glare. "Elders help us if you can get past your smooth skin and get a boyfriend. You'll leave Dorrik and I here holding our tails every night."

"Ignore him, Miss Kat," Dorrik interjected. "Kaleek is just excited to be on a damper floor. He spent the first hour bragging about how excited he was to swim and fish. Then when he realized you were late, he just started fretting."

"It's good to see both of you, too." Kat straightened up, brushing off the back of her armor. "I'm sorry for being late, I was busy unraveling the conspiracy to take over my planet, thank you for asking."

Dorrik leaned in, their eyes narrowed.

"We've found out that members of my world's leadership met with the stallesp directly to discuss taking over the planet in partnership with the stallesp," Kat continued grimly. "Better yet, a recording was made of the meeting."

"This is perfect, Kat!" Dorrik smiled, crest flaring wildly. "There isn't a lokkel enclave on the fourth floor, but I can send a message out with my next ship. With this recording in hand, the clans can convene and send out a punitive expedition to clear the moles from your orbit."

"It's not in hand." She winced. "Well, it was, but I think I sold it. Right now, we know someone who can locate it, but he's in enemy custody at the moment."

"That sounds like the opposite of in hand," Kaleek interjected helpfully. "You should try not selling critical evidence of violations of Consensus law next time."

"I'll keep that in mind, Kaleek." Kat rolled her eyes. "We're going to get the recording. It's evidence of treason by some very powerful people that want to kill my family and I. I'm not sure I would survive long enough for your fleet to arrive without it."

He clapped his hands together. "Now that we've cleared that up, let's find a map and a boat so we can hit the waves."

Dorrik's crest fluttered in distress. "I'm not sure that we should be diving into anything, Kaleek," they replied somberly. "The fourth floor isn't as closely mapped by my race as the third for obvious reasons, and if what Miss Kat's saying is true, we may have a tremendous problem on the horizon."

"I knew this was going to happen." Kaleek grinned. "So for once I planned ahead. Someone in my pod had information on a dungeon named 'Whirring Cogs.' It's about an hour away, so we'll have plenty of time to talk."

"What sort of information did you acquire on Whirring Cogs?" Dorrik asked unhappily. "It sounds like Miss Kat could use another dungeon award sooner rather than later, but I would prefer that we entertain challenges with our eyes open."

"The average enemies are called iron automatons—they have a number of blade-based and spring-loaded traps—and the boss is something called a clicking horror." Kaleek put a hand on both of their backs, pushing them toward the marketplace of the Adventurer's Hall. "The dungeon itself is metal- and clockwork-themed with the foes and traps modeled upon stylized archaic robots. Is that a good enough answer, professor? Can we go now?"

"What about that makes it a good match for our skillsets?" Dorrik squinted at the impatient otter. "Psi abilities don't usually work on robots, and I'm not sure I like the sound of traps. Having footpads or someone with a spotting skill is usually recommended for those sorts of dungeons and, as you will note, we have neither."

"Kat's basically a footpad." Kaleek squeezed her shoulder, drawing a brief frown. "Plus, I looked into it. One of the major drops from this dungeon is something called a 'soul engine.' It's a red, fist-sized ball lodged in the iron automatons' chest that lets them be targeted by psi abilities."

"Well." He twitched his whiskers in amusement. "That, and soul engines allow them to adapt to their circumstances and plan ambushes. Still, that only makes them more fun to fight."

"I don't have any footpad skills," Kat replied. "I might have the agility and reactions of a footpad, but unless your plan is for me to trigger traps and jump out of the way before I get impaled on spikes, I'm not sure how you expect me to deal with traps without the Disarm skill."

"Also," she added, squinting at the otter, "if that is your plan, I'd suggest you go first. You're pretty stout and you have heavy armor. I doubt a trap could kill you in one go. We could just heal you up and send you back into the fray after each one."

"There aren't that many traps." Kaleek fluttered his eyelashes at her. "It's mostly a monster dungeon. Just one or two to keep us on our toes."

"One question…" Dorrik rumbled, drawing an easy grin from Kaleek.

"Yesssss?" the desoph asked, drawing the word out as he smiled triumphantly at the big lizard.

"…for Miss Kat." Dorrik ignored Kaleek's dispirited groan. "How soon do you need to find this political prisoner, and how dangerous will it be to save them?"

"Tomorrow, if possible." Kat grimaced. "They're going to torture information out of him. Even if he has nerves of steel, he's going to crack if we give them more than two days. As for the danger level? I'm going into an armed prison camp blind with unknown backup. I would say somewhere between 'extreme' and 'idiotic.'"

She pursed her lips unhappily.

"Honestly?" Kat flipped some hair out her eyes with a deep sigh. "If I wasn't racing a clock, there's no way in hell I'd run the mission. There are just too many unknowns, even if we had the time to properly case the joint. It just seems like a recipe for disaster."

"Then it sounds like we need a map and a boat." Dorrik nodded somberly. "Miss Kat needs our help, but we are too far away to assist. I'm not comfortable running a dungeon with incomplete information, but if necessity can make Miss Kat step outside her comfort zone in the waking world, I don't see a reason why it can't do the same to me in the dreamscape."

She smiled gratefully at the big lizard as Kaleek cheered and ran over to a vendor. Barely a minute later, he was back, holding a map seared into leather with a coating of some sort of waterproofing slathered over the top.

They left the Adventurer's Hall, stepping out into bright fake sunlight and the smell of saltwater. The light wasn't anywhere near as oppressive as on the third floor, but Kat still shielded her eyes and looked up. Above them, the shadows of birds wheeled around in a cloudless sky, screeching at each other before they dove into the water in search of the plentiful shoals of fish.

Kaleek led the way, practically skipping, past a number of one story fishing shanties made out of a combination of mud bricks and driftwood. Kat couldn't help but notice that they received a fair share of unwelcome looks, but she put it down to the three of them being a new team on the floor. Still, her hand hovered around her knife's sheath as they chatted on their way to the city's wharves. It never hurt to be careful.

Finally, they were tromping down a weathered wooden dock past a sign that said in simple clean lettering 'boat rental.' Tethered to the expanse of wood were three older but lovingly maintained catamarans. At the end of the pier, a black-and-orange gecko with a pair of giant fins that resembled wings growing from its sides, slouched in a misshapen rocking chair made from driftwood, a reed cap pulled over their face and eyes.

"Hello stranger!" Kaleek called out cheerfully as they approached.

The gecko barely moved, body still slumped bonelessly in the chair, a single sticky black limb reaching up and pushing back the hat just enough to reveal a trio of yellow eyes.

"Lo," they replied, unmotivated and lethargic.

"I see that you have boats for rent," Kaleek continued help-fully. "It just so happens that my friends and I are looking to charter one."

The gecko shifted slightly with a slurping sound that sent a shudder down Kat's spine.

"One of your friends is a lokkel," they observed, yellow eyes blinking slowly.

"Very astute of you," Kaleek replied, a hint of uncertainty entering his voice. "Now, if you would be so kind as to give us your prices, we would love to get sailing."

"Don't rent to no lokkel." The gecko rocked forward, the chair squealing under their weight before they leaned to the side and spit a gob of something greenish into the water. "Don't rent to no stallesp either. Bad business."

"What?" the otter asked, confusion now reigning on his face as he looked back at Dorrik and Kat, whiskers twitching helplessly.

"Lotta stallesp on the floor." The gecko focused on Dorrik, nodding slowly. "Ships with lokkel on them go missing. They say it's pirates, megalodons, or living reefs, but ol' Jaffy knows better. Only stallesp and lokkel ships go missing. Then the other side has a ship come back, covered in burns and holes. Bad business."

"You're Jaffy then, I take it?" Kaleek asked, trying to turn on his charm once more. The gecko grunted in the affirmative. "Well then, Jaffy, let's say I wanted to sail out for a dungeon run anyway. What would you recommend a dashing fellow such as myself with a lokkel friend do?"

Jaffy turned their attention to Kaleek, staring at the desoph. One second faded into another and before long, the otter was fidgeting slightly, plastic smile still adorning his face.

"Won't rent, but you can buy." Jaffy jerked their head toward the smallest of the three boats. "The *Marka* has seen better days, but she's a good ship. Doesn't look pretty, but she'll get you where you need to go and she has a shallow enough draft to avoid most of the living reefs."

Kaleek looked back at the three of them uncertainly. Kat shrugged helplessly, but Dorrik nodded their approval.

"How much for the *Marka* then?" Kaleek's toothy smile was already back on his face as he addressed the gecko once more.

"Five hundred marks." Jaffy grunted without any enthusiasm. "You ain't gonna find a better ship for less. Mostly cause you ain't gonna find another ship."

Kat winced as Dorrik drew in a sharp, whistling breath. Between the three of them, they had enough, barely, but it looked like the sleepy gecko was about to take them to the cleaners.

CHAPTER TWENTY-SIX

The catamaran cut across the waves, sending a spray of saltwater into the air as it hit each rolling crest of water. Dorrik sat dead center in the ship, their black scales showing a hint of green as they clutched their legs to their chest with all four of their arms.

Kaleek, grinning like a pup, worked the vessel's sails to keep them on course. He banked suddenly, steering the ship directly into a wave to stop it from knocking the *Marka* off course. Kat staggered slightly, grabbing onto a handhold to avoid being thrown about as Dorrik gagged behind her.

"Ocean's a little choppy!" Kaleek shouted gleefully at the two of them. "But I haven't seen any signs of a living reef and the dreamscape has seen fit to bless us with a sunny day, so I would say everything is looking up."

"Looking up?" Dorrik choked out, wobbling slightly as they struggled to dig the claws of their feet into the stiff wooden reeds that made up the boat's deck. "I swear you're aiming for each and every wave just to spite me. Once we sort this business out with Miss Kat, we're staying at the next lokkel enclave for at least a month."

"Of course I'm aiming for the waves," Kaleek replied, pushing the wooden beam the sail was mounted on so the flapping cloth would catch the wind and adjust the ship's heading slightly. "They're between waist- and shoulder-high, Dorrik. I'm not going to let one catch us amidship and flip us. I mean, I'd probably be fine, but the two of you would almost certainly drown before a megalodon managed to show up and eat you."

"Can you at least stop looking so happy while you're doing it?" the lizard ground out miserably. "Even if all this water is necessary, that doesn't mean you have to be so damn chipper about it. It's unnatural."

"Oh, go sun yourself on a rock." Kaleek cackled joyously. "There's just something about the water roiling under your feet and the wind in your fur that speaks to you."

Dorrik stiffened. There was a definite note of green to their scales as they scrambled to the edge of the boat, heaving the contents of their stomach into the ocean below.

"Look at the wind whipping through Kat's hair," Kaleek continued, studiously ignoring the suffering lokkel. "She's having fun, Dorrik. That's the problem with you. You need to learn to loosen your scales and live a little."

Kat glanced back at the two of them guiltily from where she'd been standing near the prow of the catamaran, both of her hands steadying herself on the guardrail.

"I was looking for the volcanic island the dungeon's on," she replied guiltily, grimacing at Dorrik's misery. "Everything looks the same out here. I wanted to make sure that we didn't miss it and torment Dorrik any longer than necessary."

The lokkel glanced at her, a look of gratitude in their eyes before the boat crested another wave and slammed down hard enough to make Kat stumble. Dorrik lunged back to the railing, slumping over the edge and convulsing once again.

"Don't worry your fuzzy head," Kaleek grunted as he put his shoulder into the sail, steering them into another swell. "I might enjoy giving our scaly friend a hard time, but I know what I'm doing and I'm not going to prolong this any more than necessary. Given the speed of the wind and the angle of the sun, we should be about ten minutes from the island."

"Can Dorrik make it ten minutes?" Kat asked with concern. The waves were getting choppier and the lokkel was really beginning to struggle.

"I am a—" Dorrik wobbled, clutching the railing hard enough that their knuckles turned white. "A proud lokkel warrior. I can survive an unnatural collection of water. Even if I may curse its very existence."

Kat glanced at Kaleek and the otter just shrugged. She turned back to the prow of the ship, shading her eyes with a free hand while she squinted against the glare. In the distance, Kat could barely make out a dull mound of rock jutting out of the sparkling waves.

As she watched, the shape grew large, Kaleek skillfully guiding their ship through the choppy water toward it. Finally, when they drew near, the otter barked at Kat to draw her attention.

"Kat." He jerked his head toward the rope coiled around a pole near the ship's prow. "It looks like the island doesn't have anything like a dock for us to land on. You're going to need to jump onto the island and pull the ship up onto the shore once I find a beach. Otherwise the waves are going to either wash the *Marka* away, or batter it against the rocks."

She looked down at the catamaran doubtfully. It wasn't exactly a yacht, but it was more than big enough for the three of them. She'd leveled up her strength once, but Kat was hardly a bodybuilder.

"At least hold it still long enough for me to get off the ship," Kaleek begged, circling the *Marka* around the small island as he looked for a beach. "Dorrik will be useless for at least another ten minutes. This needs to be you, Kat."

"I can try to use Levitation," she conceded grudgingly. "I'm not sure it will do anything, but at least I can give it a shot."

They rounded a crag jutting out from the island as Kat unwound the rope. In front of them, a small beach of gray sand had been carved out of the jagged volcanic rock of the island by the waves. Without speaking, Kaleek curved their ship toward the relatively flat expanse, and Kat began gathering mana.

Just before the twin keels of their ship bit into the sand, she jumped out, casting Levitation on the *Marka* as she fell into the waist deep water.

It was *cold*. Positively icy after the warm but windy trip from their starting point.

Kat grit her teeth, throwing the rope over her shoulder and digging her shoes into the sand as she struggled to pull the catamaran up onto the shore. Even with its weight magically decreased and partially buoyed by the ocean, Kat didn't make much progress.

The saltwater from the frothing waves stung her eyes and face, but each grunting strain only brought the ship another handful of feet up onto the shore, only for the ocean to pull hungrily at the vessel as the water receded.

She wasn't even sure she was making progress, advancing one step only to lose it the next second, when Kaleek splashed into the water next to her. He grinned at her, whiskers twitching cheerfully, before he grabbed onto the wet rope and looped it around his forearm.

They pulled together, straining against the bucking and swaying vessel. One step after another, keels grinding against the sand as they left the water, they dragged the *Marka* out from the ocean's grasp.

"Good enough," Kaleek grunted before collapsing on the gray sand, exhausted.

Kat joined him a second later, chest heaving. The sand was coarse, each grain much bigger than expected. From the moment she sat down, Kat could feel it working its way into the cracks of her armor. She suppressed the urge to immerse herself in the roiling, white-topped waves. Right now she was covered in rope burns and abrasions. Saltwater wouldn't fix anything.

"There has to be a better way to do that," she gasped back, fighting for breath as she gingerly laid down on the uncomfortable sand. "That was absolutely awful."

"There is," Kaleek replied, laying down next to her so his head almost touched hers as the two of them looked at the sky. "It involved hiring that old grakkon, Jaffy, and having them do the dragging for us. Even better, if we had rented a boat, they would've just dropped us off. Once we completed the dungeon, we could just wait until we woke up and respawn in town the next night."

"That sounds nice." Kat reached up, wiping the water from her face.

"Oh! Look who decided to join us," Kaleek called out.

Kat glanced up. The desoph had propped himself up on his arms and was smiling at Dorrik as they staggered unsteadily onto the beach.

"The next enclave, two months minimum," Dorrik ground out, their voice haggard.

"Sure thing." Kaleek sprang to his feet as nimbly as possible when wearing bulky metal armor. "In the meantime, maybe we should look into getting some draughts to prevent sea sickness the next time we go to town. I was pretty miserable on the third floor, but you're barely functional right now."

"We don't have marks for draughts." Dorrik stumbled only for Kaleek to catch them. "We spent all of them on that blasted ship."

"I don't think they're that expensive, Dorrik," Kat grunted out as she stood up, trying to massage the burn out of her aching arms. "We should earn a fair amount in this dungeon. If it's about money, I'll buy you a couple if you want. You looked absolutely awful on the trip out here."

Dorrik opened their jaws to respond. Instinctively, Kat knew that they were about to turn her down, but then they stumbled again, barely held upright by Kaleek. Their body shuddered as they clutched onto the desoph, claws scraping across his glittering armor.

"Thank you, Miss Kat." Dorrik shot her a grateful look as they slumped onto Kaleek's shoulder. "I suppose I must accept. It wouldn't be appropriate to compromise my combat effectiveness for no reason other than stubborn pride."

"The dungeon portal is at the top of the hill." Kaleek patted Dorrik's back gently. "We should get climbing. Luckily, it's a bit of a hike. It'll give ol' Dorrik here a couple of minutes to adapt back to solid land."

"I honestly don't understand how my race makes it past this floor." Dorrik shook their head ruefully. "I'm feeling a bit better, but even the *thought* of stepping back onto a boat has my stomachs churning right now. Without help from the two of you, I'd be absolutely defenseless. If by some miracle I avoided falling into the water and drowning, the first monster that came along would simply eat me as I batted ineffectually at it."

"Isn't that the point of the tower though?" Kaleek chuckled. "It spits environments and scenarios at us that would be difficult for any one race to deal with. My theory is that the ancients designed the dreamscape to try to force the races of the Consensus to intermix and work together. After all, it's just a fact that *The Tower of Somnus* is that much easier to climb with a collection of different species."

"That may have been part of the Gardeners' point," Dorrik began, "but in Clan Ahn we are taught that the real—"

They stopped, eyes wide. Kat followed Dorrik's gaze and gasped quietly despite herself.

Half buried under the rocks of the island was the charred keel of a ship. Almost twice the length of their own, the boat originally would have resembled a galleon, a great square-rigged sailing vessel.

Now? It was a skeleton, the massive beams of timber that made up its framework heavily burned, but the rest of the vessel had long since eroded and been partially concealed by a rock slide.

Dorrik brushed off Kaleek's hand, staggering briefly as they trotted over to the wreck. Their body glowed purple as they enhanced their strength and began tossing rocks aside.

For a minute, waves and the clatter of stone on stone were the only sounds on the island as Kat and Kaleek watched Dorrik dig in silence. Then the big lizard suddenly froze.

Dorrik stepped backward, emitting a low and mournful crooning noise, their crest depressed flat against their scaly head. Kat leaned to the side, trying to see what the big lizard was upset about, but only able to make out a clawed hand covered in iridescent silver scales that stuck out from a pile of rocks.

"Clan Trassk," Kaleek said, his voice bleak. "One of Clan Ahn's closest allies and trading partners. They're a major player in lokkel politics as well as the Consensus as a whole."

"The claw?" Kat asked hesitantly.

"Likely the whole ship." Kaleek's voice was quiet, not wanting to interrupt Dorrik as the lokkel threw their head back, the croon transforming into a slow, whistling dirge. "Maybe Dorrik was onto something when they were talking about this floor being a trap for their race."

"I will kill them." Dorrik whipped around, fire in their eyes. "Each and every mole that crawls out of their subterranean warrens. The dreamscape is meant to allow challenges. It's an outlet to prevent conflict from spilling over into the waking world, but there is a method and a logic to them. No challenge or grievance has been declared, yet the stallesp choose to wage an unofficial war. Not only that, they target the lower levels."

Kat shifted uncomfortably. She wasn't exactly sure how most humans would feel having the fourth floor classified as a 'lower level.' Barely ten percent of their players had even made it this far.

"The stallesp hunt *whelps*." The giant lizard practically thrummed with purple energy. "They do not seek to follow the rules of conflict. This attack had nothing to do with resolving a dispute. It is a naked attempt to cripple Clan Trassk's next generation, nothing more or less."

"Then," Dorrik bellowed, the energy pouring off of them forcing Kat to take a step backward. "There are the disquieting rumors from Earth. They plan to break the Galactic Consensus' most sacred rule and interfere with a race that is not ready. They are a blight. A poison festering in the gut of the Galactic Consensus, eating it from the inside out."

"Allowing the stallesp into the Consensus was a mistake." Dorrik's claw flashed purple as they crushed a rock that they'd been holding. "One I will personally rectify."

"I don't understand." Kat frowned as she surveyed the destroyed ship. Now that she was looking closer she could make out a number of other silver limbs and tails sticking out from the wreckage. "We've personally seen three stallesp attacks. What makes this one different?"

"We're warriors." Dorrik slammed a clawed fist into their chest. "We are prepared to fight monsters or survive traps at a moment's notice. Attacking us is dishonorable, the action of a simpering coward, but not entirely unexpected."

"Clan Trassk are merchants and poets." The lokkel's crest futtered sadly, still mostly flat on Dorrik's head. "There might have been two or three weapons on this entire ship to ward off the attacks of monsters. One appropriately leveled warrior could have torn through them like a brick through tissue paper. This wasn't combat, it was a massacre."

"Easy now," Kaleek said soothingly as he walked up to Dorrik, patting the big lokkel on their upper right forearm. "We're with you, but we've got a dungeon to fight. Plus, I'm not sure how much longer I want to just stand out here in the open. If there are stallesp raiders about, it's best that we keep moving."

"I don't want to keep moving," Dorrik growled dangerously, their claws bunched into fists. "I *want* their raiders to try me. I will happily feed their remains to the awful aquatic predators that haunt this infernal place."

Kat blinked. This wasn't the Dorrik she was used to. She'd seen the lokkel annoyed before, but their demeanor right now was something else. Rather than their usual aloof and inquisitive nature, she was staring at blind, trembling rage.

"Come on now, big fella." Kaleek's quiet words were almost inaudible over the surf. "This isn't Bashmere Pass. Going wild now won't bring your clutchmates back. You said it yourself when we got back into the tower together. The only way to pay the stallesp back is to get stronger. As cathartic as going on a killing spree would be, you need dungeons and levels, not revenge. At least not yet."

Her heart froze. Dorrik's siblings. They were in a passenger liner when an unsurveyed asteroid 'happened' to end up in the hyperlane their ship was traveling on. Bystanders on a ship, just minding their business until the stallesp arrived.

"There's a dungeon right at the top of the hill, we can blow off steam there." Kaleek began leading Dorrik away. "We've got years and years left to live. Give it time. The stallesp will get what they deserve. Just stick to the plan."

Dorrik closed their eyes, crest flaring wildly. They shuddered. A brief moment where their entire body shook, and then, eyes still closed, they nodded solemnly.

CHAPTER TWENTY-SEVEN

Dorrik slammed their shoulder into the frozen iron automaton, sending the whirring golem into the dungeon wall with enough force that two of its eight limbs were torn from its body. The remainder were bent beyond repair, unable to support the creature's weight as it tried to lift itself from the gleaming steel floor only to collapse into a pile of scrap.

Kat glanced at Kaleek with worry as their friend kicked the pile of metal, sending it clattering into the wall once again. The otter just shrugged helplessly.

"You know you have swords, right?" Kat asked. Behind her, another five of the iron automatons lay on the ground, limbs torn off and their seeing gems dim. "I've heard from reliable sources that swords are more effective in a fight than body slamming metal opponents until they can't get up again."

"It's me," Kaleek supplied helpfully. "I'm reliable sources."

"Sorry," Dorrik replied with a grimace, shaking their leg to try to dislodge it from the automaton's limbs. "I have a lot of feelings I need to work out, and this dungeon's denizens can take a satisfying amount of abuse."

"Are you sure you don't just want to talk about it?" Kat

asked hopefully as she cast Cure Wounds I on the lokkel. "It would probably save me a lot of mana."

"I'm not sure that crying like a whelp over past grievances would change much." Dorrik held still only long enough for the golden energy to heal the cuts and blemishes to their scales. "The Galactic Consensus performed an inquiry into the death of my clutchmates and the other innocents on the passenger liner. The official cause of death was determined to be sabotage or gross negligence, perpetrator unknown. Of course, everyone knew the stallesp were behind it. They even had the temerity to try to grab some of the trade routes allocated to Clan Ahn with their grubby little claws, claiming that the 'accident' proved that we couldn't maintain our shipping lanes. It took everything I had to not use a pulser on their ambassador then and there."

"Pulser?" Kat raised an eyebrow, looking from Dorrik to Kaleek.

"Modern weaponry," Kaleek responded. "They look like a metal rod. I don't understand the specifics behind it, but you don't want it pointing at you when it goes off. Modern armor will take one to two shots, but it'll turn anything from your planet into a superheated plume of plasma."

"Not nearly as satisfying as ripping something apart with a sword." Dorrik opened the gleaming circular door to exit the room. "There's something about the bulge of muscle, pull of sinew, and the thud of metal hitting an enemy's flesh that's viscerally appealing in the way that an electric whine and an explosion can't match."

Kat shot a worried glance at Kaleek. The otter's whiskers twitched uncertainly.

Dorrik stepped through the archway, and Kat was reacting almost before she heard the click. The pseudopod she'd kept active, a tentacle of water curled about her waist, leapt forward, grabbing Dorrik and pulling them back a step.

The lokkel blinked dumbly at the two dozen spikes that had sprouted from the walls. For a second, they filled the hallway, a deadly lattice of glittering steel occupying the space formerly occupied by Dorrik's torso from the top of their waist to the bridge of their muzzle. Soundlessly, each of the metal points slipped back into the hidden slots they had sprung from.

"Okay." Kat chuckled nervously. "We're going to stop for a second and everyone is going to take a deep breath. Dorrik, this isn't like you and you know it. Usually it's your job to stop me from making a mistake, or Kaleek from doing something deliberately stupid. I understand that you're angry, but you're letting it get the better of you."

The big lizard closed their eyes and shook their head, a short violent motion from side to side. When they opened them again, Kat could see a little more clarity, but still enough rage and grief to make her worried.

"I don't think you understand, Miss Kat." They took a deep, shuddering breath, crest fluttering wildly. "Deep down, this is who I am. I was a studious youth before the death of my clutchmates, but their murder changed something inside me."

"I realized then and there that two or three levels a year wasn't going to cut it." Dorrik's voice was solemn as they recited their past. "I would need to be powerful like Eidrass. A strong enough player in the games of diplomacy that I could simply do as I willed and dare someone to stop me. Only then could I shake the stallesp's warrens until they gave me the answers I needed."

"I am not calm." They shook their head, chuckling ruefully. "Far from it. Each day as the suns rise over my training retreat, I am filled with boundless rage. Then, I bottle that rage up so that I may use it as motivation to fuel me through my rigorous training routine. My demeanor is sedate because blind anger serves no purpose. I put it aside. I let it grow and fester, knowing that one day, I will let it out on those that truly deserve it."

"That…" Kat's tongue tripped over itself as she tried to find the words. "That sounds profoundly unhealthy. I can understand revenge. Hell, I want to be part of your revenge."

She caught herself. It was true. Every relationship in her life outside of her immediate family required a careful balancing act. From humoring Jasper to working closely with someone she trusted like Xander, Kat needed to watch every word she said in order to avoid betrayal. Even her friendships required a quick bout of mental calculus to ensure that the person she was talking with would not become a liability or potential antagonist at some later date.

Despite all of that, she wanted to help Dorrik. Their goals were lofty to the point of foolishness, but that hardly mattered in the face of the raw pain wracking the lokkel's muzzle. Before anything else, Dorrik was her friend, and they needed her help.

"I can think of about six people in the entire galaxy that I would risk myself like that for." Kat pointed at the big lizard. "You, Kaleek, my mom, my sister, Xander, and Whippoorwill."

"*But.*" Kat stressed the word. "We can't hunt down the moles responsible if we get angry and arrogant and die in here. You're smarter than me, Dorrik, we both know that. That means you're definitely smarter than this."

"I hate to pile on." Kaleek clapped a fuzzy hand on Dorrik's shoulder. "But I think the girl is onto something. Not using a sword on an enemy is dumb. Charging down a hallway without checking it out despite us having an intelligence report that warned of occasional traps? My baby nephew knows not to do that, and he hasn't even opened his eyes yet."

Dorrik closed their eyes once again. They took a deep breath and then another, their chest rising and falling steadily to an unheard rhythm.

"Thank you," Dorrik replied, crest fluttering sedately above their head. "I will do my best to act more rationally."

"At the very minimum, I will begin using my swords again." They smiled weakly. "I can certainly agree that discontinuing their use was more than a bit inadvisable on my part."

"Great!" Kaleek shook the lokkel cheerfully. "Now unless one of you has learned how to disarm a self-resetting trap in the last twenty minutes, I think it's about time that we crawl under some razor sharp spikes."

The otter led the way, shimmying under the metal spears on

his stomach. Kat followed, checking the hallway for follow up traps as Dorrik barely worked their massive frame beneath the metallic thresher.

Finding none, they walked unmolested to the door for the boss chamber. As Kat was reaching for the door's knob, some sixth sense stopped her. Instead, she peered closer.

Rather than the uniform metal she'd expected, the door-knob had a number of narrow slits in it, barely visible even on a close inspection. She stepped back and poked it with her knife.

Immediately, dozens of whisper-thin blades blossomed from the doorknob, turning it into a beautiful but deadly flower made of razors and poison.

She frowned as the blades retracted back into the door. Obviously there was some sort of mechanism that powered the trap, but Kat didn't know the first thing about identifying or disarming it. Worse, it wasn't like the spikes in the hallway that they could bypass. After all, it was fairly hard to open a door without using the knob.

"Allow me." Dorrik's claw tapped her on the shoulder.

The massive lizard glowed purple for a moment before they lunged forward, planting their shoulder in the door and leaving a massive dent in the metal door. They staggered back, a dumb grin on their face.

Before Kat could stop Dorrik, they repeated the process with a grunt, throwing themselves at the door. This time, it screeched in protest, but the weight of the stampeding lokkel ripped it off of its hinges, toppling it into the next room with Dorrik just behind it.

The big lizard flopped forward, their momentum pulling them past the threshold and into the boss chamber. They stumbled immediately, tripping on the doorframe and onto the metal floor beyond.

Dorrik tried to catch themselves, claws digging furrows into the steel as the ground lurched under them. Out of the corner of her eye, Kat noticed that the entire room was filled with metal discs, each of them spinning at a different speed.

She could worry about that later. For now, her friend was off-balance, wobbling toward the edge of his platform as the disc spun incessantly.

Kat's pseudopod grabbed Dorrik by the tail, pulling her off her feet as the lokkel stumbled clumsily across a man-sized rotating disc of metal, all four of their arms pinwheeling in an attempt to regain their balance.

Mana flowed through her, casting Levitation on Dorrik just in time to stop them from falling off of the spinning plate entirely.

Dorrik took an unsteady step backward, heaving a sigh of relief. Kat hopped on to the plate with them, surveying the room and frowning.

They were in a massive chamber, easily big enough to moor the *Marka* in it a dozen times over. At the far end of the room, the dungeon altar stood on an unassuming stone pedestal. Everything else was made of steel. Brightly polished and almost blinding in the magical light…

Beneath her feet, the disc she was on whirred and rotated. At its edges, she could make out the large square teeth of a gear as it spun in time with another metal circle.

The room didn't have a proper floor. Maybe somewhere far beneath them there was a 'ground' of stone, but if it existed, it was so far down that Kat couldn't see it. Rather than steady footing, the room was populated by islands made of spinning gears, all moving at different speeds.

Some of the larger gears moved slowly enough that a person on them would hardly notice. Mid-sized cogs like the one that Kat was standing on with Dorrik made a full rotation once every two to three seconds, enough to be disorienting but not crippling if you were looking for it.

The real problem was the numerous smaller gears. Barely the size of a dinner table, they spun incredibly fast in order to keep up with the rest of the clockwork. One errant step and Kat could easily end up with her legs moving away from each other at dramatically different speeds.

Of course, a missed step that landed in the gears' teeth could easily result in a crushed extremity. Kat didn't doubt that dozens of avatars had met their fate, losing a foot, crushed under the inexorable grind of metal, before falling into the endless depths below.

The ground shook under her as Kaleek jumped onto the gear next to them. He looked around the room and grinned.

"Anyone spot the boss yet?" he asked cheekily. "I vote we check the lake."

Kat rolled her eyes, letting Pseudopod and her previous iteration of Levitation lapse, before casting Levitation on herself once again and jumping to a neighboring cog.

"I'm sure it will make itself known in due time," she quipped back. "It's spent all of this time waiting for us, it would hardly be appropriate for us to spoil its grand entrance."

Click. The sound echoed throughout the room, somehow clearly audible over the cacophony of the metal gears grinding against each other.

Click. Click. Each bass note struck Kat with the force of a drum beat, rattling her bones and resonating with the air in her chest.

Click. Click. Click. Kat felt her vision blur slightly as the sound washed over her. Underneath her feet, the cog began to spin faster, forcing her to change her position so that she was still looking in the direction of the altar.

Click. Click. Click. Click. A massive metal limb, as smooth as quicksilver, snaked up from the depths of the room, curving sinuously around the stone pillar that the altar stood on.

Click. Click. Click. Click. Click. Bile rose in Kat's throat. The combination of the bass notes and the steadily increasing speed of the clockwork she was standing on played hell with her balance.

Click. Click. Click. Click. Click. Click. The end of the limb hardened into a rectangular tooth and the metal tentacle darted downward, inserting itself between the teeth of one of the tiny gears.

The cog caught hold of the thick metal rope, its steadily turning teeth locking onto the metal and pulling it. The metal limb spooled into a spiral above the gear, the limb traveling in rapid circles around the top of the small metal disc as it interlocked with and was powered by its companions.

Kat noticed the rectangular prong at the tip of the limb pulsing and changing shape slightly to accommodate the tight space between the gear and its neighbors as the limb's owner was dragged upward, like an anchor being winched up out of the depths. Seconds later, the dungeon boss was hoisted into her line of vision by the rapidly spinning gears.

It was big, but not nearly as big as most of the boss monsters they'd had to fight. Kat would put the size and bulk of its oval core right around that of the genetically engineered cattle she'd worked on at Ike Holdings.

The mad collection of limbs sprouting from that core was a different story. The monster had four of the metal cables, each the size of her thigh, each resembling a prehensile rope ending in a manhole-sized chunk of metal that could be shaped seemingly at will. Already, three more of the tentacles had converted their tips into the same metal square it had used on the gear to pull itself up and into the chamber.

The creature had two scythe blades that swept out like the jaws of a beetle from its front. Perhaps most worryingly, the final tentacle had hardened its tip into a barbed point and the rest of the limb had coiled like a spring under the monster's main body.

Kat glanced at the rest of her party uncertainly, knife in hand and ready to spring into action as the creature let the centrifugal force of the gear whip it across the room.

Then, the other three limbs found homes amongst the whirring gears and the monster stabilized somewhat. Each extremity would spool and yank on the creature's core, pulling it in the tentacle's direction.

Once the clicking horror had established itself, a metal oval suspended in the air due to the tension of the four tentacles pulling at its core, the limbs began to dance. They would slip out of their gears for a moment, reducing the pull on the monster's body from their direction enough to send it whipping away, only to re-insert themselves a moment later.

Kat frowned grimly as the dungeon boss' main body began to see-saw back and forth between each of its limbs, the rotational forces pulling it in unpredictable directions.

With an audible 'thunk,' the first tentacle to surface pulled itself from its gear and darted in between another pair of the spinning cogs, changing the wild swaying of the monster's core slightly.

It reared back, chattering wildly from a mouth lined with literal razors that appeared in the lower third of its body, just behind the scythe blades, and launched the spear tentacle across the room at Kaleek.

One second, the cord of prehensile metal was wound tight beneath the monster's core, and the next it was frozen, just in front of the surprised otter, glittering with purple energy as *Arrest Momentum* held it in place.

Despite being taken unaware, Kaleek reacted decisively, the blade of his greatsword flashing red as he activated some skill and brought the weapon down with deceptive swiftness on the frozen tentacle.

It bent.

The monster clearly saw the attack coming, and jerked its harpoon downward to dissipate the force of Kaleek's sword. The blade hit the limb, just without the relative speed it needed to deliver a killing blow.

The slash still inflicted damage. Sparks flew everywhere, and there was more than a little silver liquid that sprayed all over the surrounding gears, but at the end of the exchange, the tentacle was returning to the creature's main body, battered but still functional.

Click. The monster's core pulsed in time with the note. Beneath their feet, the gears began to whirr slightly faster.

Kat's eyes widened.

"We need to bring this thing down *now!*" she shouted, jumping to a larger and slower moving plate of metal. "If it keeps speeding things up, it's going to spin us right into the abyss!"

"*Ego Shards!*" Dorrik replied, using an upgraded version of the psi ability as they leapt to their own gear, daggers of purple light flying across the room. Only one hit the chaotically swerving monster core, but that was enough to cause the entire creature to shudder.

Click. Click. Her knees weakened slightly as the waves of sound washed over her, attacking her inner ears and throwing off her balance.

Kat frowned, eyes following its wild swinging as it raced around the room, latching on to a new set of gears. Even a foe dodging normally would be enough to make Gravity Spike an uncertain proposition. Right now, it would just be a waste of mana.

She gathered her magic inside herself, focusing her attention instead on the array of lightly glowing gems that dotted the front of the clicking horror. If it was anything like the smaller iron automatons, those would be what served it as eyes.

"Eyes closed!" Kat shouted, screwing her eyelids shut as she rearranged her feet to counteract the slow turn of the gear she was standing on.

Dazzle flashed into existence, a riot of lights and colors erupting in a cone aimed in the monster's general direction.

Kat opened her eyes, blinking away the afterimage of the spell. She wasn't sure if the spell had partially missed the clicking horror or if the sight gems embedded in its surface just weren't as susceptible to bright lights as organic eyes, but other than a slight wobble, its core seemed unaffected.

The tentacles on the other hand, were a different story. A leg that had been in the air, seeking another gear to lodge itself in, missed its target. The square bit passed through the teeth of the gear only for the rapid turn of the smaller metal disc to grab the rope-like body of the limb, pulling it forward into the hungry maw of another gear.

With a deafening shriek of metal on metal, the metal tentacle was crushed. Although the rest of the quicksilver tendril was malleable, only the bit at the front could deform enough to survive being wedged between the interlocking discs.

The creature's body shuddered and listed to the side as it struggled to rebalance itself atop its three remaining tentacles, the injured limb too mangled to support its weight.

Click. Click. Click. Kat's vision grew fuzzy, and she fell to her hands and knees.

Acting on instinct, she rolled to the side just in time to hear another scream of metal on metal. The harpoon head of the final tentacle bounced off the steel gear beneath her in a shower of sparks.

"*Arrest Momentum,*" Dorrik shouted out from somewhere else in the room, but Kat was too busy scrambling to the side as the tentacle in front of her changed from a spear to an axe head before slashing at her throat.

Compared to its previous speed, the axe was almost sedate, moving at merely human velocities. Even on her hands and knees, Kat was able to partially dodge it, bringing up her knife in time to deflect the limb in another shower of sparks.

Then, rather than more clicking, the monster chattered angrily, withdrawing its weapon. Kat woozily regained her feet, a smile on her face.

It appeared that Dorrik and Kaleek had taken advantage of the distraction she'd provided. Kaleek stood over the remains of one of the monster's legs, whooping in triumph as the bottom portion of the limb still sparkled purple with psi energy, lodged between two of the gears.

That was one way to deal with a foe that could change its shape. Wait for it to pin itself, and then freeze it in place long enough for your fighter to land a decisive blow.

The clicking horror slammed unceremoniously onto one of the larger gears, spinning slowly as it withdrew both of its remaining tentacles to itself, the bits on their ends changing to sword blades as it prepared to defend itself.

Kat reoriented herself to face it, the smile growing on her face as she began pouring mana into Gravity Spike. The slow but powerful spell charged as she focused on the absolute center of the monster's body, enjoying the luxury of targeting a pinned foe. After all, an immobile target was her favorite kind of target.

Dorrik and Kaleek charged it, their swords batting aside the metal tentacles as they struggled against the uncertain and spinning footing to make it close enough to contest with the massive scythe limbs on the front of the horror.

They wouldn't need to. Gravity Spike crushed the monster's armor inward, crumpling the shell of steel like a soda can. As the pressure mounted, the metal it used to protect itself began to shatter and tear, transforming into an array of spikes and blades that lacerated whatever passed for the monster's innards as the spell pushed them together.

It shuddered once, and then the light in its sight gems faded. Around the chamber, the clockwork slowed as the rotation of the gears they were standing on began to grind to a halt.

Kaleek jumped heavily onto the disc next to her, no longer bothering to burn stamina to lessen the weight of his armor.

"Well," he said cheerfully. "That was fun. I think we were starting to get a bit complacent with the difficulty level of the dungeons on the third floor. I suppose that thing is a good reminder that the tower ramps up the challenge with each level you ascend."

"Either that or your intelligence report was lacking," Dorrik shouted back sourly. "That foe would have been an easy target with area of effect spells. Low hit points, high armor, high mobility. All we would have needed is an ability that could bypass the metal and attack a wide area, and the battle would have been over in seconds."

"Lightning for example," the lokkel continued, only to pause and put a claw to their muzzle pensively. "No, that might not have done the trick. The clicking horror's armor might have functioned as a faraday cage and prevented the attack from dealing damage. On the other hand, fire could do the trick. The only question is getting enough of it to heat the monster's entire body—"

"Good to have you back." Kat smiled at him in relief. "I prefer overly academic lectures to mindless rage any day of the week."

Dorrik stopped, taken aback for a moment before displaying their collection of sharp white teeth with a smile of their own.

"Then I shall endeavor to find new topics to lecture the two of you upon," Dorrik replied. "I'm sure that knowing more about the habits and ecological impacts of the fourth floor's living reefs could benefit the two of you greatly."

"I wouldn't go that far," Kaleek muttered. "Look, it's about time we all wake up. Kat, you go first and use the altar. Dorrik and I will follow in a bit. It's a shame that we won't be able to make it back to town before sun up. If we could sell the drops from here, it would go a long way toward defraying the cost of buying the *Marka*."

Kat hopped from one still gear to another, her increased agility and reactions making what should have been harrowing life or death jumps a trivial matter. Finally, she placed her hand on the altar and let the rainbow light consume her.

Congratulations, Adventurer!
You have completed the Wood Tier Level Four Dungeon, Whirring Cogs.
Three of three party members surviving. Good job!
Assigning awards:

Perk: Sensory Dampening

The standard dungeon award screen came alongside another, almost as welcome notification from the tower.

You have reached Level 7 in the skill Light I, please select a first tier spell.

~~Dazzle~~
~~Shadow~~
Laser
Mirage
Highlight
Eagle Eye

She appeared on the top of the small volcanic island, stepping carefully away from the dungeon portal and the bubbling lava of the island's caldera before making her selection and pulling up her status.

Name: Katherine Debs
Class: Elementalist Initiate
Max Level: 4
91 Marks

HP: 31
MP: 45
STA: 32

Dodge: Poor
Damage Mitigation: Insignificant

Strength: 4
Agility: 7
Fortitude: 3
Endurance: 4
Mind: 6
Reaction: 6
Charisma: 4
Spirit: 4

Spells Known:
Gravity's Grasp
Levitation
Pseudopod
Dehydrate
Dazzle
Shadow
Water Jet
Gravity Spike
Mirage

Skills Known:
Knife I - 10, 9%
Gravity I - 8, 44%
Water I - 9, 17%
Cat Step - 8, 14%
Light I - 7, 1%
Cure Wounds I - 7, 91%
Penetrate

Perks:
Nightvision
Leaping
Sensory Dampening

Quickly bringing up the entry for Sensory Dampening, Kat began nodding along as she read its description. The perk let her use her reaction attribute to automatically cut off her sight or hearing in response to an ability like Dazzle or a flashbang grenade. Hardly anything world shaking, but certainly a useful ability given how often she used Dazzle to disorient enemies.

Kat nodded to herself as Kaleek materialized behind her. She was as ready as she was going to get for the raid on Beloit, but Kat doubted that it would be enough. All she could do was hope that Davis could provide enough help to make up the difference.

CHAPTER TWENTY-EIGHT

Xander and Kat walked into the restaurant together, and the quiet conversation stopped. A dozen pairs of eyes dissected them as they stepped through the door. Kat shifted slightly, feeling exposed as every aspect of their dress and demeanor was inspected and catalogued.

It wasn't that the two of them were explicitly underdressed. Kat was wearing a fitted button down shirt with slacks. Xander's button down might have fit at one point, but after a decade or so of physical activity, he was almost bursting out of the overly tight outfit.

On the other hand, the clientele of the restaurant were all wearing tailored outfits that screamed understated wealth to those who knew what to look for. After half a semester of college, Kat knew what to look for. Nothing so crude as an actual designer label or logo, but the make of a button, the cut of a cuff, or the stitching of a lapel could be just as telling.

Studiously, the restaurant's patrons looked away from the two of them. There were good reasons for outsiders like Kat and Xander to be in a location like this, but they weren't the sort of reasons that encouraged casual curiosity.

"Ah, ah!" A man ran around a corner in an immaculate suit, bypassing the host's table and the startled woman occupying it. "Sir and madame! You must be here for Mr. Stoller's party. I'll lead you right to his private room."

"Stoller?" Xander asked, quirking an eyebrow at Kat as the maître d' led them past a number of well-appointed plush booths.

"He means Davis Stoller," Kat replied, automatically scanning the people sitting at the tables and milling about the bars for threats. A couple moved with the grace she'd come to expect from samurai and players, but all of them wore suits that exuded an aura of watchfulness and palpable menace that led inexorably to one conclusion. Bodyguards.

"An interesting man of many talents," the man leading them interjected unctuously. "When Mr. Stoller requested the private room on one day's notice... well, that was a familiar request."

"Not a good sign for the area's stability." He chuckled. "When Mr. Stoller takes an interest in something, it usually isn't healthy for those around it. Still, I'd much rather have him as a friend than an enemy, so when he asks for a favor, he gets a favor."

Xander glanced meaningfully at Kat.

"Davis has connections and moves like he's spent some time as a samurai." She shrugged, stopping as the maître d' halted in front of a heavy wooden door. "We're about to do something colossally dangerous. We need all the help we can get."

The door opened and Kat stepped through, Xander at her back. The room itself was fabulous, polished marble floors with priceless artwork covering tastefully soundproof walls, but her attention was immediately drawn to the table. Kat wasn't sure if it was cherry or oak, but there was no question in her mind that the beautifully maintained hardwood was worth more than the average employee would earn in three lifetimes.

It was set for six, Iris Leander looking out of place next to Davis, Andrew, and a stunningly attractive but bored-looking middle-aged woman in a slinky black dress. Davis' gaze pinned her to the ground the moment Kat's shoes clicked on the stone floor.

"Exe, I presume." He nodded to Xander, eyes never leaving Kat. "Is there a name you'd like to go by for these proceedings, miss…?"

For a bare fraction of a second, Kat turned her attention to Iris. She didn't want the girl to know about her, but it looked like that wasn't an option. Kat turned back to Davis' waiting expression.

She closed her eyes, exhaling. This was it. Her first real business meeting that wasn't entirely orchestrated by Xander.

"Erinyes." She opened her eyes, the indecision fleeing from her voice like the morning fog from the first rays of sun. "My name is Erinyes."

The woman sitting next to Davis erupted into a smile, her boredom forgotten.

"I knew Erinyes had to be a woman!" she purred, leaning forward, eyes glittering. "The rising star of the Chiwaukee underground. The gossip channels simply will *not* stop speculating about you."

"Where are my manners?" she asked with a smile, placing a hand in the center of her chest. "I go by Hestia, and I've heard all about you. It's a pleasure to finally meet you, Erinyes."

"The Fire Witch?" Xander cocked his head to the side. "I thought you retired?"

She glared at him for a full second before turning back to Kat, the smile returning to her face.

"It can be a bit of a sausage fest at these meetings," Hestia continued, pointedly ignoring Xander. "Us Greek girls have to stick together."

"Greek?" Iris cut in, confusion dripping from her voice. "Kat was born in Schaumburg. Also, why are you calling her—"

"Stop." Davis raised a hand. "We are planning an operation. In this room, her name is Erinyes. I've seen the footage where she earned the name and I have no doubts about her capabilities."

"Earned." Iris' eyes widened as the realization hit her. "Oh God, you're a samurai."

"An infiltrator, to be specific," Andrew supplied. "Although one a bit better known for carving her way out of jobs than getting in and out of locations undetected."

"Everyone's a critic," Kat replied with a roll of her eyes and a wave of her hand. "I haven't failed a run yet."

"Enough." Davis reached up with his left hand to massage his temples. "I swear to God, the two of you are children sometimes. Erinyes and Exe, you can refer to me as Merrimac. Hestia has already introduced herself, and 'youngster' over here—"

He hooked a thumb at Andrew. Kat frowned slightly at the emphasis on the word youngster.

"He goes by Dorian." Davis sighed. "But if I let the two of them go on, we'll be catching up on old times for the next four hours. Jasper is missing, and the only lead we have is that Iris said you wanted to call a meeting. I trust you have something that could be useful to me."

Kat looked to Xander only for him to shake his head and smile before taking his seat.

"This is your show, Erinyes." He picked up one of the restaurant's menus and began scanning it. "You called the meeting and you have the same intelligence I do. You're senior enough to lead a meeting, I don't see why you can't start now."

She took her own seat, mind spinning. Xander had sprung the lead role on her, but on the other hand, he was right. She'd been the one to call the meeting, and he had nothing independent to add. The people in the room knew her. It only made sense that she spearheaded things from their end.

"Exe and I were working another mission last night." As Kat spoke, the hitch of indecision fell from her voice. "After gathering information from a wet asset, we learned that our target has been picked up and taken to the Beloit prison camp as part of an attempted hostile takeover. The asset also revealed that a number of other individuals that could impede the takeover were picked up and shipped to Beloit around the same time."

Dorian slouched indolently in his seat, a far cry from the attentive driver that had helped Kat only a couple of days ago. Almost casually, he mused aloud, "You know, Thomas Franklin died in a car crash yesterday. Seems he drove his car drunk off of a bridge on his way out of town in the wake of something big. Security is tearing apart his suite and a lot of people are asking questions about his known acquaintances right now."

"The dean?" Iris asked, turning to Dorian. "What do you mean he's dead? He barely even leaves the college!"

"A shame," Kat replied blandly. "I'm sure he knew a lot of things that would have been useful to our current situation."

"A shame," Davis agreed, his brow furrowed. "I have to say, I'm not a fan of all this hostile takeover talk. I owe the Haupts a debt that I'll never be able to repay, and their wellbeing is very tied up in the current order of things. Even if Jasper weren't in danger, I'd be inclined to lend a hand. I'm presuming you have evidence to back up your claims?"

"Exe was recording." Kat nodded at Xander as the other man pulled his data jack from the base of his neck. Dorian stood up and walked around the table, flipping back a section of skin at the base of his skull to reveal a patch of chrome and his own cord.

The table sat in silence as the two men touched their connections together. Dorian took a step back before his eyes rolled back into his head, twitching slightly. Maybe five seconds later, he opened them once more.

"I watched the interrogation on high speed playback." Dorian returned to his seat. "The file appears to be genuine and Erinyes has represented it fairly. There wasn't any mention of Mr. Haupt's name, but with his position and the timing, I don't think there can be any doubt."

"Fuck." Davis grunted, leaning back in his chair, index finger tapping the table as he tried to gather his thoughts.

"I'll drink to that," Xander responded cheerfully, pouring himself a cup full of water from one of the crystal decanters left on the table.

"Beloit is a tough nut to crack, though." Davis turned to look at Hestia, a contemplative look on his face. "Hestia, you were on a team that was looking to extricate someone from Beloit a year or so ago. Whatever became of that?"

"Our target was killed in a bread riot before we could move, so the entire plan got scrapped." A marble of blue flame appeared in her hand, dancing over her fingers as Hestia spoke. "When we were considering our raid, the security force was two hundred guards. All of them were players, heavily chromed, or both."

Kat winced. Twenty-five security officers with subscriptions represented a major investment of corporate resources. Two hundred meant that GroCorp was deadly serious about keeping Beloit's inmates on the inside.

"The actual camp itself is a fortress." The blue flame bobbed and wove between Hestia's fingers hypnotically. "The walls are a massive, concrete octagon that surrounds the entire prison. They're sheer enough to eliminate climbing as an option, and there are enough tectonic sensors under them to rule out tunneling. Each length has six towers, four machine gun nests, and two 30mm cannon emplacements. The corners are fortified to the point that they might as well be bunkers. Between the cannons, mortars, and gun slits, I would recommend avoiding them at all costs."

"A direct attack is out then." Kat nodded slowly as she took in the other woman's words. "But that's hardly news. Even if we need to get two people out, I don't think GroCorp would take kindly to us breaking into the prison at night and wrecking the place. So long as we keep our actions to 'a discrete dispute between executives,' security will likely turn a blind eye after the fact. Actually destroying an expensive piece of corporate property like the prison camp, even if it were possible, would lead to repercussions that none of us can shoulder."

"Agreed," Davis replied. "With the caveat that we're all worm food if this doesn't work out. GroCorp will accept some damage and moderate employee deaths if it's to rescue 'improperly imprisoned executives,' but if we blow a hole in the wall and kill hundreds of senior guards, they will put a contract on us. If we don't walk out of there with an executive to corroborate our stories, that will also lead to a contract. Given that most of the people in this room have worked such contracts before, I don't think I need to emphasize how much I would prefer to avoid that."

Everyone but Iris, who looked about as confused and comfortable as a puppy in a thunderstorm, nodded solemnly. Assassination and open combat were entirely different concepts. Kat had won more than her fair share of battles against better armed and more skilled opponents due to the element of surprise. On the other hand, even if she gained another dozen levels, Kat didn't like her odds against a bomb installed inside her toilet.

"You can't be serious right now." Iris glanced wildly about the table. "We can't just raid the Beloit Rehabilitation Camp. The BRC is impregnable. I'm sure that if we start a letter writing campaign, someone in a position of power will realize that they've made an error and release Jasper before anything—"

"Oh, will you just shut the fuck up!" Hestia shouted, her ball of blue fire erupting into a quartet of burning butterflies that flapped toward Iris, circling the trembling girl's head as the angry woman ranted. "The people that put our targets there knew exactly what they were doing. We're past the point of appealing to their better nature. Hell, we were past that point well before either of us were born. Push has come to shove, and unless you're willing to kill someone to get your way, your opinion means *nothing* at this table."

Kat opened her mouth to say something, but stopped as

Xander's hand gripped her knee. He shook his head once, curtly, as Hestia stood up, stalking toward Iris, the blue butter-flies flying closer to the whimpering girl.

"I owe Merrimac a couple favors, and I agreed to take on this job for old times' sake, but I didn't agree to listen to this kind of drivel." Iris was practically a puddle, wilting in her chair beneath Hestia's wrath. "Have you ever even killed before?"

Iris shook her head, eyes wide with terror.

"Been shot?" Hestia asked heatedly. "At least been shot at?"

Iris whimpered, shaking her head again.

"Then you are not in a position to offer suggestions at this table." Hestia crossed her arms with finality. "Your pretty world of dinner parties and corporate progress is built on a founda-tion of shadow and bone. It's not polite to talk about how people got where they are or why they have what they have, but when your mommy and daddy want something done, they come to someone like me. I swear to God, about half of the 'gas leaks' that took out senior corporate officials were my doing."

"At the end of the day, sometimes the only way forward is violence." The crown of butterflies flew lower around Iris, singing her hair and almost landing on her shoulders. "Our opponents are willing to kill thousands to get what they want, so we can only answer in kind. If you want to save your friend, your hands are going to get dirty. If you don't have it in you, then so help me—"

"Enough, Hestia." Davis stood up, the red sheen of a stamina-based skill lighting up his entire body. "Miss Leander has already agreed to participate in this mission. Given how much she's heard, we obviously can't let her walk away without her assistance. The risk of her reporting on us in exchange for clemency is too high. She will be involved in the mission. If something were to happen, we will all be implicated together."

"Will I have to fire a gun?" Iris asked in a whimper, not meeting Hestia's eyes as the woman smirked down at her. "I've only ever fought in the tower before."

"Did you actually fight in the tower, or did you have a team of retainers carry you through a dungeon?" Hestia recalled her butterflies with a flick of her hand. They sailed back to her, merging into a ball of blue flame that once again began dancing over her knuckles.

"I—" Iris began to stutter only for Davis to cut her off.

"Hestia, this isn't productive." He stepped between the two women. "Take your seat so we can get on with the planning."

"What if we take down the wireless network?" Dorian asked, interrupting the argument from where he was still slouched in his seat. "Beloit has two hundred guards, but those walls have a lot of square footage to them. If we can knock out communications for an hour or two, whoever is going after the targets will only have to fight a handful of guards at a time. It's still dangerous as all hell, but not an explicit suicide mission."

"That would mean splitting the team," Kat observed evenly. "Plus, it would make remote hacking impossible. It could work, but we're already heavily understaffed for an operation like this."

"Three and three, one computer specialist with a cranial jack on each squad." Dorian shrugged, sitting up. "It would be a matter of minutes for Merrimac to figure out where the substation that provided coverage for the prison was, and a team of three should be able to keep it offline for about an hour. After that, techs and security start showing up, and the people inside the prison are on their own."

"Then how do we divide up the teams?" Kat asked, feeling her heart sinking as she already suspected the answer.

"There isn't any time for training, so each group will be people that are familiar with each other." Davis nodded slowly. "Our team will take down the substation. You will have to handle extracting the targets."

"I could go with them," Hestia offered cheerfully. "I'd love to spend some time getting to know Erinyes."

"No." Davis shook his head solemnly. "Both teams will need

a caster, and they're on a stealth mission. You're about as subtle as a hand grenade."

"Subtlety," Hestia huffed. "Why should I hide my work? I'm an artist."

Uncomfortably, Kat looked over to Iris. The other girl was quivering, eyes wide.

"I suppose that means we get Miss Leander?" Kat asked without any enthusiasm.

"Of course," Dorian interjected, a slightly malicious smile on his face. "After all, Erinyes, she's *your* friend."

CHAPTER TWENTY-NINE

"I don't see why the new girl gets to drive," Xander complained, his arms crossed.

Kat glanced back at him from the front seat of the SUV where she sat next to a white-knuckled Iris. Xander was sulking, arms across his chest in the middle row of seats.

"Because I can't drive safely in this traffic and you're a maniac," Kat responded smoothly, turning her head back toward the road. "Iris is getting us to Beloit fast enough, and without drawing attention. If you were behind the wheel, Exe, we already would have cut something like six cars off and forced at least one off the road. There's no way in hell we would make it to a sensitive location like the Beloit Rehabilitation Camp without kicking up a fuss if I let you behind the wheel."

"I could get us there faster," he muttered, glaring out the tinted windows at the decrepit outskirts of Chiwaukee as they left the megalopolis.

"I acknowledge that," Kat replied, checking the throwing knives in her bandoleer and the infiltration equipment in her carry pack for what felt like the dozenth time. "I also believe that the security guards would be able to track our arrival by the honking horns and the plumes of smoke you left in your wake."

"He can drive if he wants," Iris whimpered, merging into the slow lane to let a trio of motorcyclists clad in body armor with rifles strapped to their backs roar by. "I'm really not enjoying this. In fact, I'm pretty sure that my presence will just slow the two of you down. You don't even really need to bring me on this mission. I won't tell anyone what's happening."

"Nah." Kat could hear Xander shaking his head from behind her. "Even if I wanted to get on Merrimac's bad side, and considering his reputation, that would make me a bona fide idiot, he's right. I don't care about your family connections, if you get caught participating in a raid on the BRC, there's no way you'll be able to come out of it unscathed. This is the best way to ensure your silence."

"Plus," Kat put a hand on Iris' arm soothingly, "we will need a getaway driver. You won't even need to come inside, just protect the car until we escape with the prisoners. Remember, if you run, Jasper dies. And if Jasper dies…"

Xander snorted. "If Jasper dies, emotions will be her last concern. Merrimac will find her, and I doubt there's any place safe from that man if he's willing to sacrifice himself for a mission."

"Kat—" Iris began only for Kat to cut her off.

"Erinyes." She shook her head at Iris. "When we're in the field or planning, you need to call me Erinyes."

Iris flinched. "I'm never going to get used to that," the woman muttered. "What did you do to earn that name, anyway? I heard that a samurai needs to be pretty serious about what they do to get named."

"She killed an entire strike team," Xander volunteered gleefully. "A target that only should have had unaugmented security had multiple named samurai on site. She killed all of them and secured the objective with only offsite support. Even if the people she finished off weren't named, that's enough to earn a name in most places."

"Oh God." Iris squirmed in her seat. "Does Jasper know?"

"No." Kat chuckled. "Merrimac clearly suspected, but for whatever reason, he didn't tell Jasper. He knows I'm affiliated with 'independent contractors,' but he doesn't know my role or my seniority."

"We—" Iris licked her lips, trying to calm the stutter in her voice. "We are going to save him though, right? I know Jasper can get a little intense about his family, but he's always been nice to me. With everyone else, you can tell they're just pretending. That they're trying to squeeze some sort of advantage out of you or your family, but with Jasper it was different. He could be ruthless when necessary, but the rest of the time, he was just *nice*. The idea of him disappearing forever—"

She stopped speaking for a moment, simply staring out the SUV's front window as they wove in and out of traffic. Farm fields and windmills rolled past them.

"Most people don't come back from the Beloit Rehabilitation Center," she continued bleakly. "Those that do aren't the same. They aren't as quick on their feet, and if you even hint at questioning the CEO, they start trembling. I can't have that happen to Jasper."

"We'll get your friend," Xander said, his voice softening. "Partially because Merrimac wants him out and partially because he's connected to Erinyes, but in all likelihood, the newly picked up political prisoners will all be in the same place. They're going to want to interrogate them before releasing them into the general population. It only makes sense to pull both of them out at once."

"Thank you." Iris practically whispered the words, but it drew a smile from Kat.

There wasn't much room for mercy or good deeds on Earth. Part of that was Kat's comparative power. She'd never been in a position to help someone. In Schaumburg, she might have had a few more scraps than the other scavengers, but her position was always too tenuous. One misstep and everything would come tumbling down around her, throwing Kat back into the gutter that she'd just barely crawled out of.

She was still only a step away from the precipice, but this was one tangible way she could make the world a better place. Jasper was annoying and a bit aggressive, but as far as Kat could see, he was a good person. Well, as good a person as anyone could be.

Helping him wouldn't fix economic inequality. It wouldn't save the world, or provide blankets to the street rats shivering themselves to sleep in the bombed out buildings of the Shell, but it was something she could do here and now without appreciable added risk to the mission. It was a small step forward, but it was a step that Kat could proactively take.

"It's not *just* altruism." Kat craned her neck backward to see Xander frowning in the failing light. "If our intelligence is right, major changes are coming to GroCorp. A hostile takeover means a lot of deaths, and a prolonged disruption of business. Even if me and mine don't get caught up in the purge, there's no promise that it won't interrupt food supplies and public order."

"To those of us on the outside," he continued slowly, "cutting food and fuel will kill us just as surely as a team of corporate thugs. It'll just stretch the experience out over a couple weeks. We need people like your little friend alive and well so that he can alert the rest of the executive class to what's coming. Hopefully if enough of you have the heads up, you can nip this little revolution in the bud."

Iris whimpered slightly, and Kat patted her on the knee. She'd never been great at emotions or comforting people that were down. Her mom would probably have a whole speech to get the woman to open up and calm down, but Kat was out of her depth.

"We'll get him out of there," she finished lamely. Iris nodded, eyes moistening as she kept driving.

The minutes melted away in tense silence, the steady hum of the SUV's engine the only sound as the sun set. Finally, Iris pulled the car off the road and into the parking lot of a rest stop about a half mile from the Beloit Rehabilitation Camp.

She turned off the car, and they waited. Kat pulled the headpiece of her infiltration suit over her face and tightened her joint seals, but after that, there was nothing to do but periodically check her smartpanel for signs that Merrimac's team had been successful.

Finally, the recap of last night's episode of Chrome Cowboys cut out, replaced by an error alerting her to check with her system administrator. She turned to Xander, his face a solid oval of black fabric. He nodded back at her.

"We've got an hour, Erinyes." Xander opened the side door of the SUV and stepped outside. "Get me over the wall and to a hardwired computer hookup and I can find our boys."

"Fast and quiet?" she asked, sliding a silenced pistol into the holster on her right hip and a 5.5mm high velocity machine pistol into another.

"Don't be afraid to take someone down, but be stealthy about it," Xander responded, checking his own weapons for the final time. "Their wireless communication is down, that doesn't mean that everything is nonfunctional. Gunshots will still bring people running, and if anyone is near a wired hookup, they can sound an alarm and bring the entire camp down on top of us."

Kat nodded her acknowledgement back, and then they were off, running in a half crouch as they made their way through a farm field, the half-grown crops concealing their furtive movements. Ahead of them, Beloit itself was visible, spotlights playing their way back and forth across the empty grassland that separated it from the nearby farms.

They paused for a minute at the edge of the corn field for Kat to cast Shadow on both of them before taking off once again. She only needed to burn stamina on Cat Step to keep up with Xander twice, and then they were at the camp's walls, her chest pumping rhythmically as Kat tried to catch her breath.

"Up and over," Xander whispered, pulling a length of nylon

rope and a climbing metal stake out of his pack and handing it to her.

Kat dismissed his instance of Shadow before casting Levitation on herself. She took a couple of steps back, hopping up and down on her toes to assess her lessened weight while eyeing up the wall.

She exhaled, burning stamina to activate Cat Step once again in order to increase her speed as she sprinted at the cement barrier. At the last second, she switched to Leaping, partially crouching mid-step as her thighs burned red before launching herself into the air.

The ground disappeared beneath her as air whistled past. Just as Kat reached the apex of her leap, she stretched her arm upward, barely grabbing onto the lip of the wall with her fingertips.

With a grunt, she heaved herself over the edge, landing shoulder first onto the metal walkway. She winced at the clang and clatter as her artificially light body bounced off of the steel panels. Now that she was on the wall, Kat could hear plenty of noise from the prison camp inside, but her ascent had still been louder than she—

"What was that?" Kat froze as she heard a woman's voice coming from her right. "This is patrol Beta Forty-Four, I have an unexplained sound, investigating now."

Kat hauled herself up into a crouch, chest heaving. Shadow still clung to her, hiding Kat's outline from the guard cautiously approaching with her rifle in both hands, ready to snap it up to her shoulder at a moment's notice.

"This is Beta Forty-Four." The patrol stopped, releasing the rifle with her left hand and letting it swing backward on its sling as she pressed the now-free hand against the side of her smart-panel. "I'm only getting static here, please respond."

Kat exploded into motion, one hand whipping a dagger at the distracted guard as she broke into a Cat Step-assisted sprint.

Her target snapped her hand up in time, the knife meant for the woman's throat instead sprouting from her forearm. The guard hissed in pain, reeling backward as she tried to bring her rifle to bear one handed.

Then Kat was in front of her, driving a heel into a knee and flipping her knife into a double handed grip, one hand wrapped around the handle while the other gripped the pommel in order to drive the blade into the guard's chest.

Kat winced as, rather than snapping her target's knee back, her foot bruised itself on the metal of cyberware. Still, the blade struck true, Kat activating Penetrate to push it straight through the guard's ribs and into the organs beneath.

The other woman wrapped an arm around Kat and dropped, dragging the two of them to the metal paneling together. Blood flecked the guard's lips, and her entire body began to glow red as she activated some sort of skill.

Almost immediately, Kat felt the pressure on her back from the woman's injured arm double. Then the guard's other arm joined it, linking together in the small of Kat's back. For a moment, Kat managed to keep some space between the two of them using her own hands and elbows as a buffer, but she felt herself slipping.

The hilt of her own knife slammed into Kat's ribs as she pulled her arms to the side rather than risk breaking them under the inexorable pressure.

The other woman grinned at her, blood staining her teeth into a crimson jackal's grimace. Madness filled the other woman's eyes as her grip on Kat tightened.

Stars flashed in Kat's vision and her bones seemed to creak under the pressure as she wriggled her hands to her sides.

"Feel that, ya bitch?" the woman hissed at her, blood spattering Kat's facemask. "I've got yer hands at your side and Ferocity active. Lost HP is just making me stronger. Punctured lung is already healing, but until it does, I have fifty percent more strength to crush you with. I've fought snakes like you before. Good luck wriggling free from this."

Kat's silenced pistol left its holster, pressing its muzzle

against the bone of the guard's hip. Without saying anything, she pulled the trigger.

The gun coughed and bucked in Kat's hand.

Kat grunted. The woman's eyes widened, the red glow around her doubling in intensity as her arms crushed Kat even closer against her chest.

She shifted the aim on her pistol, aiming upward into her opponent's chest. It shuddered in her hand three more times, the force of the bearhug increasing with each bullet until abruptly the red glow disappeared entirely and the woman slumped backward.

Kat sat up gingerly, wincing at the aches covering her body. She reached down, ripping the knife from the guard's chest, leaning forward to slash open her throat before retrieving her throwing knife. With a grunt, Kat lifted the body up and toppled it over the side of the wall toward Xander.

A second later, she used Penetrate to ram the piton into the concrete and throw the nylon rope down after the corpse.

She slumped against the wall, using Cure Wounds I to fix the muscle pains and strained joints while the piton jerked and vibrated next to her. Finally, almost two minutes later, Xander clambered over the wall and slipped down into a crouch next to her.

He glanced Kat up and down. "Making friends up here without me?" he asked. She could almost see the shit-eating grin on his face under the mask.

"Just gobs of fun," Kat replied, pulling herself to her feet. "I'll let you fight the next one. I think I just dislocated every vertebrae in my back."

"Lucky. I pay a huge blond guy good money to do that." Xander nodded sagely.

Kat just stared back at him, removing the magazine from her gun and loading a couple loose rounds into it before slamming it back into the butt of her pistol.

"Anyway." Xander coughed. "Are you ready to take over

one of these towers? I'd bet my last credit that they have wired connections in them."

"Ready enough," Kat replied, sliding her pistol back into its holster and checking her mana levels. Even with a couple minutes of regeneration, she was barely over half. Enough for a quick fight or two, but a protracted engagement was an awful idea.

"Then follow me." Xander turned from her, leading the way toward one of the nearby cannon towers.

An ugly cement construct, it was barely a story taller than the wall itself. The bunker's centerpiece was a 30mm cannon, big enough to chew apart anything smaller than a main battle tank, but Kat couldn't help but notice the rifle slits dappling its walls and the spotlight on its roof, manned by a silhouette.

Xander tapped her on the shoulder, motioning for the two of them to move closer to the tower. Once he was pressed up against it, his body glowed faintly purple for a fraction of a second.

"*Compulsion.*" The word was barely a whisper. Xander held his hand up, palm outward to halt Kat.

A couple of seconds later, she heard a muffled thump from inside. Xander stood up and opened the door.

Kat followed him in, taking note of a burly man with a single chrome arm standing over the corpse of a woman, her head twisted at an unnatural angle. His eyes were blank, staring sightlessly at the computerized controls for the cannon that filled most of the room.

Without saying anything, Xander walked up to the man and placed his silenced pistol against his temple. It was like hitting a watermelon with a sledgehammer. Kat flinched as gore sprayed against the far wall.

A second later, the body crumpled to the floor, Xander stepping over it nonchalantly on his way to the computer. He pulled the cord to his cranial jack out of a flap in the back of his infiltration suit, crouching next to the firing computer.

"This will take a minute or two." Xander glanced back toward her. "Make sure there aren't any surprises while I work."

"Got it, Exe." Kat's voice was more strained than she would've liked. "I think I spotted someone up top. I'll clear them out and be right back down."

He just grunted at Kat as she put her feet to the metal rungs of the latter, burning a little stamina with Cat Step in order to prevent her footfalls from echoing and alerting her quarry. Quietly, she pushed aside the trap door and clambered up onto the tower's roof.

In front of her, a man rested his arms and torso on the spotlight, his rifle's muzzle pointing at the night sky from its perch leaning against the structure's stomach high wall.

Kat padded up behind him, each step inaudible over the steady din of the prison camp behind them. She deactivated Cat Step, noting that her constant stamina use was about to leave her critically low.

Still, there was enough left over for Penetrate as Kat's left hand snaked around and clamped itself over the man's mouth a fraction of a second before her blade sank through the back of his skull.

He twitched once, body going limp and slumping against the spotlight. Gently, Kat pulled him off, rolling him over and slitting his throat just to be sure.

Once she had confirmed his death, Kat made her way to the barricade, willing her eyes to switch back to Nightvision after the bright lights of the tower control room had shocked her out of it. She surveyed the wall. There were guards patrolling its length, but none near enough to pose an immediate threat to Xander and her.

With a sigh of relief, Kat clambered down the ladder, no longer worried about stealth. When she turned back around, Xander stiffened suddenly.

"I think I found them, Erinyes." His voice was tense and clogged with worry.

"Shouldn't that be a good thing?" Kat asked tentatively.

"Finding them is a good thing," Xander replied, turning his faceless head toward her. "Hell, they're even nearby. It's where they are specifically that's the problem. It's a biomedical lab rated for human experimentation. Both of them are registered as test subjects in some sort of black project called 'Operation Changeling.'"

CHAPTER THIRTY

Air rushed past Kat as she quietly jumped from the roof of the squat concrete building toward the ground. She hit with a muffled thud, quickly glancing back and forth for any of the guards she might have alerted with her descent.

A moment later, Xander landed next to her with noticeably less grace and more noise. She winced as he pulled himself up from the ground, dusting mostly imaginary dirt off of his infiltration suit.

They'd made it to the laboratory with only minor trouble. Kat and Xander managed to avoid all but one guard, a man that Xander had frozen with his psi abilities long enough for Kat to ram her dagger through the back of his skull and dispose of his body over the barrier wall.

It helped that the lab itself was built into the wall. Apparently, most of Beloit's administration buildings were located near the edge of the rehabilitation camp. The interior of the complex was little more than a vacant no man's land filled with tents and rival prison gangs that 'regulated' themselves.

So long as the camp's general population didn't try to break the fortified and electrified inner barrier that protected guard housing and administration, they were more or less given free rein to brutalize and terrorize their fellow inmates. The goal of the 'rehabilitation camp' was containment, and if a significant portion of the prisoners died in turf wars, that just meant that the prison administrators could pocket more in profits as they saved on food.

As for VIPs and those that might be expected to one day exit the camp 'reformed'? It sure seemed like all of them ended up in one of the three laboratories dedicated to human experimentation on site.

Xander tapped her on the shoulder, silently pointing toward the lab's entrance with two fingers before scrambling off into the night. A couple of seconds later, both of them were standing on either side of a metal door. Kat's right hand hovered above her sheathed knife and holstered pistol, ready to draw either at a moment's notice. The choice for Xander was much simpler. He stood, back to the wall on the other side of the door facing Kat, silenced handgun at the ready. Xander raised three fingers.

He put down one finger. Kat scanned their surroundings, looking for witnesses. There was a bunkhouse nearby, and beyond it a wall twice her height. The barrier was unmanned, instead motion sensor triggered turrets studded its length, facing inward toward the center of the general inmate population.

One finger remained. She took a deep breath, finally deciding on her knife. It slid out of its sheath in a single smooth and practiced motion. Kat hefted its reassuring weight thoughtfully. Xander could handle ranged targets. She would cover everything else.

Xander kicked open the door, handgun coughing twice as Kat wheeled around to follow him. She hopped over the threshold, knife at ready.

A man was on the ground, blood welling up from two holes in his chest and staining his white smock red. Shattered around the body were a number of test tubes, little more than glass shards with printed paper labels stuck to them.

The two of them rushed past a wall full of vaguely labeled stainless steel refrigerators. One or two were marked 'samples' but most simply said 'nutrients.' Kat had no idea what they were nutrients for, just that the refrigerators weren't meant to store food. After all, Kat thought as she slammed her back up against the wall next to the door to the adjoining room, the final freezer of the first room was labeled 'provisions.'

Xander nodded to her before kicking the next door open once as well. This room was a much more traditional office setting, a matrix of half cubicles complete with advanced-looking desktop computers.

A man and a woman jolted to their feet as Kat spilled into the room after Xander. The woman jerked as heavy, silenced bullets slammed into her.

Kat didn't waste a second, triggering Dazzle to disable the man before burning a small amount of stamina on Leaping in order to clear the cubicle before his. She landed on the desk in front of him, driving her knife into his neck and sawing sidewise to sever his windpipe before her struggling target could raise an alarm.

He slumped backward, clutching at his throat. Kat bit the inside of her cheek, focusing on the pain to quell the bile rising in her throat.

She stepped aside, giving Xander access to the direct port for his cranial jack on her victim's blood spattered desk.

In another life, either of the two lab assistants could have been her. Bright and eager to climb her way up the corporate ladder, fueled by a desperate desire to pay down her debts. It was like St. Louis all over again. The wrong people in the wrong place at the wrong time.

At least this time, Kat consoled herself, there truly hadn't been another option. Xander and her were racing a ticking clock. The only question was whether a dead body was found by a patrol, or whether the wireless network was restored first. Either way, an alarm was inevitable.

There simply hadn't been time to perform reconnaissance and slip into the laboratory unseen. As unfortunate as the situation was, Kat worked a messy job. She could mourn the innocent later, but for now—

"Erinyes," Xander called out, grabbing her attention. "Check the far wall."

She glanced over at him, futilely trying to read Xander's face through his opaque black mask. Giving up, she followed his gaze and froze.

The cubicles only occupied half of the room. The other half was a cluster of sterile white analytical equipment surrounding a dozen large green tubes. Each was large enough to hold an adult man curled into the fetal position, an easy fact to ascertain because two of them did.

Another four contained what could only be fetuses in various stages of development, while the remaining tubes held a variety of children and young adults.

Kat approached the equipment, squinting as she ignored the hum of a running centrifuge. Each of the tubes seemed to glow with a light of its own, as if the murky green liquid cradling the bodies was bioluminescent.

She frowned.

"Exe?" Kat asked absently, her eyes locked on the tubes. "Jasper Haupt and Colyn Raster were only picked up a day or two ago, right?"

"Yeah," Xander grunted back. "They probably only made it to this facility about twenty four hours ahead of us."

Kat reached down, running her hand over the metal nameplate on one of the tubes. 'JASPER HAUPT' was spelled out in plain font, stamped into the steel in all capitals. She stood up, lips drawn tight.

Inside the chamber was a fetus, late in the third trimester and floating peacefully in the dully glowing green soup. Faintly, she could see some shapes etched into the glass of the container. They looked like letters, but nothing in any language she'd ever heard of.

One tube down was something labeled 'COLYN RASTER.' As best Kat could tell, it was a healthy baby boy, between one and two years old.

"Have you managed to figure out what 'Operation Changeling' is?" Kat asked, concern weighing her voice as she leaned closer to Colyn's cylinder. Once again, she noticed etching in the glass, various repetitive symbols that formed some sort of pattern and glowed with their own light.

"The header is on every file in here," Xander replied in frustration, "but there aren't any electronic records of what's actually happening. Either these are the least organized researchers on the planet, or they're deliberately not recording what they're doing."

"Maybe it's paper only?" Kat ran her finger over the shapes in the glass, frowning as a thrill of mana ran up her hand from the green tube.

"I've run into that before." Xander grunted. "Everything is hackable these days, and a couple of the more paranoid execs keep their most dangerous secrets in places where they can't be downloaded. Still, it's horribly inefficient so most don't bother. I guess we just have rotten luck."

"Seems like it." Kat flinched as the child in front of her stirred, churning the murky green liquid it was suspended in.

She stepped backward, taking in all twelve of the tubes. They burbled quietly to themselves, humming and glowing as the shapes inside them twisted and grew at an almost visible rate.

"Wait!" She turned around at Xander's exclamation. "That's something. I found Jasper and Colyn. Apparently they're in the middle of something called neural patterning?"

"Whatever that is." Xander shrugged, unplugging himself from the computer. "Not that it matters. I have floor plans and room numbers. That's all we need to get them the hell out of here."

"I'm not sure I like the sound of neural patterning." Kat glanced over her shoulder at the humming tubes of green liquid as she followed Xander. "I'm not exactly up to date on the newest technological innovations, but everything in this lab seems like it's a generation or four more advanced than anything I've heard of."

"B-wing," Xander mumbled to himself, picking one of the three doors out of the office before shrugging and glancing back at her. "You're not wrong, Erinyes. I don't like jumping to conclusions, but whatever's going on here stinks to high heaven. As bad as the rehabilitation camp is, these labs are something a whole lot darker. The sooner we get our packages and get out of here, the better."

B-wing was little more than a narrow concrete hallway lit by cheap fluorescent lights. The first three doors were fairly straightforward, containing a bathroom, a kitchenette, and a supply closet.

After them, things took a darker turn. Each room had a metal door with an observation slit around eye level. Inside, they were little bigger than a dark and crudely constructed closet. Entirely innocent if it wasn't for the crude iron shackles bolted to the back wall.

"Here we are." Xander stopped in front of a metal door marked B-11. "This should be Colyn Raster. Room B-14 will be Jasper. I'll grab the target while you rescue your friend. Then let's get the hell out of here. This place gives me the heebie jeebies."

Kat rolled her eyes at him before hurrying down a couple of doors to room B-14. She stood on her tiptoes, looking through the observation slit.

Jasper was inside, suspended above the ground with his hands and feet in the shackles, bolted to the wall. On his head, a ring of golden metal glowed brightly enough to forcefully deactivate her Nightvision. Even as Kat blinked away the halo's glare, the circle pulsed ominously, the sound of static filling her ears with each flare.

She slipped inside, leaving the door open behind her. Jasper was sleeping fitfully, body jerking periodically while his eyes twitched wildly beneath their lids.

With a frown, she hooked her knife under the glowing halo. Mana surged into her body, singeing Kat's hand and filling her reserves as she quickly flipped the golden ring off of Jasper's head.

The minute it lost contact with his body, the metal circle's glow disappeared, plunging them both into twilight as their only illumination came from the fluorescent lights in the hallway.

Jasper groaned, stirring as the halo clattered to the floor. He opened his eyes, staring blearily at Kat's silhouette, confusion filling his features. He cocked his head to the side.

"Aren't you a little short for a corporate security guard?" Jasper asked, blinking at her.

Kat didn't reply, burning stamina to activate Penetrate and pierce the locking mechanisms on his shackles. As soon as his hands were free, Jasper slumped forward, unable to hold himself upright.

She caught him with a grunt, stabbing her burning red dagger through the restraints holding his ankles. Jasper stumbled down from his perch, half collapsing against one of the coffin-like room's walls as he tried to orient himself. Almost as an afterthought, Kat picked up the golden halo and tucked it into her carrying satchel.

"God," Jasper mumbled, the words slurred. "I keep remembering my childhood over and over. I swear Dad has taught me to ride a bike for the first time a dozen times in the last week. Then as soon as that's done, I'm hitting the winning double in the little league grand prix. Over and over and over again."

"They were doing something to you," Kat stated, the ring of metal in her satchel weighing guiltily against her hip. "We'll have you looked at once we get out of here, but for now there isn't much time."

"Wait." Jasper lurched toward her, losing his balance and forcing Kat to slip her head under his arm to balance him. "You don't work for Davis. I've heard your voice somewhere, but—"

"No names." Kat shook her head, half dragging him out of the room. In the hallway, Xander had Colyn's slumped body draped over his shoulder.

"But I'm pretty sure I know you." Kat grit her teeth as Jasper babbled drunkenly into her shoulder.

"We can talk when we're free, Haupt," Xander grunted, struggling under Raster's weight. Apparently he hadn't gotten all that many strength points in the tower.

"Free from where?" he asked, shifting against Kat's side. "One minute, I was having a glass of wine with dinner, and the next I could barely string two thoughts together while a pair of commandos dragged me out of somewhere."

"You're in Beloit," Kat replied as Xander leaned into the door out of B-wing with his unoccupied shoulder.

"Beloit!" She clamped down on Jasper's arm as he struggled drunkenly to escape from her grip. "What the hell am I doing in—"

The instant Kat stepped into the office area, Jasper abruptly stopped rambling. He also stopped moving.

He whimpered, body shuddering against her. In Kat's pouch, the hoop that had been over his head warmed suddenly enough that she could feel it through the fabric.

Jasper collapsed, slipping from her grasp and slapping his hands over his head, moaning as he rolled back and forth on the poured concrete of the floor.

"It's me!" he whispered urgently. "Oh God, it hurts, but it's me! I can feel it in my head, crawling around. Begging me to let it in."

Two of the green tubes up against the wall began to glow brighter, the liquid bubbling as if it was boiling. Kat didn't even need to look to determine that they were the cylinders devoted to Jasper and Colyn.

"Erinyes!" Xander hissed. Colyn had stiffened up over his

shoulder before thrashing around. The older man was wholly occupied with keeping his charge under control. "We need to stop the feedback."

She drew her silenced pistol, aiming first at the green tube linked to Jasper. The gun shuddered in her hand four times. Kat might not be the best shot in Chiwaukee, but it didn't take a gunfighter to hit an immobile tank full of glowing liquid.

Unfortunately, it didn't do anything. Each spot the bullets hit sparkled, glowing blue for a fraction of a second before the flare of light faded, leaving little more than a missing chip of glass behind.

At her feet, Jasper twisted, his body contorting with a grunt of pain as his muscles all spasmed at once.

Kat slipped her gun back in its holster. Even if she emptied both of her remaining magazines into the equipment, it wasn't making any progress. She began gathering her mana as Jasper rotated onto his back, eyes rolled up into his skull.

"Itha vokkar tammos Drapp!"

Whatever Jasper was shouting, it was something more than mere babbling. There was a structure and purpose to it that Kat couldn't parse.

A problem for another day. She squinted, launching a *Gravity Spike* at the cylinder. This time, something happened.

For a brief moment, the entire cylinder flared blue. Then, the force of the spell ripped the glass apart from the inside, shattering the tube.

Green liquid, too thick to be water and smelling strongly of sewage, splashed out onto the office floor. Almost immediately, it began hissing as it started chewing holes in the uncovered concrete, the still body in its center the only thing unaffected by its acid bite.

Jasper relaxed at her feet, unconscious.

Kat turned her attention to Colyn's tube, cracking it open with *Gravity Spike* a couple of seconds later.

"Definitely time to get moving now, Exe." She picked up Jasper, slinging him over her shoulder. Already the room was beginning to fill up with a thick yellow-green mist as whatever was in the glass cylinder interacted with the cement of the floor. Kat couldn't confirm that the gas was dangerous, but given the way the mysterious liquid had torn into and pitted the floor, she wasn't enthused at the prospect of testing her lungs against it.

He nodded back, picking Raster up and opening the door to the laboratory's cold storage room. The two of them jogged through it, eyes straining for threats but finding none. Then they were outside, stars twinkling down at them as the general unsettling shouts and screams of the nearby main prison filled the night.

Xander turned to her, shifting Colyn slightly on his shoulder.

"We're not getting out the same way we came in." He nodded toward the high outer wall. "The original plan was to use your magic to help them climb a rope, but that requires the target to be conscious. I think I saw some schematics for a waste treatment plant on the other side of the camp. We'll need to sneak over there and overwhelm the guards that are monitoring it and disable the purification system, but once we do that we'll just be five hundred yards of crawling through shit-smelling foulness from freedom."

Before Kat could respond, a low siren sounded, building in intensity until the steady tone filled the entire prison. One by one, searchlights began to snap on atop the guard towers.

"Plan B!" Kat shouted, turning toward the massive concrete wall. "Gravity Spike does more damage against heavy objects. Cover me while I blast our way out of here."

"Good enough for me." Kat could almost see the grin on Xander's face as he drew his machine pistol. "No point in being quiet now that they know we're here. We might as well break out the fun stuff."

Despite the lights, no one noticed the two of them until she used Gravity Spike for the first time. The prison was simply too large, and although it had a lot of guards, most of them were spread out, covering its massive surface area.

The wall shook, cracks running up its entire height as a massive chunk of concrete at its base shattered, crumbling into more manageable pieces. Kat set Jasper's body down and began clearing the area of debris even as she focused her mana for another strike.

Behind her, she heard the rapid crack of automatic gunfire.

"Get fucked, ya corpos!" Xander shouted, clearly enjoying himself more than he had any right to under the circumstances.

"*Psi Thrust.*" His voice was obscured by the crackle of more gunfire. Kat felt the hair on the back of her neck stand on end. A second later, there was an explosion and some screaming.

Her second Gravity Spike hit the wall, causing the entire structure to shudder. Already it was beginning to sag slightly.

She frowned. That could be a problem. If the entire wall collapsed, they'd have to climb it while every guard in the rehabilitation camp shot at them. Her original plan had been to use the spheres of gravity to drill a hole in the concrete that they could crawl through, but—

A lightning bolt snapped past her, Kat's vision dimming for a second, protecting her from its bright flash. Gravel showered down on top of Jasper and her from where the spell had struck the wall.

"*Compulsion!*" Xander shouted back, firing a shot for emphasis. "Stop throwing mana at us and burn this place to the fucking ground!"

The third Gravity Spike was enough. The wall groaned dangerously, and the tunnel she'd ripped into it was filled with fist-sized chunks of stone and rebar, but it would have to do. Xander was holding the line for the moment, but it was only a matter of time before they were overwhelmed.

"We're through, Exe," she shouted back at him, taking in the burning squat buildings of the prison administration center while Xander's machine pistol chattered relentlessly.

She didn't take the time to assess his kill-count or the full extent of the damage Xander had done, instead grabbing

Jasper by the scruff of his neck and dragging him into the tunnel.

The cement hurt like hell under her hands and knees, and Kat banged her head more than once on the narrow ceiling, but a couple of seconds later she was free, casting Levitation on herself as she slung Jasper over her shoulder. Barely ten seconds later, Xander joined her. Kat used the last of her mana to repeat the spell on him as he fiddled with something fist-sized and metal that he'd pulled from his storage pouch before rolling it into the tunnel.

Then they were running as fast as their magically lightened loads would let them. Behind Kat, there was a loud 'thump,' and then a wall of pressure and rock dust washed over her. She didn't know where Xander had gotten his hands on high explosives, but Kat certainly appreciated him collapsing the escape tunnel and part of the wall itself behind them.

Machine gun fire stabbed through the night, raking the ground in the general direction that Kat was running. Instinctively, she reached for her mana to cast Shadow, only to find her reserves empty.

One of the cannons thumped, sending a plume of dirt flying as it struck the earth some distance to her left. Searchlights were playing over the field around the prison camp, the siren changing to a louder and more insistent tone as the defenders tried to find them.

Another burst of gunfire lit up the night, this time well behind the two of them. The guards were firing blindly, hoping to get lucky or force Xander and her into a mistake while they waited for the light crews to find them.

Gritting her teeth, Kat redoubled her efforts. If she and Xander hadn't been found, it'd be just a matter of getting far enough away from the prison before a search team mobilized.

Her legs burned, and breath began to rasp in her throat. Xander kept pace with her. Despite the blood pounding in Kat's ears, she could hear his heavy ragged breathing as well. Both of them were in shape, but neither had the muscular build needed to carry a body while dodging gunfire.

More cannon fire erupted, almost drowning out the thump of mortars. The night shook and exploded around them, shrapnel flying wildly as fireball after fireball erupted in the empty field. Some were near enough to singe and batter Kat, but most missed wildly, blindly fired wastes of ammunition.

Then they were over a ridge, Beloit's bright searchlights obscured by the mound of dirt. Kat slowed to a steady jog, Xander matching pace with her. With a jerk of his head, Xander changed their course, the mapping software in his cyberware directing him to their rendezvous point.

In the distance, Kat still heard the crackle of gunfire and the thumps of explosions as the prison guards kept firing wildly. They were well out of range, but the corporate security couldn't know that. Still, that was no reason to slow down. It was only a matter of time before search parties with gene-engineered hounds were sent after them, and when that happened, Kat would vastly prefer to be in a car, on her way back to Chiwaukee.

Finally, they came upon the rest stop. She felt a layer of tension ease as she recognized Iris' SUV. The girl would have been an idiot to run. Merrimac would've ended her before she even made it back to her house, but smarter people had done dumber things while panicking.

"Oh my God!" Iris screamed at them, exiting the car and opening the sliding side door for them as Xander and Kat approached. "Is he dead? Did we really do all of this just for Jasper to—"

"Calm down," Kat grunted, slipping past the hyperventilating girl to buckle Jasper's unconscious body into the back seat of the SUV. "He's just knocked out. They were doing something to him in the camp. Now get into the driver's seat, because we need to get moving. Things are bad, and they're only going to get worse."

"I hope this was worth it," Xander muttered darkly as he

passed Colyn's body to her. "I can't say for certain, but based on what we saw in that lab, I'd say we made some serious enemies today. The kind that aren't going to care about the Code."

Kat's blood ran cold as she buckled the comatose executive in next to Jasper. She didn't refute Xander. That was a tall order when she agreed with him.

CHAPTER THIRTY-ONE

The SUV's wheels screeched against the highway, throwing Kat into the wall as the vehicle swerved through traffic, cutting off another car. Iris practically spun the steering wheel, returning them to the fast lane as she hyperventilated noisily.

Inertia pulled Kat back into her seat and the engine revved, switching gear. She glanced out the window worriedly. Luckily, the night traffic was just a shadow of the daytime chaos. Still, Iris' erratic driving would just draw attention—

Another car cut someone off without a turn signal or warning, setting off a cacophony of horns as it plowed through traffic, forcing other vehicles to get out of the way. Kat leaned back into her seat, smiling wryly as she checked her seatbelt.

She'd forgotten herself there. They were entering Chiwaukee. Honestly? Driving safely like a sane person would almost stand out more than whatever the hell it was Iris was doing. Kat just hoped that they would make it to their destination in one piece.

"Turn right on Nozick," Xander called out from the middle seat. "We're almost there."

Kat grabbed her seat-rest as Iris veered through two lanes,

forcing a truck to slam on its brakes to avoid rear ending them. The SUV groaned as it sped across the rumble strips that were supposed to separate the right lane from an off ramp.

Then they were on the open road, no cars around them as they exited the highway and entered Chiwaukee proper. Decrepit two-story structures gradually gave way to poorly maintained office buildings as Xander directed them deeper into the underbelly of the city.

Iris whimpered.

Her eyes were wild as she took in the barely lit buildings, the chromed thugs wearing leather jackets and multi-colored spikes of hair. A man and woman in gang colors were kicking a drunk curled into the fetal position outside a seedy bar, backlit by a fire burning in a metal barrel.

Iris' knuckles whitened as she gripped the steering wheel. Drug addicts hassled pedestrians for credits, while their dealers stood nearby, submachine guns displayed openly. The entire scene looked like a tableau out of an entertainment channel crime drama.

It barely fazed Kat. Things were worse than the Shell, but not by much. The only real difference was that in Chiwaukee, no one bothered to drag you into an alley before stabbing and robbing you.

She put a comforting hand on Iris' shoulder, drawing a surprised yelp from the other girl. Kat tried to paste as friendly of a smile as possible on her face, out of practice with the sort of pleasantries one would usually engage in when trying to calm someone down.

Whatever she did, it worked. Iris exhaled slowly, her hands relaxing noticeably on the steering wheel.

"Now turn up Friedman Boulevard and look for a casino called 'The Neon Dream.' We have parking out back." Xander's voice interrupted the relative calm as they passed a fizzling street light.

"Neon Dream?!" Iris yelped. "Mom yelled at my brother for

an hour when she found out that he'd gone there. She said that it's one of the most dangerous places in the city!"

"Typical corporate overreaction to the rest of us blowing off a little steam," Xander replied with a chuckle. "As long as you don't mind losing a couple credits or a little self-respect, it's safe enough."

A gunshot rang out. Iris jumped in her seat, sending the car swerving as Kat drew her pistol and frantically scanned the dark streets for the threat.

She relaxed slightly. A half block away, a drunk woman wove slightly on the sidewalk, taking a pull from an unlabeled bottle. She dropped the empty glass, letting it shatter on the pavement before raising her handgun and firing another shot, striking a street sign with admirable accuracy.

Kat holstered her gun, turning to shoot Xander a mean-ingful glare while Iris blubbered beside her.

"I said it's safe enough." He shrugged unapologetically. "I didn't say it was safe."

"That's Friedman Boulevard by the way," Xander contin-ued, pointing out the bullet scarred street sign. "It seems that turn might be a little hard to notice due to the recent vigilante redecorating."

The SUV took the corner on two wheels, roaring past the drunk and sending her stumbling to the glass-strewn pavement. Out of her side mirror, Kat saw the woman angrily wave her gun at them from where she sat, sprawled on the pavement.

Xander's calm voice guided them the rest of the way, past the Neon Dream's gaudy signs and into the quiet darkness of the parking garage. Iris practically collapsed when she parked the car, her chest rising and falling spastically as she fought to steady herself.

Kat went around back, past Xander as the older man stretched the kinks from his back, and clambered inside. She cast Levitation on Jasper to help with his weight and slipped his unconscious body over her shoulder.

"New girl," Xander called out as Iris stepped timidly out of the car. "You have to carry the second package. I need to go first to disable security."

"Does he mean...?" Iris hesitated, eyes flickering to Raster's unmoving form.

"Yep," Kat grunted back, using Levitation on the other man as well. "He should be a little more manageable now, but Exe is right. I'd prefer to have him disabling security on the way in. It beats us getting fried in some booby trap."

"I really don't think I'm cut out for this," Iris mumbled, mostly to herself as she gingerly picked up the executive's body.

"I wasn't either when I started," Kat responded, following Xander toward the entrance to the safe house. "You either get used to it, or you get soft and someone shoots you. It's not a pretty choice, but you play the hand you're dealt, not the one you wish you had."

Iris quieted, sullenly following Xander and Kat through the camouflaged doorways and into the familiar gloom of the buried outpost. As he closed the metal door behind them, locking it and re-arming the traps, Whippoorwill walked into the room, pink hair disheveled and wearing pajamas that featured cats transforming into anime girls and fighting monsters.

Whippoorwill froze, one hand stuck rubbing sleep from her blurry eyes.

"We have company," she croaked out, voice strangled. "No one told me to expect company."

"Whip." Xander pointed at Whippoorwill, before indicating Iris. "New girl. New girl, Whip."

He began wrestling down one of the wall mounted cots as he continued speaking. "Now that we're all friends, I'm going to need you to grab two doses of wakey-wakey, Whip."

"Gentle or harsh?" Whippoorwill shook her head, trying to clear the last vestiges of sleep from her brain.

Kat winced. Wakey-wakey wasn't a singular drug. More of a slang name for any number of concoctions made by back-alley chemists to keep a samurai alert and fighting. Gentle was slightly addictive, and more than enough to combat most bouts of unconsciousness.

Harsh wakey-wakey could be anything, but it almost always featured enough amphetamines and adrenaline to damage a race horse's heart. It did the trick, and it did it well, but more than one samurai had ended their career gasping for breath and begging for another hit of the concoction.

"Gentle," Xander grunted, motioning toward Iris as one of the folding beds clicked into place. "We're dealing with a friend and an asset that might pay a bounty for his release. Things are urgent, but not so urgent that we need to blow up someone's heart."

Kat deposited Jasper on a second bed with a grunt as Whip-poorwill returned with two syringes. She took a step back, letting Xander kneel next to Jasper and slide the injection into his arm.

Jasper awoke with a start, jolting up into a sitting position before crumpling forward clutching his head.

"What in Adam fucking Smith's name was that?" He groaned, voice muffled by his palms. "One minute security was asking me a question about a suspicious man spotted in the quad, and the next I was in a dark basement somewhere. Then everything went white and—"

He looked up, squinting against the dim lights.

"Oh God." He shuffled up against the bare, unpainted concrete wall, eyes wide. "It wasn't a dream. That actually happened. Where am I? Davis was there with me, is he all right?"

Kat grunted as Iris pushed past her, falling onto her knees next to the lumpy cot and grabbing both of his hands in her own.

"You're safe now," she sobbed, clutching at him like he was the only life raft in a turbulent ocean. "It's all over Jasper, you're safe."

"What happened?" Jasper asked distractedly, eyes glazed with a combination of disorientation and the drugs Xander had administered to him as he looked at Iris. "I remember reliving my life over and over again, then there was a bright light and I thought I heard Kat Debs, the new girl I brought to the meeting, but…"

"She went in and saved you, Jasper," Iris blubbered uncontrollably. "You were in Beloit. Oh God, I was so scared, but she took charge and saved you. They were shooting so many guns near the end, but she pulled you out of that hellhole."

Kat watched the two's overly damp and emotional reunion for a couple seconds before sidling uncomfortably up to Whippoorwill.

"Sooo." She struggled to keep her face straight. "I didn't take you for a fan of Chibi Princess Cats."

"Shut up, Kat," Whippoorwill replied, blushing deeply. "A couple of the kids I ran with before joining the ChromeDogs managed to scavenge a smartpanel. It only got two entertainment channels. It was either gossip broadcasts, or CPC and Star Warriors Horizon."

"God." Kat shuddered. "The voice acting on Star Warriors Horizon was awful. I could watch it with subtitles on, but even then it was a struggle."

"I know!" The other woman shook her head. "The way Garibaldi delivered his villain speeches was ridiculous. Every line was completely flat, like the voice actor was asleep or a robot."

"Or both." Kat shrugged, shaking her head at Iris' shuddering form. The last four or five hours had been rough on the girl, but still the entire performance was a bit melodramatic for her taste.

"Wait." Whippoorwill turned to Kat, confusion on her face. "You watched Chibi Princess Cats too?"

Before Kat could respond, Xander interrupted the two of them. "It looks like gentle wakey-wakey did the trick. Mild disorientation but no other side effects. It seems to be safe to use on the primary target."

"Did you just use Jasper Haupt as a guinea pig?" Kat hissed

at him, glancing furtively at the pair of corporate scions on the other side of the room to make sure they didn't overhear. "Merrimac would have killed us if something went wrong!"

"Merrimac knows the risks." Xander shrugged as he kneeled down next to Colyn Raster, tapping any bubbles out of the syringe before inserting it into the unconscious man's arm. "Sometimes not everyone survives a raid like this. We were making a significantly more dangerous run than his crew. If Jasper had an adverse reaction to the drugs needed to wake him up? Well, shit happens."

"I get that the kid is your friend." He depressed the plunger on the syringe, injecting the cocktail into Raster's arm. "But we're playing for keeps. Things are bad back at Schaumburg, and unless we can bring Williamson down, a lot of people are going to die. She might wind down all of Ike Holdings."

"But if they wind Ike down, what happens to everyone in the arcology?" Kat asked, her heart hammering in her chest. Winding down meant selling all assets and closing down business operations. At a very minimum, that would involve kicking everyone in the arcology out into the Shell. At worst? Many corporations considered employees that owed the company money to be assets.

While low level employees had jobs, it wasn't worth the company's time and money to track them down and abuse them. They did their part, serving as barely paid cogs in the massive machine, their weekly spending allotment notated in the company finances where expected maintenance costs would go on a piece of industrial equipment.

Without jobs, employees were little more than research subjects and a source of emergency organ transplants.

Xander just shook his head grimly, standing up a half second before Raster jerked up into a sitting position.

The man screamed, hands clawing through his short-cropped red hair. The noise cut off abruptly and the man shuddered, hands going to his throat.

A second later, he leaned over the side of the cot, vomiting up some sort of gray, oily discharge that splattered across the room. Kat hopped to the side, interposing Xander between her and the bile, but everyone else standing next to Raster's bed received a helping of the vile liquid.

Colyn looked up at the three of them, fear in his eyes as he tried and failed to place them. It only made sense. Xander and Kat were clearly samurai, but ones he'd never come into face to face contact with. Even when Kat had dropped the recording off with him, Colyn had used an intermediary.

"I have good news, Mr. Raster!" Xander's grim expression was gone, replaced by his trademark grin, gold tooth glinting mischievously. "While you might have enemies within GroCorp, you also have friends outside its influence! For a modest fee to be negotiated later and a couple snippets of information, you have been saved from a truly horrendous fate."

"R-Raster?" the man stammered. "Is th-that who I am? I remember green liquid everywhere. Around me. Pulsing. It embraced me, whispered that I should just let go. I fought at first, but there was this light around my head and—"

He stopped, shuddering once again. Kat bit her lip, shooting a worried glance at Xander.

"Yes, good sir," Xander continued unfazed, oozing the oily charisma of a carnival barker. "Your name is Colyn Raster, and you have the honor of being an executive working for Ike Holdings, a wholly owned subsidiary of GroCorp."

"M-Maybe." Raster looked down at his hands, turning them over in front of his eyes as if he was seeing them for the very first time.

"Mr. Raster." Xander leaned forward, gently putting a hand on his shoulder. "I have reason to believe that you were kidnapped and tortured. Forces within GroCorp wanted to know the contents and the location of a recording that you bought at an auction after it was stolen from a Millennium Company data vault."

"I r-remember the recording." Raster looked up at Xander and past him to Kat. "The light kept asking questions about it.

For some reason I w-wasn't supposed to tell the light where it was. I d-don't know why."

"I kept it secret." The scarred man beamed up at both of them. "As much as the green liquid told me to give in, and as many times as the light told me to give up, I kept it secret."

Kat glanced, at Xander, chewing her bottom lip in worry. She wasn't entirely sure what had happened to the prisoners when they were trapped in Beloit, but Colyn's descriptions were disconcerting to say the least.

"Good," Xander cooed soothingly, his hand still on Colyn's shoulder. "Now I need to know about the recording. What was so secret that you needed to hide it from the light?"

"There were people at a table," Raster began hesitantly, the stutter in his voice and the tremor in his hands fading as he spoke. "They were planning some sort of secret program. Starlight or Sunfire, something like that."

"Starfall," Xander supplied. "You're doing a good job, Colyn, now tell us what the people said."

Raster ran a hand through his short-cropped hair, closing his eyes to try and gather his thoughts before continuing. "They said that everyone needed to consolidate their power, that there would be enough alien technology to go around."

"Aliens?" Colyn opened his eyes, scratching at his red hair. "Like the people that made the tower, I guess."

"Tell us about them," Xander prompted. "Are they coming to Earth? Are they making contact with players through *The Tower of Somnus*? How are the aliens involved?"

"Both." Colyn frowned uncertainly. "I think the aliens have been helping them level faster in the game, and they talked about a ship hiding behind the moon. Apparently they've signed some sort of deal with the aliens. Once Jackson hits level twenty-four, the aliens would receive mining rights to everywhere in the solar system other than Earth. In exchange, the aliens would provide the technology needed for the human conspirators to take control of their respective organizations."

Xander glanced back at Kat, worry clouding his face.

"Colyn," he continued. "I need to know which organizations were there. Who signed this treaty with the aliens?"

"Members of Millennium and the megacorporations," Raster replied, shifting himself so that his back rested against the bare cement wall. "No other contractors outside of Millennium as far as I could tell."

"Which megacorporations?" Kat asked, careful to avoid the splatters of gray sludge as she stepped out from behind Xander. "GroCorp, VodCom, KRG Holdings, NeoSyne? Which of the companies do we need to watch out for?"

"All of them." Raster chuckled bleakly. "Each and every one had an executive or a shareholder present. If that's who you're fighting, both of you are well and truly fucked."

"Except, according to Erinyes, the aliens are breaking the rules." Xander's voice was urgent, like he was trying to convince himself more than Colyn. "That recording is evidence that they're interacting with an embargoed species. If we can present that to the authorities, poof! The aliens are gone. Plus, I'm sure the shareholders of the megacorps would be interested to know that their fellows are conspiring with the aliens to overthrow them."

Xander continued, almost pleading with the former executive. "If we can just get our hands on the recording and release it into the information channels, all of their plans would be undone in a matter of minutes. So please, Mr. Raster, tell us where you hid the recording. GroCorp hasn't found it yet, and you're our only hope."

Colyn just laughed, head thrown back and his short red hair brushing the wall behind him. Whippoorwill nudged Kat to get her attention before nodding at Raster with a frown.

Kat shrugged. She had no idea what was going on with the man. Whatever GroCorp had done to him, Raster clearly suffered from some sort of neurological damage.

"Is that what you're counting on?" Colyn cackled madly. "That you'll find a copy of the recording and broadcast it, resulting in your enemies being struck down while you ride off into the sunset on a cyberhorse like some sort of reject from Chrome Cowboys?"

"Yes?" Xander asked, without much hope in his voice.

"Good!" Colyn wiped tears from beneath his eyes. "It might even work too. The footage on the recording is damning beyond belief. I'd be surprised if anyone featured on it managed to escape being executed for insubordination."

"There's only one problem with your reasoning." Raster stared up at Xander and Kat, madness in his eyes. "I don't have the recording anymore."

"I didn't trust anyone with the data." He giggled to himself. "So I uploaded it onto a mobile storage drive that I concealed in my cufflinks. The stealth storage drives were ungodly expensive to buy, but they were worth it. After all, where would be safer to store something that valuable than on my very body?"

"Fuck." Xander spat out the word, without any emotion or inflection.

"If you want the recording, find the suit I was wearing when they grabbed me." Colyn burst out laughing, an unhealthy barking sound. "If they haven't destroyed it yet, the data is all yours."

CHAPTER THIRTY-TWO

Congratulations, Adventurer!
You have completed the Wood Tier Level Four Dungeon, Lost Forest.
Three of three party members surviving. Good job!
Assigning awards:

+1 Spirit

Kat dismissed the notification, walking away from the dungeon portal as she waited for Dorrik to exit. Kaleek and her were in a small cave, hidden behind a picturesque waterfall on a small tropical island.

The otter was grinning, his paws filled with fist-sized gemstones they'd pried from the chests of the vinecats that served as the primary antagonist. Each of the crystals glowed faintly with a prism's worth of different lights.

They'd learned the hard way that each of the stones represented a different magical ability that the gray, panther-like predators could use. Even with their new armor, Kat had been forced to heal Dorrik after a vinecat turned the ground beneath the lokkel's feet into mud, sinking them almost waist deep in slop and turning the usually agile warrior into a sitting duck.

After the headache caused by the crafty magical cats, the boss, a huge bird that reminded Kat of an owl, wasn't much of a challenge. Gravity's Grasp and *Arrest Momentum* combined perfectly to bring the feathered monster to the ground where Kaleek soundly and cheerily beat the absolute crap out of it.

By the time the boss stopped moving, Kat almost felt bad for it. Matted blood and feathers covered the forest floor of the dungeon, and one of the monster's wings had been hacked off entirely.

Still, a win was a win and Dorrik's intelligence network had paid off once again. Clan Ahn's information on fourth floor dungeons was nowhere near as complete as their compendium on the third floor, but it still gave them locations and some hints.

The lizard person shimmered into existence, a corona of rainbow light flashing into being and depositing their gray-scaled form on the stones next to the portal. They paused for a second, likely reviewing their award before nodding and swiping to the side with a claw, dismissing the pop up.

"Look at this stuff, Dorrik," Kaleek remarked, throwing a gleaming white gem to Dorrik. "It's not quite enough to make up for us buyin' the *Marka*, but I'm pretty sure that gem is used to power *Ether Bolt*. That's an iron tier wizard spell."

Dorrik snatched it out of the air, walking to the edge of the cave and slipping past the waterfall before holding the crystal up to the tower's fake sun. They inspected the stone for almost a full minute before throwing it back to Kaleek.

"Indeed." They nodded. "That gem would allow an enchanter to imbue a weapon with some of the characteristics of *Ether Bolt*, namely the ability to ignore any non-magical armor."

"That sounds dangerous." Kat perked up, a frown on her face. "If it can pierce defenses like that, the spell has to have some drawbacks, right?"

"Not really," Kaleek replied with a greedy chuckle. "Even at higher levels, it only does as much damage as an arrow, so it's not like the spell is completely overpowered, but really, that's the difference between iron and wood abilities. It'll only get more pronounced when we have access to silver tier dungeons."

"He's right," Dorrik grunted, jumping from one rock to another before landing on the mostly dry bank of the river created by the crashing waterfall. "Even the most powerful wood tier abilities in the hands of the most powerful avatars barely compare to iron tier attacks. The tower rewards us for pushing ourselves, and one of the biggest rewards is the possibility to earn an iron tier skillstone at sixth level if we take a truly great risk."

Kat followed the lokkel, skipping lightly from stone to stone while Kaleek simply barreled through the curtain of water, his hands still heavily laden with vinecat cores.

"That's why we're leveling up this fast." Kaleek waded through the chest deep water as he made his way to the riverbank. "It might be a better idea for us to slow down and practice our abilities more as we progress, but at the end of the day, if you're going to be fighting in real life, we need to iron you up as soon as possible."

"A sound plan," Dorrik agreed. "If you're going to fight in the real world, I won't feel truly comfortable until you have access to silver tier defensive skills. Iron will have to do in the meantime."

"Uh." Kat glanced at both of them as Kaleek struggled to pull himself ashore with his arms full. "Both of you do realize that I've been fighting and killing on a pretty regular basis for the last couple of weeks? Things are getting really rough back on Earth."

Dorrik leaned down, gripping Kaleek by the scruff of his neck and the small of his back and picking the otter up. The desoph scrambled away from the incline of the shore cheerfully as soon as the big lizard set him down.

Crest fluttering gently, Dorrik turned back to Kat frowning. "That may be true, Miss Kat, but I don't have to like it. I understand that your planet is a barbaric place filled with strife and blood, but the sooner you make it past the lower levels so that you can stand on your own, the happier I will be."

"That reminds me." Kat led the way through the small jungle of too-tall quasi-trees with suspiciously smooth bark. "I haven't returned to school over the last couple of days. Xander is afraid that someone will be able to put two and two together and figure out that I was involved in the Beloit raid. He doesn't think it's safe for anyone involved to show their faces in Chiwaukee."

"A wise precaution," Dorrik agreed. "For a fractured land full of minor warring polities, your Earth appears to be distressingly close to an authoritarian police state."

Kat just smiled. Dorrik wasn't wrong. Things might not be awful for every person all of the time. After all, there wasn't much profit to be made in monitoring when each office worker went out for coffee or took a crap. That said, when things began to threaten the bottom line, infighting, corruption, and inefficiency tended to disappear overnight.

Executives and managers were given free rein to fight their own hidden wars and turf battles so long as they understood that the company came first. A destructive raid on a major company asset that damaged or destroyed corporate research was sure to spark an immediate and violent reaction.

Unless Kat and her friends could retrieve the recording and convince GroCorp's shareholders that their actions were necessary, she would be forced to live her life on the run. Likely a very short life. Hiding in a hidden room behind a casino-brothel might work for the time being, but it was only a matter of time before the company managed to identify Whippoorwill and follow her back to the base when the pink-haired girl went on one of her supply runs.

"As wise as it may be," Kat replied, pushing aside a slightly too-green leaf that hung down from one of the almost-trees. "It leaves us unable to plan and coordinate. None of the parties involved in the initial raid can move freely, and we can only communicate in short coded bursts via public message channels if we want to avoid arrest and capture."

Dorrik nodded thoughtfully as Kaleek ran to where the *Marka*'s twin hulls were pushed up on the sandy beach, untying the three ropes connecting the ship to nearby trees.

"That's why Xander suggested meeting in the Snarled Net," Kat continued, grabbing onto one of the ropes as Kaleek threw it to her. "Apparently it's a bar over in the Humbrass Atoll. Once I told him what floor I was on, he managed to convince the other team leaders to descend so that we can meet."

"Oi! " Kaleek shouted, putting his shoulder into one of the *Marka*'s hulls and motioning for Dorrik to do the same. "Use Levitation so Dorrik and I can push us out while you steady her!"

Kat cast the spell, wrapping the rope around her arm to prevent a riptide from dragging the ship out to sea once her companions pushed it into the water. Kaleek had been quite clear about how much of a hassle swimming down an unmanned ship was. Apparently the otter had some experience in the field.

Sand crunched under the keels. Slowly at first, the *Marka* moved into the water, slipping away from the shore until it began bobbing on the roiling waves.

Dorrik and Kaleek ran out into the water until they were chest deep, grabbing onto the rope netting on either side of the ship and climbing aboard. Kat took a deep breath, quietly casting Levitation on herself before running toward their vessel.

Just before the waterline, she jumped, activating Leaping to send herself flying through the air. For a brief moment, she was weightless, a grin on her face and her hair whipping wildly at the back of her neck.

Then she hit the side of the ship, the enchantments in her armor trading some of her mana reserve to convert a blow that otherwise would have left her sore and complaining for days into little more than an annoyance.

Two of Dorrik's hands reached down, grasping Kat under

her armpits and pulling her aboard. She nodded gratefully to the big lizard before unwrapping the rope from around her arm and stowing it next to the chest where Kaleek had stored the vinecat gems.

Already, the desoph was pushing a large wooden pole into the sand, moving the *Marka* away from the shore. Kat hadn't quite been able to figure out what it was made of. It looked like some sort of light and pliable bamboo substitute, but it did the trick. With a grunt and the help of Levitation, they were on the open water once more.

Almost immediately, Dorrik turned green, staggering over to the storage chest and withdrawing a draught from the box. They downed it in one swift motion before shuffling to the center of the boat and plopping themself down with their back to the mast.

"The Humbrass Atoll isn't that far from our home base," Kaleek said thoughtfully, shifting the *Marka*'s sail to the side to guide the ship back in roughly the same direction they'd come from. He'd have to zig zag the ship a little to get them back to dock, but Kaleek had assured them it wouldn't be a problem.

"It's probably only six to seven hours away via ship." The otter shimmied past Dorrik, trying not to disturb their suffering friend while they waited for the motion sickness draught to kick in. "When is the meeting scheduled? We should probably head out to Humbrass at least a day before we're supposed to meet your friends."

"I think allies is a better word." Kat shuddered slightly at the mental image of Belle Donnst gossiping with her over lunch. "But we should have another four days before the meeting. Apparently some of them have to come pretty far inside the tower."

"That gives us time for three dungeons," Dorrik mused, their crest flat with discomfort. "Not enough to finish the fourth floor, but so long as things go well, we can make good progress toward reaching the sixth level before anything too serious happens."

"About that." Kat sighed, eyes tracking a trio of triangular fins as they cut through the waves. They were either normal sharks or porpoises, far too small to be a ship-wrecking megalodon. "We ran into some strange things in Beloit. I'm not sure how much time we actually have."

"Of course you have to make it sound all portentous like that." Kaleek chuckled, paw still on the wooden bar that controlled their sail. "If we weren't in the tower, I swear by the ancients that there would have been a stroke of lightning to punctuate that statement. If you have a concern, just let us know. No need to build tension like that."

"Fine." She chuckled, rolling her eyes at the desoph as Kaleek stuck his tongue out at her. "We found prisoners strapped to the wall with glowing white rings around their heads. In the next room, there were infants in some sort of luminescent green liquid. They had name plates that corresponded to the prisoners."

"More importantly," Kat continued. "When I touched the glass cylinders that the infants were in, it felt like I was touching enchanted equipment. I don't think that any humans can make something like that. At least, not for the next twenty years."

Dorrik's crest fluttered in agitation, their clawed hands gripping the wooden planks on either side of them as the ship hit a particularly large wave.

"That sounds like an illegal doppelganger operation," they said slowly, a frown on their scaled face. "The green liquid-filled cylinders are probably flash clone pods. They're only legal to use when spying on another Consensus race or infiltrating a potential member to make sure that the reported information is accurate."

"As for the metal circles?" Dorrik shook their head grimly. "Those are personality upload matrices. Highly illegal. They're used to upload the memory and characteristics of the unconscious target into a clone. The problem is that they have a tendency to burn out the neural pathways of anyone they're used on."

"Even without anything else," Kaleek chimed in, "that's probably enough to burn some of the goodwill that the stallesp have accrued. They're rich and influential enough that a lot of species give them the benefit of the doubt, but doppelgangers are more than just frowned upon."

"Well, I managed to grab one of the personality upload things," Kat replied. "Hopefully that will help smooth things out."

"It should." Dorrik nodded, their crest fluttering. "Clan Ahn has dispatched a rapid reaction force. I will make sure that they know about the doppelganger issue so that they can collect the matrix from you and lodge a formal complaint against the stallesp for their interference."

"Good." Kat slumped down, pressing her back against the *Marka*'s mast. "I just can't shake the feeling that we're missing something. The stallesp have to know that they'll get caught at some point. It just doesn't seem right for us to assume that their nefarious plot hinges on them being dumb and assuming that another race wouldn't find out about them."

"Maybe it is just that easy?" Kaleek asked, twitching his whiskers in the ocean breeze. "Sometimes people just fuck up. To paraphrase an old desoph proverb, 'don't interrupt your opponent when they're making a mistake.'"

"I suppose." Kat sighed. "I can't help but wonder why they hinged all of their contracts for mineral extraction on Mr. Jackson hitting level twenty-four. It feels like such an illogical and arbitrary number."

Dorrik froze, their eyes widening and crest stiffening in agitation.

"Miss Kat," they hissed. "This is important. Mr. Jackson is a human, correct? What level is he?"

"He doesn't publicize it," Kat replied with a frown, "but he's at least level eighteen. Speculation has him anywhere between eighteen and twenty-one."

"Well, piss." Kaleek spat out the words. "Maybe things are urgent."

"Why?" Kat asked. "What's happening?"

"Twenty-four isn't an arbitrary number," Kaleek replied, his fur-covered brow furrowed and his eyes stormy. "That's the threshold where—"

"Kaleek," Dorrik cut him off. "As a probationary race, humans are forbidden from knowing about that. It's in the rules."

"Piss on the rules," Kaleek grumbled. "The stallesp clearly don't have a problem breaking them, so why should we?"

Kat looked back and forth between her friends. This was probably the first time she'd seen them genuinely argue since arriving in the tower. It seemed like both wanted to help her, Kaleek by bringing her in on some secret, and Dorrik by protecting her from forbidden knowledge.

"Once a human hits level twenty-four, they become a racial representative." Kaleek spoke quickly, like an auctioneer trying to slip one last word in under a deadline.

Warning! As a probationary race on level 4, this information is prohibited. Your translation software has temporarily been disabled. Please contact an administrator if you wish to appeal this decision or if you believe it has been made in error.

Kaleek's words devolved into an unintelligible stream of grunts and snarls just as the popup appeared, leaving Kat with nothing better to do than stare at him blankly.

CHAPTER THIRTY-THREE

"I hope you're excited for the Humbrass Atoll," Kaleek said with a grin, plopping down on the bow of the *Marka* next to Kat and letting his paws hang over the edge. "It isn't the biggest hub on the fourth floor, but it's fairly popular. A good chunk of my pod spent time there, so I was able to get us some good recommendations for seafood places. Apparently, the Deep Delver has the freshest saltwater prawns you'll find anywhere in the tower."

"Is that just a euphemism for you trying to feed me still-living shellfish?" Kat asked, staring out at the rippling waves of the floor-spanning ocean. It was a gorgeous day, the faux sun high in the sky and not a cloud in sight. Kaleek had tied the mast in place, and other than periodically checking to make sure they were on course, there wasn't much for the cheerful otter to do.

"Well, they are really good," he responded unapologetically. "Do you think it will work on Dorrik? It would be a shame to find a traditional desoph live prawn restaurant only for everyone to just enjoy it. The screams of surprise are half the fun."

"I'm not sure how much time we're going to have for relaxing." She leaned back, focusing on the sensation of the wind blowing through her hair. "I guess you could grab a drink or something at the Snarled Net while I handle the meeting, but I'm pretty sure that most of my time will be consumed by dealing with whatever the stallesp are trying to pull on Earth. My plan is to get my relaxation in on the trip there. I doubt I'll have the time once we actually arrive."

"I'll say." Kaleek glanced wistfully at the water. "I really could go for a swim right now. If we keep this rate up for too much longer, my fur is going to lose its luster from stress. Two dungeons in two nights is a bit much. Most people spend at least six to twelve days between dungeon challenges to raise marks and prepare."

Two dungeons in two days. It hadn't been that bad, netting her a point of Mind and Agility at the expense of some minor consumable items and getting sprayed with caustic stomach acid by monsters that looked like shoulder-high dinosaurs.

Despite Kat's misgivings, the gear provided by Dorrik's clan had done the trick. They would need to replace it eventually, but for now, so long as they fought carefully, battles were no longer balanced on the knife edge of failure where a single mistake could spell an avatar's death.

She turned back to Kaleek, brushing the hair out of her face as the wind whipped it back and forth. "Speak for yourself. I've been stuck underground in a six-room complex with four other people this entire time. The first day wasn't awful, but the lack of wireless access almost drove me crazy."

"Now?" Kat shuddered. "Limited water and lack of ventilation are what's going to get me. I never realized how *bad* improper hygiene could smell."

"That's why I would suggest living on a planet covered mostly in water," Kaleek responded, whiskers twitching with amusement as he tried to maintain a serious tone. "It's hard for things to smell bad if everyone has to bathe in order to catch fish for supper."

"Speaking of which…" Kat pressed her hands into the worn and sun-bleached hull of the *Marka* to scoot back from the bow and stand up. "It's about time someone checked on Dorrik. We've been on the water for almost three hours, and even with the draughts, I don't think they're holding up all that well."

Kaleek just chuckled, flopping backward on the deck of the ship with his feet still hanging off the edge. Kat shook her head, letting her friend enjoy the breeze as she walked back toward where Dorrik sat, huddled next to the mast, legs clutched to their chest.

Just as she reached them, Kat stopped, putting a hand up to shield her eyes from the glare.

"Hey Kaleek," she called out over her shoulder, squinting into the distance. "There's nothing on the fourth floor that would make a cloud hang low over the water, is there?"

The desoph leapt to his feet, walking past Kat toward the square stern of the catamaran with a frown on his face. He stood there for a couple of seconds, staring at the faint shape on the horizon before turning back.

"That's a galleon," Kaleek said carefully, making his way over to the wooden pole that held their triangular sail and untying it. "A much larger vessel with a single keel and a deeper draft. Given the prevalence of shallower waters around the islands on this floor, they aren't in vogue for adventuring crews. You really only see them as merchants. Or warships."

"Which is it?" Kat asked, chewing her lip as she stared at the innocent tuft of white, barely visible over the glittering waves.

"A good question," Kaleek replied, angling the sail to change the *Marka*'s heading. "One whose answer I would like to avoid if at all possible. Warships often carry twenty-four or more avatars, and it isn't uncommon for a couple of them to be from higher floors. I like our odds against enemies from the fourth floor or lower, but even a single iron tier skill would be enough to dramatically change the odds."

"You're afraid of stallesp marauders," Kat stated evenly, eyes still locked on the now menacing speck.

"Primarily," the desoph agreed. "Although most war parties aren't keen on witnesses, especially when there aren't any declared and sanctioned conflicts. In short, we should try to keep our distance."

The *Marka* shifted course, angling itself against the wind as they began moving away from the galleon. Kat stood at the stern of the ship, occasionally glancing back at Kaleek steering the catamaran or Dorrik's miserable form.

After several minutes, she turned to Kaleek. "Just out of curiosity, what do we do if they try to pursue us? The *Marka* is almost certainly lighter than the galleon, so we should be able to outrun them, right?"

"Not necessarily," Kaleek grunted back, muscles bulging as he held tight to the pole that controlled their sails. "A ship like that will have a lot more canvas than us to catch the wind. Even if it's a bit heavier, it should be able to make about the same time as us."

"Of course," the otter remarked thoughtfully. "That's only if they don't have an air elementalist, a wizard, or some sort of inventor class on board. Any one of those and they could easily juice a little bit more speed out of the ship with magic."

"Huh." Kat nodded. "That would explain why it's getting closer then."

Kaleek looked over his shoulder, whiskers twitching. "Fuck." His furry face looked like he'd bitten into weak old fish. "I was afraid of that."

He leaned forward and to the side, tapping Dorrik on the shoulder with his tail. The lokkel raised his head blearily.

"You got a fight in you, buddy?" he asked gently. "Looks like the stallesp are on our tails, and I'm not sure we're getting through this without a scrap."

Dorrik staggered to their feet, their grayish black scales looking a bit green. They stumbled a step as the *Marka* skipped over a wave before catching themselves.

"The question," they said shakily, swaying unsteadily, "isn't whether I have a fight in me. The question is whether the stallesp are ready for what I'm going to do to—"

The catamaran crested a particularly large swell before smacking back down on the ocean. Dorrik fell to their hands and knees, all four of their arms wobbling as they fought to keep themselves from going snout first into the sun-bleached wood of the deck.

"Yeeeaaah," Kaleek sighed, wrenching on the sail to change their heading drastically. "That's what I thought. Time for plan B, 'do something stupid.'"

"I feel like that's the sort of statement that should worry me," Kat replied worriedly. She couldn't yet see the figures on the galleon's deck, but there was no question that it was visibly gaining on them.

"A lot of things should worry you right now." Kaleek shot her a cocky grin. "First and foremost is the marauders chasing us. After that is the fate of your troubled planet. Finally, we reach my plan. Don't get all worked up about it, though. I'm guessing we have at least a seventy-five percent chance of surviving this."

"Is there a plan available that doesn't have a one-in-four chance of dying?" Kat asked hopefully. There was no doubt about it, the galleon was pursuing them.

"Not unless you think that ship wants to catch up with us to borrow a jar of fish paste," the desoph answered with a shrug. "Even with Dorrik at one hundred percent, I don't like our odds against that many enemies. Right now? We're firmly in 'long shot' territory."

Kat chewed her lip, eyeing up the ship. The only sound was Dorrik's moans competing with the creak of the *Marka*'s wooden hull as they splashed over the increasingly choppy waves. Behind them, she could just start to make out the ant-like figures of the avatars on the opposing ship.

God, there were a lot of them.

"Do you mind telling me what this secret plan of yours is?"

Kat ripped her eyes away from their pursuer to turn and face Kaleek. "I think the speed with which they're catching up with us is making me more amenable to long shots."

"There's more than just marauders that stop ships from coming home after an expedition." Kaleek nodded grimly, inclining his head toward a flock of white birds, circling an empty patch of ocean in the distance.

Kat stared blankly at it for almost five seconds, trying to make heads or tails of her companion's words. As far as she could tell, it was nothing more than a blank patch of water with birds overhead. Maybe the waves weren't quite as pronounced there, but that could hardly be the cause of Kaleek's dramatic behavior. Finally, she shrugged.

"Are we going to try to get them lost or something?" she asked uncertainly. "You're going to have to be specific here. The only body of water near me on Earth is GroCorp Presents: Lake Michigan, and I haven't gotten a chance to visit it yet. I really have no idea what you're talking about."

"Oh, by the grace of the ancients." Kaleek snorted. "Do what you can to stop the galleon from sinking us. Just make sure to save at least a quarter of your mana, I'm going to need it."

"Stop it from—" Kat flinched as a watermelon-sized ball of *something* crashed into the water to her right. A second later, there was a bright flash of light and water cascaded upward, drenching the *Marka*.

A wave picked the catamaran up and tossed it to the side. For a moment, Kat was entirely weightless as the *Marka*'s twin hulls were entirely exposed.

Then they smashed back into the ocean, aged deck planks groaning in protest as more water splashed everywhere. Kat was barely able to maintain her footing, her enhanced reactions and agility serving her well while Kaleek hung on to the sail for dear life.

Dorrik wasn't so lucky, slamming into the bottom of the ship and rolling until they hit the railing, a rickety wooden fence the only barrier between the lokkel and the frothing ocean waves.

Promptly and without preamble, they shoved their muzzle over the edge of the ship and threw up into the ocean below.

"Spell casings," Kaleek grunted, shifting the sail to get them back on course. "That means they have a wizard and an artificer on board. Let's hope that was a lucky shot because if they're that accurate all the time, the three of us are going to have to learn how to swim in a hurry."

Almost a minute later, another gray ball arced through the air, launched by some sort of contraption on the galleon's bow. This one didn't hit the water, instead exploding into three crackling bolts of lightning well short of the *Marka*.

Kat blinked her eyes, trying to clear the white and blue after images as Kaleek steered their ship toward the circling birds.

"There we go." The desoph grinned madly back at her. "That first shot was just beginner's luck. As long as they don't get absurdly fortunate, we should be able to make it in time."

"I hate to ruin the mood," Kat replied nervously, eyeing up the galleon, its sails full and straining as some sort of spellcaster aided its pursuit, "but we aren't making it anywhere in time. I can see the stallesp from here and that thing is only getting closer."

Another gray sphere struck the water, detonating beneath the surface and sending a fountain of brine everywhere. The three of them stopped talking long enough to grab onto hand holds as the wave from the attack picked them up and pushed the *Marka* forward.

"Good," Kaleek cackled. "We want them close anyway."

"We want *what* now?" Kat whipped around. Kaleek was standing tall as he held onto the sail, making constant minute adjustments to keep the *Marka* on a steady heading as the wind tousled his wet fur. "I'm pretty sure whatever that magical cannon is, it gets more accurate when it gets closer, not the other way around."

"Just get ready to cast Levitation, Kat." He didn't look back, instead focusing on the water and the birds circling overhead. "It'll reduce our drag and give us a speed boost. Where we're going, we'll need both."

Another spell casing exploded in the air off their stern, peppering the water with dozens of razor sharp daggers of ice. Kat shook her head and frowned at the galleon.

A dozen or so of the mole-like stallesp stood on its deck, most armed with what looked like long bows as they waited for the range to close enough for their weapons to be useful despite the wind. At the prow of the ship, two figures in robes stood next to a device that looked like two ballistae welded together, one horizontal and the other vertical.

Even as he watched on, one of the figures picked up a dark circle and slid it into a housing where the two massive crossbows intersected. Then the other put a hand on the side of the contraption.

It launched another gray sphere that detonated in the air off their starboard, stabbing the waves with four eye-searing bolts of lightning, close enough that the hair on Kat's forearms stood on end.

"They're awfully close, Kaleek!" she shouted, not even bothering to look at the desoph. "If you have a plan, now is the time. I'm not sure we're going to have the opportunity in a minute or so."

"Now, Kat!" he screamed back over the wind. At some point, it had picked up into an almost gale force torrent of gusting air. "Cast Levitation on the *Marka*!"

She didn't ask any questions, placing her palm on the ship's deck and infusing the gravity magic into it.

The effect was immediate. The *Marka* bobbed up higher on the waves and darted forward, a spell casing detonating under the water in their wake.

"Oh fuck!" Kaleek's giddy madness morphed into genuine terror. "I can't believe they fucking did it! Cast it again. Now, Kat!"

She frowned, infusing more mana into the ship. It practically leapt from the water, skating up a massive swell of water that hadn't been there a moment before and sending her skittering across the deck.

Her hands hit the deck on either side of her, fingers questing for a handhold and only finding splinters. At the last second, she caught hold of one of the posts that anchored the safety railing.

Then the *Marka* was in the air, hanging for an eternal second under the power of her spells. One of the white birds swooped by, a four-winged gull of some sort. Its eyes fixed themselves on her, vivid golden rings surrounding massive black pupils. It screeched at her, entirely unafraid, and then they began to descend.

They fell almost gently, more of an uncontrolled glide really. Casting the same spell twice multiplied its mana cost, but at the same time, Kat couldn't argue with the results.

She looked back at the galleon, and a gasp tore itself from her throat. The giant swell of water was gone, replaced by two massive pillars of pink coral that affixed themselves to the sides of the enemy ship.

Spells flashed and flickered as the stallesp tried to fight off the attacker, but Kat could see that it wasn't working. The attacks were removing chips of the rocky substance, but the glittering coral towers were grinding through the ship's hull like drill bits.

Then, the water opened up in front of the galleon, a swirling vortex of water leading down into the massive pink maw of *something*. The whirlpool pulled at the galleon, forcing the vessel's nose downward as the masses of coral dragged it toward its fate.

The *Marka* hit the water, barely breaking the surface as it jolted away. Just beneath the waves, barely three feet from the bottom of their ship, jagged toothlike spears of coral stared back at her menacingly.

Kaleek began laughing maniacally. Behind them, Kat heard the snap of the galleon's massive timbers being torn apart.

"What in the name of all that is holy is *that*!" she shouted at Kaleek, pulling herself up on the railing.

"That is plan B!" he shouted back exuberantly. "Me doing something stupid!"

"Usually your stupidity doesn't take the form of some sort of nightmare monstrosity, Kaleek." She worked her way along the guardrail toward him, making sure to keep one hand on the rickety wood at any given point of time.

"The idiots didn't even know to avoid carrion gulls." Kaleek flashed her a mad smile. "Even if they didn't bother to check the charts for this area for hazards, they should have known to avoid still water and carrion gulls. That's the first lesson every pup gets when they reach the fourth floor."

"You're not being terribly illuminating here, Kaleek." Kat shook her head at him, glancing into the water once more to take in the almost endless pink blades just beneath the surface.

"*That* is why heavy vessels with deep drafts are out of favor," he replied, eyes twinkling. "As soon as your keel strikes the coral, it triggers an attack, and then almost nothing on the floor can escape, let alone defeat it."

"Say hello to Leviathan, Kat," Kaleek continued cheerfully. "She isn't the biggest living reef on the fourth floor, but I wouldn't want to piss her off."

CHAPTER THIRTY-FOUR

Humbrass Atoll wasn't what Kat was expecting. She'd expected another dingy shantytown made out of bleached driftwood and populated by half-awake locals. Instead, the *Marka* sailed past a necklace of gorgeous tropical islands filled with well-maintained and multi-story brick buildings. Here and there, a shop or house would be made of wood, but given the intricacy of the carvings on their windows and doors, she could tell that it was an aesthetic choice.

The atoll itself was a circle of islands centered around a shallow bay with a pillar to the fifth level in it. Apparently the floor guardian, something called a dread kraken, was fairly sedate except when challenged by people seeking to ascend. Then, the citizens of the islands would crowd the beaches to watch the aquatic battle while they enjoyed fruity drinks and placed bets.

The islands varied in size, with most being large enough for a mid-sized town. The biggest isle, Mount Halleka, was large enough to house both the Schaumberg arcology and the Shell combined, while some of the smaller islands were little more than sandbars. Every one of the isles was occupied with densely packed structures, packed onto the scarce land and connected with their neighbors by a series of bridges.

The Snarled Net, on the other hand, was exactly what Kat was expecting. After she, Kaleek, and Dorrik reset their spawn point to the altar in Mount Helleka, they'd sought out the bar.

Apparently, like everywhere else, there was a pecking order on the Humbrass Atoll. There was no question that the Snarled Net was one of the finest human establishments in the island chain.

Kat's nose wrinkled as she took in the beat-up collection of canoes, rafts, and ancient ships at the New Panama dock. On the atoll, going to the fanciest human restaurant was like meeting the tallest third grader. It just didn't mean much.

Kaleek started tying up the *Marka* with swift and efficient motions as Kat jumped onto the aged and worm-eaten wood of the dock and surveyed the island of New Panama. Their catamaran was almost certainly the best ship there, a sorry statement given the *Marka*'s age and repair.

As for the island? It was barely the size of the parking ramp that Xander, Whippoorwill, and her used to hide their base behind the Neon Dream. The buildings were well made if densely packed. Two-story structures constructed from wood and baked mud bricks crowded each other to the very edges of the ocean. Really, the only place with any breathing room was the Snarled Net itself, a three-story brick building directly at the base of the wharf.

Dorrik jumped on the pier after her, wobbling slightly as they tried to overcome the last vestiges of seasickness. They surveyed the island, crest fluttering in the wind as they nodded sagely.

"This looks horrifying on both a sanitary and a moral level," the lokkel said cheerfully. "Still, it's much better than another minute on that ship."

They walked past Kat a few steps before turning around and waving a claw in her and Kaleek's direction. "Come, Miss

Kat, let us meet the dregs of your society. I am sure they have much to teach us."

She snorted, following the giant lizard down the beat-up pier as it creaked in the waves. A second later, Kaleek finished tying their ship down and joined the two of them just as Dorrik opened the wooden door to the Snarled Net.

The bar was dimly lit. Oil lamps flickered through aged and clouded glass from their perches, hanging from iron rings affixed to the ceiling. The clientele was mostly human, figures hunched over any number of tables as they drank quietly from chipped mugs and steins, but a couple aliens dotted the building's main floor.

After a quick survey of the room didn't reveal Xander or Davis, Kat took a deep breath of the room's stale air before weaving her way through the tables toward the bartender. He was a middle-aged man, dirty blond hair close-cropped, his face and hands a web of scars.

"Hello," Kat said, nodding to him. Behind her, chairs scraped across the floor as various patrons cleared a path for Dorrik and Kaleek as the two aliens followed her to the bar.

The bartender just grunted, not even looking up from the mug he was cleaning with the tail end of a smock covered in indecipherable stains.

"I'm here looking for a couple friends of mine," Kat began only to get cut off by a gurgling voice booming from the bar's door.

"Jacques Terre-du-Tête! By my gills, is it good to see you again."

The bartender sighed, setting the mug opening down on the polished wood of the bar. Kat followed his gaze past her shoulder. An alien, little more than a bulbous triangular head suspended from a number of tentacles slapped his way wetly toward her, an unctuous smile on his rubbery face.

"I thought I told you that I didn't want to buy whatever it is you're peddling, Briqui," the grizzled man growled, leaning forward to put both of his mangled hands on the bar. "I don't need psychedelic fruit, narcotic powders, or euphoric tree sap. Last time you came through here, you 'forgot' to mention that Bacchus Honey causes intense shakes and nausea after the high wears off. It took us two nights to get the vomit mopped out of the floor."

"Ah!" The squid thing waved a tentacle agreeably at the proprietor. "Jacques, my old friend, you only say that because last time I did not come to you with my finest product, Dread Kraken Ink. One drop into each of your eyes and you will see things you could never even dream of. Usually I sell it for five marks per hit, but for you I could go as low as three."

Kaleek cocked his head at the overly cheerful alien, whiskers twitching thoughtfully.

"Doesn't Dread Kraken Ink put the user into a fugue state where their greatest nightmares become reality?" the otter asked quizzically. "I've heard that the Omicron Pirates are known to use it in interrogations to torture the truth out of their victims."

"Just two marks for four hours that you'll never forget!" Briqui glanced at Kaleek nervously. "From my beak to my tentacles, I swear you won't regret this."

"I can do two marks," a tall thin man blurted out, lurching drunkenly to his feet.

"Oh, sit down, Adam," another man at his table grumbled, wine-glass halfway to his mouth. "You're drunk and this is an absolutely awful idea."

Kat stood to the side, eyeing the exchange in confusion while Dorrik studied it with their usual academic fervor. Kaleek? The desoph just covered his muzzle with a paw, likely trying his hardest to hold in an inopportune snicker.

"Ah-hah!" The squid-like alien undulated toward the swaying man, beak chattering excitedly. "I knew I could find a human with a properly adventurous temperament in this august establishment."

"No, you can't do two marks, Adam." Jacques sniffed, reaching under the counter and retrieving a heavy metal mace that he slammed down on the polished wood in front of him. "You still owe twelve on your tab that you keep promising you'll pay off 'tomorrow.' And Briqui? Get the hell out of my bar."

The squid capered, bobbing its head in a half bow before it flowed back out of the building. A moment later, the general conversation and hubbub of the common area returned as muted conversations resumed and glasses began clinking once more.

"Sorry about that, miss." The bartender nodded at her. "You were saying something before we got interrupted?"

"Ah." Kat hesitated, rattled by the exchange. "I was looking for some of my friends. They were coming down from other floors to meet me, and we were going to meet here."

"I can be your friend, baby!" The tall man that had been trying to solicit drugs from the alien squid wobbled toward her, only for his companion to grab his wrist and restrain him.

Dorrik stepped in between her and the drunk, top pair of hands touching the hilts of their swords. A low growl escaped their throat, crest flat against the back of their head.

"I consider myself a student of human culture." The lokkel's voice was deeper than usual, a dangerous rumble that set even Kat on edge. They stepped toward the human, towering half a head over the tall man. "And I don't appreciate you bothering my companion. Take your seat and return to your drink, or I will become a student of human anatomy as well."

"Hey now!" Jacques' scarred hand slapped onto the table, drawing attention back to the scowling bartender. "This bar has two rules on fighting. First, do it outside. Can't have any broken furniture. Second, if you kill a man, you pay his tab. Adam owes me twelve marks. Pay up or leave the asshole alone."

Kaleek burst out laughing, unable to restrain himself as the drunk blanched and returned to his seat.

"That settles it." The otter's body was shaking with mirth. "Unless the beer here is absolute piss, I think this is my favorite bar on the entire atoll."

"They aren't completely piss," the bartender responded defensively. "You gotta cut 'em with rainwater first."

"My friends?" Kat could feel a headache beginning to press down on her temples like a vise.

"We had two groups come down the stairs and tangle with the kraken today." Jacques picked up the glass and began rubbing it with his smock once more. "Real scary blokes. Said they're waiting on someone and to send her up to them when she shows up. They've got the dining room upstairs."

"Thanks." Kat smiled back at him, struggling to be polite, but the bartender just grunted back, nodding slightly.

Giving up, she turned, following Dorrik as the big lizard cleared a path to the dark staircase in the corner. They climbed past the dirty oil lamps and into the next floor in silence.

There, things were cleaner and better lit. Magical lights dotted the old but recently washed wooden walls, and there was even a small vase with a handful of red flowers in it next to a window. All of the plants had seen better days, but it was the thought that counted.

Kat stepped past Dorrik, leading the way toward a door labeled 'dining hall' in clear, block lettering. She pushed the door open and stepped inside.

Inside the room, heads jerked toward Kat as she stepped inside, making room for Kaleek and Dorrik to follow her. The interior was little more than a small brass and crystal chandelier hanging over a large table with five of its eight seats occupied.

"Kat!" Xander sprang to his feet, richly colored cloak billowing behind him and exposing an iron breastplate covered in carvings of men and women laboring before a gleaming golden ziggurat in the center of his chest. "Come on in and introduce us to your friends."

"Oh and big guy." He pointed at Dorrik and winked. "Make sure to close the door behind you. Super secretive stuff going on in here, very hush hush."

Dorrik cocked their head and stared at Xander, crest fanning out in bemusement before they closed the door. Kat just rolled her eyes at yet another example of Xander being Xander.

"This," Kat hooked a thumb toward a waving Kaleek, "is Kaleek. He's a desoph. They're pseudo-mammals that live in mid-sized communities on mostly oceanic planets."

"Kaleek, meet Xander," she continued, nodding toward the human. "When on a job, he goes by Exe, just like I do with the name Erinyes."

Before she could continue, Dorrik stepped past her, having already closed the door.

"I'm Dorrik," the lokkel volunteered, stepping forward and inclining their head. "I like to think of myself as a student of your race's history and customs, and working with Miss Kat has been an absolute pleasure. I look forward to learning more about each of you as we work together."

"It's good to meet you, Dorrik." Belle Donnst stood up, her voice overly cultured and smooth in a way that sent shivers down Kat's spine. "My name is Belle, and I've worked with Miss Debs in the past, but I have to say that this is the first time a lokkel has actually bothered to talk to me. Usually when your people find out who I am, they look at me like I'm a half-eaten apple with only part of a worm in it."

"Belle Donnst!" Dorrik's face lit up. "Kat has told me so much about you! She refers to you as 'the toxic pinnacle of competence and treachery.' I must say, her descriptions of your callous disregard for the life and feelings of your fellow humans are *fascinating*."

"Charmed," Belle responded, a pleasant smile on her face as she motioned to a burly man sitting next to her. "I honestly couldn't think of a more fitting summary. This is my second, Jason."

"Davis Stoller, or Merrimac when I'm on a job," the older man introduced himself before nodding to the woman next to him. "This is Hestia. Her actual name isn't commonly known, so we'll keep it to commonly available knowledge."

Hestia smiled at Kat, waving quickly to her, ignoring the scowl thrown her way by Davis.

"Great," Belle said, clapping her hands together. "Hestia, if you could be a dear and activate the chandelier, our newcomers should take a seat so we can begin."

Kat pulled out a chair, noting the cushion tied to its simple polished wood. The seat wasn't anything special, but it was still a good sight better than the dimly lit rough construction of the first floor.

Hestia raised a hand, creating one mote of blue flame after another until four small balls of fire rose to the glittering arms of the chandelier. As soon as they touched the wicks of the fixture's candles, the spell disappeared.

All of Kat's hair stood on end at the same time as a static charge ran through her. Dorrik looked up in interest, inspecting the gleaming bronze carefully.

"Anti-eavesdropping and recording enchantment," Xander supplied with a grin. Absently, Kat noticed that his avatar didn't come with the older man's signature golden tooth. "Very useful for clandestine meetings like this."

"Indeed," Belle replied, her smile growing a little thin. "Now Exe, you've mentioned that Kat and you have managed to pull some intelligence out of the assets you've extracted from Beloit."

"Watch yourself," Davis growled, fixing a stormy gaze on the elegant woman. "One of those 'assets' is Jasper. Don't think I've forgotten what you did to the poor boy's father. We might be allies of convenience today, but don't think that I won't have you killed if you pull any stunts."

Belle's companion jumped to his feet, drawing a longsword in a flash as he interposed himself between Davis and Belle. Merrimac stood slowly, both of his fists glowing dully red as he stared down the younger man. Behind him, a constellation of blue flames sprang into existence behind Hestia. She licked her lips hungrily as the balls of fire began to weave together in a complicated dance.

"Sit!" Belle snapped, crossing her arms. "Either of them could take you apart with one hand, Jason. While your courage is laudable, a poodle yipping at a junkyard dog is hardly menacing. You're embarrassing me."

The man opened his mouth as if to say something, before ultimately eating his words. He sheathed his sword and sat down, staring moodily at the table before him.

"Remember your job here?" Belle asked him, her voice tinged with acid.

"Look pretty and stay silent, I should be seen, not heard," Jason mumbled back, his pleasant tenor bitter as he recited the words.

"Good," she finished, her tone of voice allowing no room for argument or compromise.

"I'm sorry about that, Mr. Stoller." Belle's wintry expression disappeared as she smiled back at the still-standing Merrimac and Hestia. "I forgot that you were still prone to bouts of sentimentality regarding the boy. I will try to watch my tone in the future."

Davis nodded slowly. Behind him, Hestia snapped her fingers, causing the foxfire to disappear as suddenly as she'd summoned it.

The older man took his seat, face troubled. Kat couldn't help but notice his slightly haunted expression. For a moment, she thought about how she would react if her family were in danger, and she couldn't help herself.

"He's doing fine, you know," Kat interjected with an awkward smile. "Jasper had some memory problems for the first day or so, but I think we got him out quickly enough. Colyn Raster, on the other hand—"

She stopped. Raster wasn't improving. He could still take care of himself, but more and more he would isolate himself, sitting in silence for long periods of time only to break out into laughter or mumbling to himself in foreign languages.

Davis inclined his head slightly, a grateful look in his eyes. For a moment, no one spoke as everyone around the table tried to find something to say that would reassure the worried Merrimac.

"Splendid." Belle broke the silence. "Now that affairs of the heart have been settled, we should talk about the conspiracy that very well may kill us all. Xander, if you will?"

"The good news is that we know that the recording exists, we know what's on it, and we know where it is," Xander replied with a grin. "Even better, the contents are incriminating enough to save all of our asses. Elements of every megacorporation on the planet are conspiring together to overthrow their existing leadership and form a cartel with the help of the stallesp."

Kat's brow crinkled slightly. Xander hadn't told her anything about the recording's location.

"Oh?" Belle leaned forward in her seat. "By all means, Xander, proceed with your highly anticipated dramatic reveal."

"The bad news is that, although we were able to track the recording through poorly secured logistics records, it was only notated as a prisoner's personal effects, after all," Xander replied, grimacing slightly. "It's located in a vault in Elaine Williamson's suite. So that's the story. We just need to break into a shareholder's fortified residence, steal the recording from a secure location, broadcast it, and hide from the fallout. Easy peasy."

For a second, a pensive silence filled the room as everyone digested Xander's words. Then, Dorrik shook their head, their voice rumbling unhappily. "Unfortunately, things will hardly be that simple. Miss Kat has mentioned that the contracts signed between the stallesp and your enemies become valid when a Mr. Jackson reaches level twenty-four, is that correct?"

"Yeah," Xander agreed, a frown on his face, "but that's years away. The other shareholders will kill off the rebels before he gets a chance. After that, the problem is settled and we all go our own ways."

"You misunderstand." Dorrik shook their head. "Something happens when a member of a probationary race reaches the twenty-fourth level in the dreamscape. I cannot tell you the specifics, but it would be safe to say that the potential harm far outstrips a petty civil war between corporations. As a race, you have two options, kill this Mr. Jackson before he achieves his goal, or beat him to it."

"I suppose the third option is being enslaved as a race to perform mineral extraction for the moles." Belle sighed, fingers tapping the table.

"Exactly, Miss Donnst," Dorrik replied, a slightly predatory smile on their face.

"Is it too much to hope that your people would help us out with this predicament?" she asked hopefully, raising a single manicured eyebrow. "As best I can understand, the lokkel aren't exactly on speaking terms with the stallesp."

"No," Dorrik declared, leaning forward with clawed hands digging furrows into the wood of the table as they grinned, "I cannot help *you*. You are untrustworthy and just as likely to betray me as the stallesp themselves. I *can* help Miss Kat."

Belle's face broke into a bright smile as she chuckled slightly. "I suppose that's fair enough. You'd be a fool to trust me, and I don't trust fools. Kat is a bit altruistic for her own good, but in all honesty, every other choice I can think of would be worse."

"Great!" Xander clapped his hands together cheerfully. "Now that we're done with all of our nefarious plots and menacing threats, who's ready to plan a raid?"

CHAPTER THIRTY-FIVE

"Three sevens beats a pair of aces." Iris laid her cards down on the cheap plastic table, drawing a groan from Jasper. The woman grinned, leaning forward to rake the pot, the metal pull tabs from some fifteen vacuum-sealed meals, over toward her.

"You should have known better, Jasper," Kat said with a click of her tongue as she collected the cards from the stained vinyl surface so that she could deal. "Iris was acting way too smug not to have a winning hand. That's why I folded right away."

"How could you know that!" Jasper leaned back into his chair, arms crossed. "There's no way you could know if she was bluffing, you folded."

Her hands flickered, barely visible as she slid cards to Iris and Jasper. Kat shook her head, chuckling. "I knew she wasn't bluffing and that's why I folded. Both of you really need to know how to rein in your body language. You're starting to make me feel bad about winning."

"I still think I'd be doing a lot better if we switched from draw to hold 'em." Jasper sulked, picking up his cards. His eyes widened and the corners of his mouth twitched. "I'm anteing three, by the way."

He slid three of the tabs from the dwindling pile in front of him to the center of the table.

Kat glanced at her hand. She had a pair of fours and a chance to draw up to three cards, but given Jasper's expression, it wouldn't be enough. She glanced down at the pyramid of tabs in front of her, half again the size of Iris and Jasper's piles combined.

"Fold." Kat put her cards face down on the table. "I'll say it again, Jasper, we can't play hold 'em, because there's only three of us. It's only really fun with four or more players. At least until you can pull someone out of the pipes, five card draw is the better choice."

"We could always ask Xander to play?" Iris asked, biting her lip as she reorganized her cards. Finally she tossed three tabs from her pile into the center. "Check."

"Xander cheats." Kat snorted as she picked up the deck. "Anyway, how many cards do the two of you want?"

"That just sounds like he's good at poker." Jasper smirked back, sliding two cards to Kat. At the other end of the table, Iris discarded three.

"No," Kat replied, dealing their new cards back to them with sure, quick movements. "He literally tells you he's cheating when you start playing. Xander uses most games and leisure activities as an excuse to train operatives in the skill you'll need to succeed on the job. The point of playing cards with him is to train your perception."

"Doesn't stop him from keeping your money, though." Kat chuckled, leaning back in her plastic and steel chair. "He'll just wink at you and say it's his fee for teaching you."

"I still can't believe you're an actual samurai," Jasper grumbled. "I had Davis look into you, and all he told me is that you worked for the ChromeDogs and that you could handle yourself."

He inspected the cards in his hand before pushing three of his tabs into the pot.

"Believe it," Iris replied, a ghost of a smile on her face as she looked pensively at her hand. "Davis and his friends were deadly serious about Kat. I didn't get a chance to see any of their operation, but there were a lot of guns and cannons firing when they pulled you and the weird guy out of Beloit."

"Check," she finished, matching Jasper's bet. "What do you have, Jasper?"

Iris laid down her cards, a pair of threes and a pair of jacks. Jasper's face broke into a wide grin as he revealed three tens and scraped the twelve tabs across the table toward himself while Iris sighed.

"How is Davis doing, anyway?" Jasper asked quietly, glancing up at Kat. "It's weird, but the first thing I thought of when Xander woke me up was Davis. Him and Andrew were my security detail for that day, and when the kidnappers attacked our car, he jumped out to handle them. I…"

The boy choked up a little, his previous elation over winning fading from his face as he set his cards on the table. Iris leaned over with a pinched expression and covered his hand with hers.

"I didn't know whether he'd made it out in time." Jasper leaned back, closing his eyes. "I just remember jerking awake and seeing all of you hovering over me, and something in my chest clenched when he wasn't there."

"He's doing fine," Kat replied, letting her face soften. "Look, it isn't weird for you to care about Davis. He might work for you, but he doesn't strike me as the type to concern himself too much about the money. If he didn't genuinely want to look out for you, he would have retired years ago."

"I guess," he began, only to be cut off as an irate buzzing tone filled the compound.

Kat jumped to her feet, checking her pistol and knife to make sure that both were ready for use at a moment's notice. Xander jogged by the three of them, nodding briefly before turning on the old smartglass display next to the door.

After inspecting a grainy image of a woman with pink hair walking down the trapped walkway toward the front door, he grunted and stepped back from the door.

"It's just Whip, no need for guns."

Kat sighed with relief, trying to calm her racing pulse in the wake of the adrenaline rush caused by the alarm. She turned to sit down.

"Don't get comfortable, Kat," Xander called out to her. "Whip is coming back from breaking into an open terminal. With any luck, she'll have some updated intelligence for us."

"Good." She nodded apologetically at Jasper and Iris. "No offense, guys, but I think I would have snapped if I had to spend a fourth day cooped up in here."

The door rang as a fist knocked against the reinforced metal. Xander pulled the eye-slit to the side, his finger hovering over a button that would activate the twin flamethrowers trained on the doorway as he visually confirmed that it was Whippoorwill at the door.

Unfortunately, as useful as technology was, every step forward came with its own perils. As Kat was well aware, spoofing a CCTV system wasn't terribly hard. That portion of Xander's security network primarily relied upon a potential invader being unaware of the hardwired observation system's existence.

For everything else, there was a weight sensor and good old-fashioned eyeballs. Between the hints of corporate strike forces equipped in optical camouflage and tower-granted magic, invisibility was a reality they had to deal with. Even if mana and technology could fool their eyes, most infiltrators wouldn't think to use gravity magic to baffle the concealed scale just outside the door.

Xander stepped back from the door, undoing the lock and letting Whip inside. The girl hurried in, shivering slightly despite the oversized hoodie she'd worn for her excursion.

"The next safehouse goes somewhere with less degenerates," Whippoorwill grumbled, glaring at Xander intently. "Either that or you send Kat with me so that people will think I have a girlfriend. I had a drunk guy follow me half a block from the Neon Dream before he tripped over a curb and I was able to lose him."

"Or maybe I can teach you how to use a gun," Xander replied thoughtfully. "I know you're not a frontline operative, but it just doesn't seem right for a ChromeDog to not be able to shoot."

"You want me to shoot random drunks now?" She pulled the sweatshirt over her head before hanging it on a metal peg sticking out of the wall. "I'm not saying no, it just seems a tad aggressive."

"Maybe." Xander shrugged sheepishly. "You might be right, it does seem a little extreme."

"Whatever," Whip responded, rolling her eyes as she pulled her cranial jack out of the back of her head. "Just download the data. I need to take a shower before the freeloaders run us out of hot water again."

Xander touched his cord to hers and for a second or two, both of them stood perfectly still, their eyes twitching rapidly beneath their lids as if they were dreaming. The moment ended with Whippoorwill stepping away from Xander and walking past Kat with a quick nod.

The older man just stood there for a couple seconds, face thoughtful as he ruminated on the information passed to him from Whippoorwill. Finally he sighed.

"I hope you're tired, Kat, because we need to go into the tower." Xander shrugged helplessly. "And if you're not, a street chemist owed me a favor a couple months back and whipped up a couple batches of the sleeping drugs the executives use to keep themselves under for hours at a time. You can't take them too often without getting the shakes, and even one dose will give you dry mouth and a headache, but—"

"But the information Whippoorwill has delivered is that important?" Kat finished for him.

"Yeah," the older man replied unhappily. "Just a second, it looks like I have to burn one of my ghosts."

He walked over to the wall and plugged himself into an outlet by the smartglass. Kat watched as Xander silently went about the business of contacting their allies.

Whippoorwill had explained the process to her, and it was suitably paranoid. None of them could directly use their e-mail or social media accounts as it would be surprising at this point if they had gone unmonitored. Instead, Xander would tap into Neon Dream's network and piggyback off of someone using an entertainment channel to send a packet of data to an offsite relay of his own design that Xander called 'ghosts.'

To the user, it would look like a couple pixels burnt out on their smartpanel for a fraction of a second. A hard to notice digital artifact under normal circumstances, it would go almost unnoticed by the drugged and drunk clientele of the Neon Dream.

From there, a bot would extract a packet of data before posting a coded message on a Chrome Cowboys fan forum. Finally, the bot and the ghost would delete themselves, a small charge slagging the thumbnail-sized piece of electronics.

Xander was limited in the messages that he could send, and he had only pre-planted a certain number of the ghosts around the city, but the chances of the message being traced back to their hideout were almost nil.

He opened his eyes and nodded to Kat. "The meeting is in one hour at the Snarled Net, we should get ready."

She followed Xander into the hideout's bunk room, and the two of them folded down the thin mattresses from where they were stored vertically against the wall. They weren't soft or comfortable, and after only a handful of days Kat was ready to return to her dorm bed, but at the same time, they had an important advantage of her 'not waking up to a corporate goon slipping a bag over her head.' It was hard to beat amenities like that.

Xander pulled an unlabeled bottle out of his pocket and

removed two pills from it. He offered one to Kat before slapping the other into his mouth, Adam's apple bobbing.

Kat swallowed her own, trying not to think about its chemical fragrance and bitter taste. She laid down on her cot, shifting her thin body to avoid the bed's numerous lumps and hard spots.

Her eyelids drooped, heavy with sleep as the drug began to kick in. Kat's thoughts slowed and became fuzzy as the room around her darkened. She blinked.

The bustle of Mount Halleka's Adventurer's Hall appeared around her. A second later, Xander appeared in a cocoon of rainbow light.

"It's still weird to see you in here." She shook her head, taking in his brightly colored cloak and simple iron armor. "It's like when my teachers in school would come into my convenience store. It's just... wrong."

"I don't know," Xander replied with a grin as he led the way out of the stone building, "you seem about the same. All dark clothes, knives, and pointy bits."

"Thanks, I guess?" Kat laughed back as the two of them walked through Halleka's crowded streets, making their way down the paved slope of the mountain and toward the bridged road that connected the various small islands of the Humbrass Atoll.

The narrow and crowded walkways were filled with aliens of all stripes, but only the occasional human. Kat and Xander drew more than one stare as eyestalks swiveled to follow their passage. Only after about twenty minutes, when the two of them were far from the main island, did they begin to see more of humanity.

People showed up in twos and threes, their armor and weapons noticeably more drab than those around them. Somehow, their envious glances as they eyed up Kat's lokkel-crafted armor was almost worse than the gawking aliens.

Finally, they reached New Panama. Other than the better maintenance, it really did remind Kat of the Shell. People were cramped and on edge. She could almost feel the eyes of scavengers tracking Xander and her as they stepped off of the rope bridge and onto the tiny landmass only to dismiss them.

The island might be full of vultures, but Xander and her moved like wolves. Actual predators that could tear through the avatars of the underequipped thugs that might only have a handful of dungeons between them.

Just as Xander reached for the door to the Snarled Net, it slammed open, the tall skinny man from the previous day slumped over his friend's shoulder.

"Get him out of here, Ben!" the bartender shouted from inside. "And remember to tell Adam that it's fourteen marks now when he wakes up!"

The mostly sober man nodded apologetically at the two of them before he brushed past, half dragging his slurring and staggering companion out into the tower's fake light.

Xander didn't even slow, wading into the morass of degeneracy like a fish slipping into the water. A couple of the bar's patrons eyed Kat up, but after noting the number of knives she carried and the easy grace in her step, they returned to their drinks.

"Jacques, you old pirate!" Xander grinned at the scarred man as he slapped his hands down on the bar.

The bartender carefully put down the mug he was cleaning before replying with a sigh, "What do you need now, Exe? I thought I was done with this shit when you made it to the fifth floor."

"Nothing much." Xander winked at the other man conspiratorially. "Just the key to the meeting room from yesterday. I have a couple of friends dropping by and if you could send them my way, I would appreciate it."

"That'll be five marks, Exe." Jacques reached inside his shirt, pulling out a keyring he wore on the end of a necklace like jewelry.

"Five marks!" Xander gasped, putting his left hand on his breast as if affronted. "After I saved you from a sand grub infestation on the third floor and mediated that dispute between you and the Cahokia Crushers?"

"It's been a while since St. Louis, Exe," the bartender grumbled, removing a bronze ring and handing it to Xander. "You can't keep relying on old times forever."

"I'll stop bringing it up when it stops working," Xander replied with a quick laugh as he made the key disappear somewhere inside his cloak. He turned to leave, but Jacques called out to him.

"Hey Exe, watch yourself. It's about time for you to retire and find something to occupy your old age like I did. There aren't many samurai with gray hair for a reason. People get slow and start making mistakes. You need to get out while you still can, spend some more time with that wife of yours."

Xander only winked back before stepping onto the dimly lit stairwell. Kat followed him in pensive silence. Finally, just as they were opening the door to the meeting room, she spoke up.

"There might be something to what he was saying, Xander. You're sharp and on top of things right now, but how much longer do you think that can last?"

"That's just Jacques," Xander replied, waving his hand and dismissing her concern. "He was always a klutz. He likes to make everyone think he earned all of those scars on runs, but it was really a forklift accident. Good guy, but a bit melodramatic."

Kat opened her mouth to reply, but stopped herself. It was clear that Xander didn't want to hear anything she'd have to say. Instead, she listened distractedly as he nattered on about the good old days back in St. Louis where he'd first met Jacques.

Finally the door opened. Belle and her companion entered, followed just under a minute later by Davis and Hestia.

Davis closed the door as Hestia lit the chandelier. Once again, Kat felt the electric thrill of the enchantment running over her as Xander stood up.

"Good news," he started cheerfully.

"It had better be," Belle cut him off darkly. "Food reserves at Schaumburg are running critically low. Already the enforcers from Millennium have put down two bread riots. With submachine guns."

"As I said," Xander continued, rolling his eyes. "Good news. It seems that Elaine Williamson has a conference in the New York megalopolis. Half of her security detail has already shifted to prepare for her arrival, and her motorcade is leaving between six and eight o'clock tonight. Her suite will still have security, but if we're going to break into that vault, tonight is our best bet."

"That is good news," Belle agreed, a rare genuine smile on her face. "I'm ready to proceed per our arrangements from yesterday. My people will make a disturbance at the Schaumburg maglev stations to draw security from Chiwaukee."

"If you give me a couple of hours, I can get some teams out to start riots in Chiwaukee too." Davis nodded thoughtfully. "I'm going into the tower, though. Even if the security detail is mostly gone, this is too big of a job for just two people."

"Unfortunately, I agree." Xander sighed. "Whippoorwill, a support agent, will be coming with us, but she won't be enough. We're going to need a full combat team if we want this to work."

Hestia grinned, giving Kat a thumbs up, eyes twinkling.

"Remember to be careful with who you bring," Xander warned. "We don't know how long Elaine has been running that cloning lab of hers. Anyone that has disappeared for more than a week could be a double."

"Don't tell your grandmother how to suck eggs," Belle replied crossly. "I've been ferreting out corporate spies and informants since the days when you were running protection for two-bit drug dealers. My people have already caught two imposters. The clones crack under questioning when you run an electrical current through them."

"That seems like a fairly obvious weakness." Davis frowned. "Elaine is a wily opponent, she wouldn't leave a loose end like that open."

"Of course." Belle tapped the side of her head. "You have to target the electricity. Scramble their implanted memories."

"Your people consented to that?" Kat asked, disbelief in her voice.

"Consent?" Belle cocked her head, bemused.

CHAPTER THIRTY-SIX

"I can't believe they offer tours of this place," Kat remarked with a shake of her head as she, Hestia, Whippoorwill, and Xander walked by the looming skeleton of a dinosaur. "It seems like a security risk to me."

"At some point, that risk became a status symbol." Xander frowned as Hestia stepped past him in order to crowd closer to Kat. "The Field Tower used to be a museum, but as the megalopolis grew, they started adding floors on top of it. They kept the museum so that us commoners can come downtown and gawk at how rich and great they are."

"Don't worry," Hestia purred, a slightly too-wide smile stretched across her face. "Only the first two floors are open to the public. After that, we'll have plenty of chances to melt and burn our way through the bad guys."

"Just a second." Kat held up a hand. "Exe and I need to change our faces."

The four of them stepped out of the walkway, letting crowds of tourists walk past, snapping pictures of the fossils and rare mineral samples with their smart panels. Whip and Hestia shielded her and Xander with their slim bodies as she recast Mirage.

Xander's features smoothed, his eyes moving a bit apart and changing colors as his nose grew slightly. Kat squinted at him appraisingly before nodding. Mirage wouldn't let her make major changes, but with proper care, it could change someone's appearance enough to fool a guard or facial recognition software.

She pulled a compact out of her purse, flipping it open so that she had access to a mirror. A second later, she touched up her own appearance with Mirage, lightening her hair, and altering the bone structure of her cheeks.

With a snap, she closed the plastic lid of the compact and slipped it back into her purse, before turning back to the rest of their group.

"I simply must pick up light magic." Hestia sighed, shaking her head. "It's not fair that you can circumvent hours of makeup and plastic surgery with a snap of your fingers. That's cheating."

Behind Hestia, Whippoorwill nodded fervently.

"Mirage is an advanced spell. It's meant for disguises and blurring your outline in combat," Kat replied with a roll of her eyes. "It isn't meant to give you smoky eyes and highlights."

"But you did give yourself smoky eyes and highlights," Whip said accusingly.

Kat blushed, opening her mouth to reply only for the museum loudspeaker to cut her off.

"It is 5:50 p.m. Visitors to the Field Tower should begin making their way to the exits as it will be closing in ten minutes. Ten minutes after that, security will apprehend anyone still in the building with prejudice."

"That's our cue." Xander chuckled, slapping Kat on the shoulder. "Let's all head to the bathroom and wait for security."

Xander led the way, doing his best to avoid the building's visible cameras. One by one, all four of them furtively entered the men's restroom, making their way to the toilets. Each of them took their own stall and climbed up on top of the porcelain seats. Once their feet were off the ground, they crouched, concealing themselves from any potential patrols.

This was the riskiest part of the operation. Whip and Hestia were both wearing a lot of makeup, but in reality, all four of them were counting on the teeming hubbub of tourists to hide their movements.

Quietly, Kat pulled her wadded up infiltration suit out of her large purse and began slipping it on over her clothes. It didn't fit perfectly—the outfit wasn't designed to have something on under it—but she could live with a couple of uncomfortable lumps for the next hour or so.

The door to the bathroom opened, and Kat's breath caught in her throat.

Heavy footsteps thudded on the tiles as someone began walking into the bathroom. Kat's arm tensed, gripping her knife as she prepared to make a silent kill. Their plan didn't include having to stash a body and race the clock against the inevitable alarm when someone came up missing, but—

The steps stopped outside of her door, the flimsy layer of metal and plastic all that separated her from what Kat could only assume was corporate security.

Her muscles burned as Kat kept herself coiled, ready to pounce on the guard the instant they noticed her. She tensed her body, hoping that the Kevlar weave of her 'street clothes' would be enough to stop the bullets if the security officer opened fire through the door.

One second dragged into another as a single bead of sweat pooled on the back of her neck and began running down her back.

Then she heard the rushing sound of water as they turned on a faucet. A second later, they began whistling the chorus to a pop song as they washed their hands.

"*Compulsion.*" A thrill ran through Kat's body as Xander's voice echoed through the mostly empty room and the whistling stopped.

The steps receded away from her, and a couple of seconds later, the bathroom door closed. Kat held her breath.

After a moment of silence, Xander interrupted her anxious thoughts.

"Everyone get your masks on. Their sweep of the floor should be done in ten minutes, so we'll head out in twenty."

Kat pulled the fabric over her face before tucking it under the collar of her infiltration suit. Nearby, the other bathroom stalls creaked open, and she joined Hestia and Whippoorwill in the main room.

All four of them were dressed head to toe in the black suits, milling about aimlessly as they waited for the hallways to clear. Xander was himself, calm and somewhat bored, while Whippoorwill managed to look both excited and uncomfortable at the same time.

Hestia? She managed to make the outfit look good, somehow avoiding any of the uncomfortable bulges of bunched clothing that were visible beneath the rest of their infiltration suits.

Finally, Xander spoke up.

"It is officially six twenty-five. Time for us to move out. Remember, the target is a security office on the tenth floor. Dorian and Merrimac have infiltrated independently and they'll meet us there. After that, it should just be a matter of disabling the upper floor's defenses and finding the secure storage center."

"Stay between Hestia and I." Kat turned to Whippoorwill and squeezed her shoulder. "Between the two of us, we should be able to keep you safe, but if someone starts shooting, dive for cover."

"Thank you for the advice," Whip's defiant voice was a bit shaky, "but getting gut shot once was already enough for me. I could go my entire life without having to hear about intestinal grafting again."

"Don't worry," Hestia purred. "Erinyes and I will keep you safe. It's not often that two experienced elementalists work together. I doubt the corpos are going to know what hit them, and even if they did, we can always just burn the entire building down."

Xander opened the door, popping his head out into the hallway to look around before turning back to the three women. Kat could almost hear him rolling his eyes.

"I would like to remind everyone that this is supposed to be a stealth mission. Any security we run into should be avoided if possible."

"If you have to kill someone." Xander stopped, pointing his black clad finger at Hestia. "I want it done quiet. No disintegrations."

"As you wish," she replied sarcastically, crossing her arms.

Xander just shook his head, pushing the door open gently and stepping out into the now-empty hallway. Hestia followed him with Whippoorwill just behind her. Kat took up the rear, hand on her silenced pistol as she surveyed the empty building.

The halls of the Field Tower were different without teeming crowds of tourists. Naked except for the blinking red lights of security cameras and an exhibit on bronze age tool making that occupied the far wall.

Quickly, she cast Shadow twice, doing her best to extend the size of the spell. They had to crowd close together for it to work, but to outside eyes, the four of them should look like little more than a mobile cloud of murky shadow.

They made it as far as the electronically-locked fire door to the building's stairwell before they encountered their first guard, a bored but alert man with a stun baton in his hand and a submachine gun strapped to his hip. His expression sharpened as he noticed the unnaturally dark section of the hallway that the four of them were hiding in, and the baton crackled to life as he stepped forward.

"*Compulsion.*" Before Kat or the guard could act, Xander stepped out of the darkness, a purple glow outlining him ominously for a fraction of a second.

Xander grabbed the man's stun baton from his nerveless

hand and jammed the crackling electrodes into the side of his neck. The security officer spasmed, eyes rolling back into his head as he collapsed bonelessly to the ceramic floor of the museum.

Kat cursed under her breath, looking down at the twitching man. Of course this would be a problem. Shadow was a great spell for fooling the eye in small, dark crevices. Instead, the huge area covered by the two concurrent spells was a bit of a give-away to any guards with discerning eyes. It was better than standing in the open, but that was about all she could say for it.

Quietly and efficiently, Xander rifled through the man's pockets. First, he crushed the guard's smartpanel, preventing him from calling for help. Then, with quick, sure motions he fastened the man's hands and feet with a pair of zip ties. Finally, he ripped off a chunk off of his captive's shirt to fasten into a makeshift gag.

After dragging the man behind a pillar of stone covered in cuneiform markings, Xander sauntered back out, flashing a green keycard between his index and middle finger. Kat rolled her eyes inside her mask as he almost casually swiped the rectangle of plastic through the stairwell's reader, opening the heavy steel door.

"Why leave him alive?" Hestia hissed as she stepped into the stairwell with them. "If he wakes up, we could be in for a world of hurt."

Xander shrugged as he began to climb the stairs, craning his head over his shoulder to respond, "If he doesn't wake up, that could set off an instant alarm. A lot of these places have biomonitors in their guards to track their heartbeat and location. Him not moving will raise a yellow flag, but if he dies, we're looking at sirens and corporate security as far as the eye can see."

Hestia grumbled something indecipherable back. Xander paused, his face hidden by his mask as he glanced back at her.

"I don't do quiet," she grumbled. "Immolating someone before they can call in backup is the closest I come to stealth."

Xander just chuckled, shaking his head before turning back to the stairs. The team followed him. At every landing, Xander would call a halt, pausing for a moment to inspect the walls and stairs around them.

Three times, he found a button to disable a trapped landing, and one time Kat had to grab his shoulder to stop him from stepping on a field of translucent needles. After a minute of searching, they found the release that pulled the tiny blades back into the floor.

Other than that, things proceeded tensely, but smoothly. On each floor, Kat kept expecting to find a guard patrol smoking a cigarette, or for Xander to step on a pressure plate and have an automated gun pop out of the cement.

Nothing happened. By the time the four of them reached the tenth floor, the clang of the gun at her hip against the metal railing sent Kat almost a foot in the air. When she came down, she was hyperventilating with her knife in hand.

A hand on her shoulder brought Kat around, knife at the ready. She let out a sigh of relief as she made out Whip's black-clad form.

"I know how you're feeling," the woman whispered, tension in her voice. "I don't want to jinx things by saying that it's *too* quiet, but... you know."

"It's too quiet," Kat sighed.

"Shush, you two," Xander called back. "We're on the tenth floor. Stop cursing us, and be quiet. We're almost to the security station and the rendezvous with Merrimac and Dorian, and that would only make blowing our cover now all the more embarrassing."

They crept through the halls, ducking aside twice as patrols came into view, but the roving guards never came close enough to be an actual issue. Eventually, after getting turned around in the winding passages of the administrative wing three or four times, they came upon the metal door of the security annex.

Xander leaned forward, touching the door. It swung gently inward, letting a crack of light spill out into the hallway. With a shrug, he put his eye to the door only to take a step back and put his hands up.

"It's Exe," Xander hissed. "Put the fucking cannon down, Merrimac."

The door opened fully, revealing Davis in a dark gray outfit that vaguely resembled the ChromeDog infiltration suits. At his shoulder, Davis held a massive weapon at the ready. Kat didn't recognize its make or caliber, but it was even bigger than the squad-operated fifty caliber machine guns she'd seen the ChromeDogs equipping their warehouse base with. Mentally, she confirmed her assessment that Davis must have some serious chrome or player levels hidden beneath his mild exterior, given the way he freely carried such a bulky weapon.

Davis stuck his head out into the hallway and scanned back and forth before motioning their team inside.

"Get in here before a patrol wanders by," Davis said, stepping to the side and lowering his weapon. "Dorian is already jacked into the network. He disabled the auto alarm for the dead guards, and now he's trying to locate the secure storage."

"Dead guards?" Whippoorwill asked as she filed into the room after Kat. "But we managed to make it here without—"

"Oh," she finished lamely, taking in the bodies of four security officers.

At least what was left of them. None of the corpses were intact, all of them sporting gaping cantaloupe-sized holes in their torsos. Three of them were missing limbs entirely, but Kat quickly located them by the blood and viscera covering a bulletin board on the other side of the room, the appendages in a twisted mess beneath it.

"Merrimac!" Hestia breezed past them and into the room. She ripped off her facemask and shook her head, letting her hair flutter in the recycled and air-conditioned air of the office building. "You've been having fun without me."

"I was a bit upset over the boy," Davis replied sheepishly. "I got a bit overzealous."

"Not to break up this love fest," Xander cut in, moving past them toward another network jack, "but I'll help Dorian with the security. One of us can handle finding the vault while the other turns off the traps and alarms."

"Don't worry about it," Dorian called out, waving Xander off. "I'm almost done. Just a little bit more and I'll have the passcode for the storage center."

"Two sets of eyes are better than none," Xander chuckled, setting the stun baton he'd liberated from the guard on the second floor as he plugged himself into the wall. "The least I can do is double check the electronic records to make sure you didn't miss anything while erasing all mention of us."

His head whipped around, the gaze of this featureless black mask on Dorian.

"Wait, why the fuck are we surround—" Xander never got to finish the sentence as gunfire drowned out his words.

Time seemed to slow. Merrimac's chest rippled as bullet after bullet thumped into him, Dorian's machine pistol chattering as it spat out rounds.

Kat tackled Whippoorwill, bringing the stunned girl to the ground and out of the line of fire. Distantly, she heard Xander screaming something, but she was more focused on dragging the trembling girl behind a metal desk.

A blast of flame seared past her, practically melting her infiltration suit to her skin as Hestia practically ignited. Kat's Sensory Dampening kicked in as the white-hot beam of fire slammed into the wall next to Dorian, filling the room with enough light to give exposed skin a sunburn.

The door to the security room slammed open, a guard shouldering her way inside with a rifle at the ready only to take a pair of bullets to the face as Xander popped up over the edge of the desk he'd taken cover behind.

A spray of gunfire drove Hestia out of cover and into the open even as a trio of blue balls, spitting flames and hotter than a stove even halfway across the room, zipped out the door. A second later they exploded, ripping the security door from its hinges and rocking the room. The lights flickered once and then died as the blasts ruptured something important.

Someone fired a shot into the room, the bullet shattering a smartglass display but coming nowhere near anyone inside. Then, the room lapsed into silence, the only sounds Merrimac's wet, ragged breathing, and the crackle of flames as a chair burned on the other side of the room.

"Why, Dorian?" Hestia begged, tears in her voice. "Merrimac has been like a brother to us for decades. How could you?"

"To Andrew?" Dorian's voice responded from behind the metal cabinet he'd flipped on its side during the brief moment of combat. "Maybe. But Andrew's been dead for weeks. Buried with a dozen other bodies in a hole outside of Beloit."

"For a group that claims to be like siblings to each other," he taunted, "none of you noticed me taking his place. I thought I was done for sure once you found out about Operation Changeling, but no one even blinked at me being 'too busy' to show up to the meeting in *The Tower of Somnus*."

Kat's heart dropped as one of the guards outside the room sprayed gunfire wildly through the gaping hole where the door had once been. Their only exit was teeming with security.

It had been too quiet for a reason as they made their way up to the tenth floor. The entire operation had been a trap.

CHAPTER THIRTY-SEVEN

Hestia fired a handful of shots in Dorian's general direction to keep him under cover. Rage twisted her face as a quartet of blue flames appeared behind her, twisting into the shapes of butterflies and drifting through the air toward the impostor's hiding spot.

"You didn't give me a chance to contact my handlers before the prison raid," the clone shouted back mockingly, tossing a small metal box into the center of the room. "But I suppose I should thank you for delaying this attack long enough for me to set up an ambush. With the four of you out of the way, no one will know enough to even slow down Starfall."

The box exploded into a flash of bright light and screeching static. Almost immediately, Kat's senses dimmed to an acceptable level as Sensory Dampening protected her from the device's effects.

Dorian's replacement broke from cover, left arm over his face while the right carried his pistol. He vaulted a desk, sprinting toward the door as Kat brought her pistol up. Her first shot missed, but the second struck him square in the flank, knocking the clone sideways.

Before she could fire a third shot, he gingerly slipped behind another cabinet, just in front of her. Kat swore to herself. She'd used her silenced pistol and, unsurprisingly, the high mass, low velocity round hadn't done much against the Kevlar weave that all of the infiltrators were wearing.

"You bitch!" he shouted, his voice coming out in a pained gasp as a trio of guards in bulky body armor stormed into the room.

Xander's pistol fire sparked off of their armor, the angled ceramic plates deflecting the low-caliber rounds. They countered, their rifles issuing a cacophony of discordant blasts as they echoed in the tiny room.

A swarm of flaming butterflies, curving back from following Dorian's clone, clustered around one of the guards. They flashed with a searing blast of blue light, sending a wave of heat slamming into Kat as they self-immolated.

Kat slammed her back into the desk in front of her, hand snaking up to grab the stun baton left there by Xander, as she began casting Pseudopod.

One of the security officers slumped to the ground, the polymers of their helmet fused to their skull by the intense heat of Hestia's spell, but the other two fanned out into the room, guns at the ready.

Xander popped up and fired a shot before their return fire forced him back into cover. Both the clone and Kat took that moment of distraction to break into the open. The false Dorian ran for the exit while she jumped into the air, immersing the crackling stun baton into the base of the tentacle of water growing from her stomach.

The rope of water blurred through the air, slapping into one guard and discharging the electricity from the baton en route to coiling around Dorian's ankle.

Then, all three of them, Kat, the guard, and Dorian, began falling together. Quickly, she removed her baton from the Pseudopod, not wanting to share the fate of the twitching security officer once she was no longer airborne and insulated.

The imposter slammed face first into the ground, nose splattering like a ripe tomato. A second later, the guard joined him, smoke coming from the joints in his armor as he twitched spasmodically.

Kat burned stamina and Leapt, landing on the final security officer's side.

The woman yelped as Kat's weight knocked her off balance, but a fraction of a second later, Kat's knife, empowered by Penetrate, slipped under the seam of her helmet. By the time the two of them hit the ground, blood was pouring from the ruptured seal in the guard's armor, and Kat's victim wasn't moving.

Another masked and armored security officer burst into the room, only for a wave of fire to erase their head and upper torso. Hestia shifted the flame lance, cutting through the clone and stunned guard's chests with an effortless twitch of her hand.

A grenade clanked on the floor, but even crouched over the body of a guard, Kat's agility and reaction attributes were enough. The tentacle of water created by Pseudopod lashed out, batting the metal oval back out into the hallway a second before it detonated.

Hestia followed the explosive outside, screaming in frustration and rage as she erupted into a corona of flame. The smell of charred flesh began to waft through the room as the walls grew hot to the touch.

"Erinyes," Xander called out. "Hestia should have the door covered. See what you can do for Merrimac. As soon as the backup generator kicks in, Whip and I will try and locate the secure storage."

"We're still going after the data?" Kat asked incredulously, kneeling over Merrimac just before she began reciting the words to Cure Wounds I.

"We have to," Xander replied grimly. "Elaine knows we're here, and I saw a lot more than a handful of corporate security guards heading our way. Williamson is in the building herself, along with at least six individuals marked as VIPs. I'm not sure we're going to be able to fight our way out of this. There's a decent chance our exit will involve a window and gravity magic. There's certainly not going to be a second shot at retrieving the data."

The lights turned back on as the secondary generator kicked in. Around them, various smartglass displays, the ones that were still intact, anyway, booted up to a number of loading scenes.

"This is do or die, Erinyes." Xander walked over to a jack, plugging himself in once more. "If we don't expose Elaine, Belle is going to be left swinging in the wind, and she's the only thing standing between our families and Schaumburg's total destruction."

Kat nodded back before focusing her attention on Merrimac. Despite the close range gunfire that had brought him down, the damage didn't seem as bad as she'd expected.

Of course, that was a relative matter. Dorian's clone had still shot him a good dozen times, and even with the Kevlar weave Davis wore under his infiltration suit, the bullets hit close enough together that at least four or five made it through the shredded fabric. It took a good half of Kat's remaining mana and almost thirty seconds for the bleeding to stop.

Merrimac jerked upward, gasping for breath, his hand reaching up to grip Kat's in a vise-like hold.

"Save your mana, girl." He choked the words out, pain clouding his words. "You're going to need it. I have perks that can heal me from here."

She glanced back to Xander only for the older man to nod. Davis grunted in pain as he slid backward on the blood-slick floor and propped himself up against one of the security room's metal desks. Reluctantly, Kat stood up just as Hestia walked back into the room, still wreathed in fire.

Hestia's hair blew back and forth, whipped about by a wind that touched only her. The arms and shoulders of the older woman's infiltration suit were burned off, exposing unblemished skin beneath. Around her, dozens of fist-sized balls of flame pulsed angrily.

Her eyes locked on Merrimac's bloody but conscious form, and the spells winked out. Hestia sprinted across the room, dropping to her knees next to Davis.

"I thought I saw you die," she whispered heatedly, hands on his shoulders. "That thing unloaded a full magazine into you when you didn't have your armor on. You should be dead."

"Luckily, Erinyes can use healing magic," he grunted back, hissing with pain as he tried to shift his body once more. "Fetch me the monitor, will you, Hestia? I don't think these assholes are just going to stop coming after us because we asked nicely."

Quietly, the woman picked up Merrimac's massive rifle, and dragged it over to the seated man. Merrimac put a hand on it, stroking the stock of the weapon lovingly while muttering some sort of incantation under his breath.

The desk he was leaning against crumpled, the metal flowing forward to encase Merrimac. Steel plates seemed to sprout from his infiltration suit, glowing gently blue as more and more of the material surrounded him until eventually, the skinny man was clad in a huge suit of armor.

"It's good to have you back." Kat could barely hear Hestia whispering the words, but even across the room she noticed that the older woman's eyes were damp. "I couldn't afford to lose both of you in one day."

Even sitting down, Merrimac was almost the size of a small car, and likely as bullet resistant. He hefted his rifle easily, his glowing armor whirring slightly as he brought the gun to his shoulder.

"I have two hundred rounds of armor piercing and fifty of high explosive," Merrimac called out, not moving from where he sat. "I can't move or it'll negate the perk keeping me awake and alive, but that should be enough to hold off whoever's after us for a little while. What's the plan, Exe?"

"Doesn't look like there are any good options, unfortunately." Xander sighed as he tucked his cord back into the cranial jack. "They've got the security station down to read-only right now. They know we're here and have all permissions for these workstations revoked. The secure storage is on the thirty-second floor and there are about a hundred guards between here and there."

"No chance of us leaving a back door and sneaking in later?" Davis asked without much hope.

"Negative," Xander replied, walking to the center of the room and grabbing a rifle. He tossed it to Whippoorwill. The girl yelped, barely catching the weapon.

"It looks like our only option is to send someone in fast and hard to crack the vault." He passed another rifle to Kat. "There are too many guards. If we get bogged down in a fight, they'll overwhelm all five of us in minutes. Someone needs to man the cameras and steer the strike team away from security, and that means leaving people here where they'll be a sitting duck for unending waves of corporate security."

"If this is about me," Davis shook his metal clad head, "I know what I signed up for. I'm not going to let my injury slow the operation down. Leave me behind. Who knows, I might even make it."

"No." Hestia crossed her arms. "You retired and I came back as a favor, so unfortunately for you, Merrimac, you're not the team lead. I'm not leaving you to die."

"Unfortunately," Xander replied, picking up a final rifle for himself, "I really do need someone to monitor cameras and comms. I'll also need some people to keep the coordinator safe. That means Whippoorwill down here with Merrimac and Hestia covering her."

"Congrats, Whip." He chuckled. "If you get out this alive, you'll have earned a name."

"I'll say," Hestia snorted, surveying the charred bodies. "We'll have enough of these to build a fairly grisly barricade before the night is through."

"But," Whippoorwill's voice was trembling but she held her rifle a steady and determined grip. "That means that you and Erinyes will have to go alone. I saw how many guards there are, and—"

"It is what it is, Whip." Kat shook her head, resignation weighing down her voice. "Exe and I have the best chance of making it to the vault before the security forces can triangulate on us. This isn't just a mission we can back out of. Everyone dies if we fail."

"She's right." Merrimac nodded, the metal of his impromptu helmet scraping against the chest plate. "The mission comes first. Even if four of us die, so long as the fifth uploads that data, we'll have saved the lives of dozens of people close to us."

"It's a tough ask for someone on one of their first combat missions." Xander walked over to Whippoorwill and put a hand on her shoulder. "I swear I meant to ease you into this sort of thing, but once again necessity has made a fool of me. You can handle this, Whip. Just follow Merrimac and Hestia's lead."

Whip nodded, hands gripping the rifle tightly as she hunkered down next to a desk.

"Come on, Erinyes." She could almost see Xander's golden tooth glinting through his mask. "It's time to go save the world."

CHAPTER THIRTY-EIGHT

Xander's rifle barked twice and the guard that rounded the corner dropped, a hole in the faceplate of their helmet. Another stepped into the open only for Kat to fire a three-round burst from her stolen weapon, missing wildly but forcing the figure to dart back behind cover.

Kat let loose a burst of stamina, pouring it into Cat Step as she blurred forward. At the last second, she dropped to the ground, letting her momentum carry her past the wall.

She could almost see the blank look of surprise on the security officer's face as her left arm grabbed him around the ankle, pulling Kat close enough to ram her knife through the side of his knee with the help of Penetrate.

The armored guard collapsed in a bellow of pain, Kat taking a brief second to straddle them and cut their throat as Xander jogged past. She snagged her rifle from the floor, and a moment later, she was matching time with him, breath coming a tad unevenly from the expenditure of stamina.

Still, she'd used a lot of mana getting to this point, and it was almost certain that she'd need more to get out. Even if Kat didn't end up needing to fight her way into the vault, she'd likely need mana to cast Levitation so that the five of them could jump out windows and escape. Spending stamina in order to conserve mana for later only made sense.

"Left!" Whippoorwill's voice erupted in her ear. "Turn left now! There's a VIP and a squad of five guards heading toward you right now."

Xander grunted, planting his foot on the tile floor and juking sideways into the small hallway. Kat followed a second later, a gunshot and some shouting chasing her down the narrow passage.

"We've been made, Whip!" she shouted in between quick gasps, offices rushing past her.

"I see that!" Whippoorwill responded, agitation coloring her voice as a rifle fired in the background only to be silenced by the thump of a heavy weapon.

"Just come in here and try it!" Merrimac thundered, his voice distant and tinny. "I've got fourteen millimeters of 'sudden and forceful employment termination' with your names on it right here."

"Uhhh, left again," Whip's voice in Kat's ear sounded distracted as more gunfire was picked up by her mic. "Wait, shit! Right, go right. There should be a fire escape at the end of the hallway."

The plaster next to Kat exploded as a gun fired three times in short succession behind them. Xander reached out with his right arm, grabbing the wall to help him turn as they came upon the cross hallway.

Kat followed him, almost sighing with relief as she took in the welcome sight of the emergency exit at the end of the hall. Then, she glanced side to side and frowned.

"Uh... Whip?" she asked as Xander ran up to the doorway. "This hallway is a dead end."

"Kinda busy, Erinyes." Kat winced, gunfire almost deafening her as Whippoorwill opened fire on a hot mic.

Xander swiped the keycard they'd pulled off the guard on the second floor through the lock on the door.

"Fuck!" he shouted. "Insufficient access?"

He kneeled down, pulling a knife out and popping the metal faceplate off of the lock.

"Erinyes." He grunted, shoving his hands into the mess of wires and computer chips that powered the system. "I need you to hold them off, this is going to be a minute."

"With what?" Kat frantically searched the dead end. "An improvised machine gun made out of a filing cabinet and a stapler? There's six of them!"

"Grenade on my belt," he replied distractedly. "Use it."

"Are you fucking kidding—" Kat muttered, lunging toward Xander and unclipping the metal orb just as the first of the armored security guards rounded the corner.

She burned some of her saved mana, casting Dazzle to stun the guard and their companion. A crackling cone of light appeared in the air, roughly at head level and a moment later, they slammed blindly into each other even as Kat hefted the primed grenade toward the intersection.

The two security officers went down in a heap, tripping a third as they ran around the corner, arm up and covering their facemask.

The grenade detonated, spraying shrapnel over the three prone forms. Kat didn't take any chances, going down to one knee and putting her stolen rifle to her shoulder. She exhaled, closing one eye as she lined up the three dots of the iron sight.

Another guard popped around the corner, and she was ready, a three-round burst catching him in the upper chest and shoulder. The bullets sparked as they hit his heavy ceramic armor. Kat couldn't see whether any of the bullets had managed to penetrate one of the thinner joints or limb protectors, but the soldier went down and that was good enough for now.

The quiet *thump-thump-thump* of a grenade launcher was all the warning Kat got before a trio of metal spheres ricocheted off of a wall and into the narrow hallway with her.

She sprang backward, burning some of her dwindling

stamina on Leaping in order to clear the area where the grenades landed.

They exploded, far enough from her that the Kevlar she was wearing under her infiltration suit was able to save her life, but near enough that she could feel the hammer blows of shrapnel slamming into her as the blast swatted her from the air like a troublesome mosquito.

Kat hit the ground, skidding across the tiles as the front of her body blossomed with pain. As soon as she bled enough momentum, Kat sat up. Her rifle was missing, tossed somewhere in the explosion.

She drew her pistol, and stared down the hallway. She couldn't see anything. The passage was filled with smoke and plaster dust from the ravaged walls.

Wincing at her growing bruises, Kat kicked off the floor, pushing herself near the wall as she cast Shadow to hide her outline. Then, she pulled herself painfully into a crouch, unsilenced pistol at the ready.

Given the quality of the weapons and armor worn by the security officers, Kat wasn't overly hopeful that her gun would do much. The lower caliber, higher velocity gun performed much better against armor than her heavy and slow silenced pistol, but if a rifle struggled to penetrate the guard's chest armor, the handgun would be about as useful as a slingshot.

Still, she brought the gun up in a two-handed grip as a silhouette loomed in the hallway, slingshots had their uses.

Her target had switched out the grenade launcher for a submachine gun. They lifted the weapon, sighting past her at Xander while he hunched over the lock to the emergency exit.

Kat's first shot hit the soldier's faceplate, snapping their head backward. Her second and third shots missed, unfortunate but hardly unanticipated given the poor visibility and chaotic circumstances.

Still, even if the follow-up shot hadn't hit the thinner armor in the suit's neck crease, the headshot did enough. The officer staggered backward, slapping a hand to the spot where Kat's bullet had hit his helmet.

She dropped her gun, springing forward and activating Cat Step to take advantage of the guard's moment of distraction. Kat's face froze in a rictus of pain as the bruises covering her front erupted in agony, but in that split second, her training took over. The knife sprang into her hand as Kat closed the last couple of steps between herself and the security officer.

The guard began swinging their gun around, trying to draw a bead on the rapidly approaching amorphous blob of darkness. Kat ducked, feeling the wind from the passage of the bullet pluck at her back as she darted in, under their extended arm, and brought her knife up into the weaker armor of the officer's armpit.

Her knife glowed red for a fraction of a second as Kat activated Penetrate, forcing her blade through a seam in the armor. Her right leg lashed out, swinging forward before catching the security officer in the back of their knees even as her shoulder slammed upward into their chest.

The guard went down, Kat landing on top of them, their gun skittering off into the choking mist of smoke.

Before her opponent could react, Kat was rewarded with a spray of arterial blood when she ripped her knife out of the guard. Her left hand thrust upward, slamming the downed person under the chin of their helmet and snapping their head back before jamming the knife into her target's neck.

For a second, Kat just sat there, straddling her opponent with her infiltration suit covered in blood, some of it her own. Then, she remembered the remaining guards, probably only stunned and injured by the single grenade.

Hissing in pain, she rolled the dead guard over, freeing their grenade launcher. A quick check revealed that the six round belt still had three shots remaining.

Kat brought the weapon to her shoulder and emptied the belt, bracketing the intersection with explosions as the grenades went off one after another. Hopefully, that would be enough to wound any of the survivors badly enough that they would stay down.

She stood up slowly, biting her lip against the waves of pain radiating across the front of her body. The spent grenade launcher fell to the ground with a clatter as Kat squinted into the smoke, searching for any movement.

"Got it," Xander said behind her, the lock on the door clunking open.

Kat sighed in relief, turning around only to throw herself to the side as her senses screamed danger. A spray of liquid splattered against the ceramic tiles just past where she once stood, hissing and bubbling as they rapidly eroded the floor.

"Erinyes." Whip's voice echoed in her ear, dripping with worry. "The VIP is almost on top of you. You need to get out of there now."

A bald man walked out of the smoke, covered in dust from the shattered walls. He wore a bulletproof vest and little else, but on the other hand, there was little else to cover. All four of his limbs were chrome, polished to a shiny silver sheen under the clinging plaster.

"I think I found him," Kat whispered back. Distantly, she heard the fire door sliding shut behind her.

He grinned, an extra mechanical arm, fixed somewhere in his back, raised above his left shoulder like a scorpion's tail. "Missed, eh?"

The man's voice was raspy, like he smoked two packs of cigarettes a day. His face twitched as he scanned Kat's battered form. He'd clearly broken the Wierzbicki Limit years ago, and never looked back.

"Name's Eli." The metal 'arm' darted past his shoulder, its four fingers blossoming open to reveal a thumb-sized nozzle. "Eli Crow of Millennium. And you must be Erinyes."

The spigot on the mechanical arm dripped, a line of clear liquid landing on the floor where it hissed, burning a lumpy divot into the tile.

"Huh." He shrugged. "From all of the stories, I thought you'd be taller."

Kat blinked at him, unmoving, her hand gripped tightly around the hilt of her blood-stained knife.

"Sorry, I guess?" she replied, eyes on Eli as she waited for the slightest twitch to betray that he was making a move.

"No matter." He sighed laconically, face twitching once more. "Mr. Jackson has put out a fairly impressive bounty on you and Exe. Once I'm done with you—"

"Duck," Xander's voice whispered in her ear, and Kat didn't stop to think, she just reacted, throwing her injured torso to the ground as the fire door hissed open behind her.

The pain of hitting the tiles stole Kat's breath even as Xander emptied his rifle into the Millennium samurai. A blast of acid missed wildly, spraying the walls of the corridor as sparks erupted from Crow's head and chest.

Most of the bullets simply creased the metal of the samurai's chrome limbs, pushing him back a handful of steps. At least a couple tore through his vest, shattering the ceramic trauma plate underneath and digging into what remained of Crow's chest.

Kat gathered her mana and began casting Dehydrate. The gunshots were clearly hurting her opponent, but they weren't dealing enough damage. Already, Crow was beginning to recover, leaning into the bullets like they were a windstorm, metal arms covering his face.

Just as Xander's magazine ran dry, she finished the spell, targeting her opponent's head and neck. This time there was a reaction.

Eli dropped to his knees, hands clawing at his face. Kat knew from experience that her spell had attacked the greatest source of moisture available, the tender membranes of his eyes and throat.

With a grunt, she pushed herself up into a crouch and lunged forward, trying to ignore the burning pain that filled her body. Kat's dagger flashed red, using the last dregs of her stamina to power her Penetrate perk and saw off the end of the mechanical hand sprouting from the samurai's back.

Almost immediately, clear acid began to bubble up through the metal limb, the valve that normally controlled its release lying on the floor along with her enemy's metal hand. Kat wrenched the limb to the side, pointing it at the writhing samurai just as it unleashed a torrent of liquid death.

He screamed, arms freezing in place as the acid burned through their armor plating and fried control mechanisms. A moment later, the scream cut off as the vapor from the liquid seared his lungs, stealing their function and forcing the man to aspirate.

"Quit playing around, Erinyes," Whippoorwill's voice interrupted her, screaming and gunfire audible over her friend's mic. "More guards are converging on your location. Exe and you need to get moving, *now*."

She dropped the convulsing body, sprinting toward the now-open fire door where Xander had been hiding. As soon as she joined him in the stairwell, the door slid shut behind her. Without saying anything, Xander drew a pistol, unloading three shots into the keypad from the inside.

"Up three floors," Whip cut in, an explosion followed by what sounded like Hestia's maniacal laughter drowning her out for a moment. "There's a service elevator on a different network. I can't control it, but it doesn't look like they've managed to lock it down."

Kat glanced at Xander, and the older man shrugged. As dangerous as being trapped in an elevator sounded, they'd only managed to make it two floors. At this rate, there was absolutely no way in hell that they'd make it all the way to the thirty-second floor.

Then the two of them took off, pounding up the metal steps of the emergency exit. They made it to the service elevator without any major problems, a trio of lost guards the only resistance as Whippoorwill managed to guide them past all other major concentrations of security.

New rifles salvaged from the dead patrol, Kat and Xander entered the elevator together. Kat panted for breath as Xander hit the stylized '32' button that would bring them to their desired floor. Her mana reserves were almost three-fourths full, but the hard run to avoid security hadn't given her much of a chance to replenish her stamina.

She closed her eyes and leaned back against the padded wall of the elevator, panting for breath. The machine 'dinged' to let them know they'd gone up a floor.

"You know, I think we're just going to pull this off, Erinyes."

Kat opened her eyes to see Xander pulling his mask off. His hair was soaked with sweat, matted to the top and sides of his head, but his eyes burned with an eager and excited light.

"We're moving too fast for the defenses to pin us down," he continued, removing the magazine from his gun to check how many rounds he had remaining. "Plus, there are about half as many guards as there should be. The riots in Chiwaukee and Schaumburg seem to be preventing reinforcements. Once we manage to get the information to Whip, Merrimac can use his connections with the Haupts. I wouldn't be surprised if half of the guards in here were ordered to arrest Elaine. There'll be more than enough chaos for us to escape."

She rolled her eyes, pressing a hand to the tender flesh of her stomach where one of the shrapnel pieces had been caught by her Kevlar.

"I'm in a building full of hostile corporate security, all of whom are better armed than me," Kat began incredulously. "I'm not sure if my ribs are broken after a near miss from a grenade, but they sure hurt like they're broken, and you're telling me that everything is going to work out?"

"What can I say?" Xander winked at her. "I'm just a glass half full kind of guy. Just keep your head down and trust your instincts. You'll get out of here in one piece. I promise you."

"Thanks, I guess?" Kat shook her head.

The elevator dinged one final time, doors opening onto what appeared to be an industrial-sized laundry room.

"Good talk." Xander smiled, slapping her on the shoulder before he stepped out onto the thirty-second floor.

Kat followed him. After the chaos of the lower levels, the building was eerily quiet. Apparently, most of the security had been sent down to deal with the five of them, and the same mandatory lockouts that prevented them from using ordinary elevators prevented the corporate guards from following them.

It was only a matter of time before the security forces figured out how Xander and Kat had bypassed them and replicated the trick, but for the moment, the two of them made it to the vault unimpeded.

The entrance to the secure storage was a massive metal door at the end of a hallway. Still, it may as well have been a continent away given the dozens of visible, laser-triggered traps that lined the walls of the corridor. For almost a minute, the two of them stared at it in silence. Without Whip to disable the defenses, they were in trouble.

Finally, Kat sighed as an idea came to her. It was risky, but she had enough mana.

"Exe?" Xander glanced back. He'd been chewing his lip, trying to figure out a way through the maze of defenses. "You're better at disabling security than me. It burns up a lot of mana, but I can cast Mirage on you twice. That should be enough to curve light around you for a couple of seconds, so long as the laser is only hitting an extremity."

"That's long enough for me to get to the lock mechanism." He nodded thoughtfully.

She cast the spell once, causing the air to blur around him, like she was looking at the man through a fun house mirror. The second time, Xander's appearance morphed further, his body thinning and almost becoming insubstantial.

Then he was off, Kat watching him with worry as he acrobatically twisted his way through the maze of lasers en route to the other end. Despite his best efforts, at least three times, she saw the ghost of one of his limbs pass through one of the lasers.

Her spell held. After fifteen tense seconds, Xander made it to the other side.

The lock itself took almost three minutes. By the end, Xander was pulling gear out of his pouch that Kat had only heard hints of on information channels. She just shook her head in appreciation. She might be an infiltrator, but Xander was absolutely an expert.

Finally, with a chunk, the door hissed open a crack. Xander put his shoulder into it, straining to push the heavy plate of metal aside so that he could slip into the vault.

Then, Kat stood alone in the pristine hallway. Once again, she felt terribly out of place. The floor under her feet was polished marble, and the walls were paneled with stained and treated hardwood. Even the fanciest rooms at the college could barely touch this building's quality.

"Whip?" Kat asked, searching for any possible threat in her placid surroundings. "What's the ETA on security?"

"—breaking up," the response was so filled with static that Kat couldn't even tell if it was Whippoorwill or one of their companions speaking.

"I said what's the ETA on security?" Kat frowned. Even if the floors were lined with lead, she was close enough that Whip and her should have been able to talk without any interference.

"—yes! G— —t —w!" Shouting and a wall of static. Hardly helpful. Kat shifted, leaning her back against the wood paneled wall.

"Erinyes."

She perked up; Xander had disabled the security from the other side of the trap hallway and he was walking back toward her, a grin on his face and something small and metal in his hand.

"I told you that this was all going to work out."

She rolled her eyes, preparing a sarcastic response. Then the world exploded.

The left side of Xander's hallway detonated, throwing him sideways into the wall with enough force to shatter the wood, revealing glittering steel plating beneath. Kat took a step forward, only for a three-round burst from a rifle to shatter the marble at her feet.

Out of the wreckage of the destroyed room strode a middle-aged woman, a massive and heavily chromed thug following her, his rifle pointed at Kat's throat.

Her heart sank. She'd read enough dossiers and seen enough pictures in the run up to the operation to know exactly who stood across from her in an immaculate pantsuit, its edges crisp and without even a touch of dust on it despite the recent blast.

"It's a pleasure to finally meet the two of you." Elaine Williamson shot her a wintry smile. "I suppose I should thank you for finding the recording. Dorian's replacement was able to discover that I had it in my possession, but he never was able to give me specific details."

"Really." She shook her head, perfectly styled hair flowing like a movie star's. "I've only heard good things about the ChromeDogs. It's a shame you know too much."

"Otto, if you would?" She nodded politely to the man at her side.

CHAPTER THIRTY-NINE

Mana swelled in Kat's chest, erupting as she cast Dazzle on the heavily chromed samurai only for him to not blink, his rifle pointed unflinchingly at her throat. He grinned without any real warmth.

Internally, she swore. Flashbangs were popular enough that it only was a matter of time before she ran into someone with an immunity like hers. Still, it had been worth a try. Knives might be her forte, but they weren't terribly useful in a situation like this.

"I remember you, girl," Otto rumbled. "You wrecked my jeep and my knee. I think I'm going to enjoy watching you bleed out."

"Oh, for the love of—" Elaine wheeled around on the samurai. "Quit playing with your food. Do you even remember what I taught you about megalomaniacal speeches?"

"That they just give your victim a chance to escape," Otto responded, voice taking on the singsong tone of someone reciting a phrase committed to memory via rote repetition. "If you're going to gloat, do it while standing atop their corpse."

"Good." Elaine crossed her arms. "Now quit dithering and shoot the girl."

Otto nodded, pressing the rifle tight to his shoulder.

"*Compulsion.*" Kat had never been so happy to hear Xander's voice. Otto froze, face twitching as he struggled with the psi ability that had taken control of him.

For a moment, you could hear a pin drop. Xander pulled his battered and bloodstained body from the rubble as both Elaine and Kat watched Otto's internal battle with bated breath.

The samurai spun around, firing a half dozen shots at point blank range into Williamson.

A shimmering field of silver light caught the bullets, slowing them to a stop just in front of the shareholder. They dropped to the marble floor, clicking impotently.

"You weak minded fool!" She sneered, backhanding Otto with enough force to send the man flying into a nearby wall. "He's using an old tower mind trick on you."

"*Compulsion,*" Xander repeated the word, his face pale as blood trickled from his mouth.

She snorted with contempt. "Your mind powers won't work on me, boy."

Xander stared at her. Despite everything, Elaine didn't have a single hair out of place. She simply glared back, not even bothering to make a move to apprehend them.

"Well," Xander muttered unhappily. "Fuck."

Kat lifted her stolen rifle, firing one three-round burst after another into the woman as she juked to the side. Her chest screamed with agony, the bruises from the grenade blasts having stiffened on the elevator ride up.

Across from her, Xander's pistol rattled with deadly accuracy, firing a dozen bullets at the shareholder's condescending smirk in a matter of seconds.

It didn't matter. The web of silver mana caught everything fired at Elaine, leaving the rounds suspended in the air for a fraction of a second before dropping them unceremoniously to the floor.

Kat's rifle clicked empty, and the shareholder just stood there. Arms crossed and a condescending smile on her face with a circle of spent lead littering the floor around her. Nervously, Kat looked over at Xander. Her companion was frantically reloading his pistol despite the weapon's complete lack of success.

Elaine reached down, picking up one of the spent bullets from the ground, rolling the copper-jacketed pistol bullet around in her hand before smirking mischievously.

"My turn," the woman said playfully. She opened her hand, letting the bullet rest on her palm before leaning forward and puckering her lips, blowing on it like a child would dandelion fluff.

The bullet disappeared, burying itself in Xander's chest.

Kat dropped the rifle, switching to her knife as she sprinted toward the shareholder. She almost made it. A step from the woman's back, a telekinetic fist closed itself around Kat, pinning her hands to her side.

Elaine turned around, the same bright smile on her face. "How precious," she purred. "You gain a couple of levels with your lokkel friends and suddenly you think you're an action hero."

The bands of invisible force around her squeezed tighter, crushing Kat's arms to her side and driving the breath from her lungs. Her knife clattered to the ground, falling from nerveless fingers.

"This isn't a movie, girl." Elaine shook her head, clicking her tongue mournfully. "And you certainly aren't anything special. I've been killing better warriors than you since long before you were even born."

Kat's spell activated, her Pseudopod thrusting itself up and out of her chest, into a sputtering fluorescent light, and down into the top of the shareholder's head. The entire room flickered, electricity flowing down the tunnel of water and into Elaine.

Whatever ability Elaine was using shorted out, dropping

Kat into a heap on the marble floor as the other woman twitched and smoked, her skin bubbling and sloughing off of her face. For a moment, Kat dared to let herself think that she'd won.

Her opponent reached up, a dainty and well-manicured hand ripping into the boiling mass of sloughing flesh that had become her face. Gobs of writhing meat spattered to the floor, revealing the matted fur and elongated snout of a stallesp beneath. Its pink nose twitched once before it spun to glare at Kat, its baleful gaze filled with a bottomless reservoir of anger.

She activated Cat Step, not even bothering to dive for her knife as the hallway blurred past her. A massive wave of reddish purple energy slammed into the spot where she'd just been laying, leaving in a crater in the floor that extended down to the bent metal structural beams of the level below.

"To your left!" Xander shouted hastily. A metal cylinder clanked onto the floor near Kat, hissing as it began releasing a thick cloud of inky smoke.

She turned the corner, finding Xander hunched over in a hallway, his left arm clutching at his wounded chest while his right slipped the recording into the back of his cranial jack.

"Whip," he began, stumbling down the corridor as smoke filled the hallway. "I'm transmitting now. Please confirm receipt."

"—nothing." Kat winced as she heard the tail end of Whip-poorwill's voice and then static.

A scream of rage echoed through the floor as the stallesp that had been masquerading as Elaine fired another blast of energy, blowing a car-sized hole in the wall next to them. Xander coughed, hand coming away covered in blood.

"Time for Plan B." He chuckled, the laughter turning into a grimace as he clutched his chest. "Follow me, I have an idea."

"You hateful pink-skinned wretches!" The stallesp's voice echoed through the maze of abandoned hallways as Kat scurried after Xander. "Do you know how much work you have put at risk?"

The building shook as the giant mole shattered another wall, sending Xander sprawling to the floor. Kat helped him back to his feet as the alien continued its diatribe.

"Years of infiltrating, drip-feeding technology to a bunch of hairless apes only for a lucky fucking hit to unmask me. The rest of my brood managed it without any trouble, but no. K'thella, you're the one who got outsmarted by a waif with a wood tier water spell."

Xander pulled Kat into a well-appointed boardroom, staggering behind a couch that would conceal them from the hallway, and let himself slump to the ground, body trembling. Kat crouched next to him, trying not to think about the blood on her hand where he'd grabbed it.

For a moment they just sat there, backs to the leather couch as Xander shook next to her. Kat looked out through the floor to ceiling windows on the neon lights and buzzing cars of the Chiwaukee night. In the distance, the garish light of the city reflected off of Lake Michigan.

"Do you think that a little smoke can hide you from me!" Kat winced as the alien shouted once again. "I can *smell* you. I can track you by the stink of your sweat and the spoor of your fear. I'll grind your bones into flour for what you've done to me!"

"A cake!" The floor rumbled under them as a blast of arcane energy removed another wall. "I'll turn you into a fucking cake and garnish it with goonya berries, just as soon as I get off of this accursed ball of rock."

Xander put a hand on her shoulder. "Kat," he whispered, his other hand, wet with blood, finding hers. "In the elevator, I promised you that I'd get you out of here alive. I plan on keeping that promise."

"How?" She shook her head. "And why are you using my actual name, we're on a mission?"

"Because I'm talking to you right now, Kat, not the persona we invented for you." He coughed wetly, pressing something slick and plastic into her hand.

She held it up the blood-covered recording, eyes widening.

"No." The word was a whisper, a denial of the inevitable.

"She's too strong," Xander shook his head. "She just stood there taking shots from both of us before sweeping us away like we were dust. Only one of us is walking out of here."

"Exe," she began, unshed tears stinging her eyes.

"Xander," he corrected. "We lived our entire life by that damn code only for the people in charge to throw everything away and sell our goddamn planet to aliens. It's a smoking hellscape, but it's ours, damn it."

"Xander," Kat amended herself. "We can go out the window. I'll use Levitation. It'll slow us enough that we can probably make it to the ground. We can give the recording to someone, and everything will be alright."

"Kat." Xander's hand reached up, cupping the back of her head. "That won't work and you know it. We'll be sitting ducks. If the mole doesn't rip us from the sky, her goons will shoot us down."

"Please." Kat heard her voice breaking, but she didn't care anymore.

"We don't have a wireless connection to Whip," he replied sadly. "The mission comes first. If we don't pull this off, Whip dies. Nina dies. Your family dies. One of us needs to make it down to the tenth floor with the recording, and that's only happening if we go through the alien."

Xander chuckled, blood trickling down his face. "We both know that ain't me ,Kat."

"But—" she began, only for Xander to shush her, his golden tooth glinting in the light shining off of the city light. In the distance, the stallesp annihilated another wall.

"My lungs are wrecked, Kat." Xander shook his head sadly. "I haven't been able to draw a breath since she shot me with my own goddamn bullet. That healing spell of yours won't be enough to fix what's wrong with me."

"I'm only upright due to chrome." He smiled weakly. "A couple years ago, I had an oxygen reservoir installed so that I could do an underwater job. I didn't think much about the duration then. Ten minutes of compressed air for an emergency seemed like plenty, but here I am. Seven minutes left."

Kat deflated, tears streaming down her face and soaking the inside of her mask.

"You're right about one thing." He grinned at her weakly. "Two people are about to go out that window. You just aren't going to be one of them."

She looked up, uncomprehending, barely even noting the screams and explosions as the stallesp drew closer.

"It's the only way to get through that shield of hers," he replied. "Spells can penetrate it, but bullets can't. You need to cast Levitation on her as soon as she gets in the room. Then we need a blow with enough momentum to knock her out the window."

"That's my job." Xander put a hand on his chest. "Once we're falling, you need to increase gravity's pull on her. I don't know how strong that shield is, but thirty stories at two G should turn her into strawberry jam."

"I—" Kat tried not to think about her hands shaking. "I can't do it."

The door to the conference room rattled as another spell exploded nearby.

"You're a good kid, Kat." He patted her on the cheek through her mask. "Tell Nina—"

He paused, the facade of confidence slipping for a second. "Tell her I'm sorry."

"Tell Whip I'm sorry."

The door to their hiding place shattered. 'Elaine' stood outside, a gross parody of a human being with her mole face sticking out from a woman's body.

"I can smell you in here, vermin." The alien's hate-filled voice rumbled through the room.

"And Kat," Xander whispered. "I'm sorry to leave all this weight on your shoulders. If anyone can see this through, it's you."

Then her hand was empty, the bloody data stick all that remained.

Xander burned purple, his remaining stamina fortifying his shattered body as he sprinted for the window. En route, he picked up a chair, swinging it in a double-handed grip with the strength of an Olympian.

The window shattered outward, shards of glass spraying into the neon lit night like a thousand stars as Xander slipped himself out onto the narrow ledge outside the windowsill.

'Elaine' fired a blast of energy, shattering the rest of the panes, but missing Xander as the older man ignored his pain and nimbly shimmied to the side. She sprinted after him, a snarl affixed to her furry face.

Eyes blurry with tears, Kat finished casting Levitation just as the stallesp reached the window and leaned outside, one hand high in the air as a crackling orb of reddish purple energy gathered between her well-manicured fingers.

Xander slammed into the alien, drawing a high-pitched squeak of surprise from the mole before both of them tumbled off the ledge and into the night air.

Kat canceled her spell and ran to the edge of the building. Even from the thirty-second floor, she could hear Xander laughing like a maniac as he pinwheeled toward the pavement below.

A bittersweet smile found its way onto Kat's face. That was just like Xander. Even in death, he was going to go out on his own idiotic terms.

She cast Gravity's Grasp twice on the stallesp, enjoying on a deep level the alien's squeals of alarm as she jerked downward, outpacing Xander in her descent until she slammed into the street below. There was a flash of white energy as the shield overloaded and failed, leaving behind a mangled cluster of limbs and abused flesh.

Kat turned away, unable to stomach what would come next. The blood-covered data stick was unbearably heavy in her hand as she left the conference room.

The next couple minutes were a blur. Kat didn't even remember retrieving her knife, let alone fighting, but the next thing she knew, she was entering the security room on the tenth floor.

She handed the datastick to Whip. For some reason, she wanted Kat's smartpanel, too.

Kat didn't argue, handing both to the woman and flopping into the corner, head in her knees. Merrimac, Hestia, and Whip were cheering, slapping each other on the back with the zeal and relief that could only be brought on by a near brush with death.

They'd won. After all of the struggle and heartache, Elaine Williamson and her conspiracy was exposed. Their families were safe, and they could return to their everyday lives from before they'd discovered Operation Starfall.

Almost.

Her body felt miles away. Intellectually, Kat knew she had a fractured arm and two broken ribs. The bruises from the grenade blast were bleeding internally now, the constant activity exacerbating the injuries.

Her infiltration suit was a mess, torn and battered from her descent to the tenth floor. At some point a bullet had creased her side, ripping a hole in the Kevlar and leaving a long, bloody gash on her flank, but none of that mattered.

It didn't even hurt.

The main smartglass display in the security room was playing picture in picture the footage of Xander and Kat killing their way up the tower alongside the boardroom footage from the Millennium meeting that had started everything. An icon in the corner of the screen indicated that the footage was being uploaded to a dozen different channels at once.

The room erupted in cheers when Kat doused the Millennium enforcer in his own acid. They gasped when Elaine's face melted off to reveal the alien underneath.

Then the footage was in the conference room. Kat's breath was coming in short, ragged gasps.

"Tell Nina I'm sorry."

The room was dead silent.

Then, Whippoorwill was crouching next to her, a hand on either of Kat's shoulders shaking her still body with a fierce urgency.

"Where is he, Kat?" The girl's voice was panicked, lost. "Where's Xander?"

Now it hurt.

ABOUT CALE PLAMANN

A lifelong fan of Fantasy and Science Fiction, I usually spent my nerdy energy creating overly elaborate homebrew RPG campaigns. As it became harder and harder to juggle schedules for a half dozen players, I eventually made the logical choice and just cut them out of the picture entirely.

Now I write novels. They whine a lot less about critical failures.

If you enjoyed what you read, please make sure to visit my website or reach out to me on twitter (where I talk about writing amongst other things) or join my discord where I almost exclusively* talk about my existing books/what I'm currently writing.

*There are also memes. Lots of memes.

Connect with Cale:
CalePlamann-Author.com
Discord.gg/xzgycqtFNe
Twitter.com/WritesCoco
Patreon.com/CoCo_P

ABOUT MOUNTAINDALE PRESS

Dakota and Danielle Krout, a husband and wife team, strive to create as well as publish excellent fantasy and science fiction novels. Self-publishing *The Divine Dungeon: Dungeon Born* in 2016 transformed their careers from Dakota's military and programming background and Danielle's Ph.D. in pharmacology to President and CEO, respectively, of a small press. Their goal is to share their success with other authors and provide captivating fiction to readers with the purpose of solidifying Mountaindale Press as the place 'Where Fantasy Transforms Reality.'

Connect with Mountaindale Press:
MountaindalePress.com
Facebook.com/MountaindalePress
Twitter.com/_Mountaindale
Instagram.com/MountaindalePress

MOUNTAINDALE PRESS TITLES

GameLit and LitRPG

The Completionist Chronicles,
The Divine Dungeon,
Full Murderhobo, and
Year of the Sword by Dakota Krout

Arcana Unlocked by Gregory Blackburn

A Touch of Power by Jay Boyce

Red Mage and
Farming Livia by Xander Boyce

Space Seasons by Dawn Chapman

Ether Collapse and
Ether Flows by Ryan DeBruyn

Dr. Druid by Maxwell Farmer

Bloodgames by Christian J. Gilliland

Unbound by Nicoli Gonnella

Threads of Fate by Michael Head

Lion's Lineage by Rohan Hublikar and Dakota Krout

Wolfman Warlock by James Hunter and Dakota Krout

Axe Druid,
Mephisto's Magic Online, and
High Table Hijinks by Christopher Johns

Skeleton in Space by Andries Louws

Dragon Core Chronicles by Lars Machmüller

Chronicles of Ethan by John L. Monk

Pixel Dust and
Necrotic Apocalypse by David Petrie

Viceroy's Pride by Cale Plamann

Henchman by Carl Stubblefield

Artorian's Archives by Dennis Vanderkerken and Dakota Krout

Vaudevillain by Alex Wolf

www.ingramcontent.com/pod-product-compliance
Lightning Source LLC
Chambersburg PA
CBHW030756260626
47169CB00001B/81